Secrets of the Jam Factory Girls

Mary Wood was born in Maidstone, Kent, and brought up in Claybrooke, Leicestershire. Born one of fifteen children to a middle-class mother and an East End barrow boy, Mary's family were poor but rich in love. This encouraged her to develop a natural empathy with the less fortunate and a fascination with social history. In 1989 Mary was inspired to pen her first novel and she is now a full-time novelist.

Mary welcomes interaction with readers and invites you to subscribe to her website where you can contact her, receive regular newsletters and follow links to meet her on Facebook and Twitter: www.authormarywood.com

Secrets of the Jam Factory Girls

Mary Wood

PAN BOOKS

First published 2021 by Pan Books
an imprint of Pan Macmillan
The Smithson, 6 Briset Street, London EC1M 5NR
EU representative: Macmillan Publishers Ireland Limited
Mallard Lodge, Lansdowne Village, Dublin 4
Associated companies throughout the world
www.panmacmillan.com

ISBN 978-1-5290-3339-7

1 3 5 7 9 8 6 4 2

A CIP catalogue record for this book is available from the British Library.

Typeset by Palimpsest Book Production Ltd, Falkirk, Stirlingshire
Printed and bound by CPI Group (UK) Ltd, Croydon, CR0 4YY

Visit **www.panmacmillan.com** to read more about all our books
and to buy them. You will also find features, author interviews and
news of any author events, and you can sign up for e-newsletters
so that you're always first to hear about our new releases.

For Bill Dwyer, my beloved late brother-in-law.
A man of great compassion and insight who
encouraged my journey and counselled me wisely
when I flagged. Miss you forever.

Chapter One

Elsie and Millie

MARCH 1912

''Ere, Elsie, mate, what does it feel like to be in charge of us and not one of us any more, then?'

Elsie had known this would come one day and was glad Ada hadn't sounded resentful or spiteful. The working conditions in Swift's Jam Factory had never been better and, because of this, the women didn't begrudge her sudden rise from being one of them on the factory floor to being one of the bosses. They seemed to forget that most of the changes had been hard fought for last year, when they had taken action and gone on strike. Instead they put a lot of their good fortune down to Elsie moving up in the world.

It had been the National Federation of Women Workers that had encouraged all female factory workers in the Bermondsey area to walk out in protest against the long hours, poor pay and hazardous working practices that had prevailed at the time. Elsie had been one of the factory-floor workers then. And, in her heart, she still was.

Deciding not to answer Ada's question, she sighed heavily as she chastised the girl for the umpteenth time. 'Ada, luv, I've told you many a time, you should sit down while you

1

work. That's why I bought that high stool for you. You can weigh the sugar batches just as easily while sitting as you can standing up.'

'You tell her, Elsie, mate. And while you're at it, tell Ada to spend less time on her back, then she wouldn't have a bun in her oven every nine months or so.'

All the women laughed at Peggy's comment. Elsie grinned. This kind of banter was familiar to her and didn't offend her, but she hoped Millie hadn't heard it. She glanced up towards the office, a room that seemed suspended in the air of one corner of Swift's Jam Factory, and was relieved that there was no sign of her.

Millie was posh and was brought up in a much more refined way than Elsie, who, before all the revelations about her real father, had known nothing but poverty and had lived in one of the many tenement blocks and slum houses in and around Long Lane, as these women around her still did.

For a moment Elsie was transported back to those days, only a few short months ago, although they seemed to be in another lifetime. She thought of Dot, her lifelong friend and, now, her newly discovered half-sister – a fact that seemed incredible whenever she tried to analyse it. Everything had changed with the horror that had happened to herself, Millie and Dot, after they'd discovered they were fathered by the same man. Now they were rebuilding their lives – well, she and Millie were. Dot was trying to, against the will of her bigoted mother, Beryl Grimes. *Oh, Dot, luv, I wish you were here – I miss you.*

As if her thoughts had transmitted themselves to the women, Peggy said, 'We've all been talking about Dot, Elsie. It must be six months since she left to look after her mum's aunt. Ain't the ole girl kicked the bucket yet?'

Although this deepened her pain of missing Dot, Elsie decided to laugh it off. She had to keep Dot's secret. 'No, but I wish she would, then we could have Dot back. It's like part of me is missing.'

Another voice piped up, 'And you're missing your brovver Cecil, too, no doubt. Good that they're together, though, eh?'

'Yes . . .' Elsie didn't like where this was leading and was glad when Peggy intervened.

'Leave it, girls – me asking about Dot weren't meant to start an inquisition. We don't want to go stirring up Elsie's sorrow. I'm sorry, Elsie, luv, I should have thought before I opened me ugly mug. Insensitive, this lot are.'

'It's all right. None of it's far from me mind, but I cope.'

Cecil, whom she affectionately called Cess, was the eldest of her brothers and only a year younger than herself. She knew these women suspected the truth about Dot and Cecil's relationship. They all knew how sweet they'd always been on each other, but she didn't want to confirm it.

'Now, let's get on – we need to get this batch in stock and get ready for the early-season fruits coming in. This is the last of the marmalade.'

The making of marmalade kept the factory in production during the early winter months of each year. The first shipment of oranges came in from Spain just after Christmas – a time that had, in the past, seen them all glad to get back to work after a forced two-month layoff, due to there being no local fruit available.

Elsie was proud to think that, with her and Millie now working as partners, and with Jim Ellington, their new manager, introducing the manufacturing of pickled onions as a new venture, the usual closure of the jam factory during

November and December hadn't happened. For the first time in her memory, the women and their kids hadn't gone hungry – something she knew they'd all dreaded each year, as she had herself when she was in their position. Since being a young girl of thirteen she'd worked here, and the starvation months had been difficult to get through as she'd tried to look after her brothers.

Although the factory remaining open hadn't been down to her, the women thought it was and this helped Elsie's situation.

Making her way up the stairs to the office, Elsie found the conversation she'd just had haunting her. She so longed to see Dot and Cecil. She knew she should feel happy and settled – grateful even that, after her life had been torn apart, she'd landed on her feet. But although everything had changed for the better and beyond all recognition, she still mourned the old days. And, more than that, she longed for everything associated with all that had happened last year to be over, and to find a niche in life and not always seem out of place. She hated the feeling that she was no longer part of the world she'd grown up in, and yet she didn't feel she belonged to this new world that she'd suddenly been catapulted into.

When two o'clock came Elsie was glad to leave the factory. She and Millie worked part-time at the moment, as they had so much stress to cope with. However, slipping into the back seat of Millie's car and greeting the driver, then snuggling into the soft leather beside Millie, only enhanced Elsie's feelings of being a misfit.

Millie sensed her mood. 'Are you all right, Elsie? You're very quiet.'

'Oh, you know, the usual: missing Dot and Cess – not to mention worrying about the future.'

Millie took her hand and squeezed it. 'I miss Dot too, and I dread what we have to face. But we cope most of the time, helping each other through it. You can always talk to me, Elsie. No one understands better than I do.'

'I know. It was the women's banter that unsettled me. They're naturally curious about Dot and Cess, and I can sense them making assumptions that aren't far from the truth. If their gossip reaches Dot's mum, she'll go completely over the top and could cause such a lot of harm.'

'I don't think she will. She might even relent and let Cecil and Dot marry, then all the gossiping will be stalled. Anyway, worrying about what might happen doesn't help us. We have to get through each event as it occurs. And we will, Elsie. Look how far we've come already.'

Elsie had no time to answer as the car pulled up outside their home – well, Millie's home really – and Barridge, Millie's butler, opened the door for them.

As they ran up the few steps and entered the hallway of the imposing three-storeyed house that backed onto Burgess Park, just off the Old Kent Road, Elsie wondered for the thousandth time if she'd ever get used to this grand lifestyle. But she had no time to dwell on this. As soon as they entered the grand hall, Millie picked up the letters from the silver salver that sat on the hall table and shuffled through them.

'There's two for you, Elsie. One looks official.'

Millie's expression told of her apprehension as she handed Elsie the envelopes and the mother-of-pearl paper knife. One of the letters matched the one that Millie had retained in her hand. The seal on both was that of Millie's solicitor.

5

Elsie's hand shook as she slit her letter open. Her eyes scanned the first few words:

I am pleased to inform you, that at this eleventh hour, the defendant has changed his plea to Guilty.

Gasping in a deep breath unleashed the tears that had gone unshed all day and they rained with the relief Elsie felt, because so much lay in that one little word 'Guilty': the release of the suffocating fear and tension that had gripped her for months at the prospect of facing the despicable Horace Chambers, a former foreman at the jam factory, in the courtroom, and of his vile rape of her coming out into the open for all to hear. But, worse than that, having to listen to every detail of the murder of her lovely mum.

With Chambers having at last admitted his crimes, she would never have to face her mother's name being dragged through the mud for being a prostitute, a stigma that didn't convey the reasons for it: how, as a young unmarried woman, her mum was made pregnant by her own boss – Millie's dad – and then abandoned by him. Nor did such a reputation encompass the good heart Elsie's lovely mum had harboured. *Poor Mum, having once trodden the path of selling yourself to get food for yourself and your child, how difficult life made it for you to change direction, especially as more children came along.*

'Elsie? Is – is it bad news?'

She looked up. Millie stood suspended, her own letter unopened. Her eyes held fear, but Elsie saw something else in her expression: the love and concern that her half-sister felt for her. 'No. It's good news, Millie. Open yours.'

As she watched Millie's shaking hands opening her letter, Elsie felt the pity of how her life, too, had been torn apart.

Millie had been brought up and loved by her father, and had suffered a tremendous shock as the revelations about him unfolded – his terrible treatment of Elsie and Dot, his two illegitimate daughters, born to different mothers, and how he had ordered Chambers to kill Elsie's mum.

'Oh, Elsie!' Millie's tears spilled over. 'Is it really over?'

She held her arms open, and Elsie came into them. 'Yes, Chambers is to be sentenced next week, and the solicitor says that the death penalty will be the most likely outcome.' As she said this, Elsie knew that on the day the noose tightened, a new beginning would dawn for her. 'We're free of it all, Millie. Don't cry, luv.'

Millie lifted her head from Elsie's shoulder. 'These are tears of relief. Oh, Elsie, I can't wait to let Mama know. She was thinking of coming down from Leeds to be at all the hearings, although I didn't want her to. I didn't want her to sit through hours of listening to my – our – father's sordid and wicked life. Nor did I want you to have to go through it all again. It truly is over, Elsie.'

Drying her tears, Millie took a deep breath and, as was her way, changed the subject to talk about more hopeful events – one being the coming wedding of her much-loved maid, Ruby. She rejoiced that she could at last concentrate on this. 'I shall feel much happier, Elsie, now that I don't have to pretend enthusiasm, as Ruby deserves more than that from me. And, oh, I cannot wait to tell Len that we can start to plan our own wedding too!'

At the mention of Len, and his and Millie's forthcoming marriage, a fresh agony assailed Elsie. From the moment she'd set eyes on Len, she'd loved him – a feeling that should be joyous, but was a jagged pain within her. And right now it was mixed with the heavy feeling she'd harboured all day.

7

I so long to go back in time and have all my family around me. I love having me little Bert here, but if only Cess and Dot, Mum and Jimmy – poor Jimmy . . . A different pain assailed Elsie at the thought of her mum and of her late, much-loved little brother Jimmy.

Millie broke into her thoughts. 'I'm sorry, Elsie, I shouldn't have jumped to more joyful events, but I find everything easier to cope with if I weigh the bad against the good. And we have so much to look forward to. Maybe your second letter will be the start of it? I can see, by the handwriting, that it's from Cecil. Open it, Elsie. We might be aunties and not know it!'

Elsie smiled and felt lifted by Millie's attitude. Her heartache paled a little, and all the sordid mess concerning Chambers and his guilty plea didn't seem to matter, as she ripped open Cess's letter and scanned the page. 'A girl! Millie . . . Oh, Millie! We've got a niece!'

'What's a niece, Else?'

Bert had crept up on them without her noticing, bringing further joy to Elsie as she looked into his big blue eyes. Ruffling his once-blond hair, which was now darkening as the months went by, she made an attempt to be cross with him. 'Bert! What are you doing down here? You should be upstairs with your tutor.'

'It's boring, Else. I know everything.'

Elsie laughed. 'Not everything: you don't know what a niece is – not that there's any reason you should. But you will now, mate. Because, buggerlugs, at five years old you have one!'

'Me? How?'

'Your big brother Cess has given her to us – well, Dot has. Dot gave birth to a little girl!'

8

'But . . . ?'

Bert didn't have time to finish whatever he was going to say because Millie clapped her hands together. 'How wonderful. Come on, let's all go into my sitting room. I can't wait to know more – I have so many questions.'

As they entered what was Elsie's favourite room in the house, the weak spring sunshine shone through the French windows, giving a bright and airy feel and an enhanced view of the garden. Elsie loved the colours that adorned the room: soft greys, with warm ruby-reds giving richness to the velvet cushions and drapes, picked out by swirls of the same colour in the circular pattern in the centre of the huge, thick grey rug.

As soon as they were settled – Bert snuggled into Elsie on the sofa, and Millie sat in the chair next to the fireplace – Millie fired off questions. 'Is the baby all right? Is Dot doing well? Have they named the baby? Who does she look like?'

How important that last question was, but although she was tense about the answer, Elsie laughed at Millie. 'I reckon it's best if I read the letter out, then we can all have the answers.

'*Dear Sis,*

I am happy to tell you that our baby girl arrived on 2 March 1912. She is so beautiful, and my Dot is a smashing mum, though very tired, and naturally a little down at how everything is.

Anyway, the best news of all is that our Kitty, as we call her – although we have formally registered her as Beryl Katherine Elsie – looks just like me, though her hair is the colour of yours and Mum's: a beautiful copper-red . . .

'Oh, Millie, they've given her mine and our mum's name!' Elsie felt joy rising within her as she said this. What did the past matter now? She had a new Kitty to love. She would never stop loving her mum, but she would let her rest now in a happy place, among the good memories she held of her.

Bert sidled closer to Elsie; she could feel his heartache, which she knew had been triggered by hearing her talk about their mum. Ignoring this, as she wanted to hold the moment, she voiced her thoughts to him. 'We have a new Kitty, Bert. A little girl who will bring us happiness and love. You'll play with her and, as you grow up, you'll become her protector, making sure she is safe. It's going to be all right, buggerlugs – everything is going to be all right!'

'But Cess isn't here. I can't look after Kitty while she lives in Leicester . . . I miss Cess, Else.'

'I know you do, mate. But we'll go and see them, I promise. Now this is no time for sadness. We have a new niece – Kitty is your niece, and you are uncle to her. Ha, such a young whippersnapper, but an uncle already!' She stood then and pulled Bert gently to his feet. 'Come on, I'm taking you back to your tutor. You're to say sorry for leaving the schoolroom, and I will ask her to explain all about family relationships to you, so that you understand what a niece is.'

'But we will go and see Cess, won't we?'

'We will.'

When Elsie returned to the sitting room, happiness gripped her as Millie, who had moved to sit on the sofa, patted the seat next to her. 'Oh, Elsie, I'm so happy that little Kitty is indisputably Cecil's child. That cloud has hung thickly over their heads.'

'So am I. No more skeletons in the cupboard. And maybe now Dot's mum will accept the child and give permission for Cess and Dot to marry.'

Although she said this, Elsie didn't really feel optimistic. Beryl Grimes didn't like giving in – she liked complete control over Dot and would try to break her resolve to marry Cecil by any means she could. A married Dot wouldn't be half as compliant as a daughter living under Beryl's roof, where Beryl could use the love that Dot craved from her as a blackmailing tool.

Brushing these thoughts away, Elsie said, 'I'll read on and see what Cess has to say about it all.' Picking up the letter again, she read:

'*When Dot saw Kitty for the first time she kept saying over and over, "Red hair: my baby, you have red hair!"*

Brought tears to my eyes, it did, Else. And then she said, "Cess, we'll try to forget all that happened now, me darlin'. We won't taint our future by thinking about that beast of a stepdad of mine and what he did to me. This is our baby – yours and mine, Cess. Her hair and her features tell us that." And Dot went on to tell me that no one in her family, to her knowledge, had ever had red hair. Anyway, you only have to look at me lovely daughter to see that she takes after me.

This is a happy moment, made all the happier for me, Else, because all through carrying, Dot's been plagued with nightmares. She even said that if the baby turns out to be her stepdad's, she didn't want to keep it.

She misses her mum, though, Else. I have written to Beryl time and again, telling her we are sorry for

taking the course we did, deceiving her and not taking
Dot to the convent she'd booked her into, but we haven't
heard back. I am praying that Beryl will relent once
she learns that the baby is mine.
    But, Else, despite it all, I am so happy.
    When can you come? Make it soon.
    Love from me, Dot and Kitty – and love to Bert.
Miss you both, and regards to Millie x'

'He writes a beautiful letter, Elsie. It's all so sad. Dot's mum should have been with her daughter when she had her first child. I would want my mama with me.'

'You're right. I'll go and see Beryl. I'll make her see that she has to change her attitude now, and try and get her to come with me to Leicester to see them. I'd like to go next week, if you can you manage without me for a couple of days?'

'Yes, of course I can, though . . . Well, do you think I would be welcome to come with you? I never dreamed I would have a niece – even a half one – as I always thought I was an only child. Now I can't wait to see her, and I so want to hug Dot.'

'That would be lovely. And you know, from her letters to us, that Dot's dying to see you as well as me.'

'It's all so exciting. We'll have to go shopping for the new baby, and the new mum. Oh, I need a hug, Elsie.'

They clung to one another, Millie's dark hair mingling with Elsie's vibrant red locks – the only difference between them, as they had both taken after their father in looks, and both had his dark eyes too.

'I'm so glad to have found out that you and Dot are my half-sisters. But I still find it hard to believe how, just a year after I was born, my father made two of his factory workers pregnant and then abandoned them.'

'I know, Millie. And a few months ago our lives were so different. If only your – our – father had left my mum alone.'

They were silent for a moment, and Elsie wondered how long it would take for every good event in their lives to stop being tainted by all the bad ones. But then it was only they who could make that happen.

'Millie, ever since we met, you've been such a support to Dot and me.'

'And you to me.'

'Well, let's help each other to put our past behind us. Everything that happened last year caused us extreme pain and almost broke us, but we pulled through it. I think we should do as Dot says and not taint our future with our past.'

'That's music to my ears, Elsie. I have prayed for the day you could feel you can do that. Because, once you can, I know that I can too, as I have felt so guilty about it all – Father's involvement, and the way your and Dot's lives were lived in such a different way from my own. And I didn't know how to lose that guilt. I couldn't do it on my own, but with you saying you will try to forget it all and look to the future, then I know I can.'

They hugged again.

As they came out of the hug, Elsie asked, 'Millie, do you remember the day we first met and you asked me to promise not to tell anyone we were friends, for fear of you being sent away?'

'Yes, of course. Why?'

'Well, that day you asked me to make a pinky-promise, and I had never heard of such a thing.'

'Ha, yes. Your face was a picture. And Dot's. Oh, Elsie, I'll never forget Dot's reaction. She looked as though touching me would set her on fire!'

The pain broke and Elsie burst out laughing. 'And that's what she believed. I can hear her now, as she asked, "That pinky-thing were a bit weird, weren't it?"'

'Pinky-thing! Oh, Elsie . . .'

Elsie loved to hear Millie laugh. She joined her and let herself feel a lifting of her spirits once more, as she told Millie, 'I want us to do that again. Make a pinky-promise that we will avoid dwelling on the past. We'll never forget it, but we won't let it spoil our future.' With this, she held out her little finger. Millie hooked hers around it. 'I promise.'

'I promise, too.'

'Eeh, promise what – or is it a secret?'

They both jumped to see Ruby coming through the door carrying a tray. A young woman a little older than themselves, she had been born and brought up in the North of England, where she started working for Millie's family in their Leeds mansion. Her official capacity was as a maid to Millie, but Ruby was much more than that – she was a wonderful, down-to-earth friend to them both.

'Eeh, me lasses, I didn't mean to interrupt owt, but I thought you'd like a pot of tea. You've usually summoned one by now.'

Elsie grinned as Millie winked at her. They both knew that Ruby hadn't been able to contain herself any longer, and wanted to know what was going on. It would have reached her ears that they had cried over a letter that had arrived for Elsie, but were now laughing together in Millie's sitting room.

Millie covered her amusement well, as she told Ruby,

'That's very welcome, thank you. But today a nice glass of sherry would actually go down better. Oh, and you have one too, Ruby. We need to make a toast.'

'Eeh, lass, naw. Housekeeper'd smell sherry on me breath a mile away and have me knicker elastic to use as a rope to hang me with.'

Their laughter rang out. Millie sobered first. 'All right. I'll tell you what: fetch Mrs Robinson and Barridge to me. We'll have all the staff join us.'

Ruby obviously disapproved of this, but she scurried away to do Millie's bidding.

'This should be fun. I love to upset the apple cart.'

Elsie wiped her eyes. 'Oh, Millie, you're a card, mate.'

'Ha! That was a bit of your old cockney self, Elsie.'

Elsie smiled, but inside she thought, *Yes, it is, and it feels good to be who I really am.*

Chapter Two

Elsie and Millie

When the housekeeper and the butler arrived, Millie gave them instructions to assemble everyone in the withdrawing room and to have a glass of sherry ready for each, telling them that she had an announcement. Barridge looked astonished, and Mrs Robinson nearly choked on her indignation, giving a magnificent 'huff' as she left the room, prompting more giggles from Elsie.

Millie joined her, but Elsie could detect her half-sister's nervousness as she held her hand to her lips. 'Oh dear, I'm in trouble now.'

'You are, but I think it's a lovely thing to do.' Although Elsie said this, she wondered how it would go and felt slight trepidation at what would be an ordeal for her.

'That was a big sigh, Elsie, are you all right?'

'Not really. I haven't said anything before, but the attitude of the staff worries me. I don't think they're happy about me, and the standing they have to show me. And I'm not sure if I'll ever get used to living above my station in life.'

'Elsie, this *is* your "station", as you call it. Or it should have been. You have as much right to all this as I have.'

Barridge knocked on the door, entering, and his stiffly spoken 'The staff are ready, Miss Millie' gave Elsie no time to elaborate on her feelings, but she determined to do so when the moment was right.

Millie took her hand. 'Come on, Elsie, it'll be all right.'

When they entered the withdrawing room, the general chit-chat quietened down as Millie addressed the staff, though Elsie noticed her take a deep breath before she spoke.

'Thank you for attending, everyone. I'm sorry to take you away from your daily routine, but my half-sister, Dot, has given birth to a little girl. I want us all to toast the baby.' Raising her glass, she said, 'To baby Kitty.'

All raised their glasses, but Elsie didn't miss the look of disdain that Mrs Robinson gave Cook. Since she'd lived here, Elsie had often noticed that the staff who served the family were far more snobbish than the upper classes themselves were.

Millie then shocked them all further by saying, 'I have another announcement to make. As from today, Ruby will no longer be my maid, but my companion.' Turning to Ruby, she told her, 'And, as a wedding gift and a thank-you for all your services to me, Ruby, I am going to give you and Tom an apartment to live in, rent-free. And you will be welcomed here as my friends.'

In the silence that followed, Elsie felt cross with Millie for a moment, for this impromptu announcement. She could tell it hadn't been discussed with Ruby, by the look of fear on the poor girl's face – a feeling that Elsie knew well, as she had felt the same way, when snatched from her own class by a loving and well-meaning Millie.

Mrs Robinson was the first to react with one of her huffs. Elsie glanced from her to Barridge, and saw a look cross his face that showed his own feelings of shock. She surmised that the poor bloke felt upstaged. As she understood it, he had been in the family's service since before Millie was born.

For once, Millie's confidence looked shaken and it was plain that her own error of judgement had dawned upon her.

Everyone raised their glass to Ruby and Tom, who stood looking at each other in dismay. That moment saw Millie recover. 'Now listen, everyone. Miss Elsie and I are in talks about rewarding you all for your loyalty, and for the way you supported my mother and me through the terrible things that afflicted us last year, and the way you have graciously taken on the duties of caring for Miss Elsie. Once we have finalized our plans, we will discuss them with Mr Barridge and Mrs Robinson. But for now, let's have a final toast to our futures.'

The atmosphere relaxed and became a happy one, as the staff began to enjoy the break from their usual routine. More than one of them had a second glass of sherry – Mrs Robinson being the first to comply. Elsie was sure she only offered the bottle to the others to cover up wanting another tipple herself.

When they had all gone back to work, with Cook and Mrs Robinson bright-cheeked and a little wobbly, Elsie giggled. 'I wonder what we will have for dinner tonight? I wouldn't be surprised if it was poisoned, judging by the look Mrs Robinson gave Cook.'

'Oh dear, Elsie, they weren't best pleased, were they? And neither would Mama be. She'd say I had made a faux pas of the worst order. I do miss her. I cannot wait to see her when we all go up to Leeds for Ruby's wedding. And I cannot wait to take you to my home there. Raven Hall is magnificent and is set in the wonderful Ravensprings Park.'

'It sounds lovely. I've never been further than when we went to Brighton. That was a lovely day out.'

'It was. I'll tell you what: why don't we give Cook the

afternoon off and go out to dinner – we have so much to discuss. We can go to Rene's shop too and have a final fitting for our wedding outfits, and then shop for the baby. What do you think?'

Elsie sighed. 'What I think, mate, is that I'd love to go down the Old Kent Road and have pie and mash at the pie-shop we pass every day on our way to work. And there's something else I think: you should consider what you just said to Ruby, and have her in for a chat. She told me that she and Tom want to go back to Leeds to live, and hoped your mother would find work for Tom. Or, if that isn't possible, then maybe you could help them by recommending Tom for a position with one of her friends.'

'Oh, Elsie, I knew that. How could I have been so insensitive and acted so hastily? I have done that with you too, haven't I – played the Crusader, riding in to save you. You're not really comfortable in my world. I know you miss your old life. I see you chatting and laughing with the factory workers, falling back into your cockney lingo. I'm so sorry.'

'Look, luv, what you've done for me and for Dot has been a wonderful thing. Neither of us has ever had a bank account before, let alone nice clothes. And, for me, a job I never thought in a million years I would have. So don't apologize. Everything you do, you do out of kindness and wanting to make everyone's lot better. And I'm really glad that you're me sister. Or, as me granny would have said, me skin and blister!'

The tension broke as they laughed.

'I know, Elsie, but it can't be easy for you. I was thinking, as you spoke, what it would be like for me, if I suddenly found myself living in the tenement block where you used to live. I don't think I could cope.'

19

'I'm glad we're talking about this, Millie. We needed to. And we did need to have this time living together. I haven't been altogether unhappy, but, yes, I do think now is the time to think differently about things. When you're married to Len—' Elsie caught her breath. She'd thought she could discuss what had been on her mind without any pain, but the knife that always seemed to jab at her heart when speaking or thinking of Len twisted inside her.

'Are you all right, Elsie, dear?'

'Yes . . . yes, I just feel that I want to say what has to be said, but I'm afraid of hurting you.'

'You want to move out? Is that it?'

'Yes. I'm sorry, but when you're married, I'll feel in the way: always that third person at the dinner table, wanting to make meself scarce after dinner, so that you two can be alone.'

'You're not hurting me. I've thought about this too. Not from my point of view, but about how uncomfortable you may feel. So yes, I will be happy to support you in any arrangement you want to make. Oh, Elsie, we must always feel that we can talk to one another. And let's do that over pie and mash! I've always wanted to try it. Come on, mate, let's get ready and go to Rene's to try on our glad rags. And then we'll go for our supper.'

'Ha, Millie, you may be posh, girl, but you're born and bred in cockney land, even if our lingo does sound funny, coming from you. And I know you'll love pie and mash. Mickey's, on the Old Kent Road, serves the best liquor ever.'

They hugged then, and Elsie felt an easing of tension. Millie and Dot were the best sisters she could wish to have. The familiar ache she often felt, at missing Dot and Cess, visited her, and now she had a new longing – to meet her new niece, Kitty. *Kitty, you'll never know, me darlin', the hope you've given me. Now I know I can go forward. I really, really can.*

Millie straightened the bonnet that Ruby had put – or, rather, plonked – on her head. 'You're cross with me, I can tell.'

'By, "cross" ain't the word, lass.' Ruby always dropped her formal term of address when out of hearing of the housekeeper. 'I felt that embarrassed.'

'I'm sorry. Elsie has made me see how it was for you. Please, Ruby, don't fall out with me. Let's talk about what you and Tom really want – is it to set up home in Leeds?'

'Aye, it is, lass. I've talked afore about this to you, and you seemed all right with it. I want to be near me ma, and the rest of me family. I've never been happy in London, but I would've gone to the ends of the earth for you, lass.'

'I know you would. Leeds it is, then. There are several cottages on Mama's estate and I know she would want you to have the pick of them. Some are in excellent condition. Or you can have one of the many terraced houses that I own in Leeds itself. My father left them to me in a property portfolio. All have been undergoing renovation, as I wanted to make them available for letting, instead of have them rotting away, as my father did.'

'Aw, ta, lass. Ta ever so much. Eeh, but I'll miss you.'

'I know you will, and I'll miss you. Oh, Ruby, you don't know how much you mean to me. I was always such a lonely girl, and you have been so much more than a maid to me. You will accept living rent-free, won't you? Only I know Tom is a very proud man.'

'He is. And it'd be better if you let us pay rent. Tom

wants to feel he is providing a roof for his missus and kids – if God blesses us with any.'

'Yes, I thought that. Well, I will be guided by you. But one thing I won't do is set the rent anywhere near what you would have to pay normally. You have to talk Tom into that.'

'I will. And ta again, lass. Eeh, I can't wait to get back to Leeds.'

Millie hung her head and fiddled with the ribbons of her bonnet. *I have to rein myself in and realize that I can't play benefactor to everyone, much as I want to.* One thing she had learned so far, since feeling responsible for everyone, was that kindness could upset people's lives as well as make them better. Soon to be twenty-one, she had considered herself grown-up enough to handle everything since her father's death: running the jam factory, sorting out all the poor people who worked there, and making the conditions better for them. And, most of all, looking after her new-found sisters, Elsie and Dot. *It seems that I got a few things wrong, but I'm learning.*

'Well, I'm ready. Do you know if Elsie is?'

'Aye, she is. She's in your sitting room, waiting for you.'

'Right, I'll go down to her. Oh, and when I'm in Rene's shop, Ruby, I'll fix up a final fitting with her for your wedding frock. Ooh, I'm so excited – it's going to be a lovely wedding.'

Ruby's wedding was something Millie hadn't interfered with or offered to pay for, as she knew, from when Ruby's mother was housekeeper in this house, what a proud woman she was. She was already saving for her daughter's big day then, and Ruby had only been fourteen years old! Now she was housekeeper to Millie's mama in her beloved Leeds, and Millie could imagine Ruby's mum having the time of her life planning everything. *I wonder how much Mama is helping her,*

because she can be meddling, too. Ha, that's where I get it from.
Smiling to herself, Millie ran down the stairs. Finding Elsie, she told her of her new resolution.

'Good for you. Like you say, there's kindness and there's meddling. Sorting the two out, when you want to right the world's problems, can get confusing. Right, mate, I've said me goodbyes to Bert – I did ask him if he wanted to come, but Tom's promised to take him into the park to play footie, and that had more appeal. So let's get going, shall we? I can't wait to see Rene, or to have me pie and mash.'

Millie laughed. She still found it funny to hear Elsie revert to her roots. Funny, but nice, as this was the Elsie she loved very much.

Going into Rene's shop and hugging her was something Millie never saw herself doing. Rene was a sort of aunt to Elsie. She and Elsie's mum used to work the streets together, but she was now a reformed character with her own dress shop – one of the meddlings that Millie was very proud of, as she had funded the shop and given Rene a lot of business. Not that Rene relied solely on Millie for orders, as she had a good side line making outfits for the theatres around the area and was doing really well.

'Good to see yer, me darlin's. I've been run off me feet, what with moving into me flat upstairs and sorting out me business, but I've never been happier, even though it's lonely at times.'

'Rene, how much of the three storeys above do you use?'

On Elsie asking this, Millie knew what she had on her mind.

'I only use the first floor; the other rooms above look like they've been empty for years. I can close the shop for a mo and take yer up there now, if yer want, Elsie, girl.'

23

'I'd love that, Rene, ta.'

'It's home from home, with all your mum's furniture in place. It was good of you to give it to me.'

'I'm glad you wanted it, luv. But you know I'd have bought you all new stuff – you only had to say.'

Ruby laughed this off.

As they mounted the steep, narrow staircase, Millie thought this place wasn't what she wanted for Elsie. *But then am I right to want her to have the same as I have? Elsie may be my half-sister, but her life has been so different from mine. I must let her do as she wants to, and if that is to live here – which is a huge step up from where she used to live anyway, and she obviously feels comfortable in here – well, so be it.*

But despite telling herself this, Millie's heart was heavy. She had so loved having Elsie with her. All her past loneliness had gone, and she and Elsie were soulmates. More so than she and Dot were, though there was still a strong bond between them.

But Dot had clung on to her mother, and with her mother's views being bigoted and unbending, Dot saw everything that Millie wanted to do for her as charity, and worse than that: handouts from the daughter of the man who had ruined her life.

The knot of pain Millie held inside her twisted and caught her breath. Even though she and Elsie had agreed to leave the past behind, could they? Would they ever truly be free? And could Dot be free of the past? Millie doubted it. The three of them were victims, but somehow they had to pick up the pieces. Helping Elsie get settled in the life she really wanted could be a part of that process. And Millie would do her best to make it so.

Chapter Three

Elsie and Millie

When they reached the top of the stairs, Rene opened the door leading to her flat on the first floor. They stepped into her living room. At the sight that met her, Millie felt even more downhearted. 'Shabby' was how she would term it. The homely bits of furniture had looked right in Elsie's old home, but here, in the darker surroundings, they looked tired and worn. The second-hand settee that Elsie's mum had bought sagged in the middle, and had large patches of bare fabric where the brown velvet had rubbed off. The sideboard was chipped and unpolished, and the table and chairs looked rickety and had long had their day. The cabinet containing china was the only good piece of furniture. Millie bit her tongue – she wanted to protest at the idea of Elsie living here, but she had to admit it could be made nice, and the good thing was it wasn't too far away from her own home.

The shop stood in the busy street of Blue Anchor Lane, in the area known as The Blue of Bermondsey, and about a mile or so from the jam factory. Outside, the hustle and bustle of trams, market traders and shoppers gave the area a feeling of excited anticipation.

Once they had walked through the large living room, Millie was surprised to see the modern kitchen and how pretty it looked. A tall cabinet stood against one wall, and through its frosted glass doors she could see that it was used to store food items. To one side of the cabinet, a door led into a small pantry with a huge cold slab for keeping perishables fresh – meat and so on. Pretty yellow-and-brown linoleum covered the floor, and a yellow cloth was draped over a small table that stood on the other side of the cabinet. The deep pot-sink and the windows had curtains that matched this. The whole effect was one of brightness, as the light of the early spring sun streamed in through the windows. There were two bedrooms, and a closet that contained a toilet and a small sink.

'I've a tin bath on the balcony. I can easily bring that in, to have a bath,' Rene told them. 'The balcony is me only bit of outside space. I'm sorting out a tub of flowers to stand out there soon, and I'll take a chair out there in the summer when it's nice. Come and have a look. Me only view is the backs of the shops, but it'll be somewhere to get a bit of sun in the summertime.'

'It's all lovely, Rene.'

Elsie sounded taken with it all, although Millie couldn't understand how she could be, after living in such a beautiful house as hers, and having a lovely view of the park from her bedroom window. Though she had to admit it was much nicer here than in the tenements on Long Lane. But she'd envisaged Elsie wanting to live in one of the houses near her that bordered Burgess Park on the Old Kent Road.

She'd only just thought this when Elsie asked, 'Rene, you know you said you were lonely? How would you feel about renting me the second floor and letting me use it as a flat?'

'Elsie, girl, I'd do a jig, but are yer sure? It's a lot different around 'ere than it is where Millie lives.'

'I'm used to worse, as you know. And I find the area exciting – bustling with life and colour. Besides, I'd be with you, Rene. Oh, Millie, I didn't mean . . . well . . . Look, Millie, luv, wherever I am – here or in your area – nothing will change. You're part of me life now, a big part of it, and we'll be together most days at work. And I can visit you, and you can visit me. It only took us ten minutes or so to get here.'

Seeing how much all this meant to Elsie, Millie decided to be enthusiastic about it. 'I think it's an excellent idea, Sis. Let's go upstairs and have a look at your space, then plan it out and . . . Well, I mean, *you* plan it out.'

'Ha, no you didn't. And I don't want you to think you're interfering every time you make a suggestion. I love sharing things with you. Oh, Millie, this would be perfect for me. Rene, are yer sure?'

'More sure than anything I've ever been sure about in me life, girl. And if you pay me rent, it'll be a massive help to me business. Now get upstairs, the pair of yer, and I'll go and put the kettle on – the one in me shop, I mean, as I have a few things to get on with.'

Millie watched Elsie skip up the stairs. Despite the feeling of loss she had inside her, she did the same.

The size and layout were the same as Rene's, only there was a much nicer view from the balcony that led off the kitchen because, being higher, a vista of London could be seen.

'Imagine that, when it's dark and London is lit up. Be smashing, Millie.'

'I bet it will, though you will need to make it safe for Bert. You know what young boys are like.'

27

'Yes, I see some of them balconies have flower pots on them – they must have secured them somehow. I'd have cacti: that'd keep Bert from trying to climb.'

They both laughed, although Millie had half-hoped that, in pointing out this safety aspect, Elsie might be put off. Feeling a bit deflated she said, 'I'd like to see the third floor. Let's go up and have a look. It might be that you could rent both and have more of a house, with lots of space for people to come and stay – Cess and Dot, for instance.'

'That would be grand, as Ruby would say. And yer know, thinking of Ruby, her and Tom could stay here too. I know they'll want to visit us all and, well . . .'

'No need to say it. I know they wouldn't feel comfortable as guests in my house.'

'Anyway, what do you think?'

Trying to sound truthful, Millie answered, 'I love it, Elsie. Come on, let's go higher.'

The view from the top was as Millie thought. And as she watched Elsie's reaction, she knew that this was right for her and told her so, adding, 'And as your landlady – well, Rene is that, as she will sublet to you, but what I'm meaning is that I have the say as to what can be done with the building – I give you permission to do as you please, and I cannot wait to see your plans. And I will ask an architect to look at the safety aspects of those balconies.'

'That would be reassuring, luv, thanks. But I wouldn't do a lot to the inside at first. I'd have the lower floor painted and the floorboards polished, then furnish that and live here for a while, before deciding what I want to do with the rest of the space. One thing I would love is a music room.'

'Oh? A room dedicated to your piano? Or one where you could hold recitals.'

'No, not put on concerts, if that's what a recital is. But, well, I ain't spoke of this before, only whenever I play and people sing, there's happiness – everyone is lifted out of their everyday drudgery. And that's down to the music.'

'I know what you mean, but what's your idea?'

'I'd like to teach folk who can't afford to pay for lessons how to play the piano, and perhaps start a charity to help them buy their own piano. Though a lot do have one – they've taken pride of place in Sunday-best rooms for a long time, but are never played, because no one knows how to play them!' Hardly stopping for breath, Elsie looked around her. 'I'd like to change that, and this is where I could do it . . . I'm sounding daft now, and a bit like you, wanting to change the world.'

'No, you're not. I think it's a wonderful idea and would love to help you achieve it. You would need soundproofing, and music books – oh, and a piano tuner to get your granny's piano up to scratch and . . . Oh, here I go again! Sorry.'

Elsie held her arms open, and Millie went gladly into them. 'Millie, don't ever stop being you. I love you as you are. We will always do things together. This can be our project. I'm so glad you like the idea and didn't laugh at me.'

'I love it. And I think this room is perfect for it.'

With the dress fittings done, they headed for the pie-and-mash shop. 'I'd have asked Rene, Elsie, but we have so much to talk over.'

'I know, mate, don't worry about it. She won't be lonely any more once I move in.'

The pie and mash and the liquor – a kind of parsley sauce – tasted heavenly to Millie, though she felt a bit out of place

29

sitting on a wooden bench at a bare wooden table. And being among a noisy, lewd roomful of others, all vying for more elbow room.

'What's the likes of you two doing around 'ere, then? A bit common for yer, innit?'

Millie felt afraid for a moment. The burly-looking man who said this had a threatening look on his face, but Elsie saved the day. 'Eating our bleedin' supper, mate. What's it got to do with you?'

The man touched his cloth cap. 'Sorry, mate – only you looked like a couple of toffs.' With this, he turned away and didn't bother them again.

The incident mortified Elsie, but she was glad to see Millie take it in her stride and carry on with their conversation. They were so deeply engrossed, talking about all the things they'd touched upon, but mostly the new flat, that they paid little attention to the loud clanging noise the cafe door made every few minutes, as folk came and went.

After the first couple of times, neither of them even bothered to look up until the same man who'd tried to insult them said loudly, 'Blimey, we've got the bleedin' wops in here now. What's the bleedin' world coming to, eh?'

Elsie nearly died of embarrassment to see that Len had walked through the door. He ignored the comment and came up to them. Although she loathed the term, and all such names used in hatred, Elsie knew what had prompted it. Len looked Italian, and there wasn't good feeling between the dockers and the Italians. She remembered that he'd told them once that his dark skin and smouldering eyes were attributed to his Italian mother. But he had an English father and had been born and brought up in Britain.

To Elsie, Len was beautiful and had a magnetism that

was all his own. Even what he said when he reached them didn't diminish him, in her eyes. She knew it was triggered by the insult he'd had thrown at him. 'Millie! What on earth are you doing in a place like this? I was coming to visit you and I saw your car outside. I suppose this is your doing, Elsie? Well, I think we should leave, right now.'

Millie looked as though this had floored her. Elsie's heart went out to her, as she could see it must seem to Millie that her two worlds – the one she'd known all her life, and her new connections in the lower-class one – had collided today.

For a moment Elsie didn't know what to say, but then the feisty side of her reared up and she did what she never thought to do. She snapped at Len, 'You may have received an insult, mate, but there's no need to insult me or me people back. Sticks and stones, and all that!'

Glad that she was sitting at the end of a bench, she rose and stormed out. Then, feeling hurt by all that had happened today – one of the first days when the differences between her and her half-sister had been highlighted so often – Elsie took to her heels. When she reached Burgess Park, she ran across it. But she hadn't gone far when two arms grabbed her and held her tightly. 'Elsie. Elsie, I'm sorry.'

Struggling, but only because it was unbearable to be this close to Len, she broke free, but he caught her arm and pulled her round to face him. His eyes bore into hers. They held anger, but something else too. Something unfathomable to her.

'Elsie . . . I – I . . . Oh my God, Elsie.' In this last saying of her name, Len's eyes clouded over as he looked into hers. His face swayed towards hers. Elsie couldn't breathe. A voice in her head told her, *No, this isn't right*, but she so wanted him to kiss her.

In a sudden movement, Len dropped her hands and turned away from her. Elsie's heart raced and her breathing laboured. Had she seen desire in his eyes? A dull ache of disappointment settled in her chest. She didn't want him to desire her, she wanted his love . . . *Oh God, what am I thinking? Len belongs to Millie!*

When Len turned back to her, he was once more in control and, as if nothing had happened, he offered her his arm. 'Come on. I'm sorry. I was wrong to say what I did. It was said in retaliation. A childish getting back at somebody for the humiliation I felt. Shall we walk back to the car?'

'It's all right. But no, I'll carry on. I feel more fit to go into the house by the servants' entrance.'

'Don't say that, Elsie – never say that. I wasn't thinking anything like that when I said what I said. No one has more right than you to enter through the front door. Please forgive me, and please forget just now. I – I don't know what came over me.'

She lifted her head. 'I didn't notice anything. Let's get back to Millie, she'll be worried sick.'

They walked in silence to where Millie stood at the edge of the park. From where she was standing she couldn't have seen the incident, and this gave Elsie a feeling of relief. She'd never want to hurt Millie, but she wished everything was different: that Len had fallen in love with her, not Millie, when he'd happened along that afternoon and had played the hero, rescuing Millie's terrified horse and seeing off the gang of boys who were throwing stones at them.

'Elsie, are you all right?'

'Yes, sorry to run out like that, Millie. I didn't mean to stick up for me folk against Len. I just—'

'Len should apologize, not you.'

'I have done, Millie. I'm so sorry for humiliating you, too, darling.'

'Well, let's think no more about it, though I understand you both. And I felt like throwing my pie and mash into that lout's face. As it is, I'm sorry not to have finished them, as it was one of the most delicious dishes I've ever tasted.'

Elsie tried to make things better by taking Millie's arm, 'Well then, why don't we get Cook to make us some one evening? She's a cockney, and I bet she can match what we've just eaten, if not better it.'

'I like that idea. I tell you what: we can have a cockney evening, with you playing all those songs you played at the factory Christmas party last year – well, not the carols. But you can write the words down to the other songs for us, and we can have a singalong. We can invite Jim too. You promised him that night that you'd take him for pie and mash, and you never have.'

'There you go again, Millie. Ha, I told you not to match-make me.'

They'd reached their cars and, as Len got into his, he called over, 'Great idea! Jim has told me he likes you a lot, Elsie. I'll help you matchmake, Millie. We'll plan it when we get to your house.'

Elsie wanted the ground to open up and, as she got into the car, she folded her arms in indignation.

'Uh-uh, that's a pose I only see when you're angry. We're only teasing – trying to lighten the moment. I hated what happened back there, and I really am very angry with Len. I want him to promise never to speak to you again like that.

Even if he is provoked. He should have remained the gentleman and got us out without a scene, or simply left.'

This defused the indignation Elsie felt. 'Don't be angry. It's all right. He knows he's done wrong, and that's the main thing. I shouldn't have flipped me lid like that. I'm sorry, Millie, luv.'

Millie put her hand on Elsie's knee. 'Come on. Let's get home, and we'll leave it there, eh? Sometimes that's the best course to take.'

'Only if you promise not to match me with Jim. We're great mates, and we will go for a pie-and-mash supper one of these days, but I'm not ready yet.'

Millie didn't answer this. In the quiet that followed, Elsie thought about the factory foreman, Jim. She knew he wanted them to be more than friends, and that was why she hadn't yet accepted his invitation to have an evening out with him.

Sighing, she looked out of the window. The light was fading, and the trees in the park were beginning to take on a shadowy appearance. She could see the one where she had felt sure Len was going to kiss her. Was it just a sudden desire for her that had prompted him? Or did Len feel more for her than looking on her as simply being Millie's unlikely sister?

Her mind told her the former was true, but her heart longed for it to be the latter.

Chapter Four

Dot

Dot looked out of the window of her own and Cess's rented flat above a shop on London Road, Leicester. She could see the busy Gallowtree Gate shops to her left. The main station was a few hundred yards to her right, but out of sight. How she longed to run down to it and get on a train that would take her back to London and her mum because, despite everything, she loved her mum.

Day after day she waited for the postman, hoping he would deliver a letter from her mother saying she had forgiven their deceit. But nothing ever came. Dot so wanted to share her baby with her mum, and to walk the familiar streets of Bermondsey, see the folk she knew and have some banter with them. Even go to Swift's Jam Factory, which, according to Elsie's and Millie's letters, was unrecognizable now.

It was strange to Dot how well Elsie had slipped into her new role. She talked as if she loved the factory, when it had been the blight of their lives as young girls. Many a time it had caused them both to break down in tears, with blistered hands smarting from fruit juice that had seeped into their broken skin. And how their legs and backs had ached, as they'd stood for twelve hours or more washing jars and stacking them for the fillers. Despite this, Dot had to admit they had some happy times, and a feeling of belonging to a large family, and that your mates had your back. But she didn't think she could ever go back and become someone she wasn't – she'd only visit.

In case she felt pressurized if they ever did get back to Bermondsey, Dot made her mind up that she'd use little Kitty as an excuse not to work in the factory, though it seemed to her that Elsie and Millie were managing fine, as their letters were full of their successes.

But at the end of the day, like her, Elsie couldn't leave her roots, and Dot felt so happy to read in her letter that she was moving out of Millie's grand house. *On the other hand, that's what's made me so unsettled. Oh, Else, I can't wait to see you, but to think when that day comes and I return home I can visit you whenever I like, without having some butler show me in, makes me want to come back now.*

A small whimper from behind her had Dot rushing over to the sofa where Kitty lay. Kitty opened her huge dark eyes and lifted a hand towards her mother. Dot took it in her own.

'Me little darlin', I love yer. Yer like a miracle to me. I'm yer mum, yer know, mate. And I'll always be by yer side.' She ruffled the mound of curls. 'I love yer hair, darlin'. It's just like yer Aunty Elsie's. Only the curls are from me. Not that Aunty Elsie's is straight, it does have waves in it. And, oh, when the sun catches it, it looks glorious. Won't be long now before yer meet her. And yer Aunty Millie. I tell yer, darlin', there's a tale to tell about the family yer've been born into. But they're all lovely. Even your Granny Grimes, though she has her funny ways. She gets something into her head and it's like trying to move a mountain to get her to think differently.' A tear seeped out of Dot's eye. 'I'll never treat yer how she treated me, darlin'.'

Picking Kitty up, Dot held her daughter to her as her mind filled with the memories of the beatings her mum had given her over the years – and not just with bare fists, but often with a rolling pin, while screaming at Dot that all that had gone wrong in her life was down to her.

'I never knew why, Kitty. And me dad – well, he turned out to be me stepdad – hated me and bullied me and . . . Anyway, I understand now: some of how he was must have stemmed from him suspecting all along that I wasn't his child, and he took it out on Mum, making her feel that I had ruined her life. But it wasn't me that was to blame. It wasn't – why couldn't she see that? Then he had his final revenge on me, Kitty, darlin' . . .' Dot let out a deep sob.

Kitty wriggled and made a distressed sound, which broke into loud crying.

'Oh, me darlin', I'm sorry. I've upset yer. I don't know what came over me.' She jigged Kitty up and down in a soothing motion. 'There, there. Mummy won't mention it all again. I'd promised not to, the moment I knew you were yer dad's child, and not that filthy swine's. And I won't. Me and you are going to be mates. I'll always listen to yer. Play with yer, make yer laugh and kiss yer better if yer hurt yerself.' Sitting on the sofa, Dot removed her breast from her blouse. 'There, there.'

Once Kitty was suckling, Dot knew a great joy to fill her.

'I'll tell yer this last bit, then I'll have it all off me chest. You see, I want yer to know that me and yer Granny Grimes made it up. I found out that she did love me, and she was sorry. I never stopped loving her, so it was wonderful for me to have her as a proper mum. She just got upset when yer dad told her I hadn't gone into the convent that she arranged for me. But she'll be all right when she gets yer dad's letter and knows that yer not . . . well, we won't go over that again. You enjoy your tea. Yer dad'll be in soon, and then yer'll have cuddles with him. Yer've got the best dad in the world, me darlin'. Yer a lucky little girl.'

Dot sat back and enjoyed the feeling of being at one with her child. Her thoughts were still in turmoil, although as she was now a mum herself, with a love for her child so deep it almost hurt, the pain of her rejection by her own mum had become raw. She longed to see her, to hold her, but at the same time wanted to scream out at her. And these mixed feelings caused Dot a painful knot that wouldn't release and give her any peace.

The sound of Cess coming up the stairs lifted her and brought back the joy that had visited her a few moments ago. When he opened the door, his face beamed.

'What a sight to greet a man.' He crossed the room, leaned over, steadied himself by holding on to the back of the sofa and kissed her lips.

Dot's heart fluttered. She and Cess had been in love for as long as she could remember. Even as kids going to school, they'd had a special bond. Along with Elsie, the three of them were inseparable.

'You've been crying, Dot! What's happened?'

'Nothing, luv, I'm all right. The women at the factory used to talk about baby doldrums – they said it was natural to cry for nothing, in the first weeks of a baby's life. One had been to see the doctor about it. Cost her three bob. And Ada, who had a few kids, told her she shouldn't have wasted her money, as she could have told her what the doctor did, and the remedy too. "Keep busy," she said. "And talk to yer mates" . . .'

This last comment triggered the tears again. Dot tried to control them, but the loneliness she'd felt since coming to Leicester, to save her baby being taken away from her, now engulfed her.

'I'm here now, Dot. You can talk to me, darlin'. Have you been out today? It's been a nice day – not so cold. The skies have been cloudless. There's a real sense of spring in the air and we've been really busy in the market. I kept looking to see if yer'd come to see me.'

Dot drew in a deep breath. How could she tell her lovely Cess that she hadn't even dressed till an hour ago? He was worried sick about her, as it was.

'Look, Dot. Let's just go, eh? Let's go back home and confront yer mum. Surely seeing you and Kitty, and seeing that her granddaughter could only have been fathered by me, will make her change her mind and she'll let us get married, instead of waiting till yer twenty-one?'

Hope dried Dot's tears. Reaching twenty-one was still fifteen months away. And though she loved Cess with all her heart, living with him and pretending to be married still felt wrong. 'Can we do that, Cess – can we go back?'

'Yes, we can. We've plenty of money. With what I've been earning, yer've hardly touched the allowance Millie gives you.'

'She's turned out to be a wonderful sister, ain't she, Cess?'

'She has. Though I still have trouble believing she is that, to you and Else. Gave me a fright when it all first came out. D'yer remember? I thought you and me were related and could never be together, until Else pointed out that me dad – whoever he was – wasn't the same dad as you and Else had. And that you had a different mum from me and Else. So, though it's weird and complicated, the upshot is that our love is legit.' He sat beside her then as she took Kitty from her breast.

'I know. It was a frightening time.' She handed Kitty to him. 'Here, you get her wind up, while I prepare the next course for her.'

Cess laughed and lovingly took hold of Kitty. As he placed her gently over his shoulder he asked, 'What do you think, luv. Shall we? Shall we go back? We've enough for me to get a stall somewhere – Petticoat Market even – cos I don't care what I sell. Alf, who I work with, reckons I could sell snowballs to Eskimos!'

This made Dot laugh, and it felt good.

'And we could find a place around that area, near to where Else is going to live. Let's just do it, Dot.'

But a doubt had crept into Dot's head. 'I don't know, Cess. I was caught up in the idea at first, but what about all me mates from the factory? You know how they gossip and even cast out someone who lives like us. They almost cut your mum off.'

'Yes, poor Mum. But we're not selling ourselves on the street, and Else used to say that she thought a lot of women were afraid of our mum. She said they thought that if they got friendly with her, she might end up enticing their husbands away.'

'Huh, I'm sorry, Cess. You know I loved your mum and miss her so much, but there is some truth in that, mate. She went with most of the men in the area at one time or another.'

Cess stiffened. 'Don't say that. Don't talk about me mum like that, Dot. You sound no better than the lot back home.'

Dot was mortified and didn't know why she'd said it. She

hadn't even thought about it before. 'Oh, Cess, I'm not meself. That was a terrible thing to say. Forgive me, me darlin'. I'll never say anything like that again.'

'Forget it. I know you're not yourself. And you never will be, cooped up in this flat, nice as it is. Look, I bought you something today. I was talking to Hattie. I can't believe what she gets on her second-hand stall. I love all the knick-knacks. I've thought I might deal in them meself when I get me own stall sorted. Anyway, she was putting out some books, and one attracted me. It was a beige colour, with what looks like a picture frame around the edge. It's called *Pride and Prejudice*.'

'A book! You bought a book for me, mate? Ha, I've never read a book in me life.'

Cess laughed with her. 'I know, but it drew me to it, and I thought you'd like to have it. Hattie said it's very popular. The lady who wrote it died almost a hundred years ago.'

'Pass me Kitty. I don't know, Cess – yer a clever bloke. Always knows a lot of facts. You should read it. You used to love reading in school.'

'Ha, I might just do that.' He passed their baby to her. 'There you go, me little darlin': time for pudding. Yer dad's envious of yer – them titties used to belong to me.'

'Cess!'

'What? Well, I miss yer, Dot. Six weeks, did yer say? Well, it's four now and I'm counting.'

Dot hit out at him. 'You're as bad as the rest of them, Cess Makin.'

They both laughed. Then Cess leaned back. 'Do yer know what I miss, Dot? Pie and mash. If we could go down the road and get some, like we did in London, that would make me day.'

A pang of guilt stung Dot. She hadn't cooked anything

41

for Cess's dinner. She didn't even have much in. *What's the matter with me? Why can't I function like I used to?* Tears pricked her eyes again. Tears so very ready to tumble at the slightest thing.

'Don't, Dot. We will go back, and that's a promise. Hang on to that, eh?'

'I've no dinner ready!' These few words triggered something in her. Without thinking, she snatched Kitty off her breast and gave her roughly to Cess. Her voice rose to a scream. 'I can't do this, Cess, I can't! I'm not a good wife, and I'm a terrible mum.'

Cess rose, putting Kitty on the sofa. 'You're not. Dot . . . Dot, don't.'

But she couldn't stop. The screams came unbidden, from somewhere inside her.

Cess grabbed her. She felt her body shaking. 'Dot . . . Oh, Dot. No, don't, please don't.'

Her body lost its strength and she crumbled. Cess held on to her.

'Dot, me darlin', I'm here. I've got yer. I won't let you fall.'

Her screams subsided. 'But I am falling, Cess. I am falling, and I can't stop meself.'

Cess lowered Dot and himself to the floor. His arms held her, giving her some comfort and a feeling of being safe. A feeling that hadn't suddenly deserted her, but had been slipping away from her since Kitty was born.

'Let me help yer up, luv. Come on. Yer know what's wrong, so don't be afraid. Look, Kitty's safe on the sofa. I'll help yer to the chair. I'll tell yer what: you can sit on me knee.'

Feeling like a child, but as if great strength had been given to her once she was sitting on Cess's knee, Dot listened to him reminding her that she'd said herself this was the doldrums that she'd heard about. 'That's all it is. And Ada said it passes, didn't she? Well, it will, luv.'

'I know, Cess, but this is different, mate. I really do feel like . . . Oh, I don't know. But, well, when I was screaming just then, it wasn't me. It was like I'd lost me. That's it. I'm lost, Cess. Sometimes I can't even function. Cess, I left Kitty in a dirty nappy for hours . . . Oh, Cess, help. Help me, luv, please help me.'

She could see the fear in Cess's face. He was quiet for a long moment. When he spoke, he surprised her. He wasn't angry, as she'd expected. 'We'll get you help, Dot. Don't you be scared, me little darlin'. We'll go and see a doctor and, if we have to, we'll ask for a specialist to help yer. Now let me get us something to eat. You sit on this chair and close yer eyes; you must be tired, me darlin'.'

'There's nothing in, Cess. I'm sorry, I couldn't go out to shop today.' Feeling inadequate and useless, Dot allowed the tears to flow once more.

'Dot, no. Try to hold yerself together, luv . . . Oh, I wish Bert hadn't gone and got that cold, then Elsie and Bert would have come, as they promised they would. But she said she would make it very soon. You'll feel better then, love.'

'I miss her, Cess. She'd have taken care of us. Elsie wouldn't have let yer go hungry, like I do.'

'No, you don't. Yer've slipped up today, that's all. Look, I'll nip out to the grocer on the corner. He'll serve me round the back of his shop. I know him – we always have a chat when I pass. Kitty's all right, so rest yourself, and I'll be back as quick as I can.'

*   *   *

It seemed to Dot that the walls were closing in on her when the door shut behind Cess. She put out her hands to push them away. Her body trembled. Something trickled down her back. Though her logical mind told her it was it sweat, she got the notion in her head that it was a creepy-crawly. *It's trying to eat me!*

Dashing over to Kitty, she grabbed her shawl and swaddled her. Lifting her, Dot staggered towards the door, all the time trying to hold back the walls of what felt like an ever-decreasing space. *I have to get Kitty out of here – we're going to be crushed!*

When she reached the stairs, the encroaching walls began to spin, disorienting her. *Where's the first step gone? I can't find it. Help me! I must get out, I must. I must save my Kitty.*

Crushing her daughter to her, Dot stepped out into what seemed to her to be fresh air – and then she was falling. 'Help me . . . H – e – e – l – p!'

Her body bumped on each step. A voice kept telling her to let go of Kitty, but she couldn't. Kitty mustn't bang her head. *I'll save you . . . I'll . . . save you.*

Each bump almost took Kitty from her, but Dot held on tightly. Suddenly the tumbling stopped and she was lying, half on the cold tiled floor and half on the prickly rush doormat. She couldn't move, and yet she felt safe. The fall hadn't hurt her. She couldn't feel any pain. She could still feel Kitty in her arms. She smiled and looked down at her daughter. She wanted to tell her lovely baby that they were all right now, but no words came. She felt so tired, so very tired.

Chapter Five

Dot

When she opened her eyes, Dot knew she was in a bed. Her back hurt and she wanted to turn over, but couldn't. Something had her held fast! *Where am I? What's happening? Kitty – where's Kitty?* She tried to move her arms, but it hurt to strain against whatever held her . . . 'Cess, Cess, help me . . . Cess.' The words came out as a whisper. Cess didn't come. 'Cess! Cess! Help me – e – e – e!'

The room suddenly flooded with light. 'What are you shouting for? Mrs Makin, you must quieten down.'

She wanted to say that she wasn't Mrs Makin. That she was an unmarried mother, living in sin, but knew she mustn't. 'I want my Cess . . . I – I can't move.'

The woman who'd come into the room wore a nurse's uniform, but she wasn't young, like most nurses. She was rounded – her round face was squashed by a veil pinned tightly around it, before falling in folds behind her head. She had a kindly face. She looked like someone Dot felt would take care of her.

'Help me . . . help me – me baby . . . me Kitty.'

'She's all right, just relax. You fell down the stairs, but

you saved your baby. She's quite safe in the nursery. Go back to sleep.'

'No. No . . . I want me Cess! Where am I?'

'You're in Carlton Hayes Hospital.' The nurse patted the top of her head. 'I'll fetch your husband. The poor man is exhausted, but he wouldn't go home, he's sitting out in the corridor. Just be quiet while I'm gone. If Sister hears you, she'll sedate you again, and I don't think that's a good thing. But don't you go telling anyone I said that. Promise me you'll be quiet.'

Carlton Hayes – Dot had heard of that! Cess had mentioned it in a joking way, telling her that if anyone did anything a bit mad, the others would say they'd end up in Carlton Hayes, the nuthouse. 'No! Why am I here . . . ? Why can't I move? Don't leave me.'

'I have to, duckie, or I can't fetch Cess, now, can I? You listen to me: you have to be good. If you aren't, God knows what will happen – a lot that I don't agree with, I can tell you.'

This frightened Dot. Something told her she must obey this woman. She stopped writhing against the restrictions that held her and lay still, clamping her mouth closed. When the nurse left, a feeling of panic came over her, but she decided she would hold herself very still. What the nurse said about things 'happening' made her tremble with fear.

A noise to the left of her had Dot turning her head. 'Cess?' But no one was there. 'Cess!' She listened. Whispers came to her. *Someone's coming!* 'Cess!'

The door opened. 'Shush, shush!' The nurse came in, followed by Cess.

'Oh, Cess, help me – I can't move.' Stinging tears fell down the side of Dot's face.

'I'm here, me darlin'.' His fingers stroked her face, drying the tears. His lovely eyes looked into hers and she felt safe again. Blocking out her world with his head, he leaned over and kissed her lips.

'Cess, help me.'

'I will, darlin'. You fell down the stairs. Why did you leave the room and . . . and little Kitty? Oh, Dot, it was terrible seeing you both lying there when I opened the door. What happened?'

'I – I don't know. I'm sorry, Cess. I – I wouldn't . . . Kitty, where's Kitty?'

His hand stroked her hair. 'She's safe. You wrapped her up so well.'

'I wouldn't hurt her. I . . .'

'I know. I know that you love our little darlin'. But oh, Dot! Dot.'

'Cess, I can't move. Help me to move. Where am I? Cess, take us home. Me and Kitty. Take us home.'

'Shush. I'm going to, but I need you to be quiet. Please, Dot. Please do this for me.'

The nurse spoke again then. 'I'll undo the straitjacket – that's what's panicking her. A necessary evil, I'm afraid, when someone can't be restrained. And as you know, we all did our best with Mrs Makin.'

'Thanks, Nurse. And you will help me, won't you?'

'It'll be your money that'll help you: a bribe in the right place. But you need to get help for Mrs Makin. You can't simply think she will get better on her own. I've seen this all too often – young women having a breakdown following a birth. They all get classed as mad, and most never see daylight again. But they're not. It's just that the birth has acted as a trigger and made whatever is frightening them rear up and become terrifying. No one understands the condition, but I was a nurse in the Boer War and I saw similar conditions in men – the fear of dying was their trigger.'

Dot listened and, as she did so, it felt to her that this nurse was someone she wanted in her life – she was someone who would help her and make everything come right.

'I understand more than most about mental illness because my husband was a doctor, and he studied a lot about the effect that trauma can have. It can unbalance the mind – make the patient behave out of character. Every day they fear what they have to face. His theory was that if you removed whatever they feared and made them feel safe, then helped them to deal with what they had been through, they could get better. But no one would listen to him, and most of the traumatized soldiers were sent home to be locked away as madmen, and can still be found in places like this – and this is one of the better places. I think the same thing can be applied to women who are suffering as Mrs Makin is.'

'Will your husband help her?'

'He can't. Sadly, my poor Denis was shot by a South African soldier while he tended to one of those who had fallen near our tent – God rest his soul.'

'I'm sorry to hear that. It must have been hard for you.'

'It was, but I devoted myself to nursing, especially in this field, hoping to inject some of his ideas, but no one listens. They end up traumatizing patients further, until some end up chained in a padded cell.'

'What?'

'Yes. But you can save Mrs Makin. There must be something that she fears, but may have been strong enough to cope with until the birth. Has she been through any trauma,

apart from the birth – which, believe me, can be very traumatic in itself and can be a trigger to unbalance the mind
in someone who is already fragile?'

Although Dot couldn't get the whole gist of all of this,
she knew that what the nurse spoke of was how she felt.
Afraid and unable to cope. And yes, she saw things, frightening things, and couldn't sort them out into anything
logical. She felt as if everyday matters would harm her.

She heard Cess say, 'She has been through a lot of things,
and has put up with a lot since being a nipper. But how can
I help her?'

'Do as you said, and get her away from here. But when
you do, she can't be left on her own, poor little duck. And
you've the baby too.'

'Once I get her out of here, I'll take her back to London,
to me family. They'll help her.'

'Well, however well-meaning they are, Dot needs proper
help. Just taking her back to the family isn't going to do it.
They love her, but they won't understand. They'll likely tell
her to pull herself together, take hold of herself. She can't
do that. She has to deal with what's frightening her first,
and as she's been through a lot since she was a nipper, then
her past may be haunting her.'

Feeling calmer and less afraid as she listened to someone
who understood, Dot wanted to scream out that it was
family, and those she loved, that scared her – their condem-
nation of her. And she was afraid of how her mum would
cast her out forever if she brought shame down on her.
'Don't take me back to London, Cess. We can't go back till
we're wed. Please!'

The fear enclosed her – and the beatings loomed up in
her mind. The rolling pin, the fist, the stinking, sweating

49

body of her stepdad pounding her, hurting her, and her mum's face, laughing – no, crying. No . . . not caring!

'Help me, Cess. Cess, help me, don't let her beat me – she'll beat Kitty. No, no, don't let her!'

'Dot, oh, Dot . . .'

Cess was crying. Her Cess had tears running down his face. She wanted to tell him not to cry, but her voice had taken on a mind of its own.

Something was clamped over her mouth. 'I'm sorry, me darlin' Dot. Forgive me, but I have to keep you quiet.'

One of Cess's tears fell onto her cheek. It registered with Dot that she had to stop shouting – her Cess wouldn't do this unless he had to stop her. She made herself calm.

'She can be helped, Mr Makin. As you can see, Dot still has some powers of rationalization. Look, what I'm about to say may seem strange – it does to me, as I'm not given to making rash decisions – but I want to help. I – I . . . well, I'm willing to come with you to look after Dot and try my Denis's methods. I can see that you are very much in love, no matter the status of your relationship or why you have chosen this path. But I can see that tragedy awaits you both, if Dot doesn't get proper help. I'm not a doctor, but I can seek one out in London who believes like me, and get her the help she needs.'

'Yes, Cess, yes, I want that. I – I don't want to stay here. Please.'

The nurse patted her hand, and the gesture held understanding. 'Look, Mr Makin, I know you would need to take a massive chance on me, but I am your only chance, and I need to get out of here. I cannot stand to see another patient who could be saved undergo horrific treatments that only worsen their condition.'

'Please, Cess, take me away and let Nurse look after me, please. I'll be good. I'll get better.'

The nurse patted her hand again. 'My name's Gertrude, after my German grandmother. Most people call me Gertie. Now don't get upset, me duck. Something about you has captured my heart and, if Cess says no, then I'll fight him. I feel that my Denis is asking me to help you. And no one wins against Gertie when she makes her mind up – even when the decision is taken out of the blue.'

Dot looked from Gertie to Cess and saw the relief in his face as he said, 'Thanks, Gertie. Me and Dot will accept your offer. I know we've only just met you, but you talk like I think. Thank you. You're like a saviour to me. But how can we do it? What do we have to do to get Dot out of here?'

'In the normal run of things I'd say go to Sister and tell her that you want to sign Dot out and take her to a private clinic. She would then put the wheels in motion – a clinic would have to be found that would accept her, and Sister would have to be satisfied that the baby was going to be cared for. And all the time, Mrs Makin might deteriorate and her behaviour might mean that she is sectioned. If that happens, you won't be able to do anything. So I'm going to suggest something that is unconventional. I'll unlock that French window, then I'll go to the nursery and collect your baby. We're short-staffed tonight and I have care of the nursery. There's only your child in there at the moment. The other child's been sent for adoption.'

Dot gasped at the horror of this.

'Don't upset yourself, Mrs Makin – that won't happen to Kitty.'

'But me mum might make it happen! Don't let her, Cess, don't let her!'

'Dot, no. I'll never let anyone take our baby, trust me, me little darlin'. Trust me, Dot, please.' Dot's panic subsided and she smiled through her tears. Cess took her other hand and spoke to Gertie, 'So I kidnap them?'

'Yes. You get Mrs Makin's coat on. It's still on the chair you were sitting on. Don't worry about her other clothes. Once I have the baby here, get through that door and to your car and leave. I can make sure nothing is noticed until the day-staff come on and then, when doing my rounds with them, I'll look as if I know nothing. The police may be involved or they may not be. I doubt it, as Mrs Makin isn't sectioned. I'll say you had asked me how you could arrange to take her to a private clinic, and that you seemed upset at how long it would take. I think that will be the end of the matter, as they will assume that's what happened.'

Gertie helped Dot out of bed, and as she did so, she said, 'Have you got a bit of paper, Cess, and a pen? Write down your address. I'll get some sleep in the morning, then I'll come to you.'

'When? Tomorrow afternoon?'

'Yes, if there's a train.'

'I'll check when the first train after five arrives in London tomorrow from Leicester. I'll be there to meet it, but if I'm not, then get a taxi to our address. I'll pay for it when you arrive. I'm going back to our flat now to collect our things, then I'm getting on the road.'

Once they were in the car, Dot and Kitty lay on the back seat, with Cess's coat over them – a precaution against the gateman stopping them. As it was, he doffed his cap and let Cess drive straight through.

'We're on our way, me darlin'. We're going home.'

Home? Where was home? Dot stopped herself asking these questions and told the voice in her head to stop asking too, then closed her eyes tightly and wrapped her sleeping baby in her arms. *I'll be all right. I will. Cess and Gertie will take care of me.*

When she next woke, cold air wafted over her, making her shiver. A noise penetrated the darkness of the car. Kitty was crying.

'Dot! Dot, wake up!'

It was Cess's voice. *Why am I here in the dark? What am I lying on? And we're moving!* 'Cess . . . Cess!' she cried.

'I'll stop the car. You're all right, Dot, me darlin'. You're all right, I'm here.' But she couldn't see him. Her head felt full of cotton wool. And she felt so cold. 'I'm here, darlin'. Come on, mate, sit up. I'll take Kitty. She needs her night-feed. Sit up, darlin'.'

'I'm scared, Cess. Where's Kitty's food?'

'Oh, Dot. Dot . . .'

'Don't cry, Cess. When I find it, I'll feed her.'

Cess gave a loud sniff. 'It's in your breast, me darlin'. You've milk in your breast, and Kitty needs to suck it out. I'll help you open your blouse. I put a blanket over you as you slept while I got what we needed from the flat. It's slipped to the floor. There now, hold Kitty like that. That's it, I'll cover you both and you'll be warm then.'

Dot felt a nice familiar feeling, and her love for Kitty surged through her.

'Now, let me tuck this blanket around you both. That's it. I'll drive steadily. Just call out if you need me. Hold Kitty firmly, Dot. She relies on you, me darlin'.' Cess touched her hair. 'We both do. We'll be all right, darlin' – we'll be all right.'

*   *   *

To Dot, it seemed that folk were always trying to wake her up, but she felt at peace when she was asleep. There it was again: Cess calling her name.

'Dot. Dot, wake up, we're here.'

'Here? Where's Kitty . . . Cess, Kitty's gone!'

'She's inside with Else and Millie, darlin'. She's slept since you fed her, but she might need feeding again when you get inside – and changing. She's made a right stink in the car.'

Dot allowed Cess to get her out of the car. The air felt damp and there was a mist swirling. She looked up at the house they were parked in front of. It looked huge. 'Whose house is it, Cess?'

'Millie's. Else and Millie are waiting inside.'

'No, it's another hospital! It's Carlton Hayes! No . . . No!' Her scream soared in the night air. As it echoed back to her, she heard a familiar voice, one she loved. 'Come on, mate. Let Cess and me help you.'

Her mind wouldn't confirm who this was, and yet Dot knew it was someone she loved.

She felt her other hand being taken. The feel of this hand gave her memories of running in the park with someone and giggling. Not as afraid now, she let them steer her towards the very bright light shining from the open doorway. A man stood holding the car door. *Is he a policeman? Is he going to take me and Elsie away again?*

'Cess, where's Elsie, where is she? We have to run!'

She heard another voice that she knew say, 'Barridge, come back inside. I think you are frightening Dot . . . Oh, my darling Dot.'

'Dot! Dot, I'm here, this is Elsie, holding your hand. You're safe now, darlin'. Safe. This is Millie's house – you remember our lovely sister, Millie? We'll take care of you, mate, let's get inside.'

'Gertie, where's Gertie?'

'Is she asking after the nurse you told us about, Cess?'

'Yes. Let's get her in, out of the cold. Come on, me Dot. Kitty needs you – she needs to feed again. She's crying for you.'

'Don't let her cry, Cess. Bring me to her. I can put her on me titty. You said you like it on me titty.'

'Dot!'

Cess sounded cross, but the woman holding her hand laughed out loud. 'That's our Cess for you, mate. And you sound as though you'd fit right back in with the factory lot. Oh, Dot, we've missed you, luv.'

A nice feeling settled in Dot as she suddenly knew who the young woman was. 'Elsie?'

'Yes, it's Elsie, mate. Oh, Dot, let me hug you.'

The hug felt so good. 'Am I safe now, Else?'

'You are, me darlin' sis.'

When they got inside, a young woman gave her a hot drink of milky cocoa. She was lovely and she kept smiling at Dot. When she'd drunk the cocoa, someone handed Kitty to her. Kitty smelled of the same lovely smell that wafted off the young woman.

'Let's get Kitty feeding, Dot.'

Dot smiled at Elsie and lifted her clothes to put Kitty to her breast.

Elsie had a lovely silk cloth in her hand. She spread it over Dot's breast. 'There, gives you some privacy. Oh, Dot, little Kitty is beautiful.' She had a tear in her eye. 'I've missed you so much, Dot. And Millie has too. We were going to make new plans to visit you, but we're so glad you're here instead.'

'Who's Millie?'

'I'm Millie, Dot.' The lovely young woman stepped forward. 'I'm your sister.'

This frightened Dot. She couldn't say why, only that she had a feeling something was at odds. 'No! I don't want a sister. Only Elsie. We've always been sisters. Haven't we, Elsie?'

Cess sat on the arm of the chair and put his arm round her. 'Don't worry about anything, me darlin'. We'll sort everything out. Just relax and feed our little Kitty.' He was crying again.

What is making my Cess cry? Dot reached up and took his hand and smiled at him. He smiled through his tears. 'My Cess. My lovely Cess. You'll keep me safe, won't you?'

'I will, darlin', I will.'

Chapter Six

Millie

Feeling sad that Dot didn't know her, but determined to make Dot, Cess and the baby feel welcome and at home, Millie set about instructing the staff to make up a room near the nursery for her guests, and to open and clean the nursery, starting with the cot.

The nursery was always kept aired and given a light clean every week, so it wasn't musty or dirty, it just needed freshening up and a fire lit in the grate. Millie supervised all the operations, though she had no need to, but it gave her an excuse to give Dot, Cecil and Elsie a few moments on their own. When she went back into the sitting room, Dot had finished feeding Kitty. She sat back on the sofa with Cecil, looking happy and content.

Millie's heart wrenched at how unkempt Dot was. How her hair – the same dark colour as her own – hung in lank, greasy strands, when normally it fell in a shining mound of curls, as hers did. That's if Dot left it to fall freely, instead of worn in a swept-back style with ringlets falling down the back, as she normally wore it.

'How are you now, Dot?'

Looking much more lucid, Dot smiled, then warmed Millie's heart as she said, 'Millie! Oh, luv, it's good to see you.'

Millie went to her. 'Yes, it's me, my lovely sister. Can I have a hug, please, I've wanted one for so long.'

Handing Kitty to Cecil, Dot stood up. Her strength seemed to have come back into her, and Millie had the uplifting feeling that everything was going to be all right with her. And that, yes, Dot did seem to have suffered some sort of breakdown, but she would recover.

They hugged as they always used to. But then Dot showed that she was still in the grip of whatever was confusing her mind, when she came out of the hug and asked, 'Do you live in London, Millie?'

'Yes, dear. This is my home, where I was born and brought up, just along the Old Kent Road from where your mum lives in Long Lane, and from where Swift's Jam Factory is.'

Dot shuddered, and Millie realized she had conjured up bad memories for her. She went to apologize, but Cess took control.

'Sit down, me darlin'. Elsie'll be back in a minute.' Cess handed Kitty to Dot as she took her seat again. A peace seemed to come over her when she held the baby. 'That's it, me darlin'.' He looked up at Millie. 'Elsie's gone to fetch Bert from the schoolroom, Millie. My, what do you think of that, Dot? It's a bit posh for our little Bert, innit? Maybe one day Kitty will have a schoolroom in our house, eh?'

Dot giggled and Millie breathed a sigh of relief.

When Bert bounded in, the atmosphere changed, in the way only Bert could make it do – as if everything was all right with the world. 'Cess! You've been gone a long time, mate.'

The brothers hugged. Little Bert – though not so little now, jumped on Cess and then leaned over to hug Dot. Dot grinned at him. 'You've grown an inch, mate. About time. I thought you were going to stay a baby forever!'

'And you look different too, Dot. You've lost your curls.'

Cess covered this up. 'No, she's still got them, she just gave some to Kitty. Let me introduce you to your niece, Bert. This is Kitty: ain't she the prettiest little girl?'

'Hmm, I like her, but she's a bit red and crumpled. How did you get her?'

Millie felt her face colour. But Cecil took it all in his stride. 'We didn't get her, we made her, and then she grew inside Dot's tummy – like you've seen other mums do when they're pregnant. But that's all I'm telling yer, as yer too young to know more. You'll find out. I did, and no one told me.'

Bert didn't comment on this, he just grinned and gazed down at the baby. 'Can I touch her?'

'Course you can. If you sit down, you can hold her on your knee.'

'Can I, Else, can I really hold her?'

Millie felt strangely left out, as if they were a family and she was an onlooker, but she didn't want it to be like this. She caught Elsie smiling at her and then, as if she'd guessed Millie's feelings, Elsie told Bert to sit next to her. 'Millie can steady you, Bert, as you hold Kitty.'

Bert climbed off Cecil's knee and came over to her. 'Squash up, Millie. There's room enough for me in that chair. It's nearly as big as the sofa we had . . .' As they all did, when triggered to recall a memory out of the blue, Bert faltered and his face coloured.

'The one in our tenement flat, yer mean, Bert? Well,

59

you're right there. It is. I like to remember the home we had, and love to hear that you remember it, too.'

Bert's grin came back. Cecil, as usual, had said exactly the right thing. They were all in tune with each other, whereas Millie often felt at a loss as to what to say, or said the wrong thing. Never before had she felt this divide between them, but then maybe it was because she was still upset about Elsie moving out soon.

Bert soon dispelled the feeling as he wriggled his bottom to sit beside her, giggling as he did so. 'Yer want some room, Millie.'

She giggled with him.

When they put the baby on his knee and told him to support Kitty's head at all times, Bert said, 'Millie will help with that. I'll put me arm on top of hers, then Kitty will be safe.'

The feelings Millie had experienced were erasing. Bert was special. And this was confirmed as he wriggled further into her heart when Kitty gave a loud burp. He looked up at her in astonishment, then leaned his head on Millie's arm in a fit of giggles. She felt in that moment as if she was his big sister, and experienced the same love that she knew Elsie and Cecil had for Bert warm her right through, as she wished that she truly was.

Something struck her then: though his colouring was different, Bert had a look of her father – hadn't she seen a photo somewhere of a relative on her paternal side who had fair hair and blue eyes? Was Bert, too, a child of her father? Hadn't he and Elsie's, Cecil's and Bert's mum had a long-term, on–off relationship? But then nothing had ever been said about her father having been around when Bert was conceived. Brushing the thought away and putting it down to a fanciful feeling, as Cecil came over and took the baby,

Millie smiled as Cecil said, 'So, Bert, what do you think, now you've held her then?'

'I love her, Cess. She makes me insides feel nice, as if something really good has happened. But she can't 'alf let wind! She's nearly stunk us out, ain't she, Millie?'

Millie grinned. 'She has.'

'Ha, that's the magic of my Kitty. She's brought something special to all our lives, and I reckon she did so riding a motorbike – or at least that's what it sounds like, when she starts.'

They all laughed. Millie had got used to the sometimes crude, but inoffensive banter of the cockneys, so she laughed with them.

'Now she'll need changing, so show us the way, Millie. Come on, Dot luv, let's go up to the rooms that Millie's got ready for us and see to Kitty. She's ready for her afternoon nap.'

Millie went to ring the bell to summon a servant, but then thought better of it. 'This way. It's up a couple of flights, I'm afraid.'

'I'll come, too. I'd like to see the nursery, and where you're going to be sleeping, Dot.' Elsie linked arms with Dot as she said this and was rewarded with a huge smile from Dot. The sight rekindled once more the hope that Millie felt for Dot.

'And me – wait for me.'

'You, buggerlugs, can get back to your tutor.'

Bert moaned, but did as Elsie told him to.

The clock had just struck four when Cecil came down the stairs and knocked on the sitting-room door. Millie and Elsie had spent most of the afternoon in what used to be Millie's father's study, but was now completely changed. Gone were the conventional red-leather, high-winged chairs and huge desk. Millie had brought in a small couch and two writing desks. The book-lined wall was no longer there, either, so now the room looked light and airy and not stuffy and unwelcoming.

They'd been planning Elsie's move to Rene's and what she wanted to do with the flat, and discussed a few matters to do with the jam factory, one being a new line in green-gage jam, a flavour they hadn't made yet and that Jim had suggested.

On her saying, 'Jim's such an asset', Millie earned herself one of those looks from Elsie that said, 'Don't start.' They giggled, but Millie wished Elsie would wake up to how taken Jim was with her. To her, they seemed a perfect match.

As soon as Cecil entered he told them, 'Dot's in a deep sleep. Ruby's watching over her and Kitty. I must say, I nodded off. It was a long night of travelling.'

Elsie got up and went to him, linking arms with him. 'You're home now, Cess. We'll all support you and Dot in any way you need us to.'

A tear slid down Cecil's cheek. Millie hesitated, not wanting to embarrass him, but then realized that wasn't what this family would do, as she remembered how Cecil had helped her when her horse had bolted last year.

Getting up, she went to him and linked his other arm, then steered Cecil towards the sofa. 'Anything, Cecil, anything we can do, we will. Do you think a . . . well, a doctor who specializes in this sort of thing would help? We can afford one, and can afford to have him come here, so Dot wouldn't have to face going to another strange place.'

Cecil sat down heavily. 'I don't know. I have faith in

Gertrude, the nurse I told you about. Were you able to find out the times of trains? I need to make sure I'm at the station for her.'

'Are you certain she will come, mate?'

'I am, Else. I've never been surer of anything. She's like no one else I've ever met. She's reassuring, and it's as if she knows things that others don't.'

Millie felt she had to say something that was niggling away at her. 'I'm worried, Cecil. Look, it may not be my place, but Dot is my half-sister and I love her very much. It's just that, well, what kind of a person gives up her job like that? I am concerned this Gertie may have an ulterior motive. I don't know what, but it all sounds so . . . so unbelievable – a nurse, of many years' standing, walking out on the many patients she can help, to concentrate on one she has only just met!'

Expecting Cecil to be cross with her, Millie was surprised when he agreed and then added, 'But she seems like a ray of hope. I am so scared. This is very sudden with Dot, and I can't get my head round it. She's been tired, yes, and touchy, and not caring about her appearance, the flat or making sure she has shopping in and my dinner ready, but I thought all of that would pass. When it all blew up, I didn't know what to do, and Gertie seemed to offer a lifeline.'

'I can have her checked out, Cecil. She won't know. I can ask my solicitor to make enquiries. Let's find out for sure that she is genuine.'

'But I can't stop her coming.'

'I know, and I have had a bedroom made up for her, and told the staff that Gertie is to have the same standing as the tutor has, and to be treated and looked after accordingly.

But if our worries turn out to be right, then she won't be here long enough to do any damage.'

'Would you do that, Millie? I'd be grateful – it would put me mind at rest. Ta.'

'So as I understand it, this Gertie says that what has happened to Dot can happen after childbirth, particularly if the woman has something traumatic in her life already?'

'Yes, Sis. And, God knows, my poor Dot has that – buckets of it. I could kill her mum. If only she would accept us and let us marry. I think the biggest thing that frightens Dot is being an unmarried mother. Not only the stigma, but everything: what her mates might say . . . all of it. When Dot realizes that we really are in London, and not just visiting a fancy house that Millie owns, I think it will trigger her off again.'

Cecil lowered his head into his hands. Millie could see the effect this had on Elsie. She went to her brother's side, her face a picture of someone lost and unable to find an answer. But then a determined look crossed her face, 'I'm going to go to see Beryl Grimes, mate. I meant to before now. I'll talk to her, I'll make her see sense. Surely she will relent, now that she knows you fathered Kitty? I didn't condone her before, but I understood. Finding themselves pregnant, but not by their boyfriends, then marrying the boyfriend was something both she and Mum did. Beryl thought Dot was taking the same route and, knowing the disaster it turned out to be for her and Mum, Beryl didn't want that for Dot.'

'I'd never have been like they were. The men who married our mum and Beryl thought they had a pure girl coming to them, and it turned them both sour to find out the truth. But I knew the score, and I made me decision to love Dot's child as me own, if it turned out it wasn't mine.'

'You're special, Cess. Look, mate, this will turn out all right. Dot needs time, care and love, and she'll get that here.'

'I know. Can we stay for a while, Millie? We won't get under yer feet. Only Dot seems settled and seems to like it here. She was like a kid looking round the room and the nursery and kept saying, "It all belongs to me sister, yer know, Cess."'

'Of course you can, and for as long as you want to. Elsie and I will be going up to Leeds the week after next for Ruby's wedding, but you will be fine here – the staff will look after you. Look, I'll get my driver to take you to the station to fetch Gertie. You can relax in the back then.'

'Ta, Millie. I feel as though you're my sister, as well as Elsie's.'

'I am. Or would like to be, Cess.'

Cecil gave a huge smile, then tutted. 'Who'd have thought, Else. Meeting Millie is like meeting a fairy godmother, ain't it? It almost makes yer feel glad that her dad walked up our alley.'

Elsie and Cecil burst out laughing, but Millie felt a bit lost. She knew it was a joke, but it hit a raw nerve. Elsie realized first and got up to come to Millie. 'Cess didn't mean it – it's just another of those cockney things that slip off our tongues.'

'Aw, I'm sorry, Millie. I meant no offence.'

Millie smiled. 'I know, I'm all right. I didn't get the meaning of this one, but I did feel a bit upset, but only because of all you have been through.'

'Nah, don't you worry about that, girl. It happened – and as much to you as to us. All we can do now is cry about it, or laugh it off and pick up the pieces. Yer've more than done that, how yer held out yer hand to us, and I for one am very grateful.'

'Me too, Millie. Come here and let me give you a hug. The day you drop those guilty feelings will be a good day . . . I know, maybe we'll get Gertie to work her magic on you!' Though Elsie laughed at her own joke, she suddenly became serious. 'On all of us. Because I think we could all do with some help, even though we show nothing but bravado at times.'

Millie knew she was right. Her maxim of keeping busy wasn't altogether working. But maybe all of them being together would work – she tried to forget Elsie's plans to move out. She couldn't bear that thought, even though she would be married soon. And even though she loved Len. Because neither of those things made up for not having her lovely sister with her.

Chapter Seven

Elsie

A strange feeling came over Elsie when she walked towards the tenement block on Long Lane a few days later. Part of her felt sad, and there was also a feeling of everything coming back to haunt her, but mostly she felt glad they had all left that life behind.

Beryl, Dot's mum, answered the door in her dressing gown, even though it was two in the afternoon. A fag hung from her mouth and she looked tired and unkempt.

'Hello, Beryl.'

'What do you want? Slumming it, ain't yer? I'd have thought yer were too high 'n' mighty to come back to yer roots.'

Some of the fear Elsie had felt as a child when Beryl would never speak to her, only glare at her – and of the beatings she'd heard her give Dot – came back to her, but she was determined to be strong. 'I want to talk to you, Beryl. Dot's not well.'

'What! Me Dot? What's wrong with her?'

This anguish encouraged Elsie. 'Nothing physical, but she is suffering from depression—'

'Huh! Her and me both. But she caused it, so what have you come here for?'

'Beryl, please. Can I come in – there is much more to it than that. Dot needs you. She needs yer help.'

'Well, she's a bit late in asking for it. Running off with that brovver of yours. You tell him I'll kill him if I ever see him, and with me bare hands, too. It would all be over by now, if he hadn't interfered. Well, you can tell them both: they've made their bleedin' bed, so now they can lie on it – aye, and in sin, too.'

Beryl went to shut the door, but Elsie put her foot against it. Her temper – rarely shown, but consuming her when it did appear – urged her on. 'The baby is Cess's baby, not the baby of that filthy swine you married!'

'Ha, pull the other one! Dot'd say anything to get her own way. Always did when she were just a tin lid.'

The cockney rhyme threw Elsie for a moment. Beryl had made it sound like an insult, but 'tin lid' for a kid was usually an affectionate term. 'The baby has red hair!'

This floored Beryl. She stared at Elsie who, not in her normal frame of mind, added a spiteful dig. 'That's right. And she's called Kitty, after the friend you abandoned because of yer bigoted ways.'

Beryl stepped back. Her face was a picture of astonishment. Her mouth opened and her fag drooped from where it had stuck to her lips, but Elsie didn't stop there, she was past the point of no return. 'Oh, yes, and now yer making Dot a victim of your nastiness – not that you haven't always. I remember her coming out of here, having been used as a punchbag by you. If you were my mum, I'd hate yer, but Dot doesn't. She loves you. She yearns to see you, and she misses you every minute of the day.

You! You scumbag, you don't deserve a daughter like Dot and, if it was up to me, I'd never let yer within an inch of little Kitty.'

Beryl crumbled; her body slumped as she backed towards a chair. When she was sitting down at the table, she put her fag into the already-full ashtray. 'I – I thought . . .'

'Yes, well, yer know what thoughts did, don't yer? It made you like you are. It was thinking my mum had it good that made you go after her meal ticket when yer knew she was pregnant. And then yer thought to cover up your own pregnancy by marrying yer fiancé, but he knew. Besides, he couldn't put a bun in the oven for trying – how yer thought he could, when he raped Dot, I'll never know.'

'She should have told me that she'd been with Cecil.'

'Tell you! Oh no, yer not getting off the hook by putting this on Dot's shoulders. If she'd have told yer that, you would have leathered her. She did what she thought best: she took the hand of the man who loves her and pretended she was going to that convent for fallen women that you'd booked her into.'

'There! I told you all of this was her fault. She'd rather disobey her mum and deceive me, and go with someone who's just a bleedin' tin lid!'

Elsie felt beaten. But she tried one more thing to shock this woman, who at this moment she hated. 'But for him, your daughter would be sectioned by now. Yes, rotting in a loony-bin. She's been tipped over the edge, Beryl, and you and that swine of an ex-husband of yours are to blame. With your support and love, this wouldn't have happened. You have it in yer grasp to help her get better, but I doubt if yer've enough love for Dot in your little finger to do that!'

Again Beryl looked shocked. This time she didn't coun-teract, but bent her head. A huge sob racked her body. 'Why, why, why? I did me best, but she always annoyed Fred. She got under his feet. She ruined me marriage to him, and I – I loved him.'

Elsie spoke in a gentler voice than she had up to now. 'No, she didn't, Beryl. You did that. Yer cheated on him before you were married. Yer made yer own bed, and yer should have lain on it, not blamed the innocent baby – your child – and now the young woman that is Dot. But you can put that right, luv. You can!'

Beryl didn't speak, but sat quietly sobbing and shaking her head.

'Please, Beryl, do this one decent thing for yer daughter. Come with me to see her and yer grandchild.'

After a long moment, Beryl lifted her head and asked. 'How will she ever forgive me?'

Elsie sighed with relief. She'd broken down Beryl's barriers. 'She has, Beryl. She is asking for yer all the time. Dot doesn't hold any malice against yer, she never has. I don't know who she takes after, luv, because it's not you, is it? And it's not our father – we all know what he was capable of.'

'Me mum. Me mum were a good soul, like Dot. She saw no bad in anyone. Huh! It didn't do her any good, either. She ended up in the poorhouse, with me as a kid, cos some bleedin' bloke hoodwinked her. I'm more like me dad. I loved and respected me dad, but he died when I was ten. "Don't let anyone mess around with you, Beryl," he used to say. "You be the one to say how things are going to be. And if anyone does wrong by you, cut them out of your life."'

'Trouble is, yer think the wrong ones are doing wrong by you. Look, I could go on, Beryl. I saw a lot when me and Dot were kids, and yes, I'm still seeing it, but it won't do any good. All of us have got to look to the future. Do that, Beryl: look to a future where yer forgiven, and let Dot marry the man she loves. Then you will have a family to love and be proud of. Or you can choose to rot here on your own, living in squalor, cos you're not taking care of yourself or your flat . . . Think about it – which way is best, eh?'

'I don't know. I don't know if I can go with you. It's the thought of living off charity. We cockneys never do that.'

Feeling her temper rise again, Elsie swallowed hard, as she knew anger wasn't going to win the day. 'If yer dad had given yer money and provided for you, would you call that charity?' Beryl didn't answer. 'No, I know yer wouldn't. Well, our dad didn't provide for us, didn't even recognize us as his. Now that he's dead, his money is as much ours as it is Millie's, and she acknowledges that. She needn't, but she does. She has made me and Dot an allowance and is going to make us partners in the jam factory. It isn't a handout. It is the money we have always been entitled to.'

Beryl shrugged her bottom lip. 'Where is she?'

'She's stopping with me and Millie, in Millie's house.' Seeing that Beryl thought this another chance for her to protest, Elsie jumped in, 'But she needn't be. If she had a mother to take care of her, Cess could get Dot her own house. He's already got a specialized nurse for her.'

'A nurse! Is she that bleedin' sick?'

'She is. Beryl, she didn't even know who I was, when they arrived a few days ago. But the nurse is working wonders with her. She was working at the asylum where Dot was taken. Millie has checked her out, and she's a lovely, genuine lady. She—'

'A bleedin' asylum. My Dot!'

Elsie nodded.

'Take me to her, Elsie. Please take me to her.'

'Thank God, Beryl! Blimey, mate, yer a hard nut to crack. Yes, I'll take yer to her, but there are stipulations.'

'What bleedin' stipulations – she's me daughter, and none of you lot are going to keep me from her, or give me conditions under which I can see her. So you can stuff that in your pipe and smoke it!'

Elsie knew this was a battle she wouldn't win. She'd have to leave that to Gertie. It had been Gertie who had said that, yes, it was vital that Dot had her mum with her, but from what she'd heard of her, there would have to be rules in place – or, far from aiding Dot's recovery, her mother would send her right over the top. Elsie agreed with that. She knew more about Beryl and her cruelty to Dot than she'd let on.

'For one, I ain't taking you in this state. You wash yerself and yer hair, Beryl, and you put on clean clothes. I never thought in a million years I'd have the courage to say this to you, but you stink!'

Beryl drew her lips together. To Elsie, she looked evil. And even more so when she opened her mouth, exposed her blackened teeth and filled the space around them with her cackling laugh. Unnerved, Elsie stared. Beryl slapped her hand on the table and said, 'Yer your bleedin' mother personified. She would have said that to me in the good ole days, when we were mates.' She crossed her fingers, 'Like that, we were. Me biggest regret was falling out with her – well I told you that at her funeral. I meant to make it up to yer and take care of yer, but all that was taken from me when bleedin' Fred did what he did to me Dot. And then the daughter of that bleeder who was responsible for it all started playing the fairy bleedin' godmother.'

Elsie kept quiet. People like Beryl would never take responsibility for their own actions. Everything was always someone else's fault. She wondered if they were doing right to get her back into Dot's life, but it was what Dot wanted – that, and to marry Cess.

Elsie had meant to tackle this subject with Beryl, but knew in her heart that she wasn't going to agree to it yet. The vindictiveness and need for revenge that Beryl had displayed all her life were still in her, and would stop her allowing it. Concern filled Elsie as she wondered how Beryl's hate for Millie would show itself. Already she had shifted some of her own responsibility for her wrongdoings onto Millie's shoulders. Well, that's something Elsie knew she wouldn't stand for.

With this thought, it came to her that she did have the strength to stand up to Beryl, because hadn't she just done so? And hadn't she witnessed that it could be done, by the way Beryl was cowed by her ex-husband. All it took was to be stronger than her. To beat Beryl with her own stick. That's what Dot should do, but even as she thought this, she knew it would never happen.

Beryl had filled a bowl from the large kettle that had been simmering away on the hob, and now she stood it on a high stool that she'd fetched from the scullery. 'I'll just wash me hair in this, then I'll take it through to the bathroom to wash in. I can rinse me hair in cold water – have done for bleedin' years. Makes it shine.'

73

Once Beryl was in the bathroom, Elsie took off her coat and rolled her sleeves up. Using the last of the hot water in the kettle, she filled the bowl that stood in the kitchen sink and gathered the dirty pots that lay everywhere – on the table, on the floor next to Beryl's chair, on the draining board and covering every surface of the kitchen. By the time Beryl came out, Elsie was wiping down all the surfaces.

'What're yer up to, girl? Blimey, yer your mum in everything. She couldn't stand a messy place.'

Beryl stood with a towel wrapped around her curly black hair, with her blue eyes twinkling.

As Elsie looked at her, she was reminded of one of her gran's sayings: 'Them as look as though butter wouldn't melt are the ones to watch out for.' And that's how Beryl looked now.

'Well, luv, if yer want to finish the job, there's a broom in the cupboard.' With this, she laughed and went towards her bedroom.

By the time she emerged, Elsie had swept the floors of the scullery, the kitchen and the linoleum that covered the living room.

'Blimey, girl, you can shift yerself when you want to. Ta for that, it's made me feel a lot better. Now, girl, how do I look? Will I do?'

Elsie saw a transformation she wouldn't have believed possible. Beryl looked like the attractive middle-aged woman she was. Her frock was almost the same colour as her eyes, and the fitted bodice and straight ankle-length skirt suited her slender body well. She wore a fox fur around her shoulders, and her lace-up black shoes had a kitten heel. Her hair had begun to dry and fluff out a little, framing her face, which had undergone the most astonishing transformation. The rouge she'd applied to her cheeks was just enough to give her a more youthful blush, and it complemented her ruby-red lips.

'You look lovely, Beryl. Like a star of the stage!'

'Well, I was always a looker. When yer mum and me went up west, we turned heads, I can tell yer.' She sighed then and shook her head. 'Where did it all go wrong, eh? We had ambitions, me and her. We were going to better ourselves. We both could sing, and used to get wonderful applause when we sang in the pub where yer gran played. She could have helped us, your gran, but although she played the music hall, she didn't want that for yer mum.'

'I know, but the pity is that Mum was going to realize that dream, shortly before she was killed.'

'Really?'

'Yes, I'll tell you about it on the way. We should get going now. Millie's driver is waiting for us.'

'What? I ain't going in no bleedin' posh car. The neighbours would hang, draw and quarter me, saying I was getting above meself.'

'No, they won't. They know the score. Most of them work in the jam factory and are happy for me and Dot – though they think Dot is looking after an old aunt in Leicester, so we've that hurdle to cross one day.'

Beryl gave a 'Humph!' to rival that of Mrs Robinson. This made Elsie giggle.

'Oh, all right then. But if I 'ear one word of—'

'Shut up and get in.' Elsie grinned at Tom, who stood opening the door. After what she had said to Beryl this afternoon, telling her to shut up was mild. Beryl did as she was told, but not without having her say. 'I've never heard the like. Think yerself someone now, don't yer, Elsie Makin? Well, watch out, cos the mighty can fall.'

'Only if they make themselves do so by their own actions – as you know, Beryl.'

There was another huff, then as she sat back Beryl said, 'Well, yer not wrong there. And I know I'm that way but, if given a chance, I can change.' She snuggled into the soft white leather. 'And this is just the chance I need.' This she said with a sly grin in Elsie's direction and, despite everything, Elsie had the feeling that she could like Beryl. But she also knew she would always mark her gran's words and be wary of her.

Chapter Eight

Elsie and Dot

When they arrived and Barridge showed them in, Cess was waiting in the hall. He must have been in Elsie's and Millie's office to see them arriving, or the dining room, as both of those rooms looked out onto the road. Upstairs rooms that did so were guest rooms that hadn't been opened up.

The nursery and the room occupied by Dot and Cess were on the third floor and looked over the park, as did Elsie's and Millie's bedrooms on the first floor. The basement was the domain of the staff, and those who lived in had their rooms in the attic.

Cess stood tall, not showing the nerves that Elsie knew he must be feeling. She smiled at him, trying to convey that this was exactly how he should greet Beryl. She only hoped that he didn't crumble under Beryl's bitter tongue-lashing.

'Hello, Mrs Grimes.'

'You! Don't yer stand there in yer fancy clothes and talk to me as if yer've nothing to be ashamed of. If me Dot's ill, it's all down to you.'

Barridge's face was a picture as he looked from one to the other. Elsie prayed that Cess would handle this in a way that would cause the least embarrassment possible to Millie. Her staff were already up in arms at having to look after such commoners, as they obviously thought she, Dot and Cess were. She'd heard a few intentionally snide remarks, such as 'Never in Mr Hawkesfield's day' and 'Miss Millie's gone mad.'

Elsie bit her lip. But Cess rose above it. 'Barridge, will yer show Mrs Grimes into the sitting room, please.'

Barridge's expression showed that Cess had gone up in his estimation. 'Yes, sir. This way, madam. Would you like tea?'

'It ain't bleedin' teatime yet – I've only just had me dinner.'

'Very well, madam.'

When they reached the sitting room, Millie was waiting for them. 'Mrs Grimes, how lovely to see you again. I have never forgotten your courage. You are a woman I admire greatly. And, my, you look so lovely. I love that frock.'

With the wind taken out of her sails, Beryl coloured. 'Well, thank you very much.'

'Sit down, dear, please.'

Recovering, Beryl said, 'I haven't come here to make small talk, mate. I want to see me Dot. I'm taking her home with me. I'll get her better – we don't need any specialist nurse.' Looking at Cess, she said, 'Nor any kidnappers who make me Dot go against me wishes.'

'I can't let that happen, Mrs Grimes. It would be against Dot's wishes, and would be detrimental to her health. Her nurse will be with us in a moment. She will explain everything to you. She is in total charge – with consent from Cecil – of all that happens to Dot.'

'Oh no, she bleedin' ain't! Nor is he. I'll go to the police and tell them that yer've all abducted me Dot and that he

78

knocked her up! Now she's in a bleedin' mess, but I'll get that sorted. Until Dot's twenty-one she is me sole responsibility, and no one else's. *I* say what she can do and what she can't, and *I* say what will happen to her and when.' With this, Beryl folded her arms across her chest and set her lips into a straight line.

Elsie had heard enough and was about to tell Beryl so, when Gertie was shown into the room.

'Ha! So this is the knight in shining armour then?'

'Mistress in armour actually, and you – I assume – are Mrs Grimes, Dot's mother.'

'I am, and I want you to stop poking your nose into mine and me daughter's affairs and take me to her – now!'

'Of course. Come along, this way.'

Elsie couldn't believe this; she'd thought Gertie would have told Beryl what to do with herself.

Beryl hesitated, then turned to Elsie. 'Will yer come up as well, Elsie. If Dot's upset with me, you can calm her.'

For the first time Beryl seemed unsure of herself. Elsie welcomed this turn of events and could see that Cess did, too. She followed them out of the room. As she got to the door, she turned and mouthed to Cess, 'Don't worry.'

When they reached Dot's room, Beryl seemed hesitant again. 'She is all right, ain't she, Elsie?'

'No, Beryl, but is it any use telling yer that? Go carefully with her.'

'Yes, very carefully. If you don't, I'm afraid you won't be able to stay.'

As if lost for words, Beryl harrumphed at Gertie. Gertie let her through and then winked at Elsie, as if to say that she'd got everything under control. But Elsie wondered if she realized what everything was, where Beryl was concerned.

Dot sat propped up in bed, her face pale, her eyes puffy and her hands pulling at the sheet.

'What's she doing in bed! I thought yer said she wasn't physically ill, Elsie? Dot? Dot, it's me, yer mum.'

As Beryl approached, Dot turned her head. Her eyes stared blankly at Beryl.

'It's Mum, Dot. Come on, girl. Hey, yer know your ole mum, don't yer? Dot?'

A bewildered Beryl turned towards Elsie. 'Why don't she know me? Elsie, tell her I'm here. Dot?' Beryl sank into the chair next to Dot's bed. Her face creased, her mouth wobbled and tears streamed down her face. 'Me Dot. What's happened to her?'

'If you had allowed me to, Mrs Grimes, I would have told you downstairs what to expect. Dot goes into periods of amnesia – memory loss. It's the brain's way of coping. Sometimes it does it against the very thing the patient longs to happen. Especially if that thing, or person, is wrapped up in the trauma they are suffering.'

'Well, how can I be wrapped up in her trauma?'

'Only you can answer that, Mrs Grimes. I do know from Cecil that you have refused to forgive your daughter for running away with the father of her child against your wishes – which were to make her give her child away and—'

'But I thought the kid was her . . . Well, it don't matter now. Anyway, Dot understood why.'

'She didn't understand why you didn't visit her, or let her visit you, nor did she understand why you wouldn't let her marry the man she loved and whose child she was carrying.'

'Because we didn't know it was his – and God knows I know what that's like. Oh, he probably promised her that he'd take care of her and her kid, but when push came to shove—' Beryl gasped as if someone had slapped her.

'Mrs Grimes, I don't know what happened to you, but it sounds to me as if you have had a raw deal along the way.'

The gentle tone of Gertie broke Beryl. She fumbled for her hanky and hid her face in it. The distressed sounds she made tugged at Elsie's heart. She went to go to her, but Gertie held up her hand.

'Mrs Grimes, I think you need a nice cup of tea and a moment to let the truth of the situation sink in, so that you can deal with it, don't you, duckie? And there's no one better than a mother to do that. Shall we go into the nursery? It's just next door, and there's two comfy armchairs in there next to the fireplace, where there's a lovely fire lit. Your granddaughter is in there with Ruby, one of the maids. I can dismiss her, duckie, and you can hold little Kitty and care for her for a while. I know your daughter would like that.'

Beryl didn't object. She stood ready to be guided wherever Gertie wanted to take her.

'Would you like Elsie to come through, or shall you and I have a chat on our own?'

'I'd like to talk in private – not that Elsie doesn't know most of it, but—'

'That's all right, Beryl,' Elsie said. 'I'll talk to Dot.'

Beryl seemed a changed woman when she came out of the nursery half an hour later, carrying Kitty.

Cess had joined Elsie, but Beryl didn't even look at him. She walked up to Dot. Dot looked at Cess – her bouts of amnesia had never affected her memory where Cess was concerned. She watched her mum approach and smiled at

81

her, but Elsie knew it wasn't a smile of recognition and prayed that Beryl would be able to handle that.

When she got to the bed, Beryl said, 'Hello, me Dot, it's Mum. I've got yer beautiful little baby. I love her, Dot, just like I love you.'

Dot looked afraid. She looked round her. 'Cess, Cess!'

'I'm here, me darlin'. It's all right, it's yer mum. Yer wanted to see your mum, didn't yer?'

Beryl's face changed. A bitter expression, full of hate for Cess, flashed across it.

Dot turned towards Beryl. 'Mum?'

'Yes, darlin', I'm here. Me and you are going to be mates again, Dot. Yer remember how we sorted everything and got on so well? You were happy then, weren't yer, girl? I was, too. We can put all this behind us. I was only trying to do the best for you, now, I can take care of yer and of Kitty, eh, girl? Yer'd like that, wouldn't yer, mate?'

Dot nodded. Elsie didn't think she'd picked up on the implications, as Beryl was still excluding Cess.

Elsie saw Cess look at Beryl. His voice held anguish as he asked, 'You will let us get married, won't you, Mrs Grimes?'

Elsie heard Gertie take an intake of breath and knew this wasn't in the plan. She wanted to ease the tense situation, but didn't know how to.

'Well, we'll see about that as time goes on, shall we? The main thing is for Dot to get better, and back to her old self. Gertie said that can happen, if we take things slowly.' Beryl's look towards Cess held so much meaning.

Cess looked devastated. He had a theory that the single most important thing for Dot's recovery was to be allowed to marry him.

'I want to marry Cess.'

Dot didn't say this to anyone in particular, but the way she said it, with distress in her voice, frightened Elsie and prompted her to say, 'You will do, Dot. Hang on to that. You will.'

Beryl made a sound that told of her disdain.

Dot whimpered, 'Will I, Elsie? Will yer help me and Cess to get married?'

'I will, mate. You leave it with me.'

Dot smiled. Beryl didn't speak. She didn't have to, as her set facial expression told of her objection.

'Right, everyone, I think Dot needs to rest now. Say your goodbyes to her.'

'Not Cess – let Cess stay, Gertie.'

Elsie wished with all her heart that Dot had wanted her mum to stay. She could see that being second best, or not even considered, was killing Beryl and increasing her hatred of Cess.

'Dot, luv, will you give your ole mum a hug, mate?'

Dot turned towards her mum and it seemed to Elsie that she really recognized her for the first time. 'Mum, you came? Oh, Mum, I missed yer so much.'

'And I missed you, girl. I'm sorry I didn't come to see you before. I – I was afraid for you, in case the baby was . . . well, you know.'

'But she isn't, Mum.'

'I know. She looks like her namesake – Kitty Makin, Elsie's mum. Well, me and you'll see that she has a better life than Kitty did, won't we, me darlin'?'

'Yes, Mum. She's called after you, you know. Her name is, Beryl Kathryn Elsie, and that's what she'll be christened, as soon as me and Cess are married, as the church ain't much for accepting children who were born out of wedlock.

I'd like her to be christened, though, Mum. We can get Rene to make a frock for her.'

This was Dot at her most lucid, a time when it was hard to believe there was anything wrong with her.

'Oh, there's no need for that. I've still got the gown you wore to be christened. And I'll talk to Father Hines. He's a good man and knows all the circumstances. He'll christen Kitty.'

'Oh, I'd love that – me own gown for me baby, and Father Hines doing the service. Will you ask him if he'll marry me and Cess, Mum?'

'We'll see. You don't want everyone knowing you had a baby before you wed, do you?'

Dot's face clouded.

'I mean, well – we can pretend you are, can't we? Anyway, we'll talk about it all when you come home. Back where you belong, eh, girl? Me and you, like it used to be.'

'As Dot's nurse, I must insist that everyone leaves now, please! She mustn't be overtired.'

Dot looked confused. Lost and as if torn in pieces. She put out her hand to her mum. 'You'll come again, won't you, Mum?' Her head swivelled to face Cess, and she said his name in a way that was a plea to him to make things right.

Cess had made Elsie proud many times, and now he made her even more proud of him. 'It's all right, me darlin', your mum's just saying what any good mum would say: that she's going to look after you. She doesn't mean anything else. She's too good a person to, and she loves you. And little Kitty. She loves our baby – her granddaughter – so she'll want to do the best for you both, to make sure you're the happiest you can be.' He looked into Beryl's eyes, full of hate, and asked, 'Isn't that right, Mrs Grimes? Tell Dot that's what you mean, so she can rest and not fret.'

Although Beryl didn't answer, she had no choice but to accept this, as Dot opened her arms to her mum. 'Oh, Mum. I love you. Thank you, thank you.'

Even the embittered Beryl couldn't mistake a glimpse of the old Dot and dampen that, could she? As Beryl handed the baby to Elsie and stood and leaned over the bed to accept the hug, Elsie prayed that she wouldn't. 'Cess is right. I only want what is best for you, darlin'. I've made a lot of mistakes, I know, but . . .'

'Hush, Mum: all forgotten. Like you said, me and you are mates and always will be, won't we?'

'We will, me little darlin', we will. And no one'll come between us. No one.'

In that moment Elsie felt a dread settle in her. Beryl wasn't going to let go of the control they'd all suspected she held over Dot, and she worried what the outcome would be.

When Beryl had gone and Dot was asleep, Elsie sat with Millie and Cess in the sitting room. Cess was relating to Millie what had happened during Beryl's visit to Dot, and was expressing his worries about Beryl's intentions.

Millie listened and then became thoughtful for a moment. When she spoke, she surprised them both. 'I think there is a solution, Cecil. You and Dot could elope.'

Like Elsie, Cess looked mystified. 'Do what?'

'Run off and get married. Go to a place in Scotland called Gretna Green. Couples can get married there without parental consent, and it is all legal and binding. Lydia and Wickham said they were heading there in *Pride and*

Prejudice.' Millie said this as if they should both know what she was talking about, but Elsie hadn't a clue. Cess shocked her by showing that he did!

'The book by Jane Austen, you mean? I've got a copy, but I haven't read it yet. So a couple does this eloping thing, but that's fiction, not real life. Me and Dot can't do that.'

'Why not? We'd have to have Gertie's backing, of course, as she would have to convince the powers there that Dot's of sound enough mind to consent. And in this, I think she is. She may be confused and forget who everyone is, but Gertie says that's part of a safety mechanism for her. But the one thing Dot is clear about, and never forgets or confuses, is that she wants to marry you, Cess. And though she wants her mum to consent and to be there, I think she would be happy when she realizes that she can go about freely – go to the jam factory and see her mates, and hold her head up high, as none of them need know that she married after the baby was born.'

Cess asked the question that Elsie wanted to. 'But what about her mum? Beryl could tell everyone and make us out to be wicked, and to have broken her heart. And she could withdraw from Dot again, and that wouldn't help Dot.'

'I don't think she will. We can talk to Beryl: tell her she can take that path, or she can take the one that will help her keep her pride, by telling everyone that she is very happy about it all and knew all along, but wanted Dot to be able to tell them herself.'

'Oh, Millie, it sounds as though it would work – after all, Beryl will have been telling folk that her daughter is looking after her elderly aunt. They've all speculated about you going off too, Cess, but I've been honest with them and have said you'd gone to be near Dot.'

'So when we tell Beryl what me and Dot have done, we can tell her to save face by saying that she knew?' Cecil said. 'I don't think she will. Do you, Else . . . really?'

'She can do what she likes, Cess – and will, knowing Beryl – but she can't get away from the fact that she told everyone why Dot was away. Is she going to want everyone to know the truth? Because we can threaten her with letting everyone know – including the police – how her ex-husband raped Dot.'

Cess flinched visibly, and Elsie felt immediately sorry that she'd spelled out the sordid facts. She was sat next to him now and reached for his hand. He squeezed it, letting her know he was all right.

A silence fell. Elsie imagined that, like her, Millie didn't want to press Cess too much. The decision had to be his. But she did hope against hope that he'd go with the idea and that it would all fall into place.

'Do you know how to get on with this type of wedding, Millie?'

'Well, I've never known anyone do it, but when we studied Jane Austen's work at school, I remember one of the things that was pointed out was that in Jane's day you could arrive at midnight and be married at dawn. But now the law of Scotland requires at least one of the couple to reside for twenty-one days in the parish they are to wed in.'

'Well, that puts paid to that idea then.'

Millie, who could always think on her feet, disputed this. 'Why should it? We can get round that. You could tell Dot's mum that Ruby has asked you both to her wedding. But instead of that, you could travel to Scotland and do whatever is necessary – we'll make sure we know exactly what is required of you before you go, by asking my solicitor. And then all you have to do is marry. In the meantime we could tell Dot's mum that Dot loved it up there with my mama and is making such progress that the two of you are staying there for a while. To make it more authentic, we can tell her that she can visit if she likes, but that you'll only stay a couple of weeks, and it is a long journey. We could get Dot to write to her, telling her herself that she has decided to stay up there. It could work, Cess.'

Cess grinned. 'It could, it really could!'

Elsie felt a lovely feeling come over her. It meant so much to her to see Cess happy. She sent up a prayer asking God to please make this happen, and for the outcome to be that they had their old Dot back, as she always used to be – timid, yes, but funny and loving, and a lifelong friend.

Chapter Nine

Elsie

Gertie had taken to the idea of helping Dot and Cecil to get married as soon as they told her about their plan, but did caution them. One of her stipulations was that she was to be left to introduce the idea gradually to Dot.

'We have to remember that she has already suffered a setback. Her mother seems to have some kind of a hold on her, and she plays with Dot's emotions till she gets what she wants. She has greatly upset Dot over the past week or so by refusing to accept Cecil and still not consenting to their wedding. I need to get her over that hurdle first.'

This panicked Elsie. 'But we only have a few days. Ruby's wedding is at the end of this week, and that would be an ideal time.' She told Gertie how Millie had said they could get Cecil and Dot on their way, on the pretext of going to Ruby's wedding. Gertie relented when Cecil suggested that she was present when he told Dot and, if it caused Dot anything but happiness, then he wouldn't go through with it.

Dot had been ecstatic about the whole idea. And so now here they were, on their journey north.

The train whistled along. Elsie kept her head turned towards the window for most of the way, enjoying pointing out the various changes in the landscape to Bert, as they left London's grime behind for the open countryside. But even though this fascinated her and she enjoyed the beauty of it all – and Bert's excitement, as he stood with his nose pressed onto the window-pane, gasping in wonderment at it all – Elsie couldn't relax, so conscious was she of Len sitting between her and Millie.

Concentrating on everything and anything else, she thought of the plan Gertie had told her that she had for Dot. 'I intend to try and help her stand up to her mum – not to fall out with her, but to have a healthy relationship, built on love and mutual respect, and not one that depends on Dot having to do all the pleasing.'

The way Gertie analysed Dot's mental state, with this and many other insights into the cause of what was happening to her, made it seem a simple task to get her well. But what Gertie said next, Elsie wasn't so sure of. 'She needs to confront all that has happened to her, to make her mother see how her cruelty affected her and, ultimately, to get an apology.'

Elsie could never see that happening.

She looked over at Cess, Dot and Gertrude sitting oppos-ite, and wished with all her heart that she could make Dot better. She looked so afraid as she clung to Cess's hand. Thank goodness Kitty had journeyed well, as this could have upset Dot further, but she was sound asleep in Gertie's arms.

On the morning of Ruby's wedding, Elsie had never known such excitement. She loved this beautiful, rambling house and the beauty of the surrounding park.

Every room she'd seen radiated a graceful splendour – her bedroom, which had two beds in it (one for her and one for Bert), was in soft blues, with deeply polished mahogany furniture and a carpet of blues and pinks that her toes sank into. And the sitting rooms, all decorated differently and yet making you feel as though you had hardly moved from one to the other, were in pale colours: lovely greens, greys, pinks and blues, with huge feather-cushioned sofas in creams, pale browns and blues. The walls were half clad in panelling, with wallpapers above that reflected the colour of each room, as did the carpets and curtains that dressed the floor-to-ceiling windows, from which you could gaze out at picturesque views of the garden and the wider vista of the park.

And now they stood in the vast hallway, an excited little group – Bert looking adorable in his jodhpur-shaped grey trousers, white shirt and brown herringbone jacket, and Millie looking so lovely, dressed in her lilac bridesmaid's frock. Lilly, a friend of Ruby's, was in a matching frock, and Mrs Hawkesfield, Millie's mum, whom Elsie adored, was looking elegant and beautiful in a light-grey silk costume, with a jacket that flared from the waist over a long, slim skirt. And Ruby's mum, who was just an older version of Ruby and as lovely as she was, was looking every bit as elegant in a maroon-coloured costume. Her jacket flared from the shoulders to her hip, and her skirt was cut straight until it reached her calves, then flared out, giving it a mermaid shape.

The first carriage, which would carry Elsie, Bert, Dot, Cecil and, to her dismay, Len, stood outside. Gertie was to stay behind and look after Kitty. The carriage behind theirs was to transport the bridesmaids and Millie's mum. And the third carriage, decked out with ribbons and flowers, was for Ruby and her mum.

The weather was lovely. A slight breeze made the swaying heads of the many daffodils seem like a moving carpet, but the sky was clear and the sun, which dappled leafy patterns through the swaying trees onto the huge lawn in front of the house, gave off a nice warmth.

'So where's the rest of us? Millie, have you seen Dot and Cecil this morning? And what about Len?'

'Yes, they all had breakfast with us. I am sure they will be down in a moment, Mama.'

Millie's mum had breakfasted in bed, and hadn't seen that everyone was up and organized for the day's proceedings. Millie raised her eyes in a mock-impatient expression. Elsie smiled at her. She felt so relaxed – so accepted here. She smiled at the calmness of Ruby's mum as she reassured Mrs Hawkesfield. 'Eeh, everything'll be grand and go to plan, you'll see, madam. There's no need to get anxious.'

'Ha! Betty, as the mother of the bride, it's you who is supposed to be nervous, not me!'

Betty giggled. She was so far removed from the impression of housekeepers that Elsie had gleaned from their own Mrs Robinson, and from the relationship that Betty had with Millie's mum, that it didn't seem as though she was a servant.

But then all of the household staff were different from what Elsie had known at Millie's. They gave the impression of being one big family, with Millie's mum as their mother, rather than their boss.

'Ah, here they are.'

Elsie turned as Mrs Hawkesfield said this and had to stop herself gasping at the beautiful picture they all presented – especially Len, in his grey morning suit and grey top hat. Cess, too, looked dapper in a suit of light grey, with a jacket cut in a similar line to a morning jacket, but with a much shorter tail. Dot looked tiny and frail – funny how she appeared smaller, and yet was the same height as Elsie herself – but lovely too, in a green satin frock, which although straight and not adorned with braiding or any decoration, was elegant in its simple lines, and was made sophisticated by the addition of a fox fur. On her lovely curly hair she wore a small black hat, with a lace veil. Elsie wanted to run to Dot and gather her in her arms, but she didn't want to make a fuss that might further frighten her.

Instead she waited until they had come to stand next to her. 'You look the bee's knees, mate.' She took Dot's hand as she said this and gave it a gentle squeeze.

'Oh, Else, I feel I shouldn't be here. Hello, Bert, mate.'

Bert had come over all shy and just smiled at Dot. Elsie ignored this, knowing how strange everything must be for him. 'I know, Dot. How did it happen, eh? Me and you hobnobbing it with the toffs. Ha, me mum'd have loved this. Anything theatrical and she was in her element.'

'I miss them days, Else. I know we didn't have much, but somehow I look back on them as me happiest times, and always thought me and Cess would have a flat in the tenements, amongst our own.'

'I know what you mean, mate. Well, we can go back – not to the tenements, but to where Rene lives in The Blue: there's some nice flats. I can't wait for you to see mine. And there's no better cockney area than there. I even saw a pearly queen standing on the corner when I went to visit the other day. I felt that proud to be able to put a shilling in her collecting tin.'

'I love the pearly kings and queens, Else: they look all sparkly, and I like to hear the rattle of their tin.' Bert's face held an expression that Elsie hadn't seen for a while – an eagerness; no, a longing.

'It won't be long now. You'll go to a proper school and have mates to play with. You'd like that, wouldn't yer?'

Bert didn't have time to answer as Dot said, 'Oh, it sounds like heaven. I always liked it down The Blue when we sneaked off down there together, do you remember?' She had come alive, too. Her eyes were no longer dull, but held an eager anticipation.

'I do, Dot. It was better than the city centre to us. And do you remember that day we hopped onto a tram? We had such a laugh.'

Dot giggled.

Cess hugged her around the waist and smiled at Elsie. For a moment it was as if Dot wasn't sick, and everything was as it was when they were just three South London tin lids.

'When you're married, Dot, that'll be our first job – to find you and Cess and little Kitty a place of your own.' Something occurred to Elsie then. 'In fact, I think I've found it!'

There was no time to elaborate on this, or to relieve the astonishment that she saw in Cess and Dot's expression, as they were being ushered down the steps and into the carriage. But once in the carriage and finding herself sitting next to Dot and opposite Len, Elsie was glad to have something to talk about. Especially as Len had held her hand to help her to board, telling her that she looked very beautiful – and his touch had zinged through her.

She'd never felt so glad to be dressed in a fitting way for an occasion such as this. Rene had made her frock, and had chosen the colour and the satin cloth, telling her that pale blue would complement her red hair. The style was fitted, but swathed around her hips to be caught up in a mock-bustle at the back. The bustle was really a draping of the lovely material, but looked very effective. She wore a fur cape over the frock, in a charcoal-grey, and a small charcoal-grey beret-style hat decorated with a feather, dyed to match her frock. She had to bend low to enter the carriage, to avoid catching it on the roof. This had given her a distraction from the pounding of her heart at being so near Len.

Once they were all seated, Elsie turned her head to look at Dot, thereby avoiding looking into Len's eyes. 'As I was saying, mate, I've a great idea. Rene's place is three storeys. I was going to have the top two floors, but I don't need both. Me and Bert can manage with the top floor. The rooms are really quite big. I can divide the living room to make a music room and . . .'

'Really! You'd share it with us, luv? Oh, Cess, that'd be perfect.' A wide grin spread across Dot's face.

'Anything that makes you smile like that, me darlin', is perfect. But what's all this about a music room, Sis? A bit posh for you, ain't it?'

Glad to have more to talk about, to keep her from thinking about the nearness of Len, Elsie told them her idea.

Len spoke when she'd finished. 'That sounds really interesting. I would love to help in some way.'

'I'm fine, thanks, Len. Millie is going to help me.'

'Oh, it's the old "girls against the world", is it? You two are so alike in your views of helping the less fortunate. Though I worry that Millie wants to go further than that and work with the Federation that was responsible for last year's strikes.' Len rolled his eyes.

Elsie had the feeling that he was disapproving, and this annoyed her. 'Well, it's easy for them who have everything to sit back and enjoy it. It takes guts to fight for others. And both me and Millie believe in doing that, and will join in helping anyone who needs us to. And if not that, then we'll start up help-groups for them. This is what my music idea is all about.'

'Oh, don't get me wrong, Elsie. I'm all for it, but you can't put everything in the world to rights. You have other responsibilities, and getting the factory on its feet has to be a priority. That's my only argument with Millie about her desire to right the world.'

'Well, you're our bank manager – you *would* think like that. But to us, it's people first, and make money second.'

'But don't you see? By making money and creating a stable working environment, you are helping people to help themselves?' Yes, Elsie did see that, and now she felt at a loss, as Len had taken the wind out of her sails.

'I think you're both right,' Cess said. 'But what Elsie is proposing won't in any way interfere with her work at the factory, mate. I think you've got her and Millie wrong. Knowing them, they'll put the factory and the workers first, but will still fight for the underprivileged and the rights of women.'

'I know you're right, Cess, but think if it was Dot trying to help everyone, and you had your nose pushed out of joint. Millie's always up to some scheme or another, and going into areas where she might be in danger. It worries me.'

'Yes, I see that, Len. She never blinked an eye at coming to the tenements when we lived there, but we all worried for her.'

'There, you see, Elsie, even your brother agrees with me. I have never forgotten how I met you both.' Len's eyes looked intently into hers. Then he coughed and carried on. 'That was typical of what I'm talking about. Those boys would have hurt Millie, if I hadn't happened along.'

'I – I, know. It's just that, well, sometimes you sound as though you are criticizing her . . . and me. I – I feel responsible, but Millie had this spirit before I met her.'

Len leaned forward and reached for her hands. Elsie jumped and he looked puzzled. There it was again: that fleeting something in his eyes. His hold on her froze Elsie, so afraid was she of showing her feelings.

'Elsie! Elsie, please don't take it like that. I'm sorry – I'm used to lively debate. None of it is personal. It would never be intended that way, I promise. I admire you more than any person I know. You have shown great courage, and have helped others too. I would never criticize, just play devil's advocate and try and help you and Millie to think before you act.'

Wanting to pull her hands away, and yet wanting him to hold them forever, Elsie nodded. 'I – I understand. I . . .'

He let go of her hands and sat back, but his gaze remained on her, unnerving her. 'I'm so glad, Elsie. Ah, here we are, I think. At least I can see a church, and some people dressed in what I think they call their Sunday best.'

There it was again: that note in Len's voice that made her feel her lower-class station in life. Angry once more, she snapped, 'And cost them a week's groceries, no doubt. But then that's what the poor have to do – sacrifice one thing for another. Looking nice for special occasions is all the luxury some people have!'

Len looked perplexed, but had no time to retaliate as the carriage came to a halt and the door was opened for them to alight.

Getting out first, Len offered Elsie his hand. This time she declined to take it and fussed over helping Bert down the steep step, so as to not look rude. Holding her head high, she marched towards the church entrance.

'Hold on, Sis. What's the hurry, mate? No doubt there's seats reserved for us – we're one of the posh lot today.'

97

Cess caught hold of her arm and turned Elsie towards him, grinning down at her. 'Them toffs don't mean any harm. They're up their own arses, we all know that, but it's just the way they are.'

'Len isn't a toff. He's upper-middle-class and he knows what it's like to be looked down on, as the toffs look down on him, and yet he still does it to others, and it makes me so angry.'

'Why does he get you going like this, Sis? We've had this all our lives, and you've always coped with it.'

'It's not Len! It's the whole thing of putting folk into categories, and thinking yourself better than them, that gets me. And it goes on among all levels of people – even servants put themselves in a high-'n'-mighty position and think it above them to do things for one of their own class. The sooner we move into our flats, the better, then I won't have this . . . oh, I don't know what to call it, but it won't happen to us, Cess.'

'Sis, what's wrong? You're crying. Hey, it's not that bad.' His arm came round her, and Dot's trembling hand came into hers. Holding on to it, she looked into Dot's frightened face and felt ashamed that she'd upset what had been an exciting day. And even more so when little Bert snuggled into her side. 'I'm sorry. Hey, come on, Bert, I was having a daft moment. I'm all right now. Oh, Cess, I shouldn't be so touchy about it. I don't know why I am.'

'Because you're a lovely person, Sis. You think of the downtrodden all the time. Even though we've risen above what we were, you haven't left your roots, mate. And that's a good way to be, not something to be sorry for. I don't tell you, but I should: I love and admire you, Sis. You've been the saving of our family. You brought us up, me and . . . and our Jimmy, God rest his soul, and little Bert. And our mum relied on you, too. She'd have gone further into the gutter, if it wasn't for you. But all that's behind us now, Sis. We've got a good future to look forward to.' He turned then and put his arm round Dot. 'Though me darlin' Dot still needs you, and I do, and so does little Bert. And all the Lens in the world can—'

'Bugger off!' Len stood there, looking ashamed, and his face held a plea. 'I'm a buffoon. I can only apologize, and I know that isn't enough.' He hung his head. 'I – I've learned a lot today. I've learned that I am insensitive to others' feelings, and I don't like that about me. What is normal to me hurts others. I'm ashamed. But, well, I can change, given time.'

Cess held out his hand to Len, who took it and shook it. He looked relieved as he said, 'Thank you, Cess. Elsie, will you forgive me? But more than that, will you keep on teaching me the error of my ways?'

She didn't want to let him off the hook, she'd done that so many times. And besides, she didn't want to take the hand he offered her. So instead she made a joke of it, knowing that she had to lighten the atmosphere. 'I'll put you on probation.' She forced herself to smile. 'If you really can change your ways, and see people as people – all doing the best they can with the hand they've been dealt – and do some acts of kindness towards them, then I will forgive you.'

As he dropped his hand, Len smiled – a heart-tugging smile. 'I think that's fair. We should all prove that we mean what we say.' He looked around him. 'Ah!' With this, he turned and walked towards a young woman who was trying to support an old lady. Len gallantly offered his arm to the old lady. 'May I help you, ma'am.'

The old lady looked up at him. 'I'm not your mam – now bugger off!'

Len's face was a picture. Elsie burst out laughing. As he came back to them, his cheeks burning, his expression said, 'What did I do?'

Elsie could feel Cess's body shaking, and knew he was trying not to laugh. But she couldn't help herself. Len looked upset for a moment, then his face creased into a smile and he laughed out loud. But he managed to contain his amusement when the young lady came up to him and gave a slight bob. 'I'm so sorry about me ma, sir. She didn't mean it.'

Elsie realized that she was one of the maids from Millie's mum's house, and felt mortified that she might have thought they were making fun of her and her mother. But mostly her look of fear gave Elsie the idea that she might also be afraid that she would be reported. Without thinking, Elsie gathered her into her arms. 'You've nothing to be sorry about, mate. We were laughing at our friend getting his comeuppance. He's a lot to learn.'

'It seems I have. Please offer my apology to your mother.'

The maid looked mystified, but smiled at Elsie. 'Ta ever so much. Eeh, I thought I'd be in trouble, then.'

'No, you can't help what your mum did.'

The girl smiled at Elsie. 'Ma's a proper tartar at times. By, when she were housekeeper to Mr Hawkesfield, the staff lived on tenterhooks. Life's a bed of roses with this new one. She even asked us all to the wedding. Me ma didn't do owt like that when I married. She thought the other servants below her station.'

'Ha! So you see, Elsie, it isn't just me you've got to educate.'

Len's grin told her that he felt as though he had won the

battle, but she gained some ground by her retort: 'Well, you're a good one to start with, mate. By practising on you, I'll be an expert by the time I get round to anyone else.'

His laugh told her he'd taken it all in good part, something she liked about him – Len could take whatever you threw at him.

'Don't worry, Miss . . . ?'

'Rose Pike, Miss.'

'Well, don't worry, Rose. What made us laugh was that I took him to task over a bit of snobbery. So now that you've pointed out your mum's way of thinking herself better than others, he's like a dog with two tails to wag.'

Rose laughed, and Elsie thought the moment lightened with the lovely sound.

'Well, Miss, good luck with that – there's a lot of it about. I find it easier to keep me place and then . . . Oh, I didn't mean . . .'

'I know you didn't. Anyway, you'd better get back to your mum, Rose, and I hope we'll see you later.'

'You will. I'll be serving you all the wedding breakfast.'

Elsie sighed as Rose left. In her heart she wished that she was happy with her lot, like Rose appeared to be, instead of feeling like a piggy-in-the-middle of two worlds. Turning then, she saw that Dot stood huddled close to Cess, looking bewildered. 'I don't change, do I, Dot, eh? I never learn.' Elsie took Dot's other arm. 'Oh, look! Here comes Millie and her mum. Ooh, don't she look a smasher, eh, Dot?'

But even as she tried in a roundabout way to comfort Dot, her own heart needed comfort as she saw Len bound across the grass to stand at Millie's side, and plant a kiss on a giggling Millie's cheek.

Chapter Ten

Elsie and Dot

Ruby looked beautiful and so happy. The wedding ceremony and the breakfast all went without a hitch. To Elsie, but for her troubled heart, it was a perfect day of the kind she never thought to be involved in.

They had just toasted the bride and groom and sat down, when Cess nudged her. 'What's wrong, Sis? I can feel you're troubled in some way. Go easy on that sherry, mate – that's the third you've taken off the tray.'

'Oh, Cess, I like it. It takes me pain away.'

'Yes, and replaces it with more troubles – you saw what it did to Mum. Don't make it so that me and Bert have that to cope with all over again.'

Elsie felt mortified. And very cross – something she knew happened often lately. As if the whole world, and all those she loved, simply wanted to make her temper rise.

'Don't be sho stupid!'

There was a hush around her. Faces, all hazy to Elsie, looked in her direction. Swallowing hard, she laughed. 'Shorry, I was talking to my daft brovver!'

'Elsie!'

'I wassh only trying to cover up. I don't think yous daft.'

'Come on. I think the speeches are over now. Let's go and get some fresh air. And you too, Dot darlin'. Let's take Elsie out for a while and have a little walk. The grounds here are lovely, and it'll do us all good.'

Elsie was aware of others getting up to leave the table, so she felt it all right to go with Cess. When she stood, she wobbled. 'Oh dear, me pins ain't me own.'

Cess laughed. 'No, mate, yours are in the bloody sherry bottle!'

'Don't swear, Cess. We're in a posh place.'

'Come on.'

Out in the air, Elsie's legs went completely and she had to slump onto Cess to be able to keep upright.

Dot giggled. 'Oh, Elsie, you're drunk!'

'It's not funny, Dot. I think Elsie's let herself, and us, down.' Elsie began to heave.

'Christ! Help me get her round to the back of the building. She's going to disgrace herself.'

Their half-dragging of her stopped the overwhelming urge to throw up that Elsie had felt, but once they stopped and propped her up against the wall, she bent over and emptied her stomach. 'Ooh, Cess, I'm shorry. I'm shorry, mate.'

'Ha, so you should be. But I'll forgive you. You missed me shoes.'

'Can I help? Has she had too much to drink?'

'Oh, Roshe, I have. Sho shorry, mate.'

'Don't worry, Miss Elsie, come with me. Eeh, Cook's tea'll soon sober you up, lass. Leave her with me, sir. You see to your wife.' Elsie felt sad then, as she saw Rose tap Dot on the shoulder. 'Now, don't you go upsetting yourself,

Miss Dorothy, lass. Eeh, we'll sort her out and have her back with you in no time.'

'Ta, Rose. I'll take Dot for a walk and come back to fetch Elsie in a while,' Cess said.

Elsie felt safe with Rose and went gladly with her.

'This way, lass. Now sit on this bench. It's where we all sit to have a brew. I'll go and whisper to Cook what we need, and I'll bring it out here to you. Then at the right moment, when the coast is clear and you're feeling better, I'll sneak you up the back stairs to your room, lass, and no one'll be any the wiser. I'll give a message to Mrs Hawkesfield and Miss Millie that you have a headache and will be back down when you've had a rest.'

'Oh, Rose, I've been a bad girl.'

'Naw, lass. By, if I had the troubles I've heard as you've shouldered, I'd drink a bottle of sherry, let alone a few glasses. Eeh, I reckon as you've learned your lesson, though. Alcohol only increases your problems, not takes them away. Just wait here – I'll not be a mo.'

It registered with Elsie that everyone knew what had happened to her and her family, and she had the urge to run and run, and rid herself of the shame of it all. She stood, but her legs had other ideas and plonked her back down again.

'Elsie! Elsie, are you all right? I saw you almost slump on Cess. What's wrong?'

She looked up into Len's eyes. He was so close, she could touch him – she wanted to. She lifted her hand. He took hold of it. Her body swayed. 'Elsie, oh, Elsie.' His arm came round her and he pulled her into his body. This is where she wanted – no, needed – to be. Her head flopped onto his shoulder. 'Len. Oh, Len.'

'Elsie, my beautiful Elsie.'

Her heart soared; all the pain left her. When Len suddenly let her go and stood, she felt confused, but then Rose's voice made her feel afraid. 'I'm sorry, sir. I didn't knaw as you were here. I've brought . . .'

'Yes, of course. I – I was just supporting Elsie until you returned. I'll leave her in your capable hands.'

Elsie felt bereft for a moment, but then her fear revisited her. 'Rose, mate, I didn't know what I was doing. I'm shorry. Pleashe, pleashe don't tell anyone!'

'I won't lass. It weren't your doing. He took advantage of you. Here, sip this. And you take care around men like that. If they're not faithful to their own girlfriends, then they won't be faithful to you, neither. Poor Miss Millie, saddled with him.'

'He's not bad, Roshe. It was me.'

'He is. And don't you go blaming yourself for everything that happens to you, lass. You've drunk too much and he shouldn't have acted in that way. You're going to be mortified when you sober up. I just hope as you don't remember it.'

Elsie's confusion deepened, but she didn't argue any further. She liked and respected Rose. She wanted her as a friend. An uncomplicated one, who took her for what she was and didn't need anything from her: not to be propped up or reassured by her, and not even to have her plug the loneliness within her. Just to be her friend.

When she woke, Millie was standing by her bed. 'Come on, you. Ha, I saw you going at that sherry. I don't blame you. How are you feeling now?'

'Oh, Millie! I'm sorry . . . I—'

'Hey, no tears. No one else noticed. Except Len, and when he came back to me he said one of the maids was taking care of you, so I thought it best not to make a fuss. Especially after Rose came to tell me that you had a headache and were lying down. I thought I would leave you for a while.'

'What time is it? Oh, my mouth is so dry, and my head's thumping.' She looked over to the empty bed beside her. 'Where's Bert?'

'Rose has left a pitcher of water here for you. I'll pour you a glass.' As she did so, Millie said, 'It's five o'clock, and Bert's fine, he's been playing with some of the children. Ha, I heard him telling them that they talked funny – then they retaliated and said it wasn't them, it was him. That took the wind out of his sails. Anyway, he went with Dot and Cess.'

'Are they all right?'

'Yes, they didn't stay at the reception long. They went for a walk. I saw them when they came back, and all three, including Dot, looked so happy. Anyway, the reception has all been cleared away and everyone is resting. Ruby said to tell you not to worry at all about having to lie down, and she hopes your headache gets better and you'll join them for the main party this evening.' Millie sat down on the edge of the bed. Her face had an unreadable expression.

'Are you all right, Millie?'

'Yes. Look, don't worry if you don't want to come down. I've got to, of course – and I want to. But . . . well, I'm having a funny day.'

'Oh, what's up, luv?' As Elsie asked this, her cheeks burned – and memory slapped her in the face. *Oh God!*

'Don't look so mortified: it's nothing you've done. I've been thinking of how this day marks me losing Ruby. She's been by my side since I first started at that snobby school at the age of twelve – she was only fourteen. I wouldn't have survived it all without her. And then it occurred to me that soon I'll be rattling around in that large house on my own again, until my marriage. But that's another source of my upset today. I don't know what's wrong with Len. He seems distant. When I talked to him about it soon being our turn, he shrugged and made an excuse and went to talk to my mama. I don't know what's come over him.'

Elsie leaned her head back onto the pillows. *Oh God, what have I done?*

'Anyway, I mustn't trouble you with it. It's probably all a bit hurried for him. We haven't been together for a year yet, and so much has happened. Maybe I should put the wedding off for a bit. Oh, I don't know.'

Unable to say anything, Elsie took Millie's hand. Guilt crowded her. *How could she have behaved like that? How could she betray her lovely sister?* But then she knew. It had been her heart that had done the betraying – she'd lost control of it. She vowed it would never happen again.

Dot stood with Cess and Gertie outside the hotel they had come to, just over three weeks ago. Her body trembled with anticipation and nerves.

What was to happen today was what she had dreamed of, and yet she couldn't stop the feeling flooding her that her life had been taken away from her. She wanted what the new life offered, but she also wanted parts of her old life back – or to come with her on this new journey. *Mum, oh, Mum, why? Why are you how you are? Why can't you be happy to see me happy?*

'Are you ready, me darlin'?'

Looking up at Cess, Dot knew that she was. His kissing

of her gently on her lips took away her sadness that her mum wasn't there to see her wed Cess.

'We're going to do it! At last, me darlin', we're going to tie the knot!'

'I'll be able to hold me head up then, won't I, Cess?'

'You can always hold your head up, in my eyes, luv. Oh, Dot, you look so beautiful. I love you with all me heart.'

Although her pulse quickened at his words, she couldn't deny the heaviness in her that they had to marry in this way, with no family or friends to witness their big day. This thought gave her an overwhelming feeling that set her body trembling, which soon turned to a violent shaking of her limbs.

'You're all right, duckie. Here, Cess, take Kitty for me.'

'Gertie! Gertie, help me.'

'I'm here, my love. And you're just fine. Bride's nerves is all it is. Don't worry, Dot, me duck. I've got your medicine for you – it will calm you.'

No, I don't want that. I want to make myself calm. I want to remember every moment of the ceremony that will see me become Cess's wife!

'Here, take this, Dot, love.'

She shook her head. Making an extreme effort, Dot controlled the shaking. 'I'll be all right, thanks, Gertie. You'll stay close, won't you?'

'I will, duckie. I'll be near to you as long as you need me to be. I'm so proud of you. This is a big day for you, and if you can get through it without having another bad attack, then you will have taken a massive step towards getting well. So do what we have been practising. Deep breathing, and think calming and beautiful thoughts. Banish all *if onlys* from your mind. And remember: what you want most in all your life is about to happen.'

'It is. Come on, my Cecil, let's get married!'

'Oh, me Sunday name, is it? Well, Dorothy, I'm all for that today. And, me darlin', this is the happiest day of me life.'

As they stood in the Blacksmith's Shop, their hands tied together with the ribbon that Gertie had bought when they'd been told it would be needed, a familiar smell of smelting iron surrounded her, transporting Dot to her walk from the tenements to the jam factory. She and Elsie used to pass a blacksmith's on their journey every day.

A horse snorted to the side of them. She and Cess watched as the blacksmith tethered it. 'Och, I'll be needing the anvil for a different purpose for a wee while, Rabbie boy. Your shoe will have to wait.'

'Hold on, mate. Blimey, you ain't thinking of marrying us over a lit anvil, are yer?'

'Ha, ken I might. I've a few scores to settle with you Sassenachs.'

Cess looked astonished, and Dot felt her uncertainty coming back. But then the blacksmith put his head back and roared with laughter. 'Och, don't be daft. Come over here. I've one that hasn't been lit forever and a day.'

They giggled as they made their way over to the anvil. Then, standing each side of it, they looked into each other's eyes. They'd been told to compose their own vows. Dot took a deep breath, but before she could utter a word, the door burst open. Turning round, the sight of Elsie and Bert coming through the door filled her with joy. 'Oh, Elsie . . . How?'

'I'll thank ye to get on with the marriage. I have another two couples waiting, and a horse to shoe, lassie.'

Dot fought the laughter that came to her and said her

109

words clearly. 'Cecil Makin, I take you as me wedded husband. I'll love you forever.'

'Dorothy Grimes, in me heart you've always been me wife, now I'm honoured to give you me name. You're me life, and I will love you forever.'

A loud banging on the anvil made them all jump. 'That's it. That signifies that ye be a married couple now, binding by law. I'll untie ye, and ye can make your payment and tack ye marriage licence.'

As soon as they were untied, Cess took Dot into his arms, rocking her from side to side. 'Me wife. At last, Dot. Oh, I love you, me darlin'.' Tears rained down his face.

Dot smiled up at him. His lips came towards hers, but she heard an irritated 'Och, ye've years ahead for that – dip ye hand and pay me dues and then be off. And I wish ye luck.'

They both laughed. As Cess sorted out the payment for the blacksmith, Dot turned and went into Elsie's arms.

'Congratulations, Dot, luv. I'm so happy for you. Me half-sister and me sister-in-law . . . Ha, we are bound forever, mate.'

'Is Dot my sis now, Else?'

'She is mate – she's your sister-in-law.'

'We did that in me lessons. When someone marries your—'

'Yes, we'll go into the nuts and bolts later. For now, congratulate your new sister, Bert. Tell her how happy you are for her.'

'Happy wedding, Dot. I'm happy you're me sis now, but you always have been really.'

'I have, Bert. Thanks, mate.'

Cess came over then and they went into a group hug, all giggling and crying at the same time.

When Dot came out of the hug, they laughingly made their way outside.

Feeling full of happiness, she felt a new strength come into her. Something felt different. She couldn't say what, only that she felt less afraid, and the things that crawled around her mind, confusing her, had gone. She turned and looked towards Gertie, lovely Gertie, who was like a mother to her. And, in Gertie's arms, little Kitty, who had completed Dot's world. Taking a deep breath, she knew she could go forward with, or without, her own mother, as long as Gertie stayed by her side.

With this thought, her head swivelled back to look at Cess, her beautiful Cess. Dot wanted to tell him: to shout it out to the world that she was released. But a sudden searing pain in her head stopped her. It enveloped her in agony. Her hands went to her temples. Voices came to her – Cess's lovely voice, above all the others.

'What is it, Dot . . . Dot! Me darlin', I've got yer . . . D – o – t!'

The pain took his voice along with everything in her world: the screams, the cry of her Kitty, and the picture of her mum that had come to her. Dot was alone now, alone with the all-consuming agony burning inside her head.

Suddenly release from it all came about. All hurt left her and she began to float in a beautiful swirl of white netting. It was supporting her, lifting her and, as it did so, she was filled with a peaceful happiness.

Chapter Eleven

Elsie

Cess's holler filled the space around Elsie. He kneeled over the unmoving Dot. Elsie couldn't help him. She'd frozen. It was as if she was suspended in an ever-closing circle of horror.

'Take the baby, Elsie . . . Elsie, please take Kitty, I have to see to Dot.'

Something tugged at her skirt. 'Else, Else!' A tear-filled, frightened voice – Bert needed her. This thought brought her out of the stupor she'd gone into. She took Kitty and held her in one arm, rocking her to try and soothe her, while bending and putting her other arm around Bert, giving – and trying to glean – some comfort. 'This isn't happening. It isn't.'

But before her she saw the proof that it was. Her beautiful half-sister lay on the floor, dead. Gone . . . Gone forever. 'No, no. Dot . . . No!'

'Else! Else, what's the matter with Dot? Why isn't she moving, Else?'

Elsie couldn't answer Bert.

Gertie had stopped trying to revive Dot and straightened her back. Still kneeling, she bent her head in despair. This revealed Cess to Elsie, and she saw that he was cradling Dot's head in his arms. His tears mingled with his snot. Terrible moans came from him.

In this unreal world, Elsie registered some giggles. She looked up and saw a young couple, who only looked around fifteen years of age, holding hands and walking past them – not seeing them, or the tragedy that held them cocooned in an unreal world.

Beside her she heard Bert sob, but could do nothing to help him.

Gertie rose. 'She's gone. Oh, Dot . . . She's gone, Elsie.'

Elsie knew her head was wagging from side to side and she could feel every part of her body trembling. A million protests rose up in her but all she could say was, 'Why? How?'

'I think, but don't know, that she suffered a massive brain haemorrhage – a bleed. If that's what happened, then no one could have saved her. I – I tried . . . I did. But you must help Cecil now, Elsie – your brother needs you. I'll take the baby and Bert and put them into the carriage. I'll get the driver to come and help to lift Dot. We must take her to the hospital. She has to be seen by a doctor, and they will do a post-mortem to determine what happened.'

Although she answered, telling Gertie that she had a car waiting for her, so they could follow and could all go with Dot, none of it had really sunk in with Elsie, only that she had to see to Cess.

Kneeling beside him, she put her arm round him.

'What – what's happened, Else? Oh, Else, save me. Save me, I'm falling, mate.'

'I've got you, Cess, luv. I won't let you go.'

'How? What?'

She told him what Gertie had said.

'No, Elsie . . . Tell me that me lovely Dot ain't dead!'

Elsie looked down on Dot. Never had she looked more beautiful. Her skin was waxy and her face had a serene expression. Her tumbling curls formed a shining halo around her head. Her pale-lemon silk bridal frock framed her tiny figure, and the sun glinted on her new wedding ring.

Elsie wanted to scream out the pain that the lovely sight gave her, but knew she had to be strong for Cess. Supporting him, she helped him to rise after he'd gently lain Dot's head down. 'We have to get her to the hospital, Cess. They will tell us what happened.'

Cess got out a huge white hanky from his pocket and wiped his face. 'It hasn't happened, has it, Else?'

'Oh, Cess, I wish with all my heart it hadn't. Our lovely Dot.'

Taking him in her arms, she held him as they gazed down at Dot. *I only found out you were my sister last year, Dot, but you've always been that to me. Friends since we were toddlers, we went through so much together. I can't go on without you – I can't.*

Five days later, two coffins lay side by side next to an open grave.

After hearing the news, Beryl had been found dead the next day – her wrists cut. Elsie had the unholy thought that she was sorry Beryl had done this, as she'd wanted the satisfaction of killing her herself.

The post-mortem had shown that Dot had had a brain haemorrhage, as Gertie had suspected. But it also found that she'd suffered many minor bleeds in her brain over the past weeks. And this, they learned, was the probable cause of her amnesia attacks.

They had to comfort Gertie, as this knowledge had given her terrible feelings of guilt. 'I should have suspected – I should have! I'm a nurse! I've seen this before. I was concentrating on her depression following the birth, and I put everything down to that!'

Only the doctor had been able to console her, telling Gertie that, even if she had suspected the condition and taken Dot to a doctor to have it confirmed, there was nothing anyone could have done about it. They had no known cure for weakness in the vascular system. It was always only a matter of time.

Cess hadn't wanted Dot's mum to be buried with her. They'd tried to persuade him that Dot would have wanted that, but in the end it wasn't up to them. Suicides weren't allowed to be buried in consecrated ground. So Beryl's body was staying with Dot's until Dot was buried, and then the undertakers would take Beryl over to the other side of St George's churchyard. Elsie was glad about this. She didn't want to visit Dot's grave and have to know that she was also visiting the evil Beryl.

She'd only just thought this when she had the sickening sight of the disgusting Fred, Beryl's ex-husband. Cess stiffened beside her. 'Ignore him, Cess, luv.'

But Cess marched over towards Fred, his fists clenched. Elsie held her breath.

'And what do you think you can do about anything, eh? I've more right than you to be here. I were married a long time to Beryl and were dad to Dot.'

A couple of the men from the tenement blocks and Peggy stepped forward. Fred looked from one to the other, spat on the ground and left.

Elsie went to meet Cess as he returned to the graveside,

but he skirted her and collapsed in a sobbing heap on the ground next to Dot's coffin. The priest stayed Elsie as she went to go to him. 'Leave him, Elsie. Dot and the Lord will give him comfort.'

Someone's arm came through hers. She turned and looked into Millie's weeping eyes.

'Oh, Millie, Millie, our lovely Dot.'

Len stepped forward, but Elsie glared at him, stopping him in his tracks.

'I've got yer both – hold on to me.' Rene's arm came round their shoulders, and they both turned and went into her hug. Len turned towards Cess.

The droning of the prayers went on, with deep moans coming from Cess, which tore at Elsie's heart. Without knowing where he had been in the last few minutes, Elsie saw Bert walk over to Cess and offer him his little hand. Cess took it as he looked up from his kneeling position, into Bert's pale face. Len offered his hand and together, Bert, but mostly Len, helped Cess to rise. Through her tear-filled eyes, Elsie watched Cess lift Bert up. Her heart was breaking as her two brothers clung to one another – so much sadness, so much.

Beyond them she could see her mother's grave: as yet, unmarked. Soon it would be, as the stone was ordered. On it Elsie had asked for the inscription 'A mother, greatly loved. A mother, who gave great love. RIP.'

'Elsie. Elsie, love. Cess is all right.'

Millie's kind voice penetrated the thoughts that had kept Elsie standing, observing all, but feeling nothing. She felt Millie's arm holding her own more tightly.

'Help me, Millie. Help me.'

'I will, Elsie. My dear, dear Elsie.'

'And I will, mate. I'll be by your side the moment you ask me to.'

'Ta, Rene.'

None of them followed Beryl's coffin when it was taken. To them, it seemed she had caused so much hurt – physically and mentally – to their beloved Dot, and they all hated her for it.

Two weeks later the June sun sparkled on the Barmouth sea as Elsie and Cess, carrying little Kitty and Bert, alighted from Cess's car.

It had been Millie's idea that the four of them should visit her Welsh holiday cottage together – it had seemed ideal. But now that they were here, memories hit Elsie and made her gasp for breath. Bert felt them, too. He clung to her hand and asked, 'We will visit Jimmy, won't we?'

'Yes, we will.' Elsie sighed. Visiting their little brother Jimmy's grave would bring back so much pain and rub salt into their raw wounds. 'When Cess is ready to.' She turned to him. 'We needn't, you know. Jimmy will understand. Besides, we don't have to see his resting place to know that he is with us. I feel his and Mum's presence all the time.'

'I wish I could feel Dot's. How did it all happen, Sis?'

'Oh, Cess, was this a good idea?'

'We can make it so, luv. I'll try. There may be a few times when you just have to let me go off, walking or driving, and not worry about me. I need solitude as well as the comfort of knowing you're here.' Bending down to Bert, he said, 'So, mate, this is where you and Jimmy were then, when the authorities took you from us?'

Bert nodded.

'Well, I can't think of a better place, Bert – that's if you had to go, which we couldn't stop. Were you happy some of the time?'

'Some of the time. Some of the sisters were nice. And . . . I loved being with Jimmy.'

'I know, mate. But our Jimmy was always sick, and God had other plans for him. I bet he's found Dot and'll take her to Mum. And they'll look after her for us.'

'Won't she go to her own mum, Cess?'

'No. And that woman won't get the chance to be near her, as she will have to take a trip downstairs and rot in hell.'

'But won't Dot miss her?'

'No, Bert. I believe that when we die, we lose our earthly feelings – we must do, as they say there is no pain, no worry and nothing but peace. But I don't think we lose the love others had for us, and they root for us every step of the way – it'll be Jimmy's job to root for you, and to watch out for you.'

Bert looked up and grinned at Elsie. She grinned back. When Cess straightened, she thought how courageous he was, and what a good man he'd turned out to be. Swallowing hard, she forced a smile onto her face. 'Come on, let's get inside.'

Bert took Cess's hand. 'There's some steps to go down, Cess, and you can touch the roofs of the cottages built lower down on the hill, as you pass them.'

'Lead the way then. And when we get in, I'll make up a bottle for Kitty and you can feed her.'

'All right, but you will have to make her burp. I can't do it. I end up bloomin' burping meself.'

They all laughed, and Elsie marvelled at how they could. Although they followed the instructions on the carton of powdered milk, she and Cess struggled to get it right. 'We should have brought Gertie with us, Cess. What if we can't manage? I know nothing about bottle-feeding babies, mate. Mum breastfed yer all until you could eat a rusk, then we just boiled cow's milk for yer.'

'You're a woman. It'll come natural to yer.'

'Ha, don't let Millie ever hear you say anything like that! She hates our roles to be defined, as she calls it.'

'Millie's a one-off.'

They'd settled Bert on the sofa, with Kitty safely propped on his lap, while Elsie took Cess to show him the rest of the cottage. 'There's only two bedrooms, so I'll have Bert and Kitty in with me, in the one I usually share with Millie. There's two single beds in there and a large set of drawers – we can use one of the drawers as a cot. There's only one bed in the second bedroom. Only I . . . well, I thought if you have a room to yourself, you can have some time on your own.'

'Ta, Sis. Yes, like I said, I do feel the need of that now and again. And a weep. I weep most nights for me lovely Dot. And that'll be no good for Bert to hear. He's been through enough, poor lad. Aunt Phyllis, Mum, then Jimmy and now Dot.' This last he said on a sob.

Elsie reached up and put her hand on his shoulder. 'When did you get so tall, Cess?'

'Ha, I can give you a good four inches, Sis. So if you see a bloke who's six foot and has my sandy hair, it could be me dad.'

Though she laughed, Elsie wondered if Cess ever wanted to know who his dad had been. She'd always longed to know hers, but when she did find out, she wished she hadn't. Even Millie, who'd loved their father and had been brought up by him, wished that. 'Maybe you're better off not knowing, Cess.'

They'd done the tour of the little cottage, with its scullery-cum-kitchen, and now stood outside, as Elsie pointed out the toilet in the yard.

'How does Millie cope with that? I bet that was a shock to her.'

'Oh, Millie's adaptable. She takes everything in her stride, though she has talked of extending to the left into the sloping garden and installing a bathroom.'

'I don't know how you've coped living in her house, Elsie. Me and Dot didn't like it – the servants mainly, they treated us like dirt under their feet.'

'I know. I'm sorry that you never made it to the flat together. Will you still move in there with me?'

'I will, if you'll have me, but you needn't make it into two flats. We can jog along together. And when I get on me feet, I'll find a place of me own. That way, you'll be able to have your music room as you planned it.'

'We'll see. You can stay for as long as you like, it'll be lovely to all be together – and for me to have that second living space as a music room eventually.'

'Didn't Len say he'd help you with that? I know you didn't want his help, but he's a clever bloke.'

'No! I mean, you know how he can put me down at times.'

'Sis? Have you a problem with him? Only Dot – you know how much she loved you and seemed to know what you were thinking at times. Well, she thought . . .'

'Oh, Cess. There *is* something. I – I will tell you – need to, as the guilt is wearing me down – but . . . I'm not ready.'

'Come here, Sis.' She went into his arms. 'Whatever it is,

we'll face it together. Just as long as he's not taking advantage of yer?'

'No, well. A bit. It was when I was drunk. But it wasn't his fault.'

'Bloody hell, Sis! I'll kill him!'

'No. Look, I'll tell you more, but not now. Forget it for now. You have enough to cope with. And . . . and I can't face me shame at the moment.'

Cess released her and looked into her eyes. 'All right, Sis. You tell me in your own time, but I will need to have a word, you know that.'

She nodded. She trusted him to make the right judgement when he'd heard all of the story. Part of her agreed that Len did need a talking to, but part of her was afraid that he might distance himself from her – not that she would mind that, as it would be easier for her to cope with her love for him, but it was her fear of losing Millie that held her back. She was wishing now that she'd never mentioned it.

The next day, they were ready to visit Jimmy's grave, and the nuns who had taken care of both him and Bert. As the convent was too far to walk to, Cess drove them in his car. The Sisters were pleased to see them and welcomed them inside the convent. Sister Rose hugged Bert, making him blush.

Bert chatted on to cover this as they went into a small sitting room, telling the Sister that he'd met another nice lady called Rose. 'I reckon all who have that name are good people, Sister Rose.'

'They are, Bert. The rose is a special flower, so we have to be special to be called after it.' She winked at Elsie and Cess. 'Oh, and modest, too.'

They both laughed, and Elsie felt herself relax.

'Now, Bert, be off with you. You'll find all the children in the yard – David included.'

Once Bert had run off, something that had been burning away at Elsie came to the fore – something Bert had once told her. 'Sister Rose, did you get Miss Hawkesfield's letter?'

'Yes, we did. I'm sorry. I know Sister Bernard is a little heavy-handed at times, but she loves the children.'

'That's not the point, Sister. The things Bert has said are really upsetting.'

'I know. And Reverend Mother didn't dismiss them. She has sent Sister Bernard away for six months on retreat, to think about her actions. We are all praying for her, and miss her.'

Though Elsie didn't think this enough, for a woman who had taken the strap to small children and had wrapped wet sheets around them if they wet the bed, before parading them in front of the other boys, she decided she would have to leave this matter to the nuns. 'I trust you, Sister Rose. I hope you'll keep an eye on that one when she comes back here, though.'

'We will. Reverend Mother is mindful of you and your sister being such wonderful benefactors to us, and we don't want to upset you in any way. She is writing to you as we speak.'

Elsie could feel her temper rising. It seemed to her that there was more emphasis put on not upsetting her and Millie than there was on keeping the children safe.

But for her heavy heart, and wanting to be anywhere but here, she would have pursued it, and would have asked to speak to one or two of the boys. As it was, she was glad when they all left the convent, even though she was not looking forward to their next stop.

* * *

122

When they pulled up outside St Tudwal's Church, Elsie had a moment when she leaned back and closed her eyes. Cess didn't speak, and neither did Bert. When she opened her eyes, she could see Cess trembling. Bert was standing on the back seat, leaning over, and had his arms round Cess. For a five-year-old, he had the kindest of hearts and showed a very caring nature. She remembered how he would love Jimmy like that. Sometimes to Jimmy's annoyance, as Bert was too boisterous with his hugging at times.

'Shall we leave it till tomorrow, Cess?'

'No. Let's go and see Jimmy.'

'Has Jimmy got a statue yet, Else?'

'No, mate, it's still too soon. We've one on order, as we have Mum's, and we'll all come up here when it's in place. Millie, too.'

When they got out of the car and she lifted Kitty out, Elsie had a moment when she didn't think she could do this. But she held the baby to her, using her as a prop to steady herself, and walked ahead.

They were rounding the church when Elsie saw a man standing by a fresh mound of earth, his head bent in sorrow. She looked over at Cess, who had stopped in his tracks. 'Are you all right, Cess?'

'Yes, sorry, Sis. Took me breath away for a mo.'

Elsie didn't miss the tear that ran down his cheek. But Bert putting his hand in Cess's seemed to give him the strength to walk on by.

They stood around the small grassed mound where a wooden cross bore Jimmy's name.

'Well, little man, your brother's here, mate.' Cess kneeled down as he said this and touched the mound. Bert kneeled with him. Elsie turned away. The scene was unbearable to her. She walked towards the church, still clinging to baby Kitty.

The man had left the fresh grave, which gave her some relief, as she hadn't wanted to witness his grief again. Calling back to the boys, she told them she was going to sit inside the church.

The door made a creaking sound when she opened it. The inside was familiar to her, with its barn-like beams forming an apex above. But, for Elsie, there was only one focus. She made for the statue of Our Lady on the right of the altar. Not seeing anything but this, she fell on her knees and sobbed, 'Help me to be strong, Holy Mary, Mother of God. Help me be a mother to Bert and now to Kitty, and to be all Cess needs me to be.' Then, not out loud as her shame would deepen even more if she spoke the words, she asked, *And please help me to get Len out of my mind and heart. I've done wrong. I've betrayed my dear sister, Millie.*

She bowed her head and gave in to the tears, glad that little Kitty slept through this.

Seeing Kitty's cherub face, Elsie vowed, *I will be strong. I have to be.*

Chapter Twelve

Elsie

'Are you all right?'

The question, asked in a softly spoken Welsh accent, made Elsie turn. Her cheeks burned with embarrassment as she looked at the gentleman standing behind her.

'I – I didn't mean to intrude. I'm . . . I lost my wife last week. I saw you come in. I was kneeling at the back.'

Elsie smiled. 'No, it's all right. I'm sorry for your loss. Yes, I'm fine. Well, grieving, like you.'

He looked down at Kitty. 'Is this your baby?'

'No, she's me brother's. We . . . Her mother died a few weeks ago – three. Three weeks ago.'

'Oh? I'm sorry. We were to have a baby. My Blodwyn died giving birth and . . . and my son died too. They're out there. Is your—'

'No. In London, Bermondsey. The grave here is me brother. Jimmy. It's a long story, and one I can't talk about at the moment.'

'Yes, it's hard. Shall we sit on the pew? My name's Daffyd – Dai for short.'

'I'm Elsie. My brothers call me Else, but only them.'

'Elsie it is then. Pleased to meet you, Elsie. I hope you don't mind me talking to you. I somehow felt I would get comfort from talking to a stranger who looks like she has been through – *is* going through – what I am.'

'No, it's fine. I'm not sure I can be of any comfort to you. I can listen, but I have no help to give on how to get through this. The pain yer feeling in yer heart does lessen, but then it becomes jagged again when something triggers it – like me visit here. And then all the pain you've suffered crowds yer.'

'Well, it's early days for us both. Others tell me that time is a great healer. I'm not sure, though, as I haven't found that.'

'No. It doesn't heal, but it helps. Do you live far from here?'

'I have a guest house. It's across on the other hill from here. Well, it was Blodwyn's mother's. She left it to her in her will, and Blodwyn wanted to make something of it – she had great plans.'

Dai was quiet for a moment. Elsie didn't prompt him, as she knew there were times when you just needed your own thoughts, or a moment to compose yourself.

Although he was a stranger to her, she felt comfortable with Dai. A tall man, he wasn't strikingly handsome, but was good-looking. His hair, she imagined, was a lot fairer than it looked, as he had tamed it with oil into a neat style, parted in the middle. His moustache was fair and neatly trimmed, and he had nice, gentle, if sad blue eyes, which showed signs of him having wept a lot recently.

Her heart went out to him.

When he did speak, he shook his head. 'I don't know what I'm going to do now. I was working in a bank, but gave that up to help Blodwyn with the renovations and intended to work with her in running the guest house, but I haven't a clue on my own.'

'You will feel lost at first, mate, it's only natural. I'd give yourself time.'

'Ha, now I know you're a cockney, with you calling me "mate". I worked in London for a while, near Tower Bridge, and I found the people so warm, friendly and down-to-earth. I loved it there, but Blodwyn wasn't happy. So when her mum died suddenly and she was so broken-hearted, I followed her wish to come back to Wales.'

'I don't live far from there in London.' But as she said it, Elsie wished she was back there, in the factory with her own people. 'At least you are back among your own folk, Dai. They will help you – your mates in particular. Family will try, but they're too close to your grief and they need help themselves.'

'I've neither here. Well, I have friends I met through Blodwyn, but we haven't been here long enough for them to become my close friends. You see, although she was from here, I met Blodwyn in Cardiff. That's about a hundred and forty miles from here. I . . . we met in tragic circumstances. My . . . my parents were killed in a train crash. They were visiting an old aunty of my mother's in Taff's Well. It was two years ago. Mother was killed outright, but Father was taken to hospital in Cardiff, where Blodwyn was a nurse. He only lived for a couple of days.'

'Blimey, you've been through a lot. I – I know how it feels, mate. I really do.' Impulsively Elsie reached out and put her free hand over his. 'I wish I could help yer, but I have no words, except to say I'll always be thinking of yer. And when I pray, which only seems to be to tell God off these days, then I'll pray for you.'

The church door squeaked open, making them both turn

round. Bert came running up the aisle. He stopped to bend his knee and make the sign of the cross before he came towards Elsie. It surprised her that he remembered this Catholic tradition, because although she and her brothers had sometimes gone to mass, they hadn't done so since Bert was about three years old, but then she remembered his days at the convent and shuddered.

Bert didn't shout to her either, but came over and whispered, 'Else, Cess wants to go, but he doesn't want to come in here.' He looked at Dai then. 'I saw you at that grave. You looked sad. We're sad as me brovver's in a grave, and me mum, and Dot. It makes you sad.'

Dai put out his hand and ruffled Bert's hair. 'You're right, it does. But you have your other brother and Elsie, and the baby. They'll keep you from getting too sad.'

'Oh, they do. Specially Kitty. I feed her, you know, but I can't make her burp.'

Dai laughed. But the laugh soon sounded more like a sob and he looked away.

Suddenly Elsie asked him, 'Would you like to meet to go for a walk tomorrow, Dai? I'd ask yer back to ours for tea, but we wouldn't be good company, especially me poor brovver, Cess. But by tomorrow he might feel up to meeting yer. If not, me and Bert would come and give Cess some time on his own, wouldn't we, Bert, mate?'

Bert nodded.

Dai turned and, although watery, his smile lit up his face. 'I would, thank you so much. There's a tea shop on the promenade. We could go there after our walk and I could treat you both to tea and cakes. Blodwyn and I never tried it, but were talking of doing so . . . once. Well, it's not to be.'

Not picking up on this, Elsie simply said, 'We'll see you tomorrow then: about two? We'll be on the prom where the old fishing boat is on the beach.'

'Thanks, Elsie. I'll look forward to it.'

'You were a long time in there, Elsie. I thought you'd never come out. Never known yer to be much of a one for the church.'

She told Cess about Dai.

'The bloke we passed, you mean?'

'Yes, that's his wife's and newborn's grave.'

'Oh, Else, yer can't go picking up all who're in trouble, mate. We've enough on our own plate.'

'I know, Cess, but it helps. When yer help others, it helps you. And even more so if they understand what you're going through. You and him have both lost the love of yer lives – yer know exactly how he feels, and he will know how you feel. It helps.'

'How?'

'For one thing, someone who knows doesn't say meaningless things. There's an understanding, which helps you to have a normal conversation without the grief dominating. Obviously yer talk about it, but what you say, they can relate to. So they don't tell yer to snap out of it or try to get on with your life, or any other well-meaning phrase. And it's all right to talk to them about how you feel – how yer loved one died, and your feelings about the future. All the stuff you keep locked away from others, for being afraid they'll think you're dwelling on it. It's a true saying, mate: Laugh and the world laughs with you. Cry and you cry alone.'

Cess was quiet for a moment. When he spoke, he didn't rule out making a friend of Dai. 'I'll see how I feel tomorrow,

Sis.' He lowered his voice, 'Right now I just want to find a corner to weep in. Somewhere I won't upset Bert.'

'I know. That's why I went into the church, though I did pray. They've a beautiful statue of Our Lady in there. She has a lovely, kind face, so I did give her me tears.'

'I was afraid to go in – I felt I would disgrace meself by shouting and screaming that there can't be a God. And, if there is, then he's not a "just" one, like they all say He is.'

They had reached the car.

'I'll drop you at the cottage and see you later, Sis. Will you manage Kitty?'

'I will, mate. You take as long as you need.'

Although thrown into taking the mother's role, Elsie found it was all coming back to her. Even the pooey nappy, which she had to deal with when they got in. Not so Bert. He was heaving at the smell. Laughing at him, she told him, 'You'll have to get used to it, mate. I did with you. It'll be a couple of years before Kitty stops doing this, and then there'll be the chamber pot to empty as it'll be a long time before she can go to the lav to do her business.'

'Ugh! I'll have to get her to warn me, cos it turns me belly over. Did yer like looking after me? Did Mum do anything for me?'

Putting Kitty back in her crib, Elsie went over to him. 'Come here, buggerlugs, you haven't given me a cuddle for ages. And I loved looking after yer. And Mum did, too. She had to earn the pennies, though, as I did. So she looked after yer during the day, and I did once I came in from the jam factory. Mum used to tickle yer tummy and make yer howl with laughter.'

Bert's lovely smile brought some sunshine to her as he

bounded off the chair he'd been sitting in and jumped into her arms, straddling her waist with his legs. 'Hey! Watch out, you're getting to be a big boy now . . . But not too big to tickle!' With this, she dropped him on the sofa and had him crying out for mercy, in between giggling his head off.

Kitty latched onto the lightened atmosphere and kicked her legs, letting out gurgles and the occasional quite loud cry of glee. Elsie had a sudden urge to go to her and pick her up and dance around the floor with her, but kept her focus on Bert. She didn't want him to feel pushed out of her main affections.

'Will we tickle Kitty like this, Else?'

'No, not till she's a lot bigger, or we might hurt her.'

'She's liking me being put through it, though.'

'Ha, she is. She's like her mum in that. Dot used to giggle if I got into trouble at school. I used to clock her one . . . Not hard. I mean, playfully.'

'I loved Dot.'

Elsie caught her breath. 'I know. We all did.'

'Was Mum wicked, Else?'

'No! Oh, Bert, never think that. We had the very best mum in all the world.'

'But . . . well, my tutor said she was. I heard her say to one of the maids that you should never be a sister to Millie, and wouldn't be if our mother hadn't been nothing but a wicked prostitute.'

'Oh, Bert. It's them servants who are wicked. They think themselves somebody. Well, we'll be out of that house soon, I promise you. Work is being done on the flat right now. And you'll go to school in Bevington Street, which only takes a couple of minutes to walk to. You'll have mates to play with, and it'll be how it's meant to be.'

'I'd like that, Else. I wish I didn't ever have to go back to that tutor again, I hate her.'

Though Elsie understood, she sighed. 'There's too much hate in the world, Bert. Settle for not liking her, and make your mind up never to hate anyone, eh, mate? That way you can avoid those you don't like, but never wish harm on them.'

Bert nodded, but she knew that stubborn look, and guessed he was only humouring her.

By the time she set out to meet up with Dai the next day, Elsie felt strangely silly about doing so. *Why did I think I could put his world to rights, when my own is in tatters?*

His greeting made her imagine he'd been thinking along the same lines. 'Oh, I wondered if you'd come. I – I, well . . .'

'Nearly didn't?'

He nodded, looking a little embarrassed.

'Don't worry. I had the same feelings. In the end I came out of politeness, but now I'm here, I'm glad I did. How are yer, Dai?'

'Well, you know. But I'm glad you did, too. I felt perked up when I saw you and Bert coming towards me. No baby today?'

'No, Cess wanted Kitty to himself for a while. He's had a bad day and night. He wanted her in his bedroom, but then brought her into me when she woke. He looked dreadful and said he wasn't up to feeding her. That was about two this morning. But by nine, when he appeared again, he looked a lot better. He'd been out for an early walk.'

'He's lucky to have you by his side. Though it must be hard on you, trying to keep yourself going for everyone when you're in the throes of grief yourself.'

'It is.'

Dai surprised her then by completely changing the subject. 'Come on, Bert, I'll race you from the boat to the end of the pier. That's an old pirate boat, you know. It was washed ashore and the pirates came into the town looking to steal and rob, but some of the townsfolk beat them back, while others stole all they had on board and carted it away. The pirates wielded their cutlasses as if they would take off anyone's head who got in the way.'

Bert was open-mouthed. 'But how did the townsfolk win? Did they have cannons and things?'

Elsie smiled as they trotted away, Dai expounding on his tale as if it had really happened, and Bert hanging on to his every word.

For a moment Elsie wondered what it would have been like to have a father, or any male, in her life while growing up. And for the lads too – someone like Dai, and Cess. Good men.

But thinking this brought to mind the beast who had fathered her, and the thought shook through her that, yes, that was her mum's fault – she could have resisted him! Only for her to feel ashamed at letting such a thought enter her head.

Feeling her legs go wobbly, she sank down on the sand and begged her mum to forgive her. 'You paid for yer mistake – oh, how you paid – and you didn't deserve to.' *I miss you so much, Mum. I hope Dot's with you, and not with her own mum.* 'Oh, Dot. Dot, I can't think of life without you.'

The sound of Bert's giggles brought the world into focus again. Elsie quickly dried her eyes. *I mustn't give in. I have to stay strong for Bert.*

Chapter Thirteen

Millie

Millie sighed. She so missed Elsie. The ten days had felt like a month. Not even celebrating her twenty-first birthday had lifted Millie. With everything that had happened lately, it hadn't been the event her mama had originally planned, but a quiet affair with just the two of them having a special dinner. *Oh, please don't let there be any delays. Please let them arrive at three, like they thought they would. I just can't wait to see Elsie again.*

'Millie, are you thinking what I think you are? You've paced that same bit of floor a dozen times.'

She turned and smiled at her manager. 'Sorry, Jim. I know you're trying to concentrate on those projection figures. I must be getting on your nerves. But if you're thinking I'm impatient for three o'clock, then you're right.'

'I know. I feel the same way myself. It seems a long, long time since I saw Elsie. I want to give her my condolences, too. Dot was a lovely person. I only wish I'd had more time to get to know her. It's tragic – and on her wedding day too.'

Cess had wanted everyone to know the truth about him and Dot. Not about the rape of her by her stepfather, but

134

how her mum had refused to give Dot permission to marry him, and the effect that had in making Dot ill.

'I'm not sure when Elsie will face coming back to work, Jim. I'm hoping to get her and Cess so wrapped up in getting their flat ready that it gives them a distraction.'

'I hope so. But she's missed here. The women want to see her, you know. And I could have done with her help, too. She has a head for charts and things. I want to get these figures right for Len. Though why he needs it, midway through the year, I don't know. We haven't all our orders in yet from the large food warehouses that supply the shops.'

Millie just smiled. She wasn't clear herself, except that Len had spoken of them maybe expanding – moving to a bigger factory, now that they were working all year round. This had been in response to Millie saying that she was struggling for space to store the pickles, as the stockroom was only designed for jam production.

Len was showing a lot more interest in the running of the factory than she ever thought he would. Oh, she knew that he would always keep his eye on the purse strings, being her bank manager, but financial advice seemed to be spreading to other advice that she didn't expect from him.

He'd been acting funny since Ruby's wedding day. Almost avoiding her, when she was used to him calling round to her house on any excuse. He wasn't so affectionate, either. Not that he had ever behaved other than impeccably towards her, but he had shown passion in his kisses before, and a longing for them to marry. Now he hardly ever mentioned it, and his kisses were . . . well, half-hearted. Until last night, when he visited.

He was always advising her over one thing or another, but last night he specifically wanted to caution Millie about taking her time over making Elsie a full partner. Especially since Dot had died. 'Imagine,' he'd said, 'what a mess you would be in now, if Dot had been a partner on paper!'

She'd found this very callous. Her heart was breaking at the loss of Dot, and all Len could think about were the legalities she would have been subjected to.

'Think carefully before you commit to anything, other than the verbal arrangement you have with Elsie,' he'd told her. 'Let me look into everything. Neither Elsie nor Dot's estate may be legally entitled to take one-third of what is yours. I need to protect your interests, darling. Of course I understand how you felt when you heard what your father had done, but you are under no obligation to put that right any further than you are already doing now. You've been very generous.'

Seeing how upset this had made her, Len had become something of his old self, holding Millie in his arms and whispering that he loved her. Telling her that they must set a date for their wedding, just as soon as it was proper to do so. 'I can't wait, my darling. I have been distancing myself a little from you because you are driving me mad. I want you to be mine – fully mine.'

Millie had thrilled at this and kissed him with all the fervour of the desire that he'd lit within her, feeling his need pressing against her. She knew she would have submitted to him there and then, but for Len pulling away from her and apologizing, leaving her feeling disappointed and embarrassed.

Len said he wouldn't call for a couple of days. 'It is torture to be with you, and torture not to be. Oh, Millie, I will miss you so much, but I do know that I can control myself better when I'm not in your company. Or if others are around. Elsie will be home then, and that will help. She is like a chaperone.'

Suddenly remembering now that Jim had spoken to her, Millie shook herself mentally. 'I'm sorry, Jim. I keep going into my own thoughts. So much has happened, I can't concentrate. But I will try. Len says he only wants a projection of how the figures weigh up against last year, and what orders we have, coupled with the likely ones. You know how some of our customers say some lines are doing better than others, or they will be wanting more next year as they ran out of a certain product this year – that kind of thing.'

'Yes, I understand, but it's not easy this early in the year. Anyway, I'm getting there. I just hope I'm not way off the mark.'

'I'm sure you won't be.'

'The thing is, these figures seem to be vital to Len. He called round at my flat the other evening, wanting to know how I was getting on. We went to his club for a drink, and he was very keen for them to look good. Something about the factory expanding. You never mentioned anything?'

This shook Millie. And angered her too. What right had Len to discuss her business with her manager? Not that she didn't trust Jim – she did, implicitly – but it still wasn't Len's place to have what sounded like a meeting with Jim to discuss the business without her being present!

Not wanting to look as though she was affected by this, Millie turned away and shuffled some papers on her desk. More out of loyalty than really thinking it, she said, 'Yes, Len does have some ideas. Some very good ones, too.'

But this didn't quash her annoyance. Why Len couldn't go along with her own suggestion of making room at the back of the factory by building a new toilet block and canteen, then converting the area currently occupied by these into a second stockroom, she couldn't imagine.

'When he told me his reasoning, he seemed to think the cost of having a London-based factory was too high.'

This was the first time Millie had heard a suggestion that a proposed move should take them out of London. Her reaction was to swivel round and stare at Jim.

'Len hasn't mentioned that to you, Millie? Look, I don't want to cause trouble. Len is an old school mate, and the general motto then was to look after each other's backs, but that didn't extend to working behind the back of someone who has your loyalty. I'm sorry, I can see you didn't know. I'd hoped that you did.'

'No, I didn't. But nothing can happen without my say-so, and I don't want to move from here. I couldn't abandon our loyal workers. They would suffer so much if we suddenly closed.' Thinking she was being disloyal now, when she'd tried not to be, Millie went on, 'Anyway, I am sure Len will discuss this with me soon. He knows how upset I am at the moment. And he knows how such a move would trouble me even more, as would him trying to persuade me to it. So don't worry about it – it definitely won't happen.' Millie told Jim then about her own ideas for expansion.

'Yes, that would work. That really would work. I'll look into it, if you like.'

'Yes, that would be helpful, I'm sure, and when Len hears the idea and sees that it will work, he will recommend that his bank backs the plan. Thinking of that, please cost it all out for me too, and I'll chat to Elsie about the idea to see what she thinks.'

'I know what she will say. She wouldn't be able to bear letting the workforce down.'

'I know. Look, I think I'll get off. There's nothing more for me to do here. I'll have a few words with the women and then slip out. I have the fruit orders all done, they just need telephoning in. And I've done an order for the orange importers, too. I've upped it on last year's, so that's something you can report on.' This last came out in a sarcastic tone, which she regretted immediately. 'Oh, I didn't mean that how it sounded. Sorry, Jim. I only meant that it would look good in the figures.'

Jim raised his eyebrows. 'I understand how you meant it. Please don't worry.'

Something told her that Jim was party to more than he'd said – or maybe it was because he knew Len better than she did. *Oh, I don't know. I wish I didn't suddenly have all these doubts.*

When Cecil's car pulled up outside the house, Millie couldn't contain herself and, as she had done many times, she raced poor Barridge to the front door. He coughed in a disapproving manner, but gave way – probably because of who had arrived. Millie hadn't missed the disdain that all her staff showed towards Elsie. She just hadn't been strong enough to tackle them about it. She dearly wished she had, and then maybe Elsie wouldn't want to leave.

This and other worries disappeared when she opened the door. 'Elsie! Oh, Elsie, you're back.' They fell into each other's arms, and both burst into tears. 'Oh, Elsie, I'm sorry, I didn't mean to get upset. I've so missed you and had no one to—'

'I know. I thought about yer, luv. But I was pulled both ways – wanting to be with you and yet needing to be with me brovvers.'

'I know, I know. I feel ashamed, breaking down like this.' She looked over at Cecil, who was getting out of the car, followed by Bert. Cecil seemed to have shrunk. His shoulders were bent, his eyes red-raw and he clung to the bundle in his arms as if it was a life-saver to him. She went over to him. 'Hello, Cecil. Let's get you inside, you must be so tired after that long drive. Shall I take Kitty for you?'

'Ta, Millie. Yes, I am shattered.'

As she took the baby, she felt a tug on her skirt. 'Bert! Hello, you look sleepy – have you just woken? Oh, it's good to have you back, young man.'

Bert smiled. 'I slept all the way. I didn't know we were even in London till we got here.'

'Did you have a nice time?'

'Yes. We met Dai. He's a smashing bloke. He's sad, too. He said he would visit us when he has his affairs in order . . . I think that's what he said.' He looked up at Elsie.

'Yes, it is. Now you've gone and got Millie all curious. Let's get inside and tell her all about it, before she starts getting ideas.'

Millie giggled, then winked at Elsie. 'Something like that did occur to me.'

Elsie hit her playfully on the shoulders. 'Well, it's nothing like that. Like Bert said, Dai was very sad. But let's get off the roadside.'

'Yes, come on inside. Gertie is waiting for you. She'll take care of Kitty and Bert, and I've ordered tea for us in my sitting room.'

Once settled in Millie's sitting room, Elsie told Millie about Dai as she sipped her tea.

'Ah, poor man. We all know what he is going through. So you were able to help him?'

'Yes, and he us. As we've said before, Millie, the biggest relief from your own troubles comes from helping others

140

with theirs, so it was a two-way thing. What he's going to do now, I don't know. He has the problem of the guest house, which he hasn't a clue how to run – especially on his own, and with no friends or family to call upon. I tell yer, luv, you think your own problems have reached rock-bottom and then you meet someone worse off.'

Millie was acutely aware of Cecil sitting drinking his tea and appearing to have closed down during this conversation. But he belied this by lifting his head, and then surprised her with his request. 'Millie, would you mind if I went back to the cottage? I'd like to spend a bit of time there alone. Yer see, I resisted making friends with Dai at first. I – I couldn't take his pain on top of mine. But when I found it wasn't like that, and we made friends, it really helped me – well, both of us. I feel I need his company for a bit longer. I've spoken to Elsie about this, haven't I, Else?'

'Yes, and if you're all right with it, Millie, I think it's a good idea. We need to speak to Gertie to see what she wants to do now, but we're hoping she will stay with us and take care of the children. I intend to throw myself into getting my flat ready and working at the factory. I thought, too, that I might do some voluntary work, I've this need in me to help better the lot of others. But also I just feel that I need to keep busy. If I don't, I think I'll go mad – besides, I've realized how privileged I am, to be taken from poverty and given all this – and a partnership in a business too! It's beyond anything I'd ever thought would happen to me.'

A small worry entered Millie. If she had made it legally binding that Dot and Elsie were partners in the jam factory, Cecil would now be in a better position, as Dot's next of kin. Why hadn't she gone ahead and got it all sorted? 'Of course it's all right. Take the cottage for as long as you need

141

it. And, Cecil, about Dot's allowance – sorry, I know how painful it is to speak of these things, but I'm willing to make it formally yours now, as her next of kin.'

'No! I mean, thanks, but no. I'll make me own way, once I can think straight. That money was Dot's birthright, but it ain't mine.'

'It is Kitty's, though, Cecil. Kitty is my father's grand-daughter, and my niece. She has a right. Will you consider me putting it in trust for her, with you having power of attorney over it, so that you can access it on her behalf whenever she needs it?'

Cecil looked her in the eyes and nodded. 'I've never met a kinder person than you, Millie. I've always said it, but yer like a fairy godmother to us. Yes, I will accept it on behalf of Kitty. I've no right not to. And I'll see she benefits from it – and in that I'll be guided by you both as to what's best for her . . . One thing: the little mite may have lost her mum, but she has two of the best aunts in the world and, no matter what, I know you'll both always look out for her.'

He ended this on a sob, which opened the floodgates for them all.

'Oh, Cecil, I don't know what to say. I gained a sister, and now I've lost her. That pain is so deep, but for you two – especially you, Cecil – I can't imagine it. I'm so very sorry and I'll do anything, anything at all, if it will help you.'

'We know you will, don't we, Cess? But we also know that you've done far more than anyone else in your position would, or would feel they had to. We're so grateful. And we both love you, Millie.'

Millie stood and opened her arms. They both came into them and she hugged them, wishing she could hug their pain away, but knowing that she could never do that. What she could do was to secure their future, though. 'Go and have a rest, both of you, and I'll order baths to be made ready for you, if you like.'

'No, don't do that, Millie. We can run our own baths. I couldn't face them maids of yours at the moment.'

Millie didn't know what to say to this from Cecil, but as Elsie agreed with him, she didn't protest. 'All right, take your time and I'll see you both at dinner.'

After they left, Millie rushed out into the hall. She had about an hour to get to her solicitor before he finished for the day. She didn't care how busy he was – she would demand that he see her.

The thought came to her of how, when she'd spoken of legalizing her gift to Dot and Elsie, her solicitor had told her to think about it all carefully for a while. She hadn't done that, she'd just let it slide. But suddenly she felt an urge to do it, because besides feeling that she'd let Dot down, she had a niggling worry that if she left it until after her marriage, she'd have a lot less say in the matter.

A lot of things had been said by Len lately that made her only too well aware that although legally, since the Married Women's Property Act had been passed some thirty years ago, she would remain owner of all she had, actually putting her wishes into practice and going against a husband's wishes wasn't that cut and dried. A husband became a legal partner in everything, and had a very big say.

Although she loved Len with all her heart, Millie didn't like some of his views – especially when he'd said he was glad she hadn't finalized things, where Elsie and Dot were concerned.

Mr Gutheridge wasn't busy, but he was more than surprised to see Millie in his office and was not particularly on her side concerning her proposal. 'What on earth has brought this on, Millicent? As your solicitor, I feel that you are being overly generous as it is to the illegitimate children of your father – taking them as your sisters, and into the business, is much looked down upon. You're setting a precedent that many people don't want to acknowledge. These sordid things are best swept under the carpet. I shudder to think what this has done to your poor mother. And I, and many more, are not at all surprised that she chose to slink off to the back of beyond, and not take her place in the society of the friends who enjoyed her company. The disgrace on her is unbearable to think of. I feel you are behaving in an appalling manner, letting your heart rule your head.'

Millie was shocked by this reaction. 'But it is the right thing to do surely? They . . . well, I – I only have one of them now. We lost my sister Dorothy, very suddenly, from a brain haemorrhage.'

'I'm sorry to hear that. But from a legal point of view, I'm glad that you hadn't made her your formal partner. You would be facing a legal mess now, especially as she no doubt died intestate?'

'Yes. It was very sudden and unexpected.'

'But she had lost her mind, I understand, which was another worry. Was she married?'

Concerned that he knew so much about Dot, which Millie knew she hadn't shared with him, she told him that Dot had married in Gretna Green.

'Gretna Green! Why? Actually, it doesn't matter why. This could work in our favour. They didn't go off to marry there in haste without a reason. If her husband does try to make trouble, claiming an inheritance, we can fight the case, on the grounds that his wife wasn't of sound mind to consent to marriage with him, and that she hadn't got that consent from a parent.'

'What? I don't understand all of this. I'm appalled at your attitude! How do you know about my sister's ill health, or the opposition to her marriage? And why are you so opposed to listening to my wishes and acting on them? All of this should have been settled a long time ago. My half-brother-in-law has a daughter – my half-niece and the granddaughter of my father! Of course they have rights. And as for my mother, she couldn't wait to get away from you all – you treated her with pity that bordered on disdain. And she felt mocked by you all, as she knew that you knew about my father's affairs. She has never been happier than she is right now – free from the stuffy, false society she was forced into. And that's exactly the course I am going to take, too. I will be instructing another solicitor to handle my affairs, and I would be grateful if you would be speedy in handing over to him all that you hold pertaining to me and my estate – and, no doubt, my mother will be doing the same, once I tell her of your behaviour. Goodbye, Mr Gutheridge.'

'But . . . Millicent! No. Please don't do this. I have been the family solicitor for a very long time. I am profoundly sorry to have offended you. I honestly believed I was acting in your very best interests, which it is my duty to do.'

'Miss Hawkesfield, if you don't mind – Miss MILLIE Hawkesfield! Good day, Mr Gutheridge.'

Once outside, Millie felt lost. Now she was adrift without a solicitor, had no idea how to get another one and hadn't achieved anything. Yes, one small victory against those who are bigoted and discriminatory, but such a tiny drop in a huge ocean of such attitudes – even from the man she loved.

Millie suddenly felt very alone and as if she was battling

against an unwinnable fight. *But I will win it! I will. Elsie and poor Dot, even though she is no longer with us, deserve justice, and I will do all I can to get it for them.*

Remembering that she'd seen many solicitors' offices here in Holborn Place, Millie signalled to her new driver – Harry, a much older man than Tom, and a very amiable man – to wait for her.

Not knowing the difference between various solicitors and their skills, she walked into the first office she came to. The receptionist put her off straight away, as her manner was aloof and at the nature of Millie's enquiry made her feel that she'd committed a cardinal sin. 'It is very unconventional to sack your solicitor, madam. I will have to have a word with our senior partner, Mr Harris. One moment.'

Still seething, Millie answered in a sarcastic tone, 'Thank you, but I will take my leave, as I do not want to employ a solicitor who has engaged such a rude receptionist!'

Turning, she fled out of the small glass-partitioned office, only to bump into a smartly dressed man who had come down the stairs next to the partition.

'Whoops! Beg your pardon, madam.'

Close to tears, Millie couldn't speak. She gave a dignified nod and went to leave.

'Excuse me, but don't I know you?'

Stopping in her tracks, she looked at him properly. 'Oh yes, we have met. You worked for Mr Gutheridge a few years ago.'

'That's right. Miss Hawkesfield, isn't it? I was sorry to hear of all your troubles. Neither you nor your mother deserve to have been through such an ordeal. You look distressed, can I help you at all?'

She told him why she was here.

'Well, look no further. I am fully qualified now. I have an office on the top floor – not a very grand affair, and a lot of steps to go up, but I do have an open mind. I'm not of the old school at all, which has had its disadvantages for me at times. And I have a very nice receptionist, who happens to be my wife – not only that, but I have the advantage of knowing your family and your business holdings, and I would be honoured to represent you.'

This was such a relief to Millie that she almost hugged him.

'Look, you seem pretty desperate. Why not come up now. Issy, my wife – Isadora, really, but she prefers to shorten it – will make you a cup of tea and we'll chat generally about why you sacked Gutheridge, and what it is that I can help you with. Then, depending on my answers, you can make up your mind if I will suit you or not.'

'Thank you very much. I'd like that. Especially the cup of tea.'

He laughed. As she followed him, he said, 'My name's Jordon. No short form for me – never has been. And I have to tell you that when it comes to corporate law, then Issy is your best bet. She isn't really my receptionist, but is my partner in everything and is highly qualified in corporate law. You know the way of it: she just cannot get proper legal standing of her own because she is a woman.'

Millie wanted to clap her hands at the way Jordon said this, as he sounded angry that Issy didn't have proper standing in the legal profession. Millie liked him – liked him a lot – and had the feeling that she'd found two champions to her cause. The world of fighting for her rights suddenly lightened.

Chapter Fourteen

Elsie and Millie

Elsie felt strangely nervous going back to work a week later. It was more the fact of facing the women and their questions. She hadn't seen any of them since Dot's funeral and knew they must have so much that they wanted to ask her.

'You know what I think, Elsie?' Millie said. 'I think you should tell them all the full, true story. Cecil has been very open about it, and you know how they took it when I was honest with them when all the horror happened and I had to take over running the business. You saw how they all got behind us then. And besides, if they know the facts, it leaves them nothing to gossip about.'

Elsie knew Millie was right, but she still worried about what their reaction had been to knowing that Dot had lived with Cess out of wedlock. They had their own moral code and that was totally against it – yes, a girl could find herself 'knocked up', as they called it, but the right thing to do in that case was to marry the bloke and make sure the kid was born in wedlock or, at the opposite end, get rid of it by adoption, or other means. Being a single mum and struggling to keep your kids, like her mum did, brought all sorts of wrath down upon your head – mostly of the tongue-wagging kind, but a lot of people ostracized you, thinking you a loose woman who might nab their man.

'That was a big sigh.'

'I just don't want anyone thinking badly of Dot . . . Oh, Millie, I can't believe she's gone.'

'I know. Are you sure you're up to work?'

'Yes, as I said the other day, I have to keep busy.'

Jim greeted her when they arrived. 'Welcome back, Elsie. I'm sorry for all you've been through. If there's anything I can do . . .'

'Ta, Jim' was all she could manage. But when she saw her desk, she felt she had to say more – a lovely vase of flowers adorned it. Not sure who had bought them, but having an idea it was Jim, she said, 'Oh, how kind. They're lovely.'

'I thought they might cheer you up.'

Blushing, she looked into his eyes and said, 'They do, and it's about time we had that pie-and-mash supper we talked of having months ago.'

His smile warmed her heart, but a movement to the side of her caught her attention – for one moment she thought Millie was going to clap her hands. Elsie glared at her. Millie grimaced, then turned and scuttled away. 'Must visit the bathroom – won't be long!'

'What was all that about?'

'Oh, nothing, Jim. Millie doesn't understand that a girl can have friendships with the opposite sex. To her, if you accept an invitation, that's as good as accepting a marriage proposal.'

'Not a bad maxim. I – I mean, well, for Millie's class, it is how things are done. Boy fancies girl and asks her out; if she refuses, then he gives up. But if she accepts, then he is in the running.'

'I know. She'd only met Len five minutes and she was engaged to be married – do anything in haste and you repent at leisure, that's what I think.' Although she said this, Elsie knew that if Len had asked her within two minutes of meeting him, she would have married him that day.

'Well, our supper date certainly hasn't been made in haste. We talked about it months ago. But, Elsie, I want you to know that what I once said – about being your friend – still stands. I think you know I feel more than that for you, but I would never press you. I want to be someone you can rely on. Someone you can turn to, who isn't family.'

'Ta, Jim, yer a mate. I'm grateful. I'm sorry I can't return your feelings.'

'Maybe one day.'

Elsie nodded. 'Anyway, I'd like to go for supper tonight, if you can? Len is coming for dinner and he hasn't been around since I got back. I have a feeling there's something in the air that Millie wants to clear up.'

'Oh, I might know what that is. She hasn't said anything to you then?'

'No. But then she's been a little unsure around me. You know – being careful of upsetting me – and yet I've known she had something on her mind.'

'I'll leave it to her to tell you, in her own time. I know she will, but maybe she wants to straighten things out with Len first.'

This shot a fear through Elsie. Millie couldn't possibly know what happened at the wedding, could she? Oh God! What if Rose has gossiped and it had got back to Millie's mother?

'Are you all right, Elsie? You've gone very pale.'

Catching her breath, the thought came to her that even if she did know, Millie wouldn't discuss such a thing with Jim. A feeling of relief washed over her. 'Yes, sorry. I . . . well, I have these moments. It was just the thought that I haven't tried to help Millie talk anything through with me. I feel the guilt of that. You can get a bit wrapped up in yer own grief at times, and not notice that others might need help.'

'I know. But don't worry. Look, if you find yourself sinking while you're here – as I know, only too well, can happen – then you only have to turn to me. I'll be your strength, Elsie.'

Elsie didn't know what to say to this. It seemed to her that Jim was a different man from the efficient and slightly aloof one she'd known him to be. But then he had shown her this side of him just before Christmas, and she remembered him telling her how he had lost first his twin brother, and then his mum. His dad had also passed away, but not before giving poor Jim years of hell with his bad-tempered ways. With this all coming back to her, she could see his concern for her in a different light. 'Ta, Jim. I will.' And then, to make sure he wasn't left in any doubt about her feelings for him, she added, 'You know, I lost a good mate – besides a sister – when Dot died, but I think I've found another in you.'

Jim smiled. Behind it she could see his disappointment, but she knew he would cope. Before he could say anything more, she went on, 'Well, I'd better go and talk to the women.'

'I'll come—'

'No, Jim, I don't think that a good idea. I can handle this.'

Once downstairs, she clapped her hands together to get their attention.

Peggy shouted, 'Elsie! I thought that was you. Good to see you back. Quieten down, you lot. Grace, you can listen while you carry on stirring that batch – I don't want it burning, or sticking to the sides.' When all was quiet, Peggy helped Elsie to begin, by saying, 'Can we say how sad we all were to hear of Dot's passing. She was lovely, were Dot. And then for her mum to follow her – well, that was tragic, but understandable.'

'Ta, Peggy.' Elsie took a deep breath. 'Look, I know there's been gossip, so I wanted to clear the air. You all know that Cess and Dot had only just married on the day she died.' Again Elsie had to breathe deeply.

A movement on the stairs behind her had her turning and glancing up. She hadn't noticed Millie coming back from the washroom that was at the back of the stairs, and was kept for them and Jim to use.

Millie smiled her encouragement. Elsie turned back to the women and told them the truth about why Cess and Dot hadn't married before. She left out the terrible part of how Dot had been raped, and there being doubt over the parentage of Kitty. She knew, from her own experience, how painful that would have been for Dot to share, so she didn't think she had the right to.

Peggy, as usual, spoke first, 'Well, Elsie, the main thing is that having got into trouble, Cess and Dot wanted to do the right thing, and we all know how much they meant to each other. I feel me heart breaking for Cess, and for all of you. But I don't feel the same pity for Beryl. I think she meted out her own just punishment, for denying her own grandchild the right to be born in wedlock. She was always bigoted, and we all knew what a dog's life she led poor Dot – God rest Dot's soul.'

Elsie nodded. She heard more than one sniffle and swallowed hard, so as not to spill her own tears. Suddenly a thought occurred to her. 'Dot was one of us. A big part of this factory, and she toiled alongside us when conditions were such that a dog shouldn't have been subjected to, let alone human beings. She walked out with us when we went on strike, and showed many a kind act. She was our friend – my friend . . . my sister.' Again Elsie swallowed hard, as she wanted to do this for Dot. 'And so I am going to have a brass plate made and have it screwed to the wall above the jar-washing area. It will be a memorial to Dot: a small part of this vast factory, dedicated to her.'

There was silence, and then a loud cheer and the sound of hands clapping. Elsie knew this would have made Dot laugh. She could almost hear her giggling. She'd be saying, 'Bloody hell, Elsie, a plaque? I said I'd never leave this bloody place!' Elsie was so caught up in the thought that she giggled herself. But the giggle turned to a sob.

A huge pair of arms came round her, and a damp face rested on her hair. 'You've had it rough, Elsie, girl, but you're strong. Yer'll get through this. Blimey, yer only have to look at how far yer've come – you're a credit to us, and to yer mum. She'd be bleedin' proud of yer, she would.'

Elsie snuggled into Peggy. It felt good to be held by one of her own, as she often felt the same way Dot had once said: as if they belonged nowhere. But at this moment all that changed, and she knew she belonged with her own people – she was a South London cockney girl, born within the sound of Bow Bells.

Peggy patted her before stepping back. 'And we're all

proud of yer too, yer know. You could've lorded it over us when yer fortune changed, but you didn't, girl. You stuck to your roots, but used your new position to change things for us, and we all appreciate that.'

'I couldn't have done that without Mill . . . Miss Hawkesfield.'

Millie came running down the few steps that she'd gone up. 'No, Peggy is right: it has been your doing. You enlightened me to the horrors that went on here, Elsie, and without your guidance, I couldn't have done what was needed.'

'No, but, Miss, you've been a champion to us as well, and we all admire yer and think a lot of yer. You've righted the wrongs of this place – both of yer have, and we're grateful. There's not a person here who doesn't feel glad to come to work now.'

'Thanks, Peggy. I really appreciate that.'

Elsie dried her eyes. 'And I do, too. Yes, me and Miss Hawkesfield have been through a lot, but you have all helped us through it. Now I know things are so much better than they were, but I'm also aware that, from time to time, there will still be upsets and things you don't like. Or you may have problems outside work that are affecting you . . .'

'Ha, we have plenty of them, Elsie, girl.' Ada patted her swollen belly as she said this and everyone laughed.

But before someone could pipe up something lewd, as she knew might happen, Elsie carried on, 'Yes, well, what I was going to say was that, as part of the management, this fact has been recognized by us all, and so we have an announcement to make. I am going to become the welfare officer for the factory.'

The women looked from one to the other. One said, 'They've got one of them at Hartley's.'

'Yes, I know. And that's what prompted the idea. Me and Miss Hawkesfield talked about it before Christmas, but it is only now that we're able to think of putting it into practice. Now I don't have all the answers to the problems you might need help with, but I will do my best – and anything I don't know, I will find out for you. So from now on, talk to me about anything you need help with that may be affecting your work. Even if it's nothing to do with the factory and the work we do here – being a welfare officer means just that: taking care of the welfare of the workforce.'

'Well, I for one think yer'll be good at the job, Elsie. Yer've always had a level head, and had to grow up quick. Yer've dealt with most problems life can throw at yer, even bringing up kids. You did a good job with them brovvers of yours. And yer know what it's like to try to feed them, when you've nothing to buy food with. I can't think of anyone I could trust with me problems more than you.'

Once more a cheer went up as Ada finished saying this.

'Ta, Ada. And all of you. Now, unless anyone has any questions, I think we should get back to work. I'll put up a notice in the canteen about how it will all work. And thanks again, everyone.'

As they went up the stairs, Millie's arm came round Elsie. 'Well, that's a weight off your shoulders, Elsie. I'm glad you found the courage to do that.'

'Ta, Millie. Now, what about you? I feel that you've stuff you need to get off your chest.'

'Oh? Well, yes I do. But not here. We'll go out to that cafe down the road at lunchtime. I do have some things to talk over, but I didn't think you were strong enough to deal with them. I can see that you are now.'

* * *

As they sat over a cup of tea and ham sandwiches, Millie wished she'd never suggested this, but then she did need Elsie to come to the solicitor's with her. *It's maybe not a good idea for me to tell her everything.*

'I can see yer struggling with something, Millie – spit it out. Mum always said, "A problem shared is a problem halved."'

'I know, and how true that is. Well, I've finally got something sorted about making you a formal, legal partner in the business, and to give you the right to be on the board. I had to sack my old solicitor to do it, but I have this really good new one. And, best of all, his partner – his wife – is an expert in corporate law, so she is not only advising me on the legalities of taking a partner, but will advise us on all aspects of our manufacturing, within the correct legal structure.'

'Aw, Millie, yer've no need to go to all that trouble. I trust you, mate.'

'But I do, Elsie. I don't want you ever to be in the position where you have no rights. If I had been able to do the same for Dot, then Cess would have those rights now, as her next of kin.'

'Oh, I see. Well, I think I do. But who is my next of kin? Is that Cess?'

'Yes. But you can make a will, leaving half of your estate to each of your brothers. It can always be changed when you're married and have children of your own. Anyway, I will need you to come with me to the solicitor's when everything is ready, as you have to sign the papers.'

'That's fine, but . . . well, I don't mean to be nosy, but what is it between you and Len? Something Jim said worried me. Does it involve me?'

Millie was surprised to see Elsie looking really uncomfortable. 'Don't worry, Elsie. It does, in a roundabout way.
I – I mean, well, it is to do with the business . . . Look, I
don't want you to say anything to Len about me making
our partnership legal and binding – not yet. Not until it is
done.'

'Is he against it then?'

'Not against it, but he has worried, since Dot . . . You
see, although I would have welcomed one-third of the business going to Cecil, Len thinks more about how the legal
tangle of it all would have affected our business, with Dot
dying intestate – without making a will, that is. You see such
things can be contested and can become messy. Oh, I don't
know. To be honest, Elsie, I'm a bit confused at the moment.
I need to straighten a few things out with Len.'

'Am I . . . am I part of that in any way?'

'No! Well, only as I have already said. Len . . . Oh, Elsie,
he's just being a man. You know the attitudes they have. I
– I thought he was different, but maybe I didn't see him
as he was. But now—'

'Millie! Don't cry. It didn't mean anything . . . It didn't!'

Shocked by this, Millie asked, 'What? I don't understand?
What didn't mean anything? Has Len been talking to you,
too?' She felt her tears dry instantly, as her exasperation rose.
'First Jim, then I suspect my solicitor, and now you! What
is Len playing at? Is he trying to undermine me?'

'What did he do, with Jim and your solicitor?' Now Elsie
looked shocked.

Is she trying to tell me something? Deciding to ignore this
– more because she felt it better not to know – Millie
explained, 'Len took Jim for a drink to his club, and ran
plans by him that he has for the factory after we're married.

And then the solicitor I have just got rid of knew things that I hadn't told him, and seemed to be of the same mind as Len.'

Elsie looked relieved, but her reaction had worried Millie. *Has something happened between Elsie and Len? No, for goodness' sake, what's wrong with me? Neither of these people I love would do anything like that to me.* Controlling herself, Millie asked, 'Has Len spoken to you of these plans, Elsie?'

More in command of herself now, Elsie smiled. 'No. I'd have told you, luv. But why do you think he's changed – in what way? And what plans is he making behind your back?'

Now Millie felt uncomfortable and wished she'd never said anything in the first place. Not only did she have a niggling worry that something might have happened between Len and Elsie, but she was in the position now of having to tell all to Elsie.

'Well, it's to do with after we are married . . .' When she'd finished telling Elsie about Len's ideas, as related to her by Jim, Elsie's expression went from shocked surprise to hurt. 'Can he do that? Can Len make you move the factory?'

'I don't think so. The days have gone when a husband took all the wife owned.'

'But yer not sure. Is that the real reason you want to make me a full partner?'

'Not the only one, but this rearing up has made me realize that I needed to protect you. As obviously when we are married, Len will become a member of the board – a third partner even. I wanted you legally able to vote with me against anything Len proposes that we don't like.'

'Oh, Millie, I don't want to ever be a reason to come between you and Len.'

Reaching for Elsie's hand, Millie told her, 'You could never be that, Elsie. Oh, my dear, you're shaking. Don't be afraid. Issy said she will make sure that all the Is are dotted and the Ts crossed, so that we are both protected.'

'But why do we need protecting in such a way from Len? Surely he'll have our best interests at heart?'

'We don't. I don't mean "protected" in that way, but be able to have our say, and our wishes listened to. I have seen and experienced how forceful men can be in these matters – ruthless, too.'

'You do love, Len, don't you, Millie? Only you said he'd changed.'

'Yes, I love him with all my heart and would do anything for him. But yes, he does seem to have changed. He's distant and doesn't come to see me so often, and – well, I wouldn't have expected him to have meetings about my business behind my back. That has upset me. And . . . Oh, I don't know, but he did express that, in his opinion, the present arrangement of my bond being my word is enough to guarantee your standing in the business. Why should he think that, or even want that for you?'

'Oh? But . . . well, if he thinks it best, I'm quite happy as I am, Millie. My allowance is plenty for me, with my job – especially with the new plans for me to be welfare officer. Maybe, if Len thinks like you say, he's right? I mean, what do I know about running a business? I'm a worker, mate.'

'No, Elsie. Trust me in this. I want to protect your rights.'

'And you don't trust Len to do that?'

Millie sighed. 'It isn't Len so much – it's men's attitude in general. We women *have* to protect ourselves, and I want that protection for you, Elsie.' She hadn't expected Elsie to be so complacent about it all. 'Just go along with me, please,

Elsie. You mean the world to me. You're my sister, and yet I have now – and have had in the past – far more than you. To me that isn't fair.'

'Oh, Millie, Millie. Yer so like me, in wanting to put the world to rights. But I'm all right as I am, honestly. There are others who need our help with their rights far more than I do.'

'Please, Elsie. Please agree with me and sign the papers when they are ready.'

'All right. If it means that much to you, I will. But, Millie, promise me, mate, that if this issue looks like threatening yer future with Len, then you'll change yer mind and leave things as they are.'

Millie could only nod. But in her heart she prayed that Elsie would sign the papers. She couldn't have said exactly why this was so very important to her, only that she had a feeling it might be. Trying to lighten the moment she said, 'Anyway, once this is done and you are settled in your flat, we can set about changing the world together, mate.'

Elsie laughed. 'Ha, yer may have been born a cockney by definition, but you'll never make a true one. I love it when you try, though.'

Millie made a pretence at laughing with her, but as she sipped her tea she so wished that the happiness and settled feeling she'd had just a few weeks ago hadn't left her. But then, she told herself, all relationships have to be worked at – they are all reliant on compromise – and that was true of sisters as well as fiancés. *Oh, Len. Len, I will work hard at our relationship, I will. I love you so much.*

Chapter Fifteen

Millie

Millie had seen Elsie off, teasing her unmercifully about her supper date with Jim, and then she'd dressed carefully to welcome Len to her home for dinner – choosing a simple, long sage-green frock with a fitted bodice and straight skirt. The sleeves came to just below her elbows and were edged with lace, but the overall formal look of the frock was made feminine by the soft neckline, which showed a small glimpse of cleavage. The addition of a pearl necklace and the dressing of her hair in a style that was swept back, leaving tiny ringlets to border her face, gave exactly the right look she wanted to achieve – a woman of sophistication, who could be taken seriously when talking of business matters, as she intended would be the main topic of conversation.

This desire almost left her when Len arrived, looking so handsome in a black dinner suit – the jacket of which had a velvet collar and fitted into his waist and over his hips, outlining his masculine figure. His shirt gleamed white in contrast, and with this he wore a white necktie. He carried a gift in his hand, which he gave to her as soon as they were alone. 'A token of my love, Millie, darling.'

Opening the dark-red box revealed a diamond necklace – a simple teardrop on a gold chain. 'It's beautiful, Len. Thank you, darling.'

His smile melted her heart. 'Let me put it on for you – you can put your pearls into the box.'

She could only nod as he turned her round. When his fingers touched her, a feeling trembled through her that made Millie catch her breath. Len was so close. She felt his warm breath, moments before his lips kissed her neck. 'You're beautiful, Millie. I love you so much. Let's settle on a wedding day tonight, please.' His arms came round her and he gently pulled her into his body, so she could hardly breathe. 'I know it is very soon after losing your sister, but . . . Oh, Millie, we had plans to marry soon anyway, and I can't wait much longer. I will be a comfort to you and will be able to help you in so many ways.'

'Yes, Len. Oh yes.' She turned as she said this and went fully into the circle of his arms.

His dark eyes clouded over, his voice was husky and filled with desire. 'Oh, Millie, my Millie. I will protect you, take all responsibilities off your shoulders and be a rock to you.'

This set off a small alarm inside her head, but her heart and the feeling pounding around her body were ruling her as she said, 'I know you will. I love you so much, Len.'

Holding her close, he whispered, 'How soon, my darling – a month? Can you be ready in a month?'

'Yes. Especially as we will only need a simple affair, with family and a few friends – we could hold it here. I know you have a standing in society, but I don't, and you can tell them it is a quiet affair because I am still in mourning, and that we'll host a ball later on to celebrate with them.'

'Ha! You little minx, you've already thought this through!

That makes me so happy, Millie. I've been worried lately that we had a little rift between us, and that is why I haven't called round so much. Oh, I know I said it was because of the passion you arouse in me and that's true also, but I felt that a little space would give us both time to evaluate our relationship. After all, we haven't known each other a year yet, and so much has happened in your life in that time that I wanted you to be able to think clearly about your – our – future, without crowding you.'

Relief flooded through Millie. 'I thought you were at odds with me, despite what you once said. There was so much that we didn't agree on. And, well . . . Len, there are things that we need to talk over – sort of straightening out our positions and our roles within the marriage, and my business.'

He stood back and looked down at her. 'What roles? You'll be my wife. Your role will be the traditional one of supporting me in my work at the bank, and of course you will step back from running the business.' Before she could protest, he continued, 'One day we will be among the richest families in the land. Because, although it will be a sad day for me, I will one day inherit the bank that I run, and my father's holdings in Harlington & Lefton's Bank in Knightsbridge. Oh, darling, I have such plans for the jam factory, too. I want to make it the largest there is: take over other smaller factories, and move operations of them all into larger premises. I can bring all the funding needed for this. The factory will expand further into the food industry – a canned-fruit department, for instance – and we can invest in bee-keeping farms and produce a range of honeys. The sky is the limit for us, darling.'

Somehow Millie got caught up in his enthusiasm and

163

forgot that Len might not be including her fully in all of this. 'It all sounds so wonderful, darling, and I know Elsie will agree with it all – well, most of it. But we may have to think carefully about moving the premises. Maybe open a second factory, rather than move the present one?'

It was then that her niggling worry became a fear, as Len stepped back from her. 'Elsie? Why should she have a say? I thought you knew how I felt about that question, darling. Elsie will be looked after, of course she will, but . . . Look, darling, you must be guided by me on this. Elsie cannot be a full partner in our business. What does she know about business anyway? Her head will be ruled by her need to please her "mates", as she calls them. You have to think of her happiness, darling – not your need to make Elsie's life what you think it should be. Elsie would be happiest with a home of her own, and giving her music lessons to those less fortunate than life has turned out to be for her. She will be supported in everything she wants to do – but it has to be what Elsie wants to do, not what you think is best for her.'

A chord was struck inside Millie. Hadn't Elsie protested at her plans? *Isn't she always trying to stop me from making decisions for her? Hasn't she said that she trusts me, and that she trusts Len? Didn't she protest about being made a full partner and want to be just the welfare officer for the factory? Is Len right, and I am so very wrong?*

'Darling? Look, my love, I know you want the best for Elsie, but so do I. Only my judgement isn't clouded by guilty feelings, which I know yours is. But you have no need to feel that guilt, Millie. You don't. You didn't cause what happened to Elsie. You only put it all right, once you heard about it. But now you must listen to her, and give Elsie the respect she deserves – allow her to shape her own destiny, while providing love and support for her.'

'Oh, Len, I got it so wrong, didn't I? You're right, I can feel that you are.' But although she said this, a part of Millie still held a slight concern. She brushed it aside. 'I will speak to Elsie again and, if she agrees with you, I will bow to her wishes. But no matter what any of you say, I want a formal arrangement – legal and binding – over Elsie's allowance. One that stands, if anything happens to either or both of us.'

'Yes, I agree, and we will both make a provision for Elsie in our wills. I will speak to Gutheridge tomorrow.'

'He is no longer my solicitor, Len.'

'What? Why?'

Millie was hesitant about telling him at first, but then decided that the truth was the best option. 'Because, with my misguided sense of wanting to force the issue of Elsie being a partner, I went to Gutheridge and he was obnoxious and spoke down to me. I will not tolerate that from someone I employ, in any capacity. He also knew things about the business and me that I hadn't told him – or was even party to knowing some of it myself. I was appalled by that. Especially as it had happened twice to me in the one day.'

'Oh?'

Millie noticed that Len coloured slightly, but he had the good grace to listen to her. 'Yes, Jim Ellington mentioned the plans to expand and move the premises, and I knew nothing about the proposed move out of London – he wasn't to know that, of course, because he assumed that I knew, as his boss and, at present, the sole owner of the factory.'

'But I told him . . . I mean, well, I'm sorry, darling, but you were so difficult to talk to, so touchy about Elsie and the role you saw her taking. I couldn't discuss anything with you. Jim is my friend. I was miserable, and unsure of you. I sought his company to cheer me up and got carried away with all the ideas buzzing away inside my head, and which I couldn't share with you. Then I realized that I shouldn't have done, not with Jim being your manager, so I asked him not to mention anything we had talked about. I'm sorry that he did, and yet I am glad now that he has, as it shows his loyalty to you – to anyone who employs him – and I like that.'

'But Jim said you asked him to draw up plans, and to give you a forecast of next year's projected turnover. You and I had talked about the need for that, but to instruct my manager actually to do it . . .'

'Oh, that's the bank manager in me. Ha, I can't even have an idea without costing it out and having a forward plan. That's something you will have to get used to, my darling – though, as it is turning out, it will be very useful to us.'

'There is an "us" in all of this, isn't there, Len? You do intend me to have a full say in everything, don't you? When you said that I should step back from running the business, you meant in a practical way, didn't you? You do know that I want to remain a full partner?'

'Of course you will, darling.'

They were quiet for a moment as Barridge poured them both a glass of sherry. When he'd left them, Millie pressed her point. 'And I want you to know that I am seriously thinking about the expansion of the building that we already have, as I don't agree with any move of our current operation to another factory, though I am very open to us having another premises to develop, as you have outlined. Maybe it will work out that the business you have in mind to take over will house your other projects – which, by the way, I am very excited about, darling.'

'I think, when the time comes, we will evaluate what is best for our business. Your head must always rule your heart in any dealings. That is the first rule of business, Millie, and it is a very valuable lesson that you must learn.'

This made her feel silly, and as if she was with her father, not her fiancé. She felt her cheeks burn and angrily protested, 'Please don't talk down to me, Len. I will not stand for it.'

'But . . . I didn't. I'm sorry if it seemed that way. It was a natural reaction to us talking about how you were letting your heart rule Elsie's life. I'm sorry, darling, so sorry.'

Feeling wrong-footed, Millie decided to clarify what her motives were, in a businesslike way, so that Len would respect her and not always judge her by how she had tried to shape Elsie's life. 'Well, I wasn't actually. I was thinking of the cost. Our workforce is very skilled in what they do, and they work as an efficient and happy team since the changes we implemented. Production has risen, accidents and sickness have lessened to an almost non-existent level, and that will show in our end-of-year-profit and the projected figures Jim is preparing for you. We have won new contracts, on the strength of our improved operation. Moving would mean practically starting from scratch. Besides that, the disruption would affect our ability to get supplies to our customers in a timely way, and that would ultimately result in a loss of business, which, believe me, is not easily regained.'

Len looked as though the wind had been taken out of his sails, but he soon recovered. 'Very valid points, darling. But have you thought about the pickled-onion production that Jim introduced, which has been an asset in providing you with the means to create steady employment during what used to be the closed season, which was an even bigger disruption – or so your father claimed, when arranging yet another overdraft at that time of year? That could suffer, as you don't have room to carry stock, let alone have a proper production area.'

'Oh, but I do.' Millie outlined her own plans. 'Jim, now that he has completed the work you set him, is engaged in drawing up the plans for me.'

There was a silence, and Millie knew she'd scored a valuable point – not only that, but she'd enjoyed doing so. She wanted to shout out, '*Touché*', but controlled herself. A knock on the door stopped any further discussion, as Barridge opened it and announced that dinner was ready to serve. It was a blessed relief to her and, she knew, to Len, as he jumped up and offered her his arm. 'May I?'

She accepted his gesture to escort her through with a gracious smile and a loving look, hoping to convey to Len that although she could match him in business, and oppose him when she felt it necessary, she wouldn't carry into their private lives any hostile feelings that might conjure up. 'Thank you, darling. Though I must warn you that I'm very hungry and will probably disgrace myself by gobbling my food down.'

He laughed out loud, and Millie felt herself relax. She laughed with him and felt that they had crossed one of the divides that she'd known existed between them.

During dinner business wasn't mentioned. Instead, Millie steered the conversation towards their wedding plans. This made for light conversation, as they were in agreement on all points – the day was to be Saturday 3 August, less than six weeks away. And yet that didn't pose any problems for Millie, as she had already given her wedding-frock order to

Rene and they had chosen the material. She'd just have to tell Rene to go full steam ahead and to get Elsie's bridesmaid's frock sorted, too. Who would give her away was also something that she'd been thinking about, and she had decided to ask Cecil, as he was the nearest to a male relative that Millie had. Len was delighted with all these arrangements.

'Just one thing, darling. I think you should leave the honeymoon to me. I would like us to go away together straight after the wedding – I do have a place in mind, so now that we have the date settled, we can both make our arrangements: me to have time off, and you to leave work.'

This came out of the blue. 'Leave work! But . . .'

'Leaving work doesn't mean giving up your position on the board, darling. It simply means that you won't have regular hours when you need to attend the factory, and no specific role – you will oversee, as I will. Nothing will be done, or decided, without our joint consent. And we will have a weekly meeting at the factory, or here, to make sure we are kept informed. The day-to-day running can be done by Jim and Elsie.'

'Oh, I see.'

'And that leaves you free to make my dreams come true. I want us to have a large family, darling, and I hope you do too? I hated being an only child.'

'So did I, it was a lonely existence. And you can imagine how happy I was to find that Elsie and . . . and poor, darling Dot were my sisters.'

'Well, I am happy for you, although I have said before, I couldn't do what you did. I would run a mile if I found out I had a brother – or any siblings born as bastards to my father!'

Millie hated this term, as it didn't fit her sisters at all, but she didn't want to cause any more friction. This was meant to be a happy evening. Changing the subject, she said, 'I'm only sorry, darling, that there won't be time for any of your uncles to come to the wedding – they'd hardly get the invitation in time, let alone be able to sort out passage on a ship to get here.'

'I know, but I have that covered. I have already written to them and told them . . . Oh, it was meant to be a surprise, but I've just realized that it can't be, as you will need to prepare. You see, I haven't seen my Italian family for about ten years, so when I met you, I wrote to tell them all about you. My *zietta* Maria – my Aunty Maria – wrote back full of excitement, saying that if you were the one, then we must marry in Italy. And I promised them we would.'

'What? But . . .'

'Not our main wedding, darling, but a second ceremony with all my family. And that is where I am planning to take you for our honeymoon. Please say you will? I am planning to take you across on the ferry from Dover to Calais, and then by train to Italy. It is a long journey, but I will book us first-class, so we will have a private carriage on the train.'

'It sounds wonderful. I'm so excited. What will I wear? What will happen?'

Len laughed as he rose. They'd finished their dinner. 'Shall we retire to your sitting room, darling? We can have a drink to celebrate in privacy then.'

He came round the table to offer her his hand and lead her out. He thanked Mabel, the maid who had replaced Ruby and who had served them, along with Barridge. She blushed crimson – a shy girl, Millie hadn't yet made a friend of Mabel, but she hoped to, as she missed Ruby so much. She knew she would even more so when Elsie moved out, too.

Dread settled in her then, to think of how lonely she would be when Len was out at work. Especially now that she wouldn't have to make the daily trip to the factory – something she knew she would have to agree to. It wasn't seemly for a wife to work and, if she insisted, she would cause Len a lot of embarrassment.

Len thanked Barridge, too, for his excellent service and asked him to thank Cook and the kitchen staff on his behalf. Millie added, 'And Mrs Robinson too. Tell her that she has done me and my guest proud, organizing such a lovely evening for us.'

Barridge had beamed at Len, but his expression changed at her addition to his thanks. When he closed the doors, Millie giggled. 'There's a lot of rivalry between him and Mrs Robinson, my housekeeper. I think he was going to lord it over her, by telling her that he and everyone but her had received our thanks.'

'Oh no. You will have to school me in the etiquette of the house, darling, seeing that this is going to be my home.' He went to take Millie in his arms, but a tap and the door opening hailed Barridge coming through with a silver tray bearing their sherries.

'Thank you, Barridge. If we need anything further, I will ring for you.'

They giggled when he left, toasted each other and drank the tipple straight back. They had hardly replaced their glasses when Len said, 'He nearly caught me red-handed, darling. I was just going to kiss you.' His voice lowered as he moved closer to her. 'I want to give you our first real kiss. I have so longed to, but now that we are formally engaged – or will be any moment – I want to express my love in a deeper way than the gentle kisses we have shared.' As he spoke, he

171

dug a little box out of his pocket. Millie couldn't speak. Her throat dried. The beauty of the sapphire ring took her breath away.

Lifting her hand, Len placed the ring on her finger. Before she could thank him, his lips came down on hers and lit feelings inside her that she never knew she could feel. Her world became whole in that moment. All the hurt evaporated and she was left floating in a sea of happiness – a feeling she could never see changing.

Chapter Sixteen

Elsie

The experience in Mickey's pie-shop was so different from the last time Elsie had been here. Jim was great company and hadn't stuck out, as Millie and especially Len had when he'd barged in. Jim looked and acted like one of the crowd and, but for his way of speaking, it felt to Elsie as if she was with a regular London lad.

'Well, that was delicious, Elsie. I can honestly say I haven't ever tasted anything better.'

Elsie beamed, feeling as though she had made the dish personally, so proud was she of her roots at that moment.

'That was our family's mainstay meal when we were all together. I still love it so much.'

'And with just cause. Now tell me, how you really are? Are you coping?'

Somehow she felt she could confide in Jim. 'Not really, but I keep a brave face on for Bert, poor little lamb. He sometimes reminds me of a misplaced person, as I am myself. I can't wait to move us in with Rene, and for me brovver Cecil to come home.'

They chatted on about her plans for her new home.

'Music lessons? Well, that sounds like a really good idea.'

'Well, not music – playing the piano. I can't read a note of music, but I play by ear: I think that's what me gran called it. I want to teach others how to play a set of tunes that are popular, so that they can enjoy singalongs with their family.' She told him how most families possessed a piano.

'But how will you do that?'

'I thought I would do it in stages. Show them the keys for a tune, perhaps one line at a time, something very simple, like "Twinkle, Twinkle, Little Star". Everyone knows that and how it goes. It's what me gran started me on. I remember how I felt when I played a real tune for the first time – it was such a good feeling. I wanted to learn more and more, and soon I was picking up tunes as if I had played them all me life.'

'I can see it means a lot to you, Elsie, but you sound as though you have a natural talent – an ear for music, as they say. You may struggle to pass that on to those who don't. They may need something more to help them learn the keys, other than just being shown them. When I learned—'

'You play!'

'Yes, but I read music. I had extra lessons at school. But when we first sat down to play the notes, our teacher marked the piano keys "one, two, three" and coincided that with the notes on our music sheet. I was thinking you could do that, but then mark the words of the song with the number of the key they need to play.'

Elsie laughed at this idea. 'That'd take me ages, mate. I'll think about it.'

'I could do it for you.'

She hesitated, but then thought that if she was serious about Jim being her friend, she had to trust his word and not think he was simply trying to get her into a situation where she

174

couldn't refuse him. 'Ta, that'd be a big help. But no musical notes, mind. They're just a lot of squiggles to me.'

'You'd be surprised. Look, I have a notepad in my pocket – I'll show you the basic ones. You would soon pick it up.'

Elsie was very surprised at how easy it seemed.

'I could teach you, Elsie, and then you can play anything, whether you have heard it before or not.'

A feeling of excitement gripped her. Discovering new pieces to play was always difficult, unless she heard someone play it first, or they sang it to her. To think that she would only need a sheet of music to be able to play anything was something she'd never dreamed of. 'I'd love to give it a go. Ta, Jim. Though if I do find it too hard, you won't laugh at me, will yer?'

'You won't do, I promise. As soon as you get into your new home, and Cecil is there with you, I'll come round and we can have our first lesson.'

This pleased Elsie, as it showed that he wasn't thinking of coming into her home unless she was chaperoned. 'Yer a real mate, Jim. I'm going to give my all to learning from you. But for my pupils – if I get any – I will stick to the simpler method . . . Though, well, I will be cheeky and ask if you would give Bert lessons? I can pay you. Only the odd time he has sat with me, he has shown real talent and has a good ear, as you call it, and as me gran would say. And a lovely singing voice, too.'

'He does – the voice, I mean. I was awestruck at Christmas when he came to the factory party and sang "Away in a Manger": his pitch was perfect and he hit every note. I'd be honoured to teach him music, and then you can teach him the piano, but in the correct way from the very beginning. We might have a star on our hands.'

'Oh, so my way ain't the correct way then? Well, it's done generations of poor folk good to have one in the family who could play it any way they could!'

'Ha, I consider myself told off.'

'Good. Now I think we'd better go – we're getting funny looks from those who want a table. They don't mind waiting when folk are eating, but the minute you finish you get glared at.'

'Oh, is that why they're staring. I was getting worried for a moment. Come on, then. Though I don't want the evening to end: can we go for a walk maybe? I – I only mean to kill time for me. Once back in my flat, it's a lonely existence. I don't talk to another soul until I come out the next morning.'

'But you have yer car here.'

'I know, but I can walk back to that.'

'All right, we'll walk along and then cross the park to Millie's. If yer lucky, you might get asked in for a nightcap.'

Jim laughed. 'Sounding better every minute.'

They walked in silence. The evening was balmy, and the smell of cut grass and the much fresher air than the streets provided gave Elsie a light-headed feeling. She began to relax, until they neared the place where Len had first shown her that he had feelings for her. *Or did he? Did that encounter with me, or the kiss he gave me at Ruby's wedding, mean anything to Len?*

'You're deep in thought.'

'Yes. Can I ask yer something, Jim? Something that may sound personal.'

'Ask away, and I'll do my best to answer. Come on, what is it?'

'Well, as a man . . . Oh, this is going to sound silly.'

'It sounds all right so far, at least you have acknowledged I am a man.' His laugh settled her. Yes, Jim truly was a mate, and she knew she could ask him anything.

'Supposing you had a fiancée, but you found yourself able to kiss another willing woman and no one would find out: would yer be compelled to, just because you could, or would doing so mean you had feelings for her?'

'Well, that's a tricky one. It's all a question of honour really. If I had feelings for this woman, I would be compelled to kiss her if she returned those feelings, but only after I had broken off my engagement to the other woman. That doesn't apply if I didn't have feelings for her and loved my fiancée. Then I would walk away from her. But not all men are honourable. Why do you ask?'

'Oh, nothing.'

'Well, have I answered what's bothering you?'

For some reason Jim's gentle tone broke the tension inside her and unbidden tears ran down her face.

'Elsie? Has something happened? Did someone . . . ?'

She nodded.

'Do you want to talk about it?'

'I – I don't know. I feel so guilty, so disloyal.'

They had stopped under a tree. Jim dug a huge white hanky out of his pocket. 'Unused, so don't worry. Dry your tears. You've shed enough of them. Though to be crying, you must be very hurt by what happened, because I know from experience that once you have tasted the ultimate grief, you don't cry easily over things that seem trivial. Tell me what happened.'

Elsie didn't think about whether she would regret telling him, but spilled out what was troubling her.

'My God! That isn't acceptable. I will have a word with him, as a friend. He should apologize to you.'

'No! I told you in confidence, as me mate. I can't bear there to be any bad feelings. He's marrying me sister! Besides, he'll probably deny it.'

There was a pause, then Jim enquired if he might ask her something. Elsie nodded.

'Do you have feelings for Len?'

Again she nodded.

Jim released a huge sigh.

They stood for a moment, not talking. Elsie hung her head, feeling the shame of what she'd revealed and her disloyalty to Millie. But also aware of how Jim must hurt, on hearing her revelation, when he had made no secret of how he harboured a hope of them becoming more than friends. 'I'm sorry, mate. I – I wish it was different.'

'So do I. And not just for my sake, but for yours. There's no future in this for you, Elsie. Look, whatever I say will sound like sour grapes, but I know you have suffered – and so have so many that you love – through the actions of Millie's father . . . Well, I worry that Len could have the same traits.'

This shocked Elsie. She stared at him.

'Look, despite me and Len being friends for a long time – or maybe because of that – I know that he does have another side to him. Right from being a boy, he . . . well, he used girls. There's been times when he fancied more than one, and made his choice by courting the girl with the most to offer. Then tried to have a clandestine relationship with the other girl. Like I say, this is all schoolboy stuff. The girls were boarding at a school near to ours, so it was all puppy love. But it wasn't how I – or most of our peers – behaved, while Len boasted about it and thought it the norm.'

Elsie began to have doubts, and concern rose inside her.

'Anyway, besides that, wealth means a great deal to Len.

He has always chosen his friends from those who have the most. Even myself at the time, as I was thought to be very wealthy and had all the trappings. You know, of course, how my father lost our string of factories. But Len is loyal – with his male friends, that is. I didn't think he was at first, as I didn't hear from him after the crash of our family business, but then, out of the blue, he helped me get this position.'

Elsie found her voice at last. 'You mean, he may fancy me and Millie equally, but chose her because she is wealthy?'

'Yes, I do. And he will make her happy, I'm sure. But you have to get over him, Elsie. Don't spend your life yearning for what can never be – or ever succumb to what Len may have in mind for you.'

The word 'never' shook through her. Could she live with that? But then what choice did she have? And what could Len have in mind for her . . . Jim's meaning dawned on her – she could end up like her mum, deeply in love with someone who used her.

Jim's voice, still sounding hurt, brought her out of these thoughts. 'Shall we go?'

She nodded and fell into step with Jim. 'Ta, Jim. You've helped me, in a way. To believe that Len thinks something of me cheers me, but I'll never act on it or let him think he can use me. Nor will I ever take too much drink again.'

Jim didn't answer. They walked on a little quicker than before. Elsie had the feeling that he wanted to get away from her as fast as he could, and this was proven when they reached the house and he refused her offer of coming in for a drink.

As he walked away, she called after him. He turned and looked at her. His look held a longing, and yet a coldness. 'Jim, I'm sorry. I shouldn't have told you.'

He touched his forelock, bowed his head, then turned and walked briskly away. Elsie stood, looking after him. *Oh, why can't I fall in love with someone like Jim – dependable and kind and, yes, funny?* As she mounted the steps to the house, she thought, *I really enjoyed being with him, but will he ever want to be with me again?* A small hurt touched her heart as she thought this. She brushed it aside as she said good evening to Barridge.

'I trust you enjoyed your evening, Miss?'

'I did, thank you. And you yours?'

Barridge looked shocked, then coughed and hastily took her wrap. 'Miss Millie is in her sitting room, not to be disturbed. Can I get you something?'

'No . . .' Elsie had no time to say more, as the door to Millie's sitting room burst open and a radiant Millie stood there. 'Oh, Elsie, we've been so longing for you to come home – we have the most wonderful news!'

The light from the gas mantle flashed onto Millie's ring finger. Elsie gasped with pain, but managed to make it sound as though she was astonished. 'Oh, Millie, your ring. It's beautiful. Oh, I – I'm so happy for you. When?'

'In less than six weeks, Elsie.' Millie cuddled herself. 'I'm so excited!'

Elsie felt as though she'd been stabbed, but she ran to Millie and held her. Over her shoulder she saw Len standing just inside the room, and his look melted her. He had a little-lost-boy expression. She wanted to scream, *Why? Why?* But she swallowed hard and looked away.

When they parted, Millie ushered her into the room. 'We want to talk to you, love. Though more me apologizing. But first – meet your new brother-in-law-to-be.'

Len laughed and opened his arms.

Elsie walked pensively towards him, with Jim's warnings still ringing in her ears. Len met her halfway. Held close to him, she felt as if her heart would burst, but knew she must stop this. She must always be in control of her feelings, where Len was concerned. He'd made his choice, and she would never hurt Millie – never.

'I'm very happy to have you as my sister-in-law, Elsie. And you will make a beautiful bridesmaid.' She had the sense that he was mocking her. She turned quickly to be released from his arms and ask Millie, 'Apologize? What for?'

'Len has made me see how I have been doing my "do-gooding" again, without any thought for you, dear Elsie. You tried so hard to tell me that you didn't want to be a partner, but I didn't listen. Now Len has made me see how unhappy you would be in that role. I'm so sorry for not listening to you. I will cancel the legal proceedings right away; you have no need to worry any further. Instead we are going to draw up a proper agreement for an allowance for you and Kitty. Hers will be held in trust for her until she is older.'

A warning bell sounded in Elsie's ear. Jim had said that Len chased wealth. For a moment she wanted to stand her ground and say that she did want to be a partner, and it was her due. That would foil him from what she now felt was Len's way of protecting all that Millie had, so that he would benefit. But she didn't want to embarrass Millie. Nor did she want to thank her for what she had allowed her. 'Well, that is the least me so-called father could have done for me, so thank you for doing it on his behalf.'

With this, she stormed past Millie and ran up the stairs. When she reached her room, Elsie locked her door, then leaned on it. The tears streamed down her face. She'd done the very thing that she'd said she didn't want to do: embarrassed Millie, and herself. All to get back at Len, who she was certain had changed Millie's mind.

I should fight this! I should. Oh, why did I try to let Len off the hook when Millie told me that he was opposed to her plan? Why didn't I speak up and say that owning half of the jam factory was my right? Because it is. Stinking Hawkesfield was my father, too!

Chapter Seventeen

Elsie and Millie

Despite telling herself over and over again that the upset wasn't her fault, the enormity of what she'd done wouldn't leave Elsie and she knew she had to put everything right.

Opening her door, she listened. All was quiet. Wiping her face on the large hanky that she hadn't given back to Jim, she went down the stairs. When she got to the sitting-room door she heard Millie crying. 'I just don't understand it. I did my best to persuade her the other day that she should be a partner – that it was her right to be – but she protested. Oh, Len, I don't know what to do.'

'I would leave it as it is. You were misguided in offering it in the first place. And you are wrong. It isn't her right. She is the bastard daughter of your father – you have no responsibility towards her, and she has no legal rights on your estate.'

'What about moral rights? And don't use that filthy word! In Elsie's case, I believe that my father loved her mother.'

'So is that why he had her murdered?'

'Len!'

'I'm sorry. I'm trying to make you see that none of this is your fault.'

'Nor is it Elsie's.'

'True. And we always intend to do the right thing by Elsie. And by Dot's child. There is no question of that, but the right thing isn't giving away half of your main income. Look, darling, we have been through all of this. This is meant to be our night to celebrate our love, and now it is spoiled. And that is Elsie's fault. If she hadn't tried to convince you the other day that she didn't want to be a partner, none of this would have happened. Come here and let me hug your troubles away. Everything will be all right in the morning. Elsie just needs time to think over what she's done.'

Elsie was seeing another side to Len now, and she didn't like it. *So he thinks of me as a bastard! He doesn't really think I have any rights – only to handouts, which he will determine the size of.*

Judging by how easily Len had persuaded Millie from her absolute determination that they would be partners, Elsie now thought of him as dangerous to her future. And yet, she had to admit, if he came out of this door now and put his arms out to her, she would go into them willingly.

Hesitating, she couldn't decide whether to go in and make things right, or fight her corner when Len wasn't around – but then she would tear Millie in two. Deciding that she had to accept the fate she had contributed to, she knocked on the door and entered.

Millie jumped back from a deep kiss. Elsie's heart tore in two. But she held herself strong. 'I'm sorry, Millie. I – I don't know what came over me. I . . . well, it hit a nerve that you had both discussed my future and presented me with a . . . a package. I thought you were so strongly for me being a partner, and I thought you would stick to that.'

'Oh, Elsie, I will, if that's what you want.'

'Millie!'

'Len, I'm sorry, but I did promise, and none of what you have said tonight has changed that. The only thing that made me waver was you saying that I was acting against Elsie's wishes.'

'So you don't mind acting against mine then? I think I'd better say goodnight, and maybe even goodbye! It doesn't bode well to be married to a headstrong woman who goes against everything I know is right for her.'

'No! Len, darling, no. Don't leave. We can talk this through.'

'We have done, Millie. We sorted out our future together. We included more than we had to, for the provision of Elsie and the child. But I was more than happy with that, and so were you. Now you are letting Elsie come between us, when nothing should. And you, Elsie, have disgusted me.' He looked her in the eye, 'In more ways than one!'

Elsie felt as though she'd been slapped in the face. But she also knew she should do something to stop this, and bitterly regretted behaving as she had. And she regretted, too, her earlier misguided opening of her heart to Jim, as that had led her to learn some worrying things about Len's true character. But so what? If Len was a money-chaser, he still made Millie happy – and that's all that mattered.

Running to Len, she grabbed his arm. 'Don't go. I'm sorry. What you and Millie propose for me is everything I need. I know it is, and I will be happy – I will, Millie. I have a lot of plans of me own. I know nothing about running a business, and I have already taken a role that I love and am suited to. I don't know what came over me. I – I . . . it's this thing of, well, of everyone seeming to be in charge of what happens to me, when I was the main pin in me

185

family for years. I did protest the other day, Millie. And it's unfair of me to go back on that.'

Len softened his stance. 'Elsie, I understand. It was wrong of us to talk about what you are entitled to. We should have all sat down together and sorted my role in the owning – or not – of my future wife's assets. And your wishes for your own future, as it is only right that you have a stake in your father's wealth.' He turned back to Millie. 'I'm sorry, Millie. I was cross just now because of the upset this has caused you, and I said things I didn't mean. And I'm worried, too, about the state of the finances of the jam factory. I want to make sure the changes you have both made, along with others that I propose, build the business up to what it should be. But I can see how that has diminished your roles. I'm sorry. Will you both forgive me?'

He opened his arms, and the look on his face melted Elsie's heart. Her love for Len surged through her, but something in her head rang an alarm bell – the owning of his wife's assets? *So he does intend to take what Millie has.* She quashed the thought. Millie had run to Len and was forgiving him. If there was to be peace between her and Millie, Elsie knew she had to do the same.

When they came out of the hug, they were laughing and the atmosphere lightened. Len had made a remark about being a thorn between two roses, and how he should mind his Ps and Qs, as it seemed he would be marrying two women. Millie had laughed out loud, and Elsie had allowed herself to join in.

Len helped the change of mood further by making a suggestion that included her. 'Let's all have a nightcap to celebrate us having cleared the air, and arrange a meeting when we all three go over what was discussed tonight by Millie and me.'

'I think we should have that meeting right now. It's not all that late, and I think Elsie will feel better when we tell her what we have planned.' Millie took Elsie's hand and smiled at her. 'I stood up for all we believe in, Elsie, and I always will do. I know that was worrying you. But our factory isn't moving to new premises, no matter what other changes we implement.'

This gave Elsie a chance to step down from her stance, and make it all right to do so. 'Oh? Well, that was a big part of me wanting to be able to have a say. But I see that I can leave it to you, Millie, to do right by our workers.'

The couple told her what other proposals they had, and it all sounded very exciting. 'And, Elsie, though you won't be involved in the decision-making, everything will be discussed with you, so that you know what is happening. And the reason for that is that your allowance will come from your own shares in the business.'

'Shares?' As Len asked this, his face showed that they hadn't discussed this angle.

'Yes, that is what I am proposing in the meeting about our future. I think Elsie's income should come from having shares in the business. That way, if we grow in wealth, so does she. I think that is much fairer to her. And besides this, she will have a casting vote!'

'No! Having a casting vote isn't fair, as you two will get your heads together over everything I propose that you don't like, and I will be foiled every step of the way. I am warming to the shares for Elsie. But as a sleeping partner who doesn't have a say in the running of the business.'

Millie turned to her. 'What do you think, Elsie?'

Again she had the feeling that not only her own destiny was at stake here, but also the happiness of Millie and Len.

'I think Len is right. Even if I thought what he proposed was good, but you asked me to vote against, I would.'

'There, you see! I wouldn't stand a chance. Whereas you and I, Millie, have proved tonight that we can sort out what each of us wants and there is no dominant partner. You should have heard Millie put me in my place over moving the premises! You'd have been proud of her. And not, as I thought would happen, by ruling with her heart, either. Millie had sound business arguments to back up her point. I respect that and always will.'

'Right. Note it down. Shares it is for Elsie, but with no vote and no veto. All agreed?'

To this from Millie, Elsie said, 'Aye.'

They both looked at her, then said, 'Aye.'

Elsie grinned at them. 'Now yer are proper factory workers. That's the common way of agreeing or not. None of your posh "I agree" or "Motion passed". Ha! That's us cockneys' term for going to the loo.' There was a short pause, then they both burst out laughing. Relief washed over Elsie; she truly felt that the horrible incident had passed, and now they seemed to be on a much better footing. 'And so I have a proposal. That we order a hot mug of cocoa, and that I take mine to bed and leave you two to say a proper goodnight.'

Both agreed with that. Len a bit too whole-heartedly. And Elsie had the feeling that she was a bit of a thorn in his side. She liked that and intended always to be one – but only to protect Millie. Never again would she allow anything to happen between her and Len, no matter how much she desired it to.

Millie felt the happiest she'd felt in a long time. Every-thing would be legally binding, where Elsie's shares were concerned. They'd agreed that, once the wedding was over and Len was her husband, he and Millie would both be allocated 37.5 per cent of the shares in Swift's Jam Factory and Elsie 25 per cent. But in any new businesses that were to be funded separately from the jam factory, only she and Len would hold shares.

Elsie had asked, if they could hold shares, whether others could start to buy some too. But Len had put their minds at rest by telling them they weren't floating on the Stock Exchange, so their shares were not for sale in that manner. It had made Millie feel a little silly that she didn't know this, but Len had been kind in pointing out that she had learned an enormous amount about business, and in such a short time, that she should be proud of herself, not ashamed.

It seemed to Millie that life was going to change from now on. That there would be no more conflict. And even her nightmares, where she was a little girl and her father had her on his knee, making her giggle before he suddenly turned into a monster, were diminishing.

Sitting with her mama on the night before her wedding day in her sitting room, which had been her mother's sanctuary for many years – a lonely place for her then, but a happy place tonight – Millie chatted on about things they'd shared together, being careful not to mention anything that included her father, although a tiny part of her was mourning the loving side of him that she had known.

Shaking these thoughts from her, she laughed at her mama's telling of a tale. 'You were three years old and we were staying with your grandmother in Leeds. Her friend visited, and she had a rather large nose. You kept looking at her and then you asked me, in what you thought was a whisper, but which carried all around the room: "Mama, is she the wolf from *Red Riding Hood*?" Oh, I was so embarrassed, I wanted to die. But the friend laughed out loud and came up to you, tickling you and saying, "Yes, and I'm going to eat you all up." You were in fits of giggles and never left her side all afternoon.'

Millie knew the story, and remembered receiving birthday messages from the lady every year until she was about eight, but she giggled along with her mama. 'She did have a huge hooter – or conk, as the cockneys call it. But she was so lovely: her name was Isobel, wasn't it?'

'Yes. And she and Grandmother died in the same week and had been friends since they were girls.'

'Well, let's hope they are still together. I remember my grandmother. I loved her very much.'

'Hmm. I expect I'll be a grandmother soon, dear.'

'Mama!'

'Well, you are getting married tomorrow and that means . . . Oh, this is just my clumsy way of getting round to asking you if you are . . . well, *au fait* with the ways of men. Are you dear?'

Blushing, Millie laughed. 'Oh, that! Yes, Mama. We had a lesson at school. And given by one of the nuns! Ha, it was hilarious, and we were so naughty towards her. Anyway, what you don't learn in a boarding school for girls isn't worth knowing.'

Mama's laugh was more of a relief than amusement. 'Oh, I am silly. Of course – and anyway, you have a lovely man in Len. He will take care of you.'

'Shall we change the subject, Mama?'

'Yes, please, dear. But I did think I should . . .'

'Have the mother–daughter conversation? Well, you've

had it now, so just forget it. And yes, no doubt you will be a grandmother very soon.'

They both smiled.

'So, to change the subject, Elsie will be down for dinner soon. She was very tired at work today and has gone for a lie-down.'

'Ah, I wondered where she was. You know, from what you have told me, she sounds as though she has been doing too much, with overseeing her flat renovations and working most days, as well as having responsibility for her little brother. I hope she'll be all right.'

'Yes, she seems to want to be constantly busy. I know she wants to be in her flat by the time Len and I return from Italy, though, so maybe that's motivating her. I can't wait for my Italian wedding. It all sounds so much fun. I'm so glad you and Len's father are going to come over for it. Imagine: six weeks of discovering Len's mother's roots.'

'She was a beautiful lady. I met her a few times at social occasions. Letitia, she was called. Len is very like her in looks. She had a natural elegance, which he has too. It is so sad that she won't be here tomorrow.'

They were quiet for a moment, and the thought popped into Millie's head that neither would her father. She'd always taken it for granted that he would give her away. The same train of thought must have been in her mother's mind. 'Darling, are you sure Cecil is up to giving a speech?'

'Yes, Mama, and knowing him, it will be the funniest one ever. He hasn't lost his sense of humour, despite all he has been through. Well, you've met him. He's a marvel with little Kitty and keeps cheerful, though I know he does have his moments.'

'Yes, a lot of those are probably when we don't see him. Will he be down to dinner?'

'No. He sent his apologies and said he was having an early night. He had a long journey yesterday, and he is so brave even to come to the wedding, after what happened on his own wedding day – let alone consent to giving me away. But he is the nearest I have to a brother, and I'm honoured he is going to give me away.'

'Yes, poor soul. I'm glad you're only having a small gathering – because of the mourning period, as well as for myself. I couldn't face all that false society lot.'

'No, but don't worry: I am no longer asked to anything. So I doubt any of them would accept an invite. My new solicitor is coming, Jordon Wright, and his wife, Issy. You will love them.'

'Darling, I can't tell you how happy I was that you sacked Gutheridge. He lived in your father's pocket. I hated him. But back to Cecil: you said earlier that he had some news?'

A tap on the door interrupted them. When it opened, Elsie stood there. She looked lovely in a grey day-frock, but it showed the divide between them, as both her and Mama were dressed in evening wear for dinner. Mama raised her eyebrows, but didn't remark on the error Elsie had made. Not that it was her fault, for they had fallen into being very casual when home alone. Millie told herself off mentally for not informing Elsie that Mama liked the old traditions.

'Elsie, how lovely. Millie and I were just discussing your brother and his news. Come on in, darling. Are you feeling better?'

Millie could have hugged her mama.

'Yes, ta. I've overdone it a bit. But I feel bright and breezy again, and excited about tomorrow.'

'So are we. Tonight's the last supper – so to speak – and it's nice that it's all girls, as that is the tradition. Oh, I didn't mean . . . well, you know. Anyway, like I was saying to Millie, Cecil has news, I believe. So now that you are here, you can tell us all about it.'

Elsie accepted the small glass of sherry from Barridge and then, when he'd left the room, she said, 'Yes, he's really sorted himself – well, it looks that way.'

Millie listened as Elsie told Mama about the gentleman they had met in Wales. 'He is so nice, and Cess got on like a house on fire with him – their friendship started over their mutual grief: it was someone they could each talk to who understood.' She explained more about Dai and the circumstances he found himself in. 'Anyway, Cess and Dai's friendship developed as they found they had similar interests. They both enjoy fishing and, although he was in banking, Dai loved buying and selling. They laughed a lot – which I found surprising, but lovely – over how Dai had disposed of a lot of the old articles in the guest house by getting good sums of money for them, when his wife had said they were junk. And so when Cess went back to Wales, they became really close and shared times when they broke down and times when they laughed too, till they both felt they couldn't do without each other – and so the idea of going into business together evolved. Cess is really happy about it.'

'Market stalls, isn't it? How interesting. I love the markets: the atmosphere, and the hustle and bustle.'

'Mama! I never knew.'

'Oh yes, I would often sneak down to Petticoat Lane. I bought many a trinket down there – bargains, all of them, as I knew their worth. And in some cases I recognized them and knew who had sold them, as a lot of the so-called society folk have to wheel and deal to make ends meet.'

Millie looked at Elsie. 'Well I never!'

'Yes, I love markets, so much that if Cecil and Dai need an investor, I'm it! I'd love to be part-owner of a stall.'

Millie folded over with laughter. She'd have never guessed this quirk about her mama in a million years.

Elsie joined her, and together they giggled till they had to wipe their eyes.

'I'm serious, girls. It would be a dream come true. And when I'm up here I'll even do a couple of hours behind the stall. I think I could sell well: "Cam on, get yer jewels 'ere, you lavely ladies, cam and look at this lot – make yer custard pies water, they will!"'

That did it. Already in pain from stretching her muscles at laughing so much, Millie could hardly catch her breath, but a small part of her felt sorry that she'd never known this fun-loving, mimicking side of her mama while she was growing up.

When they eventually calmed down and went into the dining room, the mood was one of happiness. What had troubled Elsie so that she had to rest before she came down, Millie didn't know, although she guessed that her grief had overwhelmed Elsie for a time and she'd needed to be alone. But now she was as jolly as she and her mama were, and this completed Millie's feeling of excitement about her forthcoming wedding day. *It's going to be so lovely. I can't wait!*

Chapter Eighteen

Elsie

'You look beautiful, Millie. Oh, I do love you. You're a lovely sister to me.' Elsie caught hold of Millie's hands as they stood facing each other in her sitting room.

'And you to me, darling Elsie. I trust you with my life. And I will always stand up for you, even against Len. So never be afraid of being cast out of the business, or of anything. I have established my position with Len, and he respects my opinions and decisions.'

'I know. I feel secure now with the new plans. Anyway, we won't even mention those things today. How do I look?' Elsie did a twirl.

'Stunning. That green is so soft, it is almost turquoise, and it shows off your hair beautifully. I'm so glad you consented to having it dressed in that style – you look beautiful.'

Elsie blushed. She'd wanted to wear her hair up and understated, but Millie had other ideas. And so the front of her hair was swept off her face, with ringlets falling down her back and tiny curls around her face. She loved it. And yes, she did feel beautiful.

Giggling at herself and at the joy of the moment, she told Millie, 'Cess is all ready for you, Millie, he's waiting in the hall. I've to go now with your mother, but I will be waiting for you at the church door. It's a lovely day, and you know what they say: "Happy is the bride that the sun shines on."'

As she went through the door, she heard Millie give a little excited giggle. For a moment Elsie wished it was *her* waiting to be taken to the church with Cess to marry Len, but she brushed this thought aside. It was never to be and, from now on, she vowed never to think of Len in that way, but to take her destiny into her own hands and hope that the path she took would lead her to her own love.

Cess looked so handsome as he stood in the sunbeam coming through the porthole-type window high above the front door. His sandy hair looked darker with the oil he'd used to smooth it, and his small moustache was neatly trimmed. His face was set into what Elsie knew was a courageous expression. What he must be feeling, she had no idea, but she was so glad he'd had the strength to do this for Millie. Poor Millie had no other male close to her who could give her away, and would have had to ask her solicitor – though she'd have asked Barridge as a last resort. She'd known him all her life. Elsie smiled at Cess, trying to convey encouragement, and yet to let him know that she knew how he felt.

Barridge stepped forward. 'Madam is waiting in the carriage for you, Miss Makin.'

'Thank you.'

He escorted her to the door and down the steps. As he gave her his hand to help her get into the carriage, Barridge said, 'May I say that you look very beautiful.'

This touched her, as it was the first human thing to be said to her by any of Millie's household staff since Ruby left. 'Thank you, Mr Barridge.'

He clucked his tongue, but gave her a little smile. She knew he wanted her to say just 'Barridge', but that he'd thought better of correcting her. She hoped he realized that she was trying to give him the respect his standing warranted.

At the church Elsie's resolve faltered when she caught sight of Len. He looked stunningly beautiful as he stood in the sunshine with Jim, who was his best man. The picture he made caught her breath.

'Are you all right, dear? Don't worry, you're bound to have a fit of nerves, but it will pass.'

Elsie smiled as the carriage pulled up directly in front of the entrance to the Church of English Martyrs in Prescot Street.

Jim rushed forward to open the door. He assisted Mrs Hawkesfield out and gave her his arm. His eyes never left Elsie until he had to turn towards the church. She read in them his appreciation of how she looked – and, yes, his love for her.

When he disappeared, Len helped her down. His voice tingled through her. Her legs wobbled. 'Elsie. Oh, Elsie, you are so beautiful.'

Coming to her senses, she took a deep breath. Tears stung her eyes and she wanted to scream at him, 'But I'm not wealthy enough, am I?' Instead she smiled at him and spoke in her broadest cockney. 'Millie chose me frock well, don't yer think, eh, mate?'

He laughed, looked round, then said in a soft voice, 'You would look beautiful if you wore a coal sack. Oh, Elsie . . .'

She snatched her hand from his, feeling herself weaken. 'This is your wedding day. You are marrying my lovely sister. You shouldn't speak to me in that way.'

Len suddenly became stern. 'What way? Don't be ridiculous – can't I compliment my future sister-in-law? Are you really so unsophisticated as not to know the difference between when you are being flattered and when someone is making a pass at you? I wouldn't dream of the latter.'

The tears brimmed over. Elsie dabbed them away and turned from him. At this moment she hated Len – a feeling that hurt just as much as loving him did.

'I'm sorry, Elsie. Forgive me. I – I panicked when you took my compliments the wrong way. We none of us would want to hurt Millie.'

'No, I'm sorry. Sorry for not being higher in your estimation, and sorry to have even met you.' Elsie turned then, intending to move away from Len, but Jim came through the church door and she felt trapped.

'Well, Elsie, you look like a princess. Doesn't she look lovely, Len?'

Len nodded. Jim looked deeply into Elsie's eyes and mouthed, 'Are you all right?'

Impetuously she reached up and kissed his cheek and, in a loud whisper, said, 'I am now that you're by my side, Jim.'

His smile held surprise and hope, and suddenly Elsie wanted to give him more than hope. Jim was a lovely man. She could do a lot worse, and she did like him very much. They were mates and that would be a good grounding for them, wouldn't it? She smiled back while looking deep into his eyes. The love she saw there she prayed would sustain her. His hand reached out for hers. She took his and squeezed it.

A cough made her jump. She'd forgotten Len for a moment and the feeling was a nice one, as if she was released from a great burden. Jim turned to look at Len.

'You're my groomsman, Jim – we should be getting inside.'

Jim grinned. 'You're eager. Nice to see. We've been at a few weddings of reluctant bridegrooms. Not a pleasant experience. I'm ready to escort you to the altar, dear sir.'

Len hit out with his gloves and they both giggled.

What have I done? I completely forgot how close Jim is to Len. If I take up with Jim, I'll never be able to keep away from Len. But then Elsie remembered that Jim knew all about her predicament with Len and would protect her. A funny kind of peace settled in her. To have her future settled was a nice feeling, and she felt nothing of the disappointment she thought she would feel.

When the carriage drew up with Cess and Millie in, she could do nothing but smile, for suddenly she knew that she didn't care about losing Len. She felt glad.

As she walked into the church a little voice called, 'Elsie!'

Looking in the direction it came from, she saw Bert waving frantically. Elsie waved back. He looked lovely in his knee-length trousers and frilly shirt. Gertie waved, too. In her arms was the sleeping Kitty. A wave of love for her brother and her niece washed over Elsie.

The service was lovely, but was over quickly as there was no nuptial mass, which surprised Elsie. Just a short exchange of vows, a hymn before and a hymn after, while the wedding party went into the sanctuary to sign the official register. Here the vows were gone over again. And then they were out in the sunshine, and the carriages began to draw up.

'I like your frock, Else. You look like a fairy princess.'

Elsie ruffled Bert's hair. 'I am, just for a day, Bert.'

He giggled. 'I have to go. Gertie said I could come and say hello, but I must hurry back to her.'

'Good boy. I'll see you back at the house.'

Bert ran off, waving and smiling.

There was a lovely moment then, as Millie and Len went towards their carriage. Millie's staff, all dressed in their Sunday best, had lined up and they threw rice and streamers at the cowering couple. Elsie could hear Millie's squeals of laughter. The sound held such happiness, and seemed to seal her letting go of Len.

A hand came on her arm and she looked up into Jim's face. He smiled down on her. 'I now have the wonderful job of escorting the most beautiful woman in the world.'

Blushing, she thanked him, then asked, 'What about Cess?'

'It's his job to take care of the bride's mother, though it looks to me as if someone else would like to do that.' Jim nodded in Mrs Hawkesfield's direction. Elsie turned and captured a moment that told a story. Mr Lefton, Len's father, was gazing down into the eyes of Millie's mum, who was telling him some tale or other. But the way she looked up at him as she did so showed how she was loving being in his company.

Jim whispered, 'A turn-up for the books, but not un-expected.'

'Oh?'

'There was a party – oh, about a year after Len's mum died. I forget what it was celebrating, but they seemed very close then. Hawkesfield,' Jim coughed, 'your father was, as usual, paying a lot of attention to one of the maids and had left his wife to her own devices – but on this occasion a few remarked that she didn't seem to mind.'

'But that'd be wonderful for her to find happiness! She's such a lovely lady, and full of fun. Is he a nice man? Please tell me he ain't like Len.'

'No, he's nothing like Len – who, I might add, is a very nice bloke when he isn't trying to better his position in life.'

'Do you think he really loves Millie, Jim?'

'I do. I really do. The way he spoke of her this morning while we were getting ready, I'd say he is besotted with her.'

'I'm so glad.'

'You are? Truly glad, Elsie?'

'Yes. Honestly. I am over him, Jim. It was a silly crush, which he didn't help with his actions.'

'So good to hear. And although Len did behave badly, I can see why – you would drive any man nuts.' He laughed, but Elsie knew there was some truth in what he said. She'd not been blind to the effect she had on men. The actions of her boss, the late Mr Hawkesfield – when he was her new-found father – and of Chambers, the factory supervisor of her days on the factory floor, came to mind and she shuddered.

'No more bad memories, Elsie. Look forward, not back.'

Millie's cry of 'Ready, ladies?' took Elsie's attention, so she didn't answer. She looked over to see Millie standing on the step of her carriage. Beside Elsie stood the unmarried maids of the house, all with their hands in the air. Elsie laughed, but then gasped as the flowers came hurtling towards her. Instinct had her reaching up and catching them. Everyone clapped. Elsie blushed, but had a happy feeling as she clutched them to her. Just before she turned to Jim, she caught Len's eye. His look gave her a funny sensation – as if somehow he would cause trouble for her. She looked away, then laughed up at Jim as he said, 'Now you'll have to find a bridegroom, Elsie.'

She nodded as she thought, *I think I may have.*

Taking Jim's arm, she accepted him leading her to their carriage, which had now pulled up as next in line.

As she entered the carriage, helped up by Jim, she looked back and caught a glance from Cess. He stood a little way away from Mrs Hawkesfield and, to Elsie, he looked like a butler waiting for orders. The thought came to her: *These times of feeling subservient are nearly over, my dear brother. We will be in our own place within a week.*

At Millie's house, all was hustle and bustle. The staff showed the guests onto the lawn at the back of the house, where they were served drinks. Elsie knew most of the guests now, except Len's friends and their wives.

The photographer ushered the wedding party into the withdrawing room and lined everyone up in front of the drawn curtains. There followed a series of photos of various members of the wedding party, all of which blinded them with a huge flash.

When they made their way out to the lawn again, a cheer went up. Elsie felt her nerves jangling, as now it was time for Cess to propose a toast. He'd decided a week ago that he would do this, but not try to give a speech. 'I don't know enough about Millie and Len, Else.' She'd tried to tell him that he could refer to the lovely day out in Brighton, and the time he rescued Millie after her horse bolted, but deep down she knew it would be a big ordeal for Cess. And Millie had agreed. And so Cess asked the guests to charge their glasses and raise them to the bride and groom, wishing them health and happiness.

Someone shouted, 'And lots of little troubles.' Everyone laughed, and Millie blushed. Len caught hold of her and held her close. They looked so happy.

Jim gave a long speech: funny, reminiscent of school and their growing-up years, and lovely to listen to. Elsie felt so proud of him.

It was much later, when she was coming out of the bathroom, that she encountered Len again. He passed by her, grinned and said, 'Time to check the cases are ready. I'm so excited to be setting off for Italy, Elsie.'

Elsie conquered her nerves enough to smile and say, 'It was a lovely wedding. I hope yer have a good time with your family.'

'Thank you, Elsie. All problems between us buried, then?' He was so close to her by now that she could feel his breath on her cheek.

'Yes. You're me brother-in-law now, Len. Think nothing of it all.'

He paused. Then shocked her by saying. 'It wasn't nothing to me, Elsie.'

'Don't, Len. We have to forget it.'

His nearness was affecting her. She didn't want it to. He leaned closer. His eyes closed. His lips puckered. Elsie didn't know what happened to her resolve, or her new-found dislike of him. She found herself in his arms, his kiss burning into her lips.

'Oh, Elsie, you do things to me.'

Suddenly Elsie came to her senses and pushed him away. 'Stop it! You're married to Millie!'

He stepped back. 'You tempted me.'

'I didn't. I just came out of the lav and you were there. You could have walked past me. I've told Jim how you treat me. He—'

'Treat you! How's that then – like a slut? That's what you

203

are, Elsie. A slut who is after getting all she can out of Millie. You take advantage of her – you and those brothers of yours. Well, it's going to stop. I'm telling you now, if you don't refuse those shares when you are due to sign the papers on Monday, then I will tell Millie how you tried on three occasions – one of them being on our wedding day – to tempt me to kiss you. Oh, and I'll embellish the truth and make it sound as though I was trapped by you. So, think on.'

'Millie won't believe you.'

'Oh, won't she now? She's my wife. Is she going to believe you over her husband? I don't think so. Besides, why shouldn't you do what I ask? You'll still have a nice income, my dear. More than you ever dreamed of having in your life . . . But if you sign those papers, I warn you, all of it will crumble.' Len's look held a threat as he added, 'See you in six weeks.'

He walked on by without looking back. Elsie stood still. Stunned, she couldn't put her thoughts together. When she did, a tremble went through her body. Len was a monster! But she knew that no one would believe her if she told them – well, maybe Jim would, but even he was besotted with Len, and hoodwinked by his charm. *Would he believe me? Would Jim do something? But then he already knows what my feelings were for Len – will he truly believe that I'm not to blame, and that I no longer love Len?*

Elsie didn't think so. She knew one thing, and one thing only. Len Lefton had a side that not many knew, and in that lay her damnation – everyone would take his side over her. She had no choice. She dare not counter-sign the papers that were already signed by Millie and Len: she had to refuse to do so.

What did it matter anyway? Len had said that she would

keep her allowance. That would be enough to pay for her flat, and to take care of Bert, Cess and Kitty, too, till Cess got sorted. And she'd ask for a wage for her work at the factory, too. After all, the two things were separate. One was what her father owed her, and the other she would work for. Len had to see that, didn't he?

Trying to compose herself, Elsie wondered if she would ever have the courage to face up to him. For now, he held her in fear, with the way he was blackmailing her. It was all so unfair.

Chapter Nineteen

Elsie

Once Elsie had steeled herself to return to the party, Jim caught up with her. 'I missed you, you've been gone for ages. I wanted to ask if you would have dinner with me tonight – no pie and mash, but dinner, somewhere quiet. I think we need to talk.'

'Oh?' Elsie looked round. She could see Len, his arm around Millie, his head back, laughing. Had he said anything?

'Elsie? Elsie, please say yes. I feel that you . . . well, may have second thoughts about us? Am I right?'

Relief washed over her. She looked up at him. Good, trustworthy Jim. 'Yes. You're right.'

'Oh, Elsie.' Jim looked down at her and then frowned. 'Elsie, is there something wrong?'

'I – I, no. I had a moment in the bathroom, that's all. You know: the wedding, Dot . . . seeing my lovely brother looking so lost. Missing Dot so much. And, well, wondering what the hell me and Cess are doing here. Little Bert's all right, he's young enough to take everything in his stride, but this . . .' She spread her arms out. 'It's all so strange to us. We don't fit. I just want us to go back to Rene. Back where we belong.'

'Dear Elsie, I understand. Millie should never have put you in this position to salve her own loneliness. I know you love her very much, but it would have been far better if she'd bought you a house very near her, where she could visit when she wanted to, or stay over when she needed to.'

'You're right, mate. That would have been better for me and me brovvers.'

'We'll talk tonight, Elsie. You will come, won't you?'

'Yes, I will. I'll put me best frock on and . . . Oh, Jim. Ta for being you, and standing by me.'

Jim whispered, 'Always.' Then found her hand and held it.

A flurry of activity changed this. Millie and Len were ready to set off. Everyone was crowding around them, when Millie suddenly broke free and ran over to Elsie. Her arms were open. 'Oh, Elsie, I wish you were coming with me.'

Elsie, comforted, and warmed by Jim's assurance, laughed. 'On your honeymoon! You daft thing. Besides, me and Jim have a date, don't we Jim?'

Millie looked from one to the other. 'You mean . . . ?'

'Yes. Well, we haven't spoken to each other yet, but we know.'

Jim stepped forward and put his arm round Elsie. She leaned into him, feeling loved and protected. She'd thought she would feel shame when she spoke to Millie, but that hadn't happened. Nothing that had gone on had been her fault – not the initiating of it, anyway. So she held her head high.

'But when did this happen? You said you were only mates!'

'Today. On your wedding day. You and . . . Len made it happen. Your love triggered something in me. I'm so happy, Millie. Really happy. You go and have a lovely second wedding and honeymoon. We will see yer when we come back and tell you all about it then . . . after all, we haven't told each other yet, mate.'

'Elsie, oh, Elsie, I'm so happy. I had Jim earmarked for you from the start.'

Len's car hooter sounding got Millie turning. 'I must go. Wish me luck, my darling sis. See you when I get back. I'll sort your wedding out then.'

'Ha! No, you won't – Jim hasn't asked me yet! Bye, dear Millie. Be happy, mate.'

When she'd gone, Jim drew Elsie closer. 'Is it true, Elsie? Do you love me?'

She turned to him. 'I do, Jim. I can't believe it meself, but suddenly I know. I do love you.'

Jim had tears in his eyes. Elsie felt surreal. Part of her felt full of joy, but a big part of her was consumed with a feeling she couldn't name. Guilt? *No, I refuse to feel any guilt over that bastard. I'll do as he says, and that'll be the end of it. How could I even have wanted more than I have? They say greed leads to bad things happening – well, it did for me. But I'll learn from this. I will* . . .

'You've made me so happy, Elsie. I have loved you almost from when I first set eyes on you. Oh, Elsie, I love you, I love you!'

Elsie laughed as Jim's voice rose and a few people turned to look in their direction. 'Shush, Jim.'

'I can't, I want to shout it from the treetops.'

'Shout what from the treetops?'

'Cess! I didn't see you coming over – where have you been?'

'Up in the nursery, Else. Kitty was a bit upset. I stayed up there with her and let Gertie come down with Bert to get something to eat. Look, Else . . . I'm moving out today.'

'Today? But you've only just got back. Where will you go, mate? The flat ain't ready till the end of the week.'

'I can't stand it here any longer. Now that the wedding's over, I want to take Kitty and leave. I'm going to stay with me mate, Bootsie. Well, in his flat – he's not here, he's at sea. He gave me a key at Dot's funeral and said I was welcome to stay there any time, and for as long as I like. He rents the flat in the tenements that he and his mum had, before she died. I'm going to load what I need for Kitty and go. I've told Gertie, mate. She's fine. She's going into a boarding house until I've got me own place, but I can take Kitty to her whenever I want to.'

'Oh, Cess, I don't blame yer. But as soon as my place is ready, you will move in with me, won't yer?'

'I will – well, if I ain't found anywhere by then. I'm looking to lease a house that's big enough for Gertie to have a room, and Dai too, when he finally sorts everything out in Wales, as we want to look into setting up our business.'

'When did you decide all of this, Cess? I thought we'd live together, mate. I was looking forward to it.'

'I know. And we will for a bit. But I have to get meself sorted, Else. I've plenty of money, and I can afford somewhere of me own.'

Elsie's heart ached for him. 'I know, mate. I'll always be there for yer, and you won't be far away, will yer?'

'No. I want to be in the same area as you. Anyway, what were you and Jim cooking up when I came up to yer? Sounded exciting.'

'It is, Cess. Today, out of the blue, I – I, well, I feel daft saying it, but I fell in love with Jim!'

'That's great news.' Cess shook Jim's hand. 'I don't know you well, mate, but from what I've seen and what I've heard,

I'll be very glad that our Else is in safe hands. I'm happy for yer, Sis.'

Elsie opened her arms to him and Cess came into them and hugged her. She thought she heard a small sob, but didn't remark on it. She just patted Cess on the back.

As he came out of the circle of her arms he asked, 'Else, can I take Bert with me? He'll be company, and a comfort to me. Besides, with Gertie gone, who'll take care of him while you're at work? Or are you seeing to things at your flat this week?'

'That's a good idea, Cess. It's only be for a few days, but I'll feel more rested knowing he's with you than leaving him here with the staff. I'll come and see you on Monday. I'm not going into work that day, as I've to go and see Millie's solicitor.'

'Oh, yes, I remember. I can't believe it, though – you, officially part-owner of the jam factory. We've come a long way in a short time, Else.'

'We have.' She didn't want to tell Cess now that she was refusing the offer of shares, as she needed to tell Jim first. And in such a way that it didn't arouse his curiosity as to why she'd suddenly changed her mind.

Millie's mum didn't protest when Elsie told her that she was going out to dinner. Elsie was glad of this, and then found out the reason just before she left the house. The doorbell had rung and she'd skipped down the stairs, expecting it to be Jim. But when Barridge opened the door, Len's father stood there. He looked nothing like Len; he wasn't as tall, and he was fair, rather than dark, in everything: fair hair, fair-skinned and his eyes were blue. It was as if he had played no part in Len's creation.

He smiled at her as Barridge took his coat from him. 'I don't believe we have been formally introduced, my dear. I'm Harold Lefton.'

'Elsie.'

'Yes, I know. You're Millie's half-sister.'

There was no accusation in his voice, or any mocking of her. Elsie's thoughts suggested that Len hadn't spoken to his father about her. This made her relax. 'Pleased to meet you.'

'Yes, and I you. Abigail has talked a lot about you. She is very fond of you. I hope you are more settled now, after all the things you have been through. I was very sorry to hear of them. I knew Hawkesfield. Not a nice man at all. Are you going out, or shall we have more time to chat over dinner?'

'Yes. I'm going out – oh, there's the doorbell now.'

'Have a nice time.' He chuckled then. 'I know I will . . . Oh, Jim! Hello, young man.' Mr Lefton looked from Jim to Elsie. 'Well, well.'

'Hello, sir. I didn't have time to chat much at the wedding today. I hope you are well.'

'I am – I am indeed. Well, so you are Elsie's date. Good, good. Have a nice evening. Now, Barridge, kindly show me the way.'

When he'd gone with Barridge, Elsie smiled at Jim. 'I'm ready, Jim, but I want to go up and make sure that Cess and Bert are all right. They were nearly ready to leave.'

'Does Mrs Hawkesfield know?'

'Yes, I had a word with her, and she understood.'

'Can I come with you?'

'Yes, of course. This way, mate.'

'Ha! I love being your mate, Elsie.'

Elsie felt a warm feeling creep over her, until they reached the spot where Len had kissed her earlier – then her skin crawled with disgust.

'Are you all right, darling?'

The endearment didn't feel strange to her. It was as if Jim had always spoken like this to her. Turning towards him, she said, 'Hold me, Jim. Just hold me close for a moment.'

In his arms she found peace.

'You're shaking, my darling. What's wrong?'

Taking a deep breath, she lifted her head and managed a smile. 'I'm in the arms of the man I love – it's a natural reaction, ain't it?'

His lips came onto hers. The kiss was light at first, but deepened, giving Elsie the feeling of drowning in his love. It dispelled the horror of what had happened in this very spot just a few hours ago. She clung to Jim. When they parted, she said, 'You'll never lose your trust in me, will you, Jim?'

'Never, Elsie. You are the most honest person I know. You told me everything when we were last alone together. You were honest with me then, so I have no reason to doubt you. Has something happened that you need to tell me about?'

'N – No. I . . . everything is fine now.' And it was. Jim's kiss had sealed the way she felt about him and had dispelled the feeling of the kiss Len had given her – a kiss that took from her, not gave. As had happened before, she felt fear where Len was concerned, and made her mind up to avoid ever being alone with him again.

Waking early the next morning, Elsie stretched her limbs. She knew she must get out of bed and begin the packing process

– not that she had much to take from here: only her clothes, toiletries and shoes. Nothing else belonged to her. *I'm like a cuckoo in someone else's nest. Well, that changes this week, and I can't wait.* This thought had her jumping out of bed, eager to get everything done. But then memories of the day before hit her and she lay back down and snuggled under the one sheet she'd had covering her during the warm, sticky night.

What a day: a mixture of happiness, fear, guilt, discovery and then bliss as she'd dined with Jim, and found a side to him that she hadn't permitted herself to see before – a romantic, loving man.

Hugging herself, she marvelled at how she'd rejected Jim all these months. And at how she could have been so taken in by Len. Her body shuddered. *Please God, let him be kind to my dear sister – don't let Millie ever see the side to Len that I have seen.*

But thoughts of Len put a dampener on what she really wanted to remember, so she banished him from her mind and instead basked in the aftermath of the feel of Jim's kisses and his arms around her, and how . . . She hesitated at this thought, as her body flushed at the memory. Then she giggled. The feelings she'd felt of wanting Jim to take her – fully take her and make her his – had been something she wanted to savour, and yet daren't visit.

She'd felt how much Jim had wanted her as she'd snuggled in close to him. But he'd taken control and stepped away. Taking her hand, he'd suggested that they walk some of the way home, before getting a cab.

This had lightened the moment and sealed her love for him – that he could respect her in that way, and not take from her what he knew she wanted to give, but what they would both come to regret. *Oh, Jim. My Jim, I love you.*

As they walked, he'd asked Elsie to marry him. She smiled as she remembered how casual he was about it. 'Well, how soon can I make you Mrs Ellington?'

She'd stopped and gaped at him. 'Really? You want to marry me?'

It was a silly question and Jim had answered with a silly answer, 'No, but I feel compelled to.' She'd hit out at him playfully and he'd grabbed her arm and taken her into a kiss that held such passion that they'd clung to each other afterwards. Jim had whispered, 'Make it soon, my darling. Become Mrs Ellington very, very soon.'

Thinking about it all now, it seemed to have happened so fast, and yet it had been staring her in the face all the time – why had she wasted so much emotion over someone who didn't deserve it?

Finally getting out of bed, Elsie had her packing done in no time, leaving only a couple of outfits out, which she might need for the next few days. In the breakfast room she found Mrs Hawkesfield already sitting at the dining table.

'Well, good morning, my dear. What a lovely day we had yesterday!'

'Good morning. Yes, the wedding went off without a hitch. I'm so happy for Millie.'

'Oh, I was talking about you and me, dear. Sit down.' Abigail's girlish giggle belied her age – which Elsie knew was mid-forties. She was a beautiful woman, with that lovely contrast of dark hair and deep-blue eyes – a feature that Millie had said she wished she had inherited, instead of getting so many of her looks from the man who had fathered her and Elsie.

Elsie knew that her colour had risen, but she giggled too.

'I need to tell somebody how happy I am and, as you're the only one here, it has to be you, dear. Sorry.'

'Don't be, I need to do the same. And I'm happy for you, mate. Oh, I mean . . .'

'Ha! You should never apologize for being you, my dear. We love you as you are. You know, I have never said – I haven't had much chance to – but I am sorry about the hurt my late husband caused you and your family. How are you? I mean, really? I know you are a very brave girl and are all things to every one of those you love, but you have to think about yourself sometimes.'

'I – I, well, it's hard, but I try to think of something good every day. About me mum, and me little brovver Jimmy, and Dot. I . . . Oh, I'm so – orry.' An unbidden sob caught Elsie's words, and a tear trickled down her cheek. She wiped it away.

'You don't have to bottle it all up, dear. I understand. I know my troubles were different, but that feeling of being alone and of no one knowing what you are feeling is so terrible. If ever you want to talk, you can seek me out, and you will always be welcome in my home.'

'Ta. That's kind. I thought you would hate me. After all, I'm part of the hurt that you were caused.'

'No, you're not. Well, not a bad part – a good part. They say that good things come out of bad, and that's what you are. Out of all the pain, I have you as compensation. We need to get to know one another better. I'm only sorry that I didn't know Dot well. She was poorly when I met her at Ruby's wedding, and I didn't like to intrude too much. But I think of her a lot, and of the pain she was caused by the actions of my late, despicable husband.'

'Dot was lovely.'

'Poor girl. You must miss her. And I was sorry to hear that Cecil wanted to move out so quickly, but I understand. I wanted to give him my condolences, but I have had no opportunity to. And to talk to him about his ideas for a market. I meant what I said: I would love to be involved.'

'He felt out of place. Oh, it's not you. It's the servants.'

'I know – bloody snobbish lot! Ha! And that's swearing.' She turned her head and looked towards the door. 'And I hope you're listening!'

There was a sound of someone scurrying away. Elsie giggled. She'd never met anyone like Mrs Hawkesfield.

'Anyway, now that we've got rid of the listening ears, my dear, I want to talk about our conquests. You and Jim, and me and Harold! Must have been the romance in the air, but I had the most wonderful man – whom I have admired for years – declare his love for me. What about you?'

This was so matter-of-fact that again it made Elsie giggle. 'Yes, me too. Only I didn't realize before – I thought Jim was just a mate. Now he's asked me to marry him!'

'And you said yes?'

'I did.' Feeling emboldened, Elsie asked, 'And you?'

'Ha, yes. I was asked too, and I said yes! Cheers to us both!'

They lifted their teacups and clinked them together. A feeling came to Elsie that here was another mate for her. Not only someone she could talk to and look up to, but someone who cared about her too.

But what Mrs Hawkesfield said next changed the atmosphere a little. 'I'm so pleased that everything is changing for you, my dear. Millie tells me you are to go into the solicitor's tomorrow to sign papers giving you shares in

Swift's? That is well deserved and, in my opinion, it should be even more. You should be an equal partner, but Millie has been guided by Len.'

'She hasn't actually. Len didn't want me to have any part of the factory. Only to receive an allowance. But Millie insisted that I got some shares. However, it's all too much for me. I'm no business person, so I'm not going to sign. There's an alternative paper that's been drawn up, at Len's request, giving me the right to my allowance – and it's not being a payment made as a favour, so to speak.'

'What? I'm sure that Millie knows nothing of this. You're not going to sign it, are you? Len has overstepped the mark. He may be her husband now, but you have a far bigger claim on the shares in the factory than he has.'

'I know, but I don't want to cause any problems. I'm happy with what I have. It's more than I ever dreamed of having.'

'Well, if you're happy I won't interfere, but I do worry about what Len is up to. His father has told me on many occasions – we've kept in touch, you understand – that Len can be ruthless when it comes to business. And yet he is the sweetest, kindest man when there isn't any money involved.' Elsie knew this only too well. 'Well, my dear, if you are sure. You must do what you are happiest with, and not what someone may have bamboozled you into.'

'I – I am.' Elsie had the overwhelming urge to confide in this lovely lady, but stopped herself. But she did add, 'And what I think is best for Millie too.'

'Hmm, well, I can see you want to leave it at that. I respect that, dear, but think hard before tomorrow. Now, how can I get to speak to your brother?'

'I am calling in to see him today. I was going to leave it

till tomorrow, but I want to share me news with him and Bert. I can see what Cecil says and let you know tonight, if you like?'

'Thank you. Now that I have the idea in my head, I can't rid myself of it. I'll see you later, dear. You finish your breakfast. I have to get ready. Harold is taking me to lunch and maybe even to the jewellery shop.' Her eyes twinkled. 'I'd rather he took me to Petticoat Lane, but I don't think he's ready for that side of me yet.'

Her lovely laugh faded as she went out of the door, and Elsie was left with a good feeling, as if she'd just had a chat with a real mate.

Chapter Twenty

Elsie

It wasn't easy for Elsie to go back to the Long Lane tenements. As it had the last time, when she came to confront the evil Beryl, memories flooded her of her mum, little Jimmy, and now of Dot – especially Dot. She saw her in her mind's eye: them playing together as toddlers and going to school together, holding hands, with herself cajoling Dot along, and then both going to the jam factory. She saw Dot's black eyes and bruised face, from the beatings her mum gave her, and Elsie's heart felt heavy.

Taking a deep breath, she looked up towards the flat Dot had lived in. It was hard to believe everything that had happened to them. But one thing she would never forget: the bond they had always had between them.

Avoiding walking past the door of the ground-floor flat where she'd lived with her family, she ran up the steps, past Dot's old flat, and knocked on the one next door. A tired-looking Cecil answered it. 'Sis, you didn't let the grass grow, did yer? Come in, mate.'

The flat was the same as all of them: a small hallway with a door leading to the lav. Through the hall was the living room. In here, the furniture was old – Bootsie hadn't replaced anything of his mum's, and Elsie could almost see her sitting in her rocking chair next to the grate.

'I couldn't wait, Cess. I have news, but besides that—'

'Else! Else!' Bert came charging out of the door that led to the bedroom and nearly knocked her over.

'Ha, Bert, it's good to see you, too, mate. But you've only been gone for a short time – one night.'

'Sometimes it seems as if you've all gone, Else.'

She was mystified, but cuddled him to her. 'I have news, mate, and I hope it's going to make you very happy. I know it will Cess – well, he already knows most of it. Anyway, you like Jim, don't you?'

'Yes, he's a nice bloke.'

This made her smile. Sometimes Bert used words she didn't expect him to. 'Well, I more than like him, Bert. I've fallen in love with him.'

'That's sloppy. That Lizzie who lives in the next block, she used to want to be me girlfriend, but I didn't want her to be. But what about me, Else?'

'You should be happy for Else, not think of yourself, Bert. That's not like you, mate.'

'No, but it's understandable, Cess. The poor boy must feel that he has no place in everything.' Elsie went down on her haunches. 'Bert, you will always be with me, and will always be my number one.'

'And mine, mate – well, number two after Kitty, of course.'

'I don't mind being number two to Kitty. She's only little and it's my job to watch out for her, but Jim's big.'

'He is, and that means he will watch out for you. Just as me and Cess do. You'll never be left out of anything – you're our brovver, mate.'

'What about when you marry?'

'Ha! I was coming to that. Jim has asked me to marry him, and I've said yes!'

'That's great news, Sis.' Cess opened his arms to her.

Elsie stood and went into them, laughing, but wanting to cry at the same time. Bert grabbed her round her hips.

'Hey, between you, you'll have me over!' As she came out of the hug, she bent down and hugged Bert. 'You used to grab me legs, and now it's me hips – soon you'll be big enough to grab me waist.'

They all giggled.

'Right, you fill the kettle, Bert. There's a stool in the scullery if you can't reach the taps. And I'll get the teapot ready. Kitty'll wake soon as well, so we'll want some hot water for her bottle. She likes it ready for her the minute she wakes.'

'How did you cope last night, Cess?'

'It was a doddle. Don't forget, mate, that I used to help you with Bert and Jimmy, didn't I?'

'You did. Has it all come back to you then?'

'Well, not all. Let's just say I managed – Kitty made me, with her yells.'

'Ha, I sometimes wonder how we did it, you know.'

'Me too, but it was needs must. And we'll do whatever faces us now, Sis. I'm glad that you're happy. No one deserves it more. When do you take over part of the factory?'

'I don't.' She told Cess what she'd rehearsed. He was with her every step of the way. And she was so pleased to hear him agree that he would sign the papers, as Kitty's guardian, for her rights and dues, too.

'That's settled then. Good. Now, where's that cup of tea? I want to hear more about your plans, and I have a surprise for you.' By the time she got round to telling Cess about Mrs Hawkesfield's offer, he was astounded. 'It's true, mate. And she wants to stand on the stall when she's down here. You should hear her cockney – it's so funny.'

'I'll be blowed. And I couldn't wait to leave there, but then I didn't know we had a mate in the camp – after Millie left, that is. Ha! I might just hear what she's got to say. Not that we need a partner. Dai has plenty of money to invest, and I have too. We just need him to sell his guest house.'

'It seems like fate, meeting Dai, Cess. I'm glad you got on so well, mate. It's good to have someone who understands.'

'It is, and I'm missing him already. So, when will you wed, Else?'

'Oh, not yet. I need to get settled.'

'Don't leave it too long. You know Jim well by now – you've worked with him for months. Take all the time you can get together.'

'When Millie's home, I'll start to plan it.'

'You want a big wedding then?'

'Yes, I do. A proper wedding, with all me mates from the factory dressed in their Sunday best, and a band so we can have a sing-song and do a few jigs.'

'Sounds good.'

Elsie didn't miss the wistful note in his voice, but she carried on, as Cess wouldn't want her to make a fuss every time he felt his pain. 'Yes. And a winter wedding, so that we can all be cosy in the church hall. It don't half get cosy in there when that big stove's lit, and we can have pie and mash . . . That's my idea of a wedding, but I'll have to talk to Jim, see what he wants.'

'Sounds like you've got it all planned out, and it sounds smashing, too. What do you think, Bert?'

'Now I'm used to it, I feel excited.'

'And I tell you something else, Bert. Jim can play the piano and read music. He's going to give you proper lessons.'

Bert clapped his hands. Elsie was glad he was happy about it all now. It would have spoiled it for her if he'd continued to be upset.

By the time Millie came home, Elsie had arranged a November wedding.

She couldn't remember feeling as happy as she did as she eagerly awaited Millie's visit today. She couldn't wait to show her the flat and tell her all her news. She'd been on pins since she'd received Millie's note telling her that she wasn't going into the factory at all this week, but so wanted to visit her. And now the time they had arranged had come.

The coast was clear for them to have a good chat with no interruptions. Bert was out at school, Cess had taken Kitty over to Gertie and had gone to view a house – something he seemed in such a hurry to sort out. And Rene had shut up shop for a while and gone out to get some thread of a special colour that she needed.

Elsie stood by the window of her second-floor flat and looked down into the street. Then turned to make a last-minute check of her home.

The grey floral carpet looked lovely against the white-washed walls and set off her rose-coloured sofas. Cream curtains with a rose-patterned border lightened the look. And in pride of place, against the back wall, stood her mum's cabinet. Rene had insisted that she have it. Though for now the flat looked a bit bare, she was waiting to fix a date for a shopping day with Millie, as it would be fun to have Millie with her, helping her to pick the best pieces. The kitchen had been painted a lovely yellow, and had new cupboards and a new sink. Elsie loved it, and enjoyed cooking in there. It was equipped with everything she needed and had a shiny, brand-new gas stove, too.

She, Cess and Bert each had a bedroom of their own, and Jim was turning the large living room upstairs into a music room.

Satisfied that all was in order, Elsie turned to look down at the street again. But she jumped back as if someone had slapped her. Len was coming towards her! Nerves made her tremble. Was there something wrong with Millie? But that wasn't the only reason she felt afraid.

The doorbell sounded, loud and echoey. Elsie froze. Then she looked up and down the street, willing Rene to appear on her way back. But she was nowhere in sight. And Len knew that she was in, as she was expecting Millie.

Taking her courage in both hands, she went down the stairs. Opening the door, she stood there, not inviting him in. 'Hello, Len. You look well. Where's Millie?'

'Am I to talk on the doorstep?'

'Well, there's no one in . . .'

'So? Oh, come on, Elsie. You're not afraid, are you? I – I apologize for my behaviour. It was the drink. I mean, look, you're quite safe. I'm married to your sister, and very happily. We can put the past behind us, can't we?'

Feeling foolish, Elsie opened the door wide and invited him in. Len took the stairs two at a time. She followed, dragging her feet.

'So this is the new haven, eh?' He looked round her living room. 'Not bad.'

'Ta. I like it.'

'Good. Well, I hope you'll be very happy. You have news, don't you?'

'I – yes, I'm marrying Jim. In November.'

'That was quick.' He stepped closer to her. 'Rebound?'

'No! I – I love him.'

'Oh? Why the hesitation then?'

'I do. Anyway, what business is it of yours?'

He leaned closer. 'I'm your brother-in-law and, as such, I want to look after you, Elsie.' His tone was low, the lids half-closed over his eyes. 'You drive me mad, you know that, and you play on it.'

'I don't. You should leave, mate. Cess will be back in a minute.'

'Oh? Well, he'll find out what his big sis is really like then, won't he?'

His hand shot out and he grabbed the collar of her blouse and pulled her to him. Before Elsie could move away, his lips were on hers. She felt nothing but disgust, when she'd been afraid that he might still have the magnetism that had once made it hard for her to resist him. Hitting out at him, he let her go.

'You know you want to, Elsie. Why the fight? We're on our own – no one will know. You know how I feel about you. You really do drive me wild. I have to have you, Elsie.'

'No! I feel nothing for you other than hate! You're disgusting. Millie trusts you. She loves you. You were going to be so different from all she'd known. I hate you. I hate your guts!'

Len's face changed. Anger and spite leaked from his vile expression. 'And you think you've found what you want in Jim? That nincompoop? He's always been soft. He never won anything at school: no sports or races, only a prize for music! What does that say about him, eh?'

'Don't you dare even mention Jim's name – yer not fit to.' As it had done in the past, something snapped in Elsie. She went for Len, with her fists flailing and her nails scratching. But he warded her off and caught hold of her arms.

'You little money-grabber, you. A bastard who thinks she's done good. Well, you watch out, Elsie, because I won't let all of this continue.' His push unbalanced her. She fell to the floor, landing on her back. Her legs went up in the air. She hardly had time to draw the breath back into her body before Len pounced on her.

'No . . . No! Stop, don't – please don't.'

But although she struggled, she was no match for him. He held her down.

Her worse fears clutched at her as she felt him struggling with his trouser buttons. 'Please . . . pl – e – a – se. Think of Millie. Len, don't do this. Don't.'

But as she gasped out this plea, she felt the sensation that she remembered so well. The rough pushing into her that haunted her nights – she couldn't breathe as Len pounded her, making her sore, tightening her knicker elastic around her thighs: on and on, harder and harder. Her gasping out for him to stop made no difference, until suddenly his moaning had more urgency and she heard her name spoken over and over again. She knew his moment was upon him. The strength she'd had at this moment when Chambers did this to her came to Elsie, and she heaved her back into an arch to dislodge him – but it didn't happen. Instead he hollered her name once more and she felt him pulsating inside her, all the time releasing an animal-like sound.

When at last it came to an end, he rolled off her, sweating and gasping for breath.

There was a silence, broken only by his sobs.

'Why? Why?' He thumped his fist on the floor. 'You bitch! Why did you make me do that? Oh God. Oh, Millie, my Millie.' As he pushed himself up to a standing position, Elsie, weak and unable to move, looked up at him. Tears streamed from Len's eyes, and snot ran from his nose. His face was twisted into an ugly grimace. 'Why? Why did you torture me like that?'

Elsie couldn't speak. She rolled over and sobbed. Everything was ruined: her love for Jim was tainted. Her love for Millie was broken. She had a feeling in her that she didn't want to live.

'Get up. You got what you asked for. Maybe now you'll leave me alone!'

Elsie got up and straightened her skirt. She was nothing. She was dirt – filth, nothing but the slut that Len once called her.

'Where's the bathroom in this hole?'

She pointed to the door that led to a small hall, which in turn led to the bathroom and her bedroom.

When Len closed the door, she slumped down on the sofa. The dampness trickling from between her legs reminded her of the horror she'd just been through. Her mind searched for what she should do now. Nothing occurred to her. She couldn't tell anyone, for fear of hurting Millie. But what about Jim? *Oh, Jim, this means the end of us. How can I live a lie with you? I can't face you. I can't.*

The door opened.

'Right, we carry on as if this never happened. It was nothing to me anyway. And I'm warning you, Elsie.' Len's finger pointed at her. His face looked ugly – had she ever thought him beautiful? 'If you tell a soul, I'll break you. I'll make Millie see that you're a liar, and that you tried to make me kiss you, and told me you wanted me and could give me more than she could. And Millie will believe me. She won't take your word against her husband's. Besides, what kind of a person are you, eh? Tempting men. You know you've wanted me from the beginning, haven't you?'

Elsie didn't answer.

'Then on my wedding day, when it was clear you'd lost out, you set your sights on Jim, poor bugger. He'll never know a minute's peace, married to a slut like you.'

'Shut up! Shut up and get out of here, now!' Standing, Elsie felt herself snap. She grabbed the poker from the pendulum set. She heard the other implements clang against one another, raised her hand and charged at Len.

He dodged her, pushing her harder than he had the first time. She crashed into the wall and fell to the ground.

'That's where you belong, Elsie. In the gutter, like the rest of you people from the slums. I'm going now. You remember what I said . . . Oh, and by the way, Millie has a cold and sent her apologies. I came here to tell you, not to be beguiled by you. You're nothing but a prostitute, just like your mother!'

As she gasped in her pain, Len put his hand in his pocket and threw some coins in her direction, and then he was gone.

Elsie collapsed in a heap and sobbed out her despair. *Mum, Mum, help me . . . Help me – e – e!*

Chapter Twenty-One

Millie

Millie lay propped up in bed on a mound of feather pillows, nursing an all-consuming, thumping headache. She half-hoped – with Elsie knowing by now that she was unwell – that Elsie would come back with Len to see her. She was longing to share how her wonderful trip to Italy had gone, and to hear all Elsie's and Jim's news.

Closing her eyes, she let herself drift back to her wedding day. It had been the happiest of days, and to think that Mama and Elsie had found happiness on that day, too.

Her mind took her back to the moment when Mama had told her of her own and Harold's plans. The sun had shone relentlessly, baking dry the lush green hills and distant mountains of Tuscany. Villa De Luca – the beautiful home of Len's family that sat on a hill surveying the vast lands they owned – was the perfect setting for her second wedding celebration. She could still hear the music, see the dancing and taste the wonderful food they'd served on long wooden tables.

After the meal she'd sat under a tree, with Len on one side of her and her mama and Harold on the other, until

Mama suddenly made the announcement that she and Harold were engaged.

As these memories assailed her, Millie stretched out her body and smiled as she thought of how happy she was, and how wonderful Len was: a kind, gently loving man, who'd been so patient with her when making love to her.

Just thinking about it made her want to make love, right now.

When the door opened not many minutes later and Len popped his head round it, her headache was forgotten as she beckoned him in, throwing the covers back off her near-naked body.

He gave her a look that she couldn't discern, but which made her feel dirty in some way, as he came fully into the room and closed the door. His attitude was that of someone seething with anger, as he tore off his clothes and got into bed beside her.

'Len? Is everything . . . Len? What? Len, please!'

Not taking the usual route of kissing and caressing her, he grabbed her roughly, straddled her and entered her before she could even catch her breath. Fear clutched at her. And the feeling of being used disgusted her.

No words of love were spoken, no kisses were ground onto her lips. It was just his body frantically working away at her, as if she was a . . . prostitute! Yes, that's what this unmerciful thrusting, and the sound of his guttural moans, made her feel like. Ignoring her cries and struggles, he relentlessly pounded her as she begged, 'Len . . . Len, please, stop!'

It was as if she hadn't spoken.

'Len!' She thumped his chest with her fists, but still he

thrust, harder and harder, until a sound came from him that disgusted her, as he groaned out filthy language and bore down on her, almost suffocating her. When he rolled off, panting for breath, a tear seeped out of the corner of Millie's eye. Its path stung her sore cheek where Len's face had rubbed against hers in his relentless quest. In that moment Millie understood what rape felt like.

All was quiet for a moment, then into the silence came some deep, rasping sobs. Her Len was crying.

'Len. Len, what is it? What made you behave like that? It was the worst experience of my life. Oh, Len, why? Why?'

'Leave me alone, Millie, you've done enough damage.'

To Millie, it was as if the great happiness she'd found dissolved in that moment. She didn't understand how something so beautiful could suddenly go so horribly wrong.

'What have I done? Tell me!'

'You've diminished me, as a man and a husband.'

'What? How?'

He sat up and turned his back to her. His head bowed. His sobs tore at her. 'Len. Len please, talk to me. Tell me what went wrong. You were so loving this morning when I felt unwell. This isn't like you. What's happened?'

'No man should have to put up with a wife who wants to run everything. You're not natural, Millie. You're just a girl, you have only a few months' experience and yet you consider yourself to be a better business person than me: your husband. I'm going to be a laughing stock. Everyone is going to look on me as a kept man. I have nothing – a third share in your business, that's all. I run my father's bank. I have nothing of my own. I *am* nothing. I was so shocked when you divided the business up as you did, giving a girl from the slums part of what should have been mine

231

as the head of this household. We have to live in *your* house, and I'm not even on the title deeds.' He gave a deep, disgusting cough. Finding his handkerchief, he spat into it.

Millie waited, unable to speak.

'I tell you, Millie, it all crowded in on me when I saw Elsie today – there she is living how she knows, one step up from the slums, and yet she can lord it over me! She told me that she had decided to relinquish the gift you should never have given her. And I felt diminished. Her share will revert to you, and I will still only have a one-third share. I am so angry – so hurt. It all came to a head in me and I took it out on you. I punished you, and it's your fault that I did.'

Millie couldn't believe what she was hearing. Had she done wrong? She hadn't thought the ownership of the business was that important to Len. And why did Elsie change her mind about the shares? *Oh God, what is happening? What have I done? It's always been the natural way that the man takes all and cares for his wife. Why am I so different in wanting to retain what is mine? Is anything mine any more? Aren't I now married and should therefore be dependent on my husband? No. No! Stop this. Women have fought for these rights. I have fought for rights for women, and I intend to carry on doing so. I'm not going to give in, I'm not.*

'We no longer live in a world where a husband can take ownership of everything the wife owns, Len. If Elsie has pulled out – and I can't imagine why she should do so – then we can be equal partners, as we were, only with more shares each. I have said that I won't work in the factory, but will simply attend the weekly meetings we planned.'

'So, that's it? A half-share! I thought you loved me, Millie. I know that the wife can retain ownership of her property, but how many do so? Tell me that. Most women relinquish everything to the husband's care. I feel as though I am only half a man. Tied to my wife's apron strings. I should be a man of wealth. My father owns a half-share in one of the biggest banks in the country, and in the smaller bank that I run. Yes, I get a good salary and a generous allowance, but they feel like handouts. I didn't bring any real wealth to this marriage.'

'Why do you care about wealth so much? You brought love to me – gentleness, caring. What you just did was animalistic and disgusting. How could you do that to your wife simply because you think you have been hard done by in the money stakes. I'm not a wealthy woman. You know the poor financial state that my father left the factory in. Yes, I have a property portfolio and this house, but I have had to put half of it up for collateral to keep the factory afloat.'

'That's just it. The factory is prospering, but that seems to have gone to your head. You seem to forget that you couldn't have done it without me. I was the one who advised on the best route to take. I found you a manager who steered you in the right direction. You've done nothing towards turning the fortunes of the factory around.'

Millie felt as though she was in the room with a stranger. She wanted her Len back. She loved him. Needed him. Wanted the happiness he'd shown her that could be hers. And he was telling her that she could have that, for the price of the factory. What did it matter? Maybe, with the business completely in Len's hands, she could concentrate on the work she felt passionate about – improving conditions for the women workers. And work more closely with Mary Macarthur, leader of the National Federation of Women Workers, to improve the conditions for women who laboured in the factories. And maybe she could join the struggle towards winning the vote for women. That was an important cause. *Why shouldn't we vote? Why shouldn't we have a say in who runs our country?*

The women who worked towards these causes were taken care of financially by their men, and didn't have to worry about business matters. But she did need to see that her properties were being run properly. She'd never given them much thought: who rented them? And exactly what were they? Oh, she knew there were about forty houses in Leeds – cottages mainly and terraced properties – but were her tenants happy? Were their houses maintained? She hadn't got round to checking. She'd left everything in the hands of the estate agents. That's something she could do, if she was released of the running of the factory.

Making up her mind to do all she could to save her marriage and regain the happiness she'd had for such a short time, she put her hand out and touched Len's back. 'Len, I'm sorry. I didn't know it meant so much to you, but I can see it does. I will sign the factory over to you.'

Len sat up straight and turned to face her. It cut her in two to see his swollen eyes and hurt look.

'Oh, Len, I've been such an idiot.'

'Oh, my darling. I love you. You are my world. I'm sorry I hurt you.' Tears streamed down his face. 'How could I have treated you in that way? How will you ever forgive me? How can you forget what I put you through?'

'I can. As long as you promise never to treat me like that again – I don't deserve it. I didn't realize how important it was to you to be seen as the one with the wealth in our marriage, but to punish me in such a way is abhorrent – I couldn't bear it again, Len, nor will I!'

'But it wasn't just your insistence on demeaning me – you actually put Elsie before me.'

Millie knew she hadn't done this, but she wanted no further arguments. 'It may have looked that way, but I was only trying to be fair – anyway, that problem is solved now.'

Again the silence.

'Len, I am not going to apologize for something that you perceive I did on purpose – but I don't want us to be at odds with each other. I am going to do as you ask of me. And I'd like to put this behind us now.'

'I would like that, too. I will apologize, but I can only say in my defence that I felt I had lost myself. I felt like nothing – as if my wife pulled all the purse strings. But now I'll make you proud, Millie. I will. I know how much you think of that factory. I will make it the biggest and the best. I'll expand until we own an empire.'

Millie couldn't help but smile at his enthusiasm. And although a big part of her still hurt, she sat up and opened her arms to him. When Len came into the circle of them, she felt she had done the right thing, and yet she couldn't help holding on to a niggling worry. 'You will take care of the workers, won't you, Len?'

He pulled back. His swollen eyes looked into hers. 'I will. I promise. For one thing, I have seen that you doing so has greatly increased your output and profitability. I'll even let you inspect the conditions from time to time, and have a say in any improvements that I make. I will value your opinion, because you are amazing. I know I advised you, but a lot of the ideas were yours, Jim's and Elsie's.'

'Thank you, darling. I have worked hard – we all have.' Suddenly she wanted it all to be properly better, to get back on a loving footing with Len. 'Hold me, please hold me, darling. I feel so afraid. I nearly lost you, and I couldn't bear that to happen. I love you and feel so lucky to have you as my husband.'

'Thank you. You've restored my manhood, and I feel empowered again. I feel that I am capable of taking care of my wife and our family. Oh, darling, the icing on the cake would be if you are pregnant. Surely you should be, as we have made love enough times.' He laughed. 'And if you're not, well, I can make love some more, and more, and more.'

His voice had lowered, and his kisses on her neck in between each time he said 'more' thrilled Millie. A familiar feeling tickled her stomach. She clung to him.

'Can I? Can I love you again, my darling? Can I make you forget that horrible experience you made me do to you?'

Not liking the inference, but roused by Len and wanting to blot out the awfulness of what had happened, Millie put an urgency into her voice as she answered, 'Yes. Yes, please, help me to forget it.'

As he lay her down, Millie felt a worry coursing through her at how Len hadn't taken any responsibility for his actions. But then, that was men for you. Hadn't her father been the same?

'Darling, you shivered. You're not well. Oh, my darling, I'll leave you alone. You need to rest.'

'No. No, make love to me, Len. Make love in your natural, gentle way. I want to forget . . .'

His kiss took her words away. Gentle at first, it deepened into a passion she hadn't known.

Until what had happened a few moments ago, he'd only ever been gentle, but now he was demanding and Millie responded with all of herself. She wanted closure on the terrible incident. She wanted to show him love, and to pleasure him – give him everything he ever dreamed of – and, in doing so, she reached new heights herself. This wasn't a gentle pleasure; this was raunchy, thrilling and made her seek something. Something she wanted, but didn't know what it was. Something that had been missing.

Not content with having him thrust at her, Millie rolled herself over until she was on top of him. Len's look was one of surprise, and then his eyes veiled as she moved on him. The urgency in her increased, and her movements became frantic. Then it happened. Her whole self burst open as an intense feeling took her. It swept through her body in wave after wave of ecstasy. She called out his name. She moaned and hollered like an animal as she held herself still, wanting to clench the feeling and never let go of it. When it did fade, she flopped off Len and lay gasping. Len climbed on top of her. Now she accepted his hard thrusting of her, and welcomed it, felt fully receptive of it. She clung to him, reawakening the feeling and letting it consume her, until Len burst into her and their cries of love joined them in a deep bond.

As she lay in the circle of his arms, still feeling the aftermath of the earth-shattering experience, she told Len of her deep love for him. He kissed her over and over – tender kisses that sealed the way she felt for him.

All her doubts left her. Millie knew the decision she'd taken had been the right one and that she would go further, if it took that, to make Len happy – this house even. Yes, she would consider putting it in his name, but she would never part with her portfolio. The income from that would give her some independence. Nor would she part with her little cottage in Wales that she loved. No matter what.

Chapter Twenty-Two

Elsie

Elsie lay in the bath, trying to soothe the bruises on her legs, thighs and back, but she couldn't soothe her bruised heart, or the feeling that she was nothing. She asked herself over and over again, *Why? And how could Len turn into such a monster? How has he deceived us all – and bewitched me?* Even Jim was blind to Len's true character. And that knowledge frightened her, as her doubts as to whether Jim would believe her, if he ever found out, assailed her once more.

So afraid was she that she vowed he would never find out. Never! And neither must Millie. Oh God. Poor, poor Millie, married to such a beast – it was like history repeating itself. *No, don't let it be. Please don't let Len have made me pregnant. I couldn't bear it.* Oh God, what if he has?

Panic gripped her. She thought of Dot – poor Dot, not knowing if her child was her stepfather's or Cess's. What must that have felt like?

Then her mum and Beryl Grimes came to mind. They had to try and pass their babies off as their husbands', and it hadn't worked: both had suffered terrible consequences. *Can I do that? Can I deceive Jim?*

Dot had been honest with Cess, and he'd accepted the situation because he loved her, but could Jim? Yes, Jim loved her, but what if he doubted her? She'd only just made him believe that she didn't love Len.

Sinking further into the water, she sought to drown her misery and uncertainties, but nothing helped.

'Elsie? Elsie, luv, I'm back. Elsie!'

'I'm in the bath, Rene . . . Rene, wait, don't open the shop!'

Rene's voice sounded nearer now as she said, 'Why, luv, what's wrong? Are yer all right? 'Ere, what's gone on? What's all this bleedin' mess about, luv? One of your chairs is upended, and your vase of flowers is smashed. Elsie? Elsie, luv!'

The bathroom door burst open.

'Oh, Rene, help me – help me.'

'Oh, me Elsie, me little luv, what's happened? Let me help you out of the bath, me darlin', the water's bleedin' cold.'

Once wrapped up in a huge towel and with a steaming mug of tea in her hand, Elsie sat on the sofa. Her eyes leaked tears, and her despair consumed her.

'Right, let's have it. Who did this to yer – and no telling me yer fell, cos I can tell something's gone on here.'

'It was Len. Oh, Rene, he . . . he raped me!'

'What? That bleedin' sod! Oh, Elsie, me luv. Let me hug yer, me darlin'. We'll sort this. I'll have him, you know.'

'No, Rene, you can't. It would kill Millie. I can't bear for her to know. Len said he'd tell her that I enticed him. I'll lose her, I know I will. And you can't tell Jim, either. No one must know. But, Rene, what if I'm pregnant? I can't . . . I can't live me mum's life over, I can't.'

'The only way is honesty, luv. It's either you suffer, or Millie does. A rough choice for you, me darlin'.'

'I would rather suffer, Rene, but in doing so, will I make Jim suffer? What if I'm having Len's baby?'

'Well, you can pass it off as having it early. But, look, I can get yer seen to, if yer like. Once we know yer've got a bun in the oven, I can get you to someone who can take it away.'

A little hope entered Elsie, but then she thought, *No. I can't do that. It's murder. I can't kill my child, whoever put it there.* She slumped onto Rene's shoulder. Rene rocked her backwards and forwards. Neither of them spoke. They were locked in the misery of all that women of their standing had to put up with.

'Do you think he treats Millie all right, Rene?'

'I doubt it. A bloke capable of doing this has no respect for women. But Len seems a charmer to me, and he'll probably twist her around his little finger and keep her there by a combination of love and cruelty. I've known a few like him. You wonder why the women don't leave them, but they never do. If he can do this to you, he'll do it to others – Millie included. Then he'll make them feel it's their fault. He's done that to you, hasn't he?'

Elsie nodded.

'Well, don't bleedin' let him. This is not your fault, Elsie. He took advantage of the fact that he found you alone and defenceless in this house. And knowing men as I do, I'd say he's been fantasizing about you. And if I'm right, then he won't leave you alone. If this had been a one-time slip, he'd have been sorry and begged your forgiveness. Did he?'

'No. He blamed me, and called me a . . . a prostitute. He threw money at me.'

'The bleedin' bastard! You've got to do something, luv. Believe me, if you don't, you'll make a rod for your own back. Cos I'm telling you, I know men – men like him: manipulative, sneaky, vile creatures. Do something, Elsie, please.'

'What should I do? What can I do?'

'Tell Jim. I'll go and fetch him now, and you can tell him. He'll be at the factory, won't he?'

Elsie nodded.

'Right, I'm off. You lock the doors, girl, and don't answer to any bleeder. Len could come back when he's had time to think about it all – he could come back to make sure he gets your silence. Don't let him in.'

When Rene had gone, Elsie felt like calling her back. Fear gripped her. *Oh God, what will happen now? Millie . . . Oh, Millie.*

Within minutes Rene was back. 'I got to the end of the road, me darlin', and I knew that telling Jim is the wrong course. I thought about Millie, and how lovely she is, and I didn't know what to do. I thought we'd talk it through. Me first reaction was to expose him, but now I'm not so sure. Len may always be the loving husband to Millie. We can keep our eye on that one – but exposing him will break her.'

'Oh, Rene, I'm so glad. The fear of what might happen by telling Jim was much greater than my fear of coping with what's already happened.'

'You've two choices. If you've caught for a baby, then I can help you get rid of it, or you can pass it off as Jim's.'

'There's a chance that I might not. I got in the hot bath right after, so maybe I . . .'

'It don't work like that, luv. If you're releasing eggs, then

241

his sperm will fertilize one – it's as simple as that. Now, let's do some maths. When did you last see your monthly?'

'Two weeks ago.'

'Right, do you remember what Dot did? She went with Cess straight afterwards, and that's what you've got to do with Jim.'

'But he's an honourable man. He – he, well, he controls himself. I'd have to . . . Oh, Rene, I'd have to behave in a way that I would hate, and then I think Jim would be ashamed of giving in. He might even blame me.'

'Luv, when a man's worked up, he has to relieve himself somehow. If that can be with the woman he loves, then that's how it should be. Your wedding's only weeks away. Now the date is fixed, he'll be a pushover, scruples or not. A standing dick don't have no scruples – well, not often. Men like Jim can deal with it in a different way maybe, but not many can. You've got to be receptive to him. Let him see you want it. Don't act all shy. Take the bull by the horns . . . Ha! Or the horn by the hand.' Rene burst out laughing, and Elsie couldn't help joining her. Rene had always been crude – salt of the earth, but crude with it, was how Mum described her, but oh, she had you in stitches.

Suddenly the black cloud hanging over Elsie lifted. And though it wasn't a road she wanted to take – deceiving Jim – she knew she had to. Otherwise, so many would be hurt: Millie, Millie's lovely mum and Len's dad. And Jim, Cess and Bert. No, she must never tell another soul. Never.

Rene pulled her to her. 'We can do this, luv. But you've got a big part to play. You've to behave as if nothing has happened. And that's got to last your lifetime, because the one who did this to you will be in your life forever. You've got to agree to me tackling Len. I'll threaten him. I know

242

folk. I could have him disappear, never to be seen again. And no trace would be found of him. You leave it with me.'

Elsie didn't want this, and yet a big part of her did. Rene had said that if Len got away with what he'd done, he'd do it again. The thought of that was too much to bear.

'Ta, Rene. With you by my side, I can do this.'

'Right, your job is to get Jim to make love to you. Leave Mr High-'n'-Mighty Lefton to me: he's going to get the biggest scare of his life. And a good punching to cement it.'

At first Elsie went to protest, but then the thought of Len receiving a pasting made her feel that it would be the best news she'd heard in a long time. And she wanted it to happen – and wished she could be present to spit in his eye as he lay in agony.

'Rene, you were me mum's best friend, and now you're mine. Always be near to me. I feel safe when you are.'

'I will, me darlin'. Your mum asked me to look out for yer, and for the lads, if ever anything happened to her, and I'll keep that promise till the day I die.'

Elsie began to feel safe again. She didn't usually like Rene's methods of solving problems, but this time she did. Len deserved all he'd got coming to him.

By the time Jim was due to pick her up that evening, Elsie was in charge of her emotions. She'd cried it all out – come to terms with it as best she could, and was ready to be herself with Jim.

He came bounding up the stairs carrying Bert, who'd run down to let him in, then took one look at Elsie and immediately became concerned. 'Darling, what's wrong?'

She blushed. 'Nothing, why?'

'You've been crying, and you look – well, sad.'

'Oh, I was being a baby earlier. I fell over. Went flying. Bruised me legs, and broke that lovely vase we found on the market.'

'Ah, come here and let me give you a hug. Did Millie come? Has she told you all about her Italian trip?'

'N – no. Len delivered a message to say that she was ill with a cold.'

'Oh? Did he take you to see her?'

'No. He – he was in a hurry, and was going to the bank, not home. Anyway, he said she wouldn't welcome visitors today. Maybe tomorrow.'

'Oh? I called by the bank in my lunch hour as I wanted to see Len, thought we might grab a sandwich together, and they told me he wasn't in until next week.'

'I – I don't know then. I thought that's what he'd said, but I can't have heard him right. I'm sorry.'

'Hey, it's all right. Anyone can make a mistake. You look mortified, my darling. I'm not a bit bothered about missing him. I am concerned about you, though. You're very pale and seem to be in pain. Have you seen a doctor?'

'No. I'm fine. I – oh, Jim, can we just go? I've been cooped up here all day. Millie not coming left me out on a limb.' Coming out of his arms, she spoke to Bert. 'Go on up to Cess and tell him that Jim's arrived and we're going soon, there's a good boy.'

When Bert disappeared through the door, Jim looked at her intently. But then he seemed to make his mind up not to pursue the topic of what was wrong with her, but instead said, 'Never be out on a limb, darling. You only have to come to the factory. I'll always be glad to see you. I could have done with you coming in today. The women were up in arms.'

As he was laughing, she made light of asking, 'What was wrong with them – were they teasing you again? They love to do that. You shouldn't blush so easily.'

'Ha! I knew it would be my fault. No. Ada came in with a black eye. The others were all angry about it, and there was a bit of a spat between Peggy and that other one who always gets on her nerves – Irene. It appears that Irene made a joke about Ada . . . well, you know how it goes, especially around poor Ada. She seems to have a brute of a husband who's got no respect for her. And she is often the brunt of the others' jokes.'

Elsie moved closer to him. Jim opened his arms to her once more. She snuggled in close, even though this increased the soreness of her back, but she needed comforting even more now, as his tale about the women had hit a nerve. Something Rene had said about women of their standing. Why was it so?

She looked up at Jim – good honest Jim – and had an overwhelming urge to tell him the truth, but clamped her lips together.

'Darling, there's something wrong, I can tell. What is it? Let me help you.'

Elsie swallowed. She tried so hard to stop the tears, but they flowed.

'Elsie, my darling!'

Held closely by him, she suddenly knew that no matter the consequences, she must tell Jim. What she'd agreed to do with Rene now appalled her.

'Oh, Jim.'

'Elsie? Elsie, talk to me. What's wrong?'

She heard the door behind her open and gasped in her sobs. It closed again and she guessed that Cess had been

245

with Bert and had taken him back to his room to give her and Jim privacy.

'Let's sit down, my darling.'

His gentleness helped her. 'I – I'm going to hurt you very much, Jim, but please believe me that none of what has happened is my fault.'

'What is it? Elsie, tell me.'

'I'm trying, but it's so difficult. I – I'm afraid. You see, I did think myself in love with Len, but I wasn't. I know that now. I know now because of how I feel for you, so please, please believe me.'

'Has Len done something? My God! Has Len hurt you? Tell me, Elsie, please tell me.'

'He – he ra – raped me.'

There was a silence. When she looked up, she couldn't tell what Jim's expression meant. She saw horror and anger, but did she see disbelief?

'No! When? What? Oh, Elsie. Elsie, tell me what happened.'

As best she could, she told him. Jim sat still. Many emotions passed over his face.

Word for word, blow for blow, the violation of her tumbled out as if she was watching it happen. When she'd finished she said, 'I – I wasn't honest with you before, Jim. I tried to protect you, but on the day of the wedding . . .'

Emotionally drained when she had finished telling how Len had kissed her and threatened her, she leaned back and closed her eyes. Jim didn't speak. Her sobs filled the space, but then a different sound joined hers. She opened her eyes to see Jim hunched over, crying.

'Jim, my Jim. I'm so sorry.'

Between his sobs he told her, 'You have nothing to be

sorry for, my darling. I – I am just so devastated. For you. For us. And for Millie, and the friendship we all have. How will we go forward?'

'We can, darling Jim, if we stick together and stay strong. That beast cannot break us.'

'I've never known anything like this to happen. Len always went after a pretty face, but he acted the gentleman where women were concerned. So to do this? I cannot take it in.'

Elsie couldn't speak. Was he blaming her? Was he just saying that he believed her, when, deep down, he didn't?

Rene stopped this train of thought as she called up the stairs, 'Cess, I'm off out. Are yer both all right?'

Elsie jumped up. 'I must stop her!' Running to the top of the stairs, she shouted after Rene.

'Blimey, girl, I thought you'd left! What's up: is there a fire?'

Going down the stairs, Elsie whispered urgently, 'Oh, Rene, I've told Jim.'

'What? Oh, girl, I told yer not to do that. What's happening – how's he took it?'

'I – I don't know. He's stunned and angry, but I'm scared, Rene. I'm not sure that he believes me.'

'Huh, well, I can tell him how true it was. I saw the state of yer, and of the room. Anyway, I take it you don't want me to warn Len? Well, let's see what Jim has to say, eh?'

As she came back upstairs, followed by Rene, Elsie felt her heart in her mouth. She knew that, no matter what she said, Rene wouldn't be swayed from her mission. But everything got worse when she went back through her own front door, because Cess stood there with his hand on Jim's shoulder. 'Sis? What's going on? I can't get anything out of Jim.'

'Bert won't come down, will he, Cess?'

'No, but he's scared. I told him that he must stay there while I find out what's happened. What *has* happened, Sis?'

'I'll tell yer what's bleedin' happened, mate. That bastard – thinks-himself-better-than-us Len – has only gone and raped our Elsie!'

'What? Elsie! Oh my God! When?'

'This afternoon. I came back from me errands and found this room looking like a burglar had done it over: chairs were upended, the vase that stood on the sideboard was lying in smithereens on the floor, and poor Elsie was in a bath of almost-cold water. Her thighs are black and blue from where she's struggled and he's forced her. And her back, well, I've never seen the like, and that's saying something, with what I've seen in me lifetime.'

Cess didn't move. His face had gone white. Anger trembled through him. When he did speak, it was in a low voice. 'I'll kill him!'

'You won't, Cess. You'll leave this to me. I know folk who'll scare the shit out of Len. He won't touch our girl again after they've paid him a visit. And that way Millie needn't know. Though we'll keep an eye on her for any signs that she's being knocked about.'

'No! You can't do that, Rene. It's up to me to talk to Len. We should go to the police really, but, like you, I'm thinking of Millie. And not just of her. Oh, Elsie, my darling. I'm sorry. I couldn't speak with the shock and horror of it all, and the pain at the thought of you being hurt.' Jim stood and now had his arms out to her.

Elsie went to him. 'I understand.'

'Look, I'm going to talk frank here, as someone has to. There could be consequences coming from this . . .'

'No, Rene. We know what you mean, but I think that me and Jim should talk about those possibilities.' Elsie felt her colour flare up.

Cess sat down. 'Oh, Sis. It's like it's all happening again.'

Seeing Cess so distraught gave strength to Elsie, and she went to her brother. 'It is, Cess, but we'll deal with it, eh? Mum had no one to stand by her, but our lovely Dot had you and, thank God, her child turned out to be yours. Well, I've got Jim, and you and Rene. Between us we'll find a way.'

Once more Jim looked shocked, as if the truth had only just dawned on him. Elsie felt fear filling her heart. Would Jim stand by her, if she was having a baby by another man? What he said next increased her fear. 'That bloody bastard! He's taken everything from us, Elsie.'

Cess stood. 'You will stand by me sis, won't you, Jim? None of this is her fault.'

Jim wiped his hand across his face. He looked haggard. Elsie held her breath, then cried out in pain as Jim stormed past her and Cess and left the room, slamming the door behind him. She felt as if all the stuffing had been knocked out of her. She slumped down onto the sofa.

'Well, that bloody bleeder! The spineless git! Good job you found out what he were like, girl, before you tied the knot.'

Tears wet Elsie's face. Out of the corner of her eye she saw Cess move. 'No, Cess. No.'

'Look, Else, I know what he's going through. It happened to me, remember. This might not mean that Jim's running out on yer. He needs time. What's happened has turned his world upside down. You never knew, but when Dot told me what her stepdad had done to her, I ran and ran. I couldn't stop.'

'Oh, Cess.'

'Go after Jim, Cess,' Rene said. 'You're the best one to do it. At least we'll know one way or the other then. What a bleedin' carry-on! And all down to that pig, who acts as though butter wouldn't melt in his mouth. He's bad news, Elsie, girl. We all thought Len a charming bloke, just right for our Millie. Now I fear for her.'

Elsie wiped her face. She had no words. The happiness she'd found had tumbled apart and lay in tatters. She didn't try to stop Cess a second time, but hoped and prayed he'd come back with news that she wanted to hear, and not news that she couldn't even bear to think about. *Oh, Jim, I love you. I can't bear to live without you.*

Chapter Twenty-Three

Millie

Millie couldn't understand why Elsie hadn't been to see her, or hadn't contacted her. *She knew yesterday about me not being well – so why? Is she unwell herself?*

Deciding to call at the factory to see if she was there, Millie got out of bed. Her legs felt wobbly, making her giggle at the reason. Len's love-making had left her feeling weak. This thought made her clutch her body with her arms, in a self-hug that contained all of her happiness. She didn't let herself think of the first time yesterday afternoon. When she did, she still felt hurt and confused.

Crossing over to the hook behind the bedroom door, she took down her robe and wrapped it around herself. As she did so, she had a queasy feeling. *Oh God, I'm going to be sick!* Rushing through to her bathroom, she only just made it to the lavatory in time.

Rinsing her mouth out after the bout had passed, Millie wondered if she was more unwell than she'd thought.

It wasn't until after she'd washed and was dressing herself that the thought struck her. *I can't be! . . . Oh, but I can!* She smiled as she remembered the first time they had made love on the night of the wedding, six weeks ago. A tentative awakening for them both – or at least it was for her. They had never discussed whether or not Len was experienced. But surely it must have happened then, for her to have symptoms already? She remembered the girls at school talking about sex, and how you only had to do it once to become pregnant. Could it really be so? Could her dreams be coming true? Could she really be pregnant? And so soon? She giggled. *Oh, I can't wait to tell Elsie.*

Jim answered the phone. He sounded cold – distant. 'Jim? Is everything all right? Have I called at a bad time? I just wanted a word with Elsie. Is she there? Is she all right?'

'I am fine, thank you. Busy – you know, always a lot to see to.'

'Jim, something's not right. Can't you talk?'

'No, erm, I have a buyer with me – a potential new customer.'

'How exciting. I'm going to miss working with you. We must have a meeting very quickly, as there have been other developments. Is Elsie all right? I thought she was in work today.'

'No, she fell over . . . yesterday – bruised herself badly.'

'Ah, that'll be why she hasn't contacted me. Poor Elsie. Anyway, I'm feeling a lot better, so I'll get my driver to take me over to see her. I'll talk to you soon . . . What? Sorry, did you say something?'

'No . . . no. All right, speak soon.'

The phone clicked. Millie replaced her receiver on the hook on the wall. She stood for a moment. She was sure Jim was about to stop her going to see Elsie. A worry settled in her. What could have happened? Len had said that Elsie was all right when he saw her. Was her fall a really bad one? But if so, why didn't someone come and tell her?

Feeling a little afraid, as she sensed something more was wrong than she was being told, Millie dressed hurriedly and went downstairs to order Barridge to have the car brought round.

Rene met her at the front door and greeted her cheerily.

'Millie! Well . . . the blushing bride! Millie, girl, it's good to see yer. I was just down to open the shop. So, how was yer trip?'

'Marvellous, thanks, Rene. Is Elsie in? Is she all right? Jim tells me she had a fall.'

'You've seen Jim?'

'No . . .' Something felt odd. 'I phoned him. Rene, is everything all right? Has something happened?'

'No, why d'yer ask that? We've all been carrying on while you've been swanning across the world, you lucky bleeder. Oops, sorry, Millie.'

Millie laughed. At least Rene was her usual swearing self. 'Oh, good to hear it. Well, I'll go up to Elsie's, shall I? I'm dying to see her, and what's she's done with the flat.'

'No. You hang on 'ere a minute, Millie, luv, while I pop up and see if she's decent. I won't be a mo.'

Elsie being decent wasn't something that would worry either of them.

Rene was away for a few moments, before Millie saw her rushing back down the stairs. 'I'm sorry, Millie. Elsie's not well enough. She, um . . . she banged her head when she fell. She's lying down with a cold cloth on her forehead. I just gave her a drink of water while I was up there. She said she's glad you're better, but can you give her a few days? She needs that, girl.'

Convinced now that all wasn't right, Millie stood her ground. 'Rene, stop this. Tell me what's going on! Elsie wouldn't refuse to see me unless there was something she doesn't want me to know, or something really bad has happened that involved me . . . I haven't offended her in some way, have I? Oh, Rene, please tell me the truth. Why is everyone being cagey – Jim on the phone, now you; and Elsie not wanting to see me, and Cecil even. I would have been the first one he came to tell after Jim, if Elsie had hurt herself.'

'Well, she didn't want you to know, but her and Jim have had a break-up. She's in a bad way over it. She – she won't say what it was all over, but she's distraught. If I persuade her to let you see her, you won't question her, will you?'

'No. I promise, Rene. But I'll go mad if I don't see her for myself.'

'Wait there then, luv.'

Rene seemed to take an age. Millie knew she must be trying to convince Elsie to see her. When she came down, Rene released a huge sigh as she spoke. 'I'm sorry . . .'

Millie waited until she was fully downstairs, then pushed past her. 'I'm not taking no for an answer, Rene. You'll have to physically stop me, to prevent me seeing Elsie.' She ran up the stairs, glad that Rene didn't try to hold her back. Finding the door to Elsie's flat was open, she burst in, then stood stock still. Elsie lay on the sofa. Her face was awash with tears, and her whole demeanour was one of extreme misery.

'Elsie! Elsie, darling.'

Elsie jumped. Millie thought she saw fear cross her face.

'Elsie, I'm here for you, my dear sister. Don't shut me out. When you hurt, I do. Whatever happened between you and Jim?'

'Oh, Millie, I don't want to talk about it.'

'He didn't hurt you, did he?' Millie had reached the sofa and was on her haunches in front of Elsie. 'He didn't make you fall? Where are you hurt?'

'No, Millie. Jim hasn't hurt me. Ple – a – se, I just want to be left alone.'

Millie felt lost. The happiness she'd felt earlier dissolved. Elsie looked broken. Millie took her hand and held it in hers, glad that Elsie didn't resist. 'Would you like me to talk to Jim?'

'No. Millie, please leave us to work this out. I know you love me and want to help, but you can't. Let me do this on me own.'

'All right. But fall back on me whenever you want to. I am your sister. I will always be strong for you – just as you have for me.' Standing up, Millie asked, 'Can I make you a cup of tea, love?'

She was rewarded by Elsie smiling. 'You wouldn't know how.'

'I can try. I've seen you do it enough times.' Millie giggled as she said this.

But Elsie rose. 'I'll make it.'

'No, show me how to. You may want me to another time, and I want to feel I'm doing something for you.'

By the time the tea was made, the atmosphere was a lot better between them. Millie wished she could say that it was normal, but that was too much to hope for. Elsie had obviously been devastated by something terrible. Millie couldn't think of anything Jim could have done to cause this. He was such a nice, gentle soul.

As they drank their tea, they sat side by side. Elsie's long red hair hung limply, covering her face as her head bent forward. Millie instinctively brushed it back for her and tucked it behind her ears. 'You have the most beautiful hair, Elsie, but you never let it get like this, darling. It seems to speak of your misery.'

'Oh, Millie, Millie.'

Elsie put her cup down on the small table at the side and leaned into Millie. Millie didn't ask any more questions. She could feel Elsie's pain. She just stroked her hair gently.

Between sobs Elsie said, 'Me mum used to do that. She'd play with me hair for hours.'

Still Millie waited.

'It'll be all right between me and Jim. Cess has spoken to him, and Jim said he needed time.'

Still unable to think what could have happened between them, Millie said, 'Sometimes we all need that, dear.'

'I don't. I want him here. How could I have been so blind as to not know all these months that he was the one? And then for it to hit me out of the blue, like it did . . . It hurts to lose that, Millie.'

'Yes. I understand that. Len and I had a . . . well, a sort of falling-out. Something that came between us, and the way he reacted hurt me badly. But we've sorted it out and you will, too.'

Not wanting to burden Elsie with any decisions she'd made regarding the factory, Millie didn't say any more, but she did ask, 'Len tells me that you decided to change your mind over the shares: what brought that on?'

'Oh, I – I just felt that I haven't a business head. I've hardly got any education and I might be a liability. I had time to think about it, with you both gone. I felt ashamed of myself. I acted in a greedy way, trying to grab all I could get. I'm sorry, Millie. I'm not entitled to anything from our father. And you've been so generous trying to make things up to me. I'm happy with my allowance, and Len . . .'

'Len what? He didn't persuade you, did he?'

'N – No. I was going to say that Len said he would make my allowance a legally binding amount, so that it was safeguarded.'

'Oh? Well, yes of course. I had already done that. I'm sure he knew that. Perhaps he was simply reassuring you.' Panic seized Millie then. *Will my decision affect what arrangements I put in place for Elsie?*

'Yes, I think he was . . . He tried to make me change my mind, but when I was adamant, he said that.'

'Oh, I see. I'm so glad you and he had a talk about these matters, Elsie. Len is very concerned that the right thing is done by us all. So whatever he has asked you to do concerning your allowance – sign papers, that sort of thing – make sure that you do it, my dear.' Millie wanted to say what a relief it was to her to be free of all the responsibility, but she held back, as she wasn't ready to tell Elsie everything yet, and needed her to follow Len's instructions. It occurred that changing the subject might be the best course now, so as not to alarm Elsie. 'So, are you ready to hear some good news?'

'Yes, I am, Millie. I'm sorry that the first time you see me, after coming home, you find me like this. But what about you? How are you feeling? Len said you had a cold.'

'More of a bad headache, which I put down to the travel. It was a very long way, Elsie. And although I wouldn't have missed it for the world, I wouldn't go again in a hurry.'

'But you had a good time?'

'I did . . . lovely. His family were so nice. And the different customs were all fascinating, and such fun. I'll tell you all about it when you feel better, but there is something I've just got to share. I did think my headache was down to the journey, but I don't know. Elsie, I may be pregnant!'

Something fleetingly crossed Elsie's face that Millie couldn't decipher. But she recovered. 'Oh, Millie. Really? How do you know that, mate?'

'Well, I was sick this morning.'

For the first time Elsie let out a spontaneous laugh. 'But you're not well – it could be to do with that. At the factory they judge by your monthlies. If any of them misses one, they say you've a bun in the oven.'

'Ha, I've heard them say things like that. And yes, I am late. I had a period three weeks before my wedding day, and nothing since. What do you think?'

'I think you've a good chance of being right.'

That was it. No congratulations, and again that look: a sort of fear. But what could Elsie be afraid of? *Oh no! I wonder if . . . No.* But the thought had planted itself: had Jim taken advantage of Elsie and they'd realized she was pregnant and he'd run out on her?

Fear took root in Millie. She wanted to ask Elsie, but thought better of it. 'I hope so, as there's nothing that would make us happier than to start a family. Len wants ten!' But although Elsie laughed, Millie knew it was a false laugh and her fear deepened. But what could she do? Elsie just didn't want to talk to her about it.

'Elsie, can I ask something? You say that everything will be all right – that Jim needs time. Does this mean that your wedding will still go ahead?'

'Oh, Millie, I don't know. I don't know how much time Jim wants . . . needs. I just don't know.'

Her distress came to the fore again, and Millie decided that she had to act. 'Look, dear, you're exhausted. Get

some rest, and I'll call again tomorrow. But in the meantime, if you need me, send Cess to me. Where is he, by
the way?'

'He takes Kitty to Gertie during the day while he hunts
for a house to rent. He wants a decent one, and they ain't
easy to find around here. He may have to go more towards
where you live.'

'Oh? Well, I know there's a couple around me that are
empty, but I don't know if they are for sale or for rent.
Clarke's and Vernon's are the usual estate agents for property
in our area. He could try them. You know, I wish you had
rented around there, Elsie.'

'I know. Jim . . . well, it has been mentioned. But for
now I want to be with Rene, and Cess as well, but that's
not to be.'

'I'm sure it will all sort itself out. Well, I have to go now,
darling. But please send for me if you need me. Or there's
an open door for you at my house, of course.'

They kissed and hugged, but something felt different to
Millie. Elsie was holding back something of herself, and
Millie was mystified as to why. It made her feel that she was
in some way responsible for whatever had happened and it
wasn't a comfortable feeling.

Once in the car, she asked her driver to take her to the
factory.

A cheer went up when Millie walked in. She smiled and
thanked the women. Remarks came her way: 'You looked
beautiful on your wedding day,' and 'You married a smasher.'
There were a few more comments spoken in a lower tone
as she ascended the stairs, but she tried not to hear them,
and couldn't have repeated them.

When she entered the office, Jim was sitting at his desk. He looked awful.

'Jim? Jim, what's wrong? I've just come from Elsie's – she looks dreadful. She can't stop crying. Oh, Jim, I'm not judging, but don't you think she's been through enough in her life?'

He swivelled in his chair and looked away.

'Jim, we're friends enough by now to be able to be frank with one another. Look, if you can't talk to me, why don't you talk to Len? I can get him to meet you tonight, although I won't let you keep him out late. I'm missing him already, and he only popped out to do some business with our solicitor.'

'No. I don't want to talk to Len, or anyone.'

'But Elsie is like a broken person. How can you treat her like this? I don't understand.'

This seemed to get through to Jim. He turned to face her. 'What do you mean: broken? I know she's upset, but—'

'She's more than upset, Jim. Whatever happened between you needs to be put right, not avoided. I fear for her. This could tip Elsie over the edge. She can't take much more, Jim. You made her so happy. You accepted her. You loved her, you made her feel loved. I know I only saw you together as a couple on my wedding day, but all of that shone from her. I went away feeling so happy that you loved each other. And then Len told me yesterday that you were planning a wedding very soon. How has it all gone wrong?'

'How did Len know about the wedding?'

'He called round there yesterday to tell Elsie about . . . But why? Jim, has this anything to do with Len?'

Jim didn't answer for a moment. When he did, his 'No' was hesitant.

Then something occurred to Millie. 'It was Elsie's idea to give up the shares in the business, Jim. Not Len's. Is that what's made you this angry?'

'No! Look, Millie, I'm sorry, I – I . . .'

'Jim! Oh, Jim, I'm so sorry. Please don't cry, I can't bear it. Please go and see Elsie. She loves you with all her heart, and you love her. Don't let whatever it is fester.' Millie hurried to his side – all she wanted was to help them both. 'Will you take my car and go round to Elsie's, Jim? I'll stay here and see to anything that occurs, and you can send my car back to me, so that I can get home when the factory closes.'

Jim rose. He blew his nose loudly. 'Thanks, Millie. I wanted to go, but I couldn't leave here.' This cheered Millie.

'You go – go on. Sort it out, Jim. Whatever it is, it isn't worth breaking both your hearts over.'

When he had gone, Millie sat down and let out a huge sigh. *Please, God, don't let it be something my Len has done. I couldn't bear to have a rift between me and Elsie.*

Chapter Twenty-Four

Elsie

Elsie felt drained. She hadn't slept for more than thirty hours, and for most of that time she'd been weeping. The strain of Millie's visit had taken its toll on her, too. And now her mind kept going over the possible outcomes of all that had happened. The one that gave her the most despair was that both she and Millie could be having Len's babies.

Then there was Jim. *Oh, why did I tell him?* Now he has to live with this for the rest of his life! Cess had said everything would be all right – Jim just needed time – but how much time? She so wanted him here with her. She needed his love and support.

But then another fear entered her. *If Jim cannot come to terms with what has happened, then I might end up being an unmarried mother. Oh God, the shame – I can't bear it, I can't!* Rene's suggestion of visiting someone who could put this right suddenly seemed the best option.

As if she'd been in tune with Elsie's thoughts, Rene knocked on the door and opened it. 'How did it go with Millie, luv? I've been tied up with a customer and couldn't get up to see yer. This woman wants four outfits, as she's going to Paris with her husband for Christmas, so I'm set for the winter months now. I've got plenty of work to keep me going.'

'I'm glad, Rene. You work hard and deserve your shop to do well, mate.'

'I hope it does, and then I'll be able to pay Millie back her investment. Anyway, how are you feeling? Have yer had a chance to think things through?'

'Some, but everything is *what if*? It's hard to sort out what to do, because some things, or all, might not happen.'

'Yer have to be in charge of yer own destiny, girl. Take decisions that'll get you out of this mess. That's how me and yer mum went on for years. I know we didn't always make a good job of it, but most of the time we got by. You did wrong telling Jim. I know: you're an honest girl and like to be straight with everyone, but now the problem is his, too.'

'I know, but you've seen what happens if you hide these things – look at what Dot went through because her mum married her boyfriend, without telling him she was pregnant by another man. And my mum, doing the same thing, caused her husband to take his own life. I'd rather live without Jim than live with him, under those circumstances. Rene, I want to get rid of the baby – if there is a baby. I mean I don't want to, but I've no choice.'

'Even if Jim still wants to marry you and take the child on as his?'

'Yes. Even more so then. He may think he can handle it, but what if he can't? What will that do to him? This is the only way. If Jim still wants to marry me, I'm going to put me wedding off till after Christmas. I need to know if I'm having a baby, before I marry. But if I am, Jim will never know. I'll always let him think it didn't happen.'

263

'Well, luv, I think yer doing right. But don't think of it as a baby: it ain't. I've helped at getting rid of many, and all that comes away is a blob – like a blood clot – if it's done early enough, that is.'

'How soon?'

'As soon as yer miss yer first monthly. You said yer last one was two weeks ago, so yer've two weeks to wait. Are yer regular, Elsie?'

'Yes, like clockwork. Mum used to make sure I had plenty of rags ready, as she knew the day.'

'Well, let's hope you come on, but I'll have everything in place if yer don't.'

'Ta, Rene. Will you be there with me?'

'If yer want me to be, girl – I'll always be by your side, Elsie, luv.'

Elsie stood up and went to her. 'Give us a hug, Rene. When yer do, it's like me mum is hugging me.'

When Elsie was in Rene's arms, Rene said, 'She is, me darlin' – these are her arms around yer, girl, and always will be. We'll get through this, I promise yer. But yer've got to fight it, Elsie. Be strong and rise above it, or it'll drag yer down and ruin the rest of yer life.'

Elsie knew this was true. She wasn't sure she could do it, but she wasn't alone: she had the support of Rene, Cess, and the love of little Bert, who depended on her, to help her through it all. And maybe, if she was lucky, of Jim too.

Rene patted her back. 'Right, go and tidy yerself up before Bert comes in from school. He's worried out of his little mind, bless him. And that's another thing that will help yer, Elsie – concentrating on others, especially those who depend on yer.'

As Elsie lay in a warm bath, she began to feel more hopeful

about the future. She had a plan, and that helped. And she had Bert to care for. She'd start by being cheerful when he came in. Maybe take him for a walk and buy him an ice-cream. Then they'd come home and make tea together for when Cess came in. And she'd sit holding Kitty for a while. Playing with Kitty and making her giggle always lifted her spirits. And . . . well, if Jim came round: what then?

Squeezing the sponge so that water trickled over her, Elsie decided that she'd have to wait and see. Jim might be ready to pick up the pieces with her, or he might not, but she would face that when it happened.

Feeling much better, Elsie got out the bath and dried herself vigorously, before putting on her underclothes and searching for something cheerful to wear. It had been a sunny day and, judging by what she could see through her window, it still was nice and warm, as the women walking by were dressed in just their frocks – no one wore a shawl or had a jacket on. She smiled as she saw a sea of bonnets and straw boaters bobbing along the street: her view, looking down on them, gave the top of everyone's heads until they'd passed, and then she saw the rest of them.

She chose to wear a white blouse that buttoned to the neck and had a stand-up priest-like collar edged with lace. The lace then bordered the pleats that were on each side of the blouse's pearl buttons. With this, she teamed a long plain-blue skirt, which was the colour of the sky. Brushing her hair, Elsie coiled it on top of her head, before dabbing her puffy eyes with witch hazel and applying a wisp of rouge and some red lipstick. Standing back from the mirror, she felt pleased with her efforts.

Going through to the living room, she crossed to the French doors and stepped out on the balcony. From here she would see Bert coming home, but checking her clock she realized it was a little early. She was about to turn to go back in when her heart skipped a beat at the sight of Millie's car pulling up. Leaning over the railings gave her a view of Jim alighting from the back. He looked up and waved. She waved back and smiled down at him.

As the car sped off, he stood there for a moment, gazing up at her. Her heart swelled to see that his face held love and gentleness. Running to the stairs, Elsie skipped down them and was at the door, opening it, and within his arms in seconds. 'Oh, Jim. Jim, me love.'

His hug told her that her prayers were answered. He still loved her, and Jim kissing her hair gave her some hope that he didn't blame her.

'My poor darling, I'm sorry. I didn't help you – I only added to your distress. Millie came to the factory and said you were broken, and that hurt me so deeply. I'm sorry. I – I made things worse for you when I should have made them better.'

'Millie? You didn't tell her anything, did you, Jim?'

'Let's go in.'

'Jim? Tell me that you didn't tell Millie the truth.'

He steered her inside and up the stairs. Once in her living room, Jim held her to him. Elsie could feel him trembling. 'I – I think she may have guessed this had something to do with Len. She suggested that if I wouldn't talk to her, I went out with Len for a few drinks and talked to him. I protested in a way that raised her suspicions, but I think she had the idea that I was angry because I thought Len had talked you out of your shares – we know he did, but that is the lesser of the evils he has done. I don't think for a minute Millie suspects what has really upset me.'

'It would kill her. She told me that she thinks she is pregnant, and she was so happy about it.'

Jim was thoughtful for a moment. When he spoke, he surprised her. 'I don't think we have any option but to take up Rene's suggestion.' For a moment she thought he meant getting rid of the baby if she was pregnant, but Jim went on, 'Len needs frightening off. If he thought he got away with it, then he might try again. I've thought and thought about it, and I want to tackle him myself. I'm not afraid to but, like you, I want to protect Millie.'

'Are we doing right in that, Jim? I mean, will Len treat Millie well and respect her?'

'I think so – I hope so. He can be petulant if he doesn't get his own way, but he's a gentleman among his own class. It's with anyone he considers beneath him that he shows little respect.'

Jim told her then about a young man that Len's father had taken on. 'He was the son of his father's housekeeper, and she'd worked and sacrificed to get him an education – he was exceptionally clever and gained a scholarship. His application to the job that Len's father gave him saw him being promoted within a year, to the same level as Len. Len worried that when the manager of their family bank retired, this chap might be chosen instead of him, as his father used to have a bit of a thing about Len – I think he saw his real character and so was a little hard on him at times. Anyway, Len framed the poor chap, made it look as though he'd fiddled the books, and he got the sack.'

'And Len told you this?'

'Not until years afterwards, when it was too late to do anything. By then I was dependent on Len's help. The job at the jam factory is the saving of me. I had nothing, and no prospects. I hadn't any skills, other than what I'd learned about business from my father. And I had no one to turn to, as my father had alienated everyone we knew – borrowed money off most, and not paid it back. Most people in our circle who could offer me a job were creditors of my father's bankruptcy. Len offered me a lifeline.'

'Oh, Jim, how were you living?'

'I have a legacy from my mother and grandmother. They both tied that up in such a way that my father couldn't touch it. I came into it when I was twenty-five, just as my father died. But it wasn't enough to start a business with, or to fund me to retrain for another career. I invested it when I got this job – I enjoy playing the stock market, and although I haven't made any losses, my gains are small, and I still need the job at Swift's – even more so when we marry.'

This caught her breath, as Elsie had the feeling that Jim was talking about anything and everything in order to avoid the real issue. 'You still want to marry me, Jim?'

'I do, my darling.'

She went into his arms, and a kind of peace came over her. 'Oh, Jim, I love you.'

'And I love you, my darling Elsie. Can you forgive me for running away like that?'

'There's nothing to forgive. Cess told me the feelings he had when he was in the same situation, so I understood, but it has been a harrowing few hours for me.'

'I know. I can see how exhausted you are – though you do look beautiful.'

'Well, I did have the hope that you would come back, and Rene goaded me to sort myself out before Bert came home. Poor little boy has had enough sorrow and upset around him. He wet the bed last night, and that isn't like him. Well, he did so in the convent I told you about, but that shows it is stress that makes him do it. I thought I would take him for a walk when he comes home from school, and get him an ice-cream for a treat.'

'Can I come? That seems like such a normal thing to do.'

She smiled up at him. 'I would love that, Jim.'

His head came down towards her and his lips touched hers, and Elsie knew that no matter what happened to them, their love was strong enough to fight it.

Chapter Twenty-Five

Elsie and Millie

Elsie and Jim walked the quarter-mile to Southwark Park, chatting about this and that, with Bert holding their hands and jumping up and down.

'You've so much energy, Bert. I wonder if you will sit still long enough for me to teach you music.'

'I will, Jim, I promise. But I saw the squiggles you drew for Elsie and they looked very funny. I'm not sure I'll understand them.'

'You will, son. I promise you.'

'I wish I was your son. I like it when you call me that.'

'Well, you will be, in a kind of way, when I marry Elsie. I can be your dad or another big brother. Whichever you like.'

'I've got a big brovver, but not a dad. I did have a mum, but she's in heaven now.'

'I know. Dad it is, then. You can call me Pops. It's a short form for Poppa. I think it will suit us two, but we should ask Cess what he thinks of the idea, as he will act as your guardian in all things.'

'What's a guardian? Does that mean he has to guard me?'

Jim laughed. 'Well, yes, in a way. It means that if there

is anything official that has to be signed for you, then Cess will be the one to sign as your next of kin.'

Bert looked up, squinting into the sun. 'It all sounds a bit daft to me.'

Elsie joined Jim in laughing at this. It felt good, and she could sense the tension easing from her tired limbs.

The park looked lovely and memories flooded her of playing here with Dot, dancing around the bandstand, then going up onto the podium and pretending to be in a show, singing. Her eyes filled with tears, but she blinked them away.

She had no recent memories here, because when they started to work long hours in the jam factory they were too tired to walk further than St George's churchyard. But now, as she looked around, she realized what she had missed. Coming here was a true oasis – a piece of the countryside that left you feeling that The Blue, with its hustle and bustle, market stalls and sometimes rowdy Blue Anchor pub, was a million miles away.

Bert let go of their hands and ran over to where some boys were kicking a ball about. Jim moved closer to Elsie. 'It's lovely, so peaceful. Shall we sit on the bench?'

When they were seated and holding hands, Elsie began to let go of some of her pain and, yes, her guilt too, because those feelings had crept into her. She thought of how she must have come across to Len, especially in the early days of meeting him: he must have known how she felt about him, and had used that ever since. He seemed so nice back then. The day they went to Brighton, for instance, he was good fun and took care of them all. How could she have made such a wrong judgement of him? And, worse, how could she ever have thought herself in love with him?

'You're deep in thought, darling. Can I intrude?'

'Yes, sorry, Jim. Just memories.'

'So many things will provoke those for you. I hope it was a good one?'

'It was – Dot and I giving a pretend show on the bandstand. Ha, we thought we were the stars of a music hall.'

'I love to hear tales of you growing up: your gran, and how she played the piano, and her funny sayings. I would have loved to have met her. And your mum, who always sounds so courageous when you talk about her, despite her drink problem.'

'She was. She kept us together and did her best for us.'

'It sounds to me as if you played a big part in keeping you all together. I cannot believe what you did for your family, when you were only a child yourself.'

'It was hard at times, but we had good neighbours. They would always watch out for you, and even though they had very little themselves, they shared what they had. I must visit them sometime and see how they are.'

'Is there something else on your mind, darling? I . . . well, I mean other than what is weighing us both down. I'm not ready to talk about that yet, but we will, if you want to.'

'That is on me mind, of course. I can't forget it, but there is something more. I – I want to . . . well, I don't want you to take this the wrong way, Jim, but because of what has happened, I want to delay our wedding.'

'What?'

'Only till Christmas, or just after. I'm sorry, but I think it will take that long for me to be ready – I mean, for a celebration, and to have to socialize with Len.'

'Oh, yes, I hadn't thought about that. And there's no chance we can leave them off the guest list. All right, darling. I'm disappointed, as I wanted to shout to the world, and to Len in particular, that I am your husband.'

Elsie squeezed his hand. 'You're me saviour, me mate, and I love you.'

'Ha, wait till I add husband to that list. Then I can show you how much I love you.'

Elsie blushed. She smiled up at Jim, but inside she was screaming with fear of that side of their marriage. Her only experiences so far had been among the worst ordeals in her life.

'You shuddered, darling. Don't be afraid. We love each other, and nothing will happen until you're ready.'

Elsie wiped a tear away. She couldn't speak. Suddenly the horror of yesterday was vivid in her mind, and she wondered if it would ever leave her. *Will I be able to be a proper wife to Jim?* At the moment she felt she never wanted another man to touch her ever again – not even Jim.

When Millie got home that evening, Len had returned from the solicitor's and was annoyed with her. 'Where have you been? I left you in bed, not feeling well. And I come home with news of all I have achieved today and you're not here. You never said anything about going out, nor did you leave a message as to where you were going.'

'Whoops, sorry, darling – I've got to get used to having a husband around. I just didn't think. Anyway, all of a sudden I felt much better and went to see Elsie. She was in a terrible state, she and Jim—'

'I don't want to bloody know about them. We have enough business of our own to tend to.'

Shocked, Millie stood staring at him. 'May we please go into my sitting room? I don't want to discuss everything here in the hall.'

'No, we will go into my study. I have taken possession

of what you told me used to be your father's study, but which you and Elsie have been using. I've had the staff working for this last hour, taking out what I don't want in there and putting in what I do. I think you may recognize it, as Barridge told me it is like it was in your father's day.'

'Oh? Yes, all right. I'll have tea sent in. I'll be with you in a moment, darling.'

Len sighed heavily. Millie felt on edge. Len had been so different since they'd come home from their honeymoon. It was as if everything got on his nerves, and she hated his new stance towards Elsie, and now towards Jim. She made her mind up to get to the bottom of it.

When tea was served, Millie took a very welcome sip. Her headache had come back and was now weighted with stress. 'So what did the solicitor have to say? Did you discuss everything? The transfer of the factory and the house?'

'Yes, we did. He is drawing up papers as we speak, but wants to see you before they are completed, which is understandable and is the right thing for him to request. After all, I could be trying to embezzle everything from you. I left there as soon as I could, to see if you were well enough to come with me, but found you gone! Anyway, we also discussed the property portfolio.'

'Oh? We didn't mention that yesterday. What were you thinking? Because I want to keep that in my name. I feel that Father put it together as a sort of insurance policy, as the properties were in a different holding name from the factory, and he probably worried that the factory would fold.'

'I know. My father advised him to do that. He told your father to build a second asset for just that purpose, and to protect it, in case of bankruptcy. And I know you feel it is your asset, darling, but I wanted to be a partner in it. Together we could build the portfolio up. Buy more properties in this area. The shop that you lease to that seamstress below Elsie is a great acquisition – you got it for a snip. But you are not charging enough rent, and that is where I could come in, as I can evaluate these things and make sure we are getting a proper return.'

'I don't know. I let it to Rene, who as you know is a sort of aunt to Elsie, on the basis of profitability: low rent for two years, then we will look at what she can afford for the third year. I wanted to give her a good start, and help her to get out of the lifestyle that had claimed her.'

'Claimed her? Look, I know what Rene used to do. And that life is a choice, Millie. Oh, Millie, please stop trying to save the world and everyone in it. What you and I must do is secure our future, and that of the family we want to build.'

'I know, but within that, there is room to help others. I will never stop doing that. In fact now that you are taking over the running of the factory, I intend to do more of it.'

'Oh, what exactly? Darling . . . darling, listen to me.'

'Work with the Federation of Women Workers, for one. And towards decent housing and conditions for the people of Bermondsey.' Warming to her theme, Millie went on, 'I've learned of an Ada Salter, who was a councillor for this borough, setting up food kitchens for the dock-workers who went on strike, and I'd like to contact her.'

'Oh, Good Lord! She is an activist, a troublemaker.'

'Men may think so, but women don't, and neither does her husband. He supports her in everything she does. I would like to have that from you, Len.'

'I despair. All right, I won't interfere with your property portfolio, but don't come crying to me when it lies in ruination . . . No, in fact, I *will* interfere. I want to have some say in what you do with it, Millie. I must protect you.'

'As long as I retain ownership and have the majority say.'

'Which leaves me without a leg to stand on. Well, don't forget that my bank holds some of it as collateral against the jam factory's overdraft.'

Forgetting everything except that this was a business meeting, Millie said, 'But I no longer own the jam factory, or won't, so some other form of collateral will have to be put up to secure its debts, as you cannot hold my property in hock for your property.'

'Millie, for God's sake! You wouldn't do that to me, would you?' But then Len's face changed and she saw the anger that she'd glimpsed when he raped her, and she became afraid. He stood and came over to her chair. His stance threatened her. 'The factory needs that collateral. If you keep your portfolio, I insist that you sign to say that you guarantee the factory loan.'

'Please sit down, Len. We are conducting a financial meeting and I have a right to speak, and to my opinion. I am signing this house over to you. It will be more than enough collateral for you to give your bank.'

Len sat down, but remained angry.

'I cannot work with you in this fashion, Len. I will be afraid that every time you want your own way, you will bully me. That's not fair on me, and it is very damaging to our marriage. I want to retain something of my own. I don't want to come to you to make decisions that are needed. I have given you a huge amount of my estate. That should be enough.'

'Well, it isn't. But I will wait for you to fall flat on your face and come crawling to me to rescue you, and then we will see who has the upper hand.'

This appalled Millie. She got up. 'Meeting closed!'

'Come back here or—'

'Or what? Will you beat me . . . or rape me? Well, you do either and I won't sign a single damned thing over to you, and I will file for a divorce!'

With this, Millie stormed out and slammed the door behind her. Her natural instinct was to run to her room and sob her heart out, but she was afraid to. She felt the need to stay around the staff.

Once in her sitting room, she sat in the chair near the window. Her body was shaking all over. She felt sick, but mostly she felt heartbroken. *How could it all have gone wrong so quickly? What have I done? What have I done!*

Len didn't come running after her, something she was glad of. But at the same time it left her unsure what to do next. Part of her wanted to flee – to get the car and go to her mother's. But she worried about leaving Elsie. Elsie was in such a state, she needed her.

Millie pondered what could have happened between Elsie and Jim. She could think of nothing other than that Len must have had a hand in it in some way. Was it Len who forced Elsie to give up her shares? Jim wouldn't have wanted her to do that, but would he have upset Elsie as much as this, simply for shares in the jam factory? It was very dear to his heart, and he might feel that Elsie having shares secured his position. *Oh, I don't know. I only know that, after less than two months of marriage, I have never felt so unhappy in my life. And I don't know what to do. I don't.*

A knock on her door made her stiffen. Her 'Come in' was tentative. Her stomach churned when Len put his head round the door.

'Can I really come in? I don't deserve to.'

277

Millie sighed, 'No, you don't. But you can, if you have come to apologize.'

'I have, my darling.' He came further into the room and walked towards her with his arms open.

Without going towards him, Millie said, 'Len, we need to talk, not hug and forgive and forget – at least not until we have come to some agreement about our relationship, and our positions within this marriage.'

'I know.' He sat down on the chair opposite her. 'You start, and I promise not to lose my temper.'

His eyes twinkled, making it difficult to remain serious, but Millie felt determined. 'When I met you, in our first conversation you said: "When I take a wife, she will be loved, respected and will be my partner in all decisions." That sentence endeared you to me, Len. I believed it, and I didn't see any reason not to trust you as a man of your word. What changed? Or was that all part of a plan to ensnare me, to get what you want out of life?'

'What? How can you think such a thing, Millie, darling?'

'Because of your behaviour since we came home. You haven't shown me that you will always respect me. Or a willingness to listen to my opinion, when we need to make a decision – and you have acted in blackmailing ways to procure everything I own, not even wanting me to keep my property portfolio. What else am I to think?'

'Blackmail!'

'You raped me – and I will never look on that incident as anything else. Then afterwards, blaming me, you made me feel that was the treatment I deserve, and will be subjected to, if I don't give you what you want.'

'Millie, I'm shocked you think this. You are throwing in my face what *you* caused. I told you that you made me feel diminished as a husband, by wanting to work and run a business, owning every asset in our marriage. I had yet to bring anything to you. I will of course when I inherit, but I cannot do so now and for a long time, as Father is in his prime – as he is proving by remarrying. It could be years before I have a standing in the wealth stakes that is anything like yours.'

'I understand all of that, but don't think it excuses you. We could have talked it over and come to an understanding. And then just now, not content with everything I am willing to hand over to you, you want it all: everything I have. How can you think that is right? I need to keep something or I will be no better than a kept woman. I'll have no pride, no means of my own and will become a beggar to my husband. Well, I won't do it, and am reconsidering all that I have agreed to.'

'Oh, darling, I didn't mean to come across to you in that way. I was only doing what any husband would do, but I can see now how my actions looked, and I am mortally sorry for my roughness with you. Look, why don't you keep the house and I will take the portfolio, except for the holiday cottage in Wales, which I know is dear to you? Doesn't that make more sense? Then I will have my rightful position as owner of our business interests, and you will be the owner of two valuable properties.'

'And how will I run these households? I have staff wages, food, heating and lighting and maintenance costs, and no private income.'

'I will make over to you a generous budget for the house, and an allowance for your personal needs – your clothes, any entertaining you want to do, that sort of thing.'

Millie considered this for a moment. Would she ever know any peace if she didn't concede? And surely, if she fought for a fair and decent allowance, she'd be in a better position than if she had to juggle an ever-changing property market to make some money of her own?

'I agree, in principle, but I won't sign anything until I am satisfied that I am being given a proper allowance. I want my personal-allowance agreement worded as if it's payment for the sale of my businesses, not as a gift from you. That way I will feel that I am earning from my inheritance, not being handed a grace-and-favour gift from my husband that can be taken from me at a moment's notice. And you will feel that you have more right to the businesses and will have earned them, not taken them.'

'My God, I am seeing a side to you that I didn't know you had – but I admire it. You have a better business head than any man I have ever met. I agree to your terms. And I add a couple of terms of my own.'

'Oh?'

'Yes, I want you to love me no matter what my mood, because I am what I am. I want you always to give me your willing love, and I want you to give me the ten children that I ordered before we were married.'

Millie laughed out loud, and when Len stood and opened his arms, she went willingly into them. He held her close and planted kisses in her hair.

'Oh, my darling, I thought I had lost you. I deserved to, I know. Can you forgive me?'

'I can, of course I can, darling. I love you, and I have news too.'

'News?' This came out of an incredulous laugh. 'Oh, Millie, you really are the most wonderful person – you go from being headstrong to springing surprises in the bat of an eye. Well, what is this news?'

'I think we may be having number one of the ten!'

'What? Oh my God, Millie. Sit down. Oh, what a pig I've been. My darling, my darling. Do you want a stool to put your feet up on? I feel so bad: I've been so horrid to you. Oh, Millie, how can I ever make it up to you?'

'Ha, you can stop fussing, for a start. If I am pregnant – and I do have the initial signs – then I will only be doing the job I was created for. Well, in the beginning, that is, because women have evolved to become much more than baby machines. But I am perfectly healthy, and once I realized why I felt so sick, I jumped out of my bed and got on with it. I'll be fine. I'm so very happy, especially now that we have finally sorted everything out.'

Millie snuggled into Len. The last thing she needed was to sit down and be cosseted. She had to show him that she was strong, and a force to be reckoned with. There were still the finer details of the deal between her and Len to be thrashed out. *And I need to be strong for dear Elsie, too. I have a feeling that she will need me to be.*

Chapter Twenty-Six

Elsie

Elsie sat at her desk. Jim had left the office to her. This was her first day of holding a clinic, as she had called her one-hour-a-day slot as welfare officer. She had an open session, because an appointment-based system hadn't worked. Often the workers' problems were immediate and not something they could wait to talk over. Now they knew they would have a chance to have a private chat, as the coast would be clear.

Jim worked on the factory floor at this time, checking quality and cleanliness, and keeping records of the stock.

It had been comforting to return to work: to hear the familiar sounds of glass tinkling, machines whirling as they pulped the fruit, and the women's chatter. And to smell the jam boiling and see the haze of steam, the hive of activity and, from her high-above-it-all position, the white mob caps, all moving in a particular pattern according to what process of the jam-making their wearers were involved in.

A knock on her door hailed her first customer. 'Morning, Ada, luv. You look peaky, are you unwell?'

'Hello, luv. No, just worn out. I was up at four this morning, feeding me latest and getting me copper on the boil and me step scrubbed – it's me usual routine, but I get more and more weary as time goes on.'

Elsie wasn't surprised. Anyone with Ada's brood and a lazy husband, who was meant to be unwell but had energy enough to keep making Ada pregnant, would be tired – not to mention that she had a full-time job as well.

'Well, I can't do a lot about your tiredness, Ada. But I will try to help if you tell me the particular problem you want to talk about.'

'Housing. Oh, I know it ain't an easy question to solve, but I thought, well, you being placed how you are now, Elsie, you might be able to help. You know where I live on Salisbury Street, and what me place is like.'

Elsie did. Rene used to live there, and Elsie, though poor herself at the time, was always appalled by the conditions she saw when she visited. The tiny cottages were in a bad state of repair and had no proper sanitation, and she couldn't think how Ada managed in a cottage with twelve or so of them – she'd lost count of the actual number of children Ada had, but knew she had a child only weeks old.

She'd wanted to do something about it for a long time, but it hadn't been her place. And even now, in her new position, Jim had cautioned her to wait until someone came to her with a problem, because what she perceived as a problem might not be, to the person living it. Elsie might therefore end up insulting rather than helping.

'I will try, Ada. How much rent can you afford?'

'Well, since the pay rise last year, after we went on strike . . . Oh, Elsie, that was a few days, weren't it? And do yer know, I were better off, as the ladies from the Federation gave me food and clothes – good ones, too. Anyway, I can afford a bit more than I pay now: a couple of bob more, so three shillings a week. How does that sound, eh?'

'That's a good start. I'll have a look around for you. How are all the kids, Ada?'

'They're all right – the usual. One has measles, so the others who haven't had it yet will get that. It's always a long haul when there's any bug going around.'

'I know. If one of us got anything, the others always followed on. I've seen times I was up all night with one or the other of them, and still had to trudge into the factory.'

'That's what's good about working here now, Elsie – oh, not what yer went through as a young girl, but that yer now in a position to help us, and yer understand how it is for us. Nothing makes us lot down there happier than to know yer up here, taking care of our corner for us.'

This gladdened Elsie. She had worried so much about how she would be perceived. She could easily have been labelled a jumped-up cow, as the women called anyone who got above their station in life. 'I will always do me best, Ada. You only have to ask. Millie – sorry, Mrs Lefton – has all of your welfares at heart. We're talking about a lot of changes: maybe a hot meal a day for you all, and something along the lines of taking care of your health – employing a nurse perhaps, that sort of thing. Nothing's settled, but we are looking at making further improvements. A lot depends on our output. If there's profit enough, then everyone will benefit.'

'Ta, Elsie, I'll put the word round. I'll get back to me bench now, as I think Irene wants a word – she's a one, so you watch her. She reminds me of that Ruth. Oh, sorry, luv, she's the last one yer want to be reminded of, after what happened to yer over her death.'

Elsie sighed. 'I'm reminded every day I come into work,

Ada. I see her falling into that boiling vat, and replay the horror of me and Dot being accused of pushing her. I can never get it out of my mind, especially the time we spent in the cells.'

'I know, luv. I shouldn't 'ave mentioned it.'

'No, it's all right. If the circumstances had been different around Ruth's accident, she too would have a plaque near the bench she worked at, like Dot has.'

'Ha, if yer did that, the women would spit at it. Things can be a bit nasty down there at times, especially with Irene showing the same tendencies to cause trouble as Ruth had. But with Peggy as supervisor, she don't get much chance to use her wily ways.' Ada stood. 'I'll leave that with yer then, Elsie, girl. I know yer'll do yer best for me.'

As soon as she left, Irene came in. Elsie knew it was spiteful of Ada, but had to smile at the way she purposely closed the door and didn't hold it open for Irene, leaving Irene to have to knock.

Irene was about the same age as Ruth had been – around twenty-two, with the same brassy appearance – and her cheeks were reddened with rouge and her lips painted bright red.

'How can I help you, Irene?'

'I feel as though everyone picks on me, Miss.'

'Call me Elsie. And tell me what's been happening.' Elsie could feel her nerves jangling – she had no experience of dealing with this sort of thing and was happier with practical problems.

'I can't do nothing right for that Peggy, and because she's top dog, the others take her side.'

This was something Elsie could deal with. She knew Peggy only too well. 'Irene, let me give you a little tip. With the Peggies of this world, those who aren't local to her need to prove themselves. Peggy is what we call a "mother" to us all. She will fight our battles and watch out for us. And will shout down anyone she thinks is making trouble.'

'But I don't make trouble. I just try to be one of them – oh, I know I were chosen from the factory gate, over some who live around here, but that ain't my fault. I feel like Peggy's trying to get me to leave . . . or the sack, or something.'

'She's not vindictive, Irene.'

'Not to you, Elsie.'

Elsie was at a loss. If she tackled Peggy, she might make things worse for Irene. 'You do respect Peggy's position, don't yer, Irene? She is the supervisor, and if she clicks her fingers, everyone has to do as she says. And believe me, Peggy is a good supervisor, and won't ask anything of you that yer not capable of. You should have been here before and worked under the bloke . . . Anyway, believe me, Peggy is a diamond.'

'Everyone says that. But I think Peggy is a tyrant. But I know what you mean, and I do resent her a bit.'

'Well, that'll be it. Try to give her all the respect she deserves and has worked for. Peggy knows every job in the factory, and the best and safest way to do it. If you work hard at everything she sets you, and do it her way – and not yer own – then yer'll find everything is better for you, and you will be accepted. Give that a try, eh?'

Elsie was relieved when Irene said she would. 'You've given me a reason for the trouble I'm in, Elsie. Ta for that. I'll change. I like working here.'

'Good. Get back to work, and I promise I will keep an eye on things. If anything unfair happens, I will tackle it, but you may not think I am.'

Irene left looking a lot happier.

As there was no one waiting to see her now, Elsie went to the window and looked down on the women. She could see Jim working on the pulping machine. They really needed a new one, but Jim managed to keep it going. Millie had promised it would be the first thing she looked at buying in the new year. She needed a year's books first, to prove that she was good to borrow the money.

Elsie wondered how it would all pan out, having Len on the board and able to influence Millie's decisions. The thought of him made her shudder, but she'd made up her mind to sort out that problem and not let Len spoil her life. She'd watch, too, to make sure Millie was all right, and would be there for her, if Millie needed her.

She saw Irene cross the factory floor and head towards Peggy. Her heart jumped into her mouth. If Irene was a troublemaker, as Ada had said she was, would she lie to Peggy about what had been said between them? *But Peggy knows me. She won't believe that I said anything bad about her.* But still Elsie held her breath while Irene was talking to Peggy.

Peggy turned towards Irene and put her arms round her, while the other women looked on in astonishment. For Elsie, it was a wonderful moment of relief, and she felt as if someone had given her a medal for doing a good job. Going back to her desk, Elsie made a note to herself to call into the estate agency in The Blue and ask about properties to rent. *If only I can help Ada, then I really will feel I am doing a worthwhile job.*

With the hour over, Jim came up the stairs. 'Well, the pulp machine is pulping again. I think this is down to the hullers. I've had a word with Peggy. She needs to check that they are hulling and stoning the fruit properly. If a stone gets through, it blocks up the works, and I think that's what's happening.'

'Oh? Well, Peggy'll sort that out. It might mean I'll get a few more complaining about her, though.'

'Has someone complained then?'

She told him about Irene, and the outcome.

'Clever you! I knew you would be good at being a welfare officer. You're just what the women need, and they love and trust you. I've noticed Irene being petulant when asked to do something – she's really got under Peggy's skin. But I haven't seen Peggy being unfair to her, only firm. Anyway, it's nearly lunch. Shall we grab a sandwich together, darling?'

'That sounds a good idea.'

They swivelled round to see the door to the office opening. 'Millie! We weren't expecting you.'

'Len's here too, Elsie. We need to talk to you both. I came up to ask you to dinner at mine tonight.'

Elsie gasped. It was as if someone had struck her.

'Elsie, what is it? Are you unwell?'

Beside her, Elsie felt Jim stiffen. His arm came round her. In his attempt to reassure her, he squeezed her waist tightly with his fingers. The feeling was as if he had tickled her and she burst out laughing. She could feel Jim's astonishment, and could see Millie's. But then Millie laughed with her.

'I don't know what's funny, but I didn't expect that reaction.'

'Oh, don't mind me, mate. I've had a busy morning dealing with the problems of a couple of the workers, one of whom reminded me – not unkindly – of me roots. And then you walk in and ask, "Would you like to come to dinner?"' Elsie mimicked Millie's posh voice.

Millie laughed again, and Elsie could tell it was with relief. She was relieved herself to have thought so quickly on her feet.

'You idiot! Oh, I miss our giggles, Elsie. And it's so nice

to see you back to normal. But if anything ever hurts you that much again, I want you to promise you will reach out to me. I'll always help you.'

'I know you will. You would put all the world right, if you could – and me in particular. But in this instance I had to sort it out meself. It was too private. I'm all right now.' Elsie made herself laugh as she said this.

'Oh? What is it I've heard the women say, when someone like me interferes – an "old biddy".'

'Yes, a nosy old biddy.'

They both giggled, and the horror that Elsie had felt lifted, although she could still feel Jim's anger.

'Well, what about dinner? We have some important changes to discuss.'

'I'm busy, I'm afraid,' Jim said. 'I've promised to give Bert his first music lesson, and to bath him and put him to bed. Then I thought I would read to him . . . You see, he has asked me if I will be his dad. I'm honoured, and I don't want to start by letting him down, with this being my first promise to him.'

'Oh, that's lovely, Jim. No, Bert must come first. Poor boy has had to take a back seat on so many occasions. And his life has been disrupted this last year. I'm so glad you get on so well with him.'

Elsie could see Millie's disappointment, but she didn't try to persuade Jim to do anything other, as she knew how much Bert was looking forward to his evening with Jim. Cess had been really happy about how things had turned out, especially as Jim had told him that, in any matter needing a guardian, Cess was that. Cess was still a bit lost, and it was enough for him to cope with what he had to deal with, without worrying about his young brother.

'What about now, Millie? You said a sandwich sounded like a good idea, and we could all go together.'

Elsie felt Jim stiffen once more, but she had to ignore it. She had to think of Millie's feelings and do all she could to stop her worrying that something was wrong.

'Yes, that's an excellent idea. But not in the local cafe. We need a little privacy. I'll get our driver to take us to that restaurant you and I went to once, Elsie. Peggy can see to things for a couple of hours, unless you have anything pressing at the moment that you have to be back sooner for?'

'No. We're fine. I've things to tell you anyway, Millie, so I hope we get a chance to talk. It's about the hot meal that we said we would think of supplying to the workers, and employing that nurse we talked about.'

'They're just the things we need to talk to you about, Elsie. Shall we go?'

'I'll be with you in a moment. I'll go and see Peggy first.' With this, Jim left Elsie's side and almost ran out of the room.

Elsie picked up her handbag. 'I need to go to the bathroom first, Millie. I'll come out to the car with Jim.'

Millie didn't seem to detect that anything was wrong, and Elsie was glad about this. If Millie did, she would have asked. Elsie smiled to herself as the thought flitted through her mind that the Millies of this world couldn't stop themselves from doing so.

Hurrying after Jim, she saw him head for the bathroom. As she rounded the bottom of the stairs, she called to him, 'Jim! Jim, wait a moment.'

He turned and glanced over to the work benches, but no one was looking at them, then took her arm and led Elsie to the out-of-sight area under the stairs. Looking out as if he was spying, he told her, 'It's all right – Millie's gone. Oh, Elsie, I can't . . . I can't be in Len's company. Not so soon, I can't.'

'You've got to, Jim. What would I say?'

'I don't know.' He half-smiled. 'But judging by what happened upstairs, you're good at it – you'll think of something.'

'I won't, Jim. We have to do this, for Millie. She already suspects something. And the best way is to brass it out. Don't let Len see that anything he has done has affected us.'

'But then he'll think he can do it again . . . I can't bear it, darling. I want to thump him till he begs for mercy.'

'I know yer do. And I love you for it. But do it this way for me, please, Jim. Len will get his warning – don't worry about that. He's being watched. He'll be left in no doubt about what will happen if he comes near me again. And you won't be involved in any way. It has to be this way, Jim: it has to.'

They'd been over and over this. She saw Jim's battle with it. But in the end he nodded.

'Right, I'll just freshen my face quickly. You go and see Peggy, then we'll go out to the car together.'

When Elsie got to the bathroom, she swilled her face in cold water. Then she clung onto the sink, trying to steady herself. The moment was upon her when she had to dig into her courage. She had to get through this.

Creaming her face and applying a little face powder, she licked one of her fingers and ran it along her eyebrows, then did the same to her lashes, dispelling any stray powder that had clung to them. Applying her lipstick wasn't easy, as her hand was shaking, but Elsie managed to smear some on –

again with one of her fingers, as she didn't think she could keep her hand steady enough to use the brush.

Feeling that she looked good – her grey costume with its flared jacket and long skirt, teamed with a white blouse, would take her anywhere – she took her hat off the stand next to the mirror and donned it. 'You'll do,' she told her mirror image. 'You can take anything on, girl.'

That thought dissolved when she saw Len's mocking face looking at her through the car window. Her legs turned to jelly. Jim helped. 'Let me assist you, darling.' Elsie took his hand and eased herself into the car. Luckily Len was sitting in the front with the driver. She couldn't have stood having to sit next to him.

'Hotch up, darling.' To her relief, Jim sounded normal. Once in, he said, 'Good afternoon, Len. I hope you are well? You're being very elusive. I thought we'd have caught up with one another before now.'

Elsie felt so proud of him. She took courage from him and spoke to Len, 'Yes, nice to see you, Len. It's seems a long time since the wedding.'

Len seemed taken aback. He coughed before answering. 'Sorry. I've been very busy since we returned. That's why I suggested dinner tonight, but I gather you will be playing at being a daddy, Jim?'

Jim laughed. 'Comes to us all, in time.'

Len looked back at Millie and winked. For a moment he was the old Len, as his expression held love and tenderness. Elsie caught hold of Millie's hand and squeezed it. With all the tension, she'd forgotten about Millie thinking herself pregnant. But with that memory, her own fear came back to her and she prayed to God to let it not be so.

Chapter Twenty-Seven

Elsie and Millie

When their driver parked in George Yard and they all alighted to walk the short distance into St Michael's Alley, Millie felt more relaxed. The atmosphere was much lighter now, as she walked with Elsie and the two men followed. She could hear them chatting, and nothing seemed amiss.

After a few yards the very old Jamaican Coffee House came into view. It occupied the corner of two alleys and always looked charming to her.

Once inside, they chose a table near the window and ordered coffee and sandwiches.

'You're brave, Elsie. The last time we came here, you wouldn't try the coffee.'

'I know. But I do fancy giving it a go.'

'Well, it has a strong taste, but it has goodness in it – not least warding off sleep, if you're very tired but need to be alert. Millie and I drank lots on our journey from Italy, didn't we, darling?' Len said.

'We did. I can't wait to tell you all about our trip, Elsie. We need a trip out by ourselves. Perhaps if you like the coffee, we'll come here again.'

'Yes, good idea. I like to think of my two favourite girls out together.'

Millie thought she saw Elsie flinch as Len said this, but no, Elsie was smiling. *What is wrong with me? Why am I watching so closely for signs that Len had something to do with Elsie and Jim being as traumatized as they were? It's the past now, and they're here. I have to stop this.*

Deciding to steer the conversation on to more of a business footing, Millie said, 'Well, chit-chat over for now. Len and I have something to share with you. We wanted to tell you first, and then we will tell the women at the factory.' Elsie glanced at Jim. Millie saw a worried look cross Jim's face. 'There's nothing to worry about. Not much will change, but from now on, Len is the sole owner of the factory.'

'What? I mean, we have so much that we were working on, Millie.'

'I know, Elsie, love, but nothing along those lines will change. Len and I have talked about it all.'

'Well, it won't change,' Len said, 'but the timescale by which everything will be implemented will be something I will look at. I can't sanction anything until I am absolutely certain I can fund it without borrowing too much, and that could be quite a while in the future.'

'But you said . . . I, well, I thought the existing plans would go ahead,' Millie replied.

'Darling, your social justices don't always marry up with a sound business plan. I need to evaluate the projection figures Jim gave me, and be certain that I can afford them – what's the use of putting things in place concerning the welfare of the workers, if that means they lose their jobs because I go out of business?'

Millie felt her anger rising. This was totally the opposite to what Len had promised, and she was furious with him. Calming herself, she told Elsie and Jim, 'Your positions are safe, though, and we will rely on you more and more, as I won't be coming back to the factory to work, and Len has his bank to run.'

'Darling, will you please stop this. You have no right to make any statements about what is my business now. You signed the papers earlier, remember? All decisions regarding the staff are mine. However, Jim, it goes without saying that your job is safe and will even be enhanced, because now you will be in full charge of the day-to-day running of the factory. But, like me, I know that you won't want your wife to work, so I am expecting to lose you, Elsie. I am therefore scrapping the welfare officer's role for now.'

Elsie looked at Millie. Millie felt so hurt to see that the look held anger, and felt as if she had betrayed her lovely sister. 'Elsie, I knew nothing of this. Len, you promised me. How could you?'

'If you have anything to say to me, Millie – concerning the business, and how I intend to run it – please do so when we are at home. You are getting far too emotional: a typical woman, eh, Jim? Rules with her heart, not her head.'

'I don't agree actually, Len. I think Millie has done a tremendous job in turning the fortunes of the factory around, and a big part of that has been taking care of the welfare of the staff and improving the conditions they work under. And as for Elsie working, no, I wouldn't like that, but it will be her choice, not mine.'

'Oh, you always were a modernist. You even put forward a motion at school to allow girls to attend. Ha! You were laughed off the debate – which, if I remember correctly, was about modernizing some of the school practices, not changing the whole structure of it.'

'I agree with you there. And you're just the opposite: you don't think women have a place. Anyway, we'll have to agree to disagree. But I would urge you strongly – from a business point of view – to think carefully about reversing some of the measures that we now have in place aimed at caring for the workers. A happy workforce – one that feels it matters – produces more, has less days off sick and, therefore, increases the profit.'

Len was quiet for a moment, but the look on his face told of him trying to control his anger. When he spoke, it was in a measured tone. 'I respect women, and hate them having to work to earn money – especially when they have no need to. They haven't been schooled in running a business, only in running a household and how to keep their husband and children cared for and happy. The women who have to work are not happy, for that reason, and they should be at home, being wives and mothers. My own mother was a very happy woman, and that made for a happy home. Let's ask the women what they think, shall we?' He turned to Millie.

Millie felt intimidated, but wanted to be honest. She knew that, in being so, she would upset Len even more than he already was. 'I think you are right, darling, but where a lot of men go wrong is that, within what you say, they devalue women. Diminish their capabilities – think of them as lesser beings, incapable of doing what men can do. But the only thing a woman lacks is physical strength. Her mental capacity is as good as, and in a lot of cases better than, a man's. Intellectually, we are equals. And a business takes more intellect to run than physical strength. Therefore women are just as capable as men.'

'Ha, I don't stand a chance. I have a modernist as a friend, and a women's-rights activist for a wife. But none of it matters, because ultimately all decisions regarding the jam factory are now mine.'

Millie was already bitterly regretting signing on the dotted line. Why hadn't she taken the time to find out this side of Len's nature before she married him? She knew why: she'd been hopelessly in love with him – in all the horror, he'd seemed like a shining light. He'd given her respect and been a true gentleman, but it felt as if now he was a different person. She turned to Elsie. 'Well, Elsie, do you want to be the little woman at home, having children and looking after Jim? Would you feel fulfilled doing that?'

Elsie surprised them all with her answer. 'No. I'd want to do something to earn money – I will have to, as I am refusing from this moment to take me allowance. When it came from you, Millie, it seemed right. You were sharing with me what our father had left you and, as his daughter too, I had a right to be looked after out of his estate – he owed me that. But you've given away what he built up, and so I no longer have a right to it. It's suddenly become a handout from Len.' She stood. 'And I want nothing from you, Len!'

Millie could only stare. She was mystified at Elsie behaving in this way. But before she could speak, Elsie turned on her. 'Didn't you even think to ask my opinion on what should happen to our father's assets? Well, it's obvious to me that you didn't consider I had any rights all along. I were just part of your do-gooding – taking care of me and Dot eased your conscience. Well, it's over now. And I hope you can live with the consequences of what you've done!'

'Elsie, no! I . . . Elsie, don't go.' Millie felt distraught. She couldn't bear to lose Elsie. As she went to chase after her, she was suddenly frozen to the spot by seeing Jim stand up and lean over Len, grabbing him by the collar.

'You swine. You bloody swine! You raped my wife-to-be – then you strip her, and your own wife, of all they had.' With this, Jim brought his fist back and smashed it into Len's face. Len's body crashed to the ground and his head banged on the tiled floor. He let out a moan and then lay still, his eyes closed, his face unrecognizable, as his nose appeared twisted to one side, and a gaping slit split his cheek.

On a deep, painful gasp, Millie heard herself screaming Len's name. She looked around. Jim was gone – and for a moment the world seemed empty of people. Millie had an overwhelming feeling of being alone and having no one.

But then strong arms held her and dragged her away from Len's side. She heard someone say that he was a doctor, and let him through. She looked this way and that, but recognized no one. In the distance she heard a whistle blow, and within moments was surrounded by police. One was asking, 'Which way did he go?'

In that moment Millie knew that everything would be changed forever.

Elsie couldn't stop running. She could hear Jim calling her name, but she didn't want to talk to him. Her whole world had crashed. Millie had betrayed her. The hateful Len had taken everything: her dignity and self-respect, her sister, her feeling of having a right to what she had – everything!

She felt Jim's hand on her arm, but pulled it away.

'Elsie, please. Elsie, stop, please!' His pull was more forceful this time and brought her to a halt. 'Elsie . . . I – I've killed him!'

The breath she gasped in hurt her lungs. Her head filled with screams.

'Elsie, no, don't . . . Oh God! God, help us.'

His plea dissolved into a surge of blue uniforms and shrill whistles.

Horror gripped Elsie as she saw her darling Jim wrestled to the ground. One of the policemen took hold of her. 'You're all right, mate. We've got him – he can't hurt you now. You're safe now.'

She wanted to tell him that Jim would never hurt her, but the world spun and took her into a swirling darkness.

'Elsie . . . Elsie.'

A voice penetrated the blackness, but Elsie didn't want to leave the peace it gave her.

'Elsie! Elsie, wake up. Open your eyes.'

As she gradually went towards the man's voice calling her name, she had the sensation of being in motion. She opened her eyes. Nothing seemed real or in place. She was on a bed – a moving bed. Bells rang out an urgent sound. The ceiling above her wasn't a proper ceiling, but a shiny yellow that had reflections in it. She turned her head and saw Len lying on a bed next to hers. 'No . . . no. Make him go away!'

'You're all right, love. You're in an ambulance going to hospital. No one's going to hurt you. Calm down now.'

'He will. Don't let him wake up.'

'No, he's not the man who tried to hurt you, luv. He's a victim as well, and a very poorly one.'

Confused, Elsie wanted to put this right. 'No – it was him: he raped me! He . . . he hurt me. Where's Jim? I want my Jim.'

'She's injured more than we thought. Put your foot down, Alf. That bloke must have hurt her, before the bobbies got to her.'

'No!' Elsie tried to sit up.

'Lie still now. Everything's all right.'

'I want Jim. Where's my Jim?'

'You mean the fella who did this? Is he something to do with you then, Miss?'

'He's my fiancé. He didn't hurt me. That man lying there – he . . . he raped me, and took everything I had, and from my . . . my sister! Don't let him near me, please.'

'Oh, right. Well, he ain't going to hurt you no more. He'll be lucky to come out of this alive. That fella of yours cracked his head open.'

'I – I hope he dies. I hate him!'

'Now, now, that's no way to talk. We've reached Barts Hospital now, mate, so you can tell your story to the bobbies. They'll be waiting here, no doubt. And your sister will be here, too. She was distraught. She's following on behind.'

Elsie didn't want to see Millie. It was her doing – all of this could be put down to Millie. She felt the pain of this, as she loved Millie dearly. *But she can't really have thought of me as a true sister. Not equal with her, as she's always saying she did. No real sister would have done what she's done.*

'I just want to go home. Me brovver'll be coming in from school and he'll be wondering what's happening.'

'See what the bobbies have to say, first. Is there someone at home for your brovver?'

She nodded. Cess was going to be in for Bert. But she wanted to be there. She wanted to be with both her brothers, and little Kitty, and Rene – a proper, normal family. Family who didn't do bad things to you, or caused you deliberate hurt by their actions. Her gran's words came to her. Overhearing Gran tell Mum that she had been offered a job in a show that was going to take the West End by storm, Elsie had felt mystified as to why Gran refused the offer and gave up the theatre: 'No good can come from getting above yer station, girl. There's those who'd kick yer back down, and the fall is a harder one than staying where yer are. Better to live amongst yer own folk and work at making their lives better. I do that with me playing, in the local pub. Folk come along and have a singalong. A happy hour to break the drudgery of their lives. Besides, as long as yer can keep warm and have food in yer belly, everything is hunky-dory in yer world.'

How true. Elsie knew that she'd stepped above her station in life, and now the fall was hard, so very hard.

After a nurse had checked her over, Elsie lay, wanting to go to sleep and yet wanting to get up and run and run until she reached home. She'd been told that Millie was waiting to see her, but had begged the nurse not to let her near her. Now she waited – alone and afraid, and desperate to know what was happening to Jim.

'Now then, Miss. The nurse tells me you're able to answer a few questions. I'm PC Higgins. I need to take a statement from you. Tell me your full name and date of birth and then, in your own words, exactly what happened.'

Elsie told him everything. The policeman sat quietly, taking notes, not interrupting her. When she'd finished he said, 'I remember some of that happening. You've had a bad deal of the cards in your young life, Miss. And now history is repeating itself for you. I feel sorry for you. Not even half of what's happened to you should happen to anyone.'

'Is . . . is Len going to die? I want him to, but I'm scared for my Jim. He'd never hurt anyone, but what Len did to me tested Jim beyond what he can stand.'

'I don't know the answers to your questions, Miss. But I think it would be better to hope that the victim lives.'

'He's not the victim, Officer. He's the instigator of everything that's happened.'

'Well, I must say your story does seem to point that way, but I can't pass judgement. In any case, causing someone's death is a very serious crime, Miss. So, like I say, for your fiancé's sake, you'd better start praying that Mr Lefton lives.'

Elsie did pray. She prayed so hard to God, and begged Him to listen to her. *This time, please, God, hear my prayer and make everything come right.*

Chapter Twenty-Eight

Elsie

Elsie held herself together as she sat on her sofa. Tea had been an ordeal. She hadn't been able to eat much of the stew Cess had made, but had tried to keep everything light-hearted for Bert. Mercifully, he'd accepted that something had kept Jim from keeping his promise and it would happen another day. Cess had taken Bert to bed and was reading him a story – in the way that kids have of bouncing back, this was fun compensation to him for missing out on his music lesson.

'I've never known the like, Elsie, girl.' Rene took another drag of her umpteenth fag. For once she seemed at a loss as to how to offer any help, but then who could? She leaned back into the sofa. 'How this can happen to yer, when yer've already been through so much, beggars belief. And poor Jim.'

'I wanted to go and see him, but the policeman told me I wouldn't be able to. I'm only staying strong for Jim. If I break, who's he got to rely on?'

'Yes. Poor bloke'll need yer, Elsie. Keep hanging onto that.'

'I'll go to the police station tomorrow and ask again if I can see him.'

'In the meantime, that bobby were right. We've got to pray that bleedin' Len don't die, even though it would relieve this world – and us – of a festering boil. But honestly, darlin', I wouldn't blame Millie for this. It's that bleeder's fault. He's the cause of all this.'

'But why did she give everything to Len, without considering me? I know it was hers to give, but she always said that I had as much right to it all.'

'But you refused it, remember? You told Millie yourself that you didn't feel you had any right to it . . . Look, luv, think about this. Think how that bastard treated you. Don't you think he's capable of treating Millie the same way?'

Elsie did think about this and, as she did so, it struck her that Rene was right. 'My God! Len blackmailed me into saying that I didn't want me shares, and so he could have done the same to Millie.'

'He bleedin' did what?'

'It was at the wedding – he, well . . . Oh, Rene, I imagined myself in love with Len. It happened the moment I met him. It was as if he consumed me. But I tried to carry on as normal because of Millie: she loved him and I never wanted to hurt her. But then at Ruby's wedding . . .' As the sordid story unfolded of her drinking too much, shame entered Elsie. 'And then at his and Millie's wedding, Len was a different person. Oh, Rene it happened again – I mean, I didn't get drunk, but he waylaid me. Only this time he threatened to tell Millie and make it look as if I seduced him, if I didn't refuse to take up my shares. After that, I had to make up the lie that I hadn't wanted them. But I *did* want them, Rene. They were my right.'

'He's more of a bleeder than I thought. It's like I said: he's more than likely done the same to Millie – made her think she had to give him her factory, and God knows what else. Probably the whole of her fortune.'

'Oh, Rene. Yes, I can see it now. Millie wouldn't have done this willingly. And the most innocent in all of this – me darling Jim – is locked up. I can't bear it all. I just don't know what to do!'

'Nothing for now, love. You can't get to see Jim, and Millie's at the hospital with Len and that's enough for her to cope with. Besides that, she now knows what he did to you.'

'But I'm adding to her hurt. I told Millie that I wanted nothing more to do with her. I have to go to the hospital. I have to.'

'I'd tread carefully, girl. What if, in her mind, you've become the instigator of it all? I'd wait and see, because if Millie doesn't think that of you, then she will come to you when she can.'

A turmoil of emotions bubbled within Elsie. She knew Rene could be right, and yet she so wanted to go to Millie.

Cess came back into the room. He sat beside Elsie and put his arm round her. 'Well, me darlin', I feel like ripping Len's head off. And we thought him such a nice bloke. You know, I reckon he targeted Millie. It's a bit convenient that he holds the accounts for the factory and then turns up as a knight in shining armour when Millie is at her lowest. Don't yer remember, Sis, you told me that he said he'd passed the three of you many a time? Well, I reckon he were just waiting for his moment to pounce. He got that when Millie's father died. And I knew how you felt about him, and so must Len have done. That was a bit of a bonus for him – two for the price of one, so to speak. You were both used by him, Sis. None of this is yours, Millie's or Jim's doing.'

'My God, Cess, you're right, I know you are. Me and Rene have just been saying something along those lines, but now you've hit the nail on the head for me. It all fits: why Len was so charming in the beginning, until he didn't need to be any more. And Jim, too! Perhaps Jim was a part of Len's plan – to have a friend right where he needed one?'

'That's my thinking, too. What we need to do now is go and see a legal bloke. A good one. We've both got a bit of money: we can pool it and get this sorted the proper way. I know you meant well, Rene. But I can't believe you and Jim went along with Rene's plans, Else.'

'It might have worked, Cess,' Rene said. 'What's ruined it is all this blowing up before the blokes that I know got to Len.'

'It was never going to work, Rene. What triggered all this today would still have taken place. You should both have let Jim go to the police, as you tell me he wanted to. And I'm mad that you didn't tell me about it all.'

'I'm sorry, Cess. I wanted to protect you from further pain and, well, I thought you might go mad and do something to Len that would land you in trouble. But now you no longer feel like someone that I have to care for, but it truly feels like you're me big brovver and someone who'll look out for me.'

'I am. I may be younger than you, but everything I've been through has made me into a man, and I'm strong enough to take on the cares of all me family. So no more trying to protect me, Else, luv. Everything that happens in this family is my business, and I can sort it – well, I'll try me best to. This family can't survive on secrets. We have to stick together. We've never been an ordinary family, but we're even more extraordinary now that we have connections to the upper classes. It's never a good mix. Them and us should go our own ways.'

To Elsie, it suddenly felt that Cess, the brother she'd taken care of all her life, was her saviour – her guardian – and that gave her a sense that he would make everything right. She told him all that she'd told Rene. He was shocked that she'd endured such treatment from Len on her own, but understood her motive in doing so.

'It's all misguided, Else. In protecting Millie, you gave Len the freedom he needed to carry out his plan. And in the end you haven't protected her, because she knows everything now, and she's lost everything, too. But, me darlin',' and he squeezed her closer to him, 'I know you had the best intentions for us all. You're not to blame, Sis. I'm just trying to show you that you should never bottle anything up. And no offence, Rene, but you're not the best person for Elsie to turn to. You've given us love and been there for us, and I think the world of you – you're family. But in future you advise her to come to me, or tell her that you will.'

'Yer right, Cess. I've only one way of dealing with things, and I know it ain't the right way. I feel now, though, that this family's got a man at the helm. Oh, I ain't saying we women aren't capable, but it feels good to have a man to head us, and to turn to.'

Cess beamed. Elsie was reminded of when he was a kid, and how he thought himself a man even then. She smiled at him. Suddenly she felt that, with the logic Cess had shown and good common sense, this awful time would – and could – come right.

* * *

307

When Cess pulled the car up outside Millie's house the next day, Elsie saw him visibly shudder. Elsie hadn't thought what an ordeal it would be for him to come back to this house. There was nothing she could say, so she just reached for his hand and squeezed it. He smiled in a way that reassured her.

Barridge let them in, his manner treating them as if they were strangers. 'I will inform Mrs Lefton that you are here.'

They were shown into Millie's sitting room. Millie sat in the winged armchair facing the window. When she turned her head, she looked lost and unsure. Elsie ran to her. 'Oh, Millie, Millie.'

Millie stood and, to Elsie's relief, came into the hug she offered. Her body trembled as Elsie held her.

'I'm sorry, Millie. I'm sorry for all I said, and . . . well, for everything. Forgive me, Millie, luv.'

'I just don't know what to think. I – I feel my world has tumbled apart these last two years. What happened, Elsie? Tell me what has been going on? I'm nearly out of my mind with worry and fear, and I – I feel so lonely.'

'It's all my fault. I tried to protect you, luv, but Cess has made me see that, in doing so, I've made things worse.'

'No, it's none of our faults, Elsie. Though nothing much is clear to me, that is: we have all been duped. Hello, Cess. It's nice to see you, though I'm sorry it's at another bad time for us all. Let's sit down. Do you want tea?'

'Not yet, maybe when we've talked and . . . well, tried to sort this mess out, Millie. And it's nice to see you, too. And yes, I can't believe we're all in such a mess so soon after all we've been through.'

Millie dabbed a tear from her eye as she sat on one of the sofas, then looked up at Elsie as she tapped the place next to her. The gesture meant so much to Elsie. They held hands. Millie's hand felt cold.

'How's Len? Is . . . is he going to be all right?'

'Yes. Oh, Elsie, what a mess everything is. How are we ever going to sort it all out and get back to the way we were? I – I want to know: is it true? Did Len . . .'

Elsie nodded. 'And . . . Oh, this is so difficult, Millie. Everything I say will hurt yer, luv, and that's what I've tried not to do.'

'I know. But it's time for the truth. Always, always tell me anything that may affect either of us, Elsie. I had my doubts about Len, but he charmed me out of them. But now . . . Anyway, tell me what else he's done to you.'

Elsie told it all. She faltered many times, but Millie encouraged her by telling her, 'You cannot hurt me any more than I am, my dear sister. And none of this is your fault.'

'But it is. I should have told you that first time. I'm so sorry, Millie.'

'My mama always said that a whole new world could be built on *should haves* – and what a better world it would be. But none of us can go back. We have to deal with what we have now. We've been through a lot, Elsie – much more than anyone else I know, and that isn't our fault. No *should haves* would have prevented it.'

When the sordid tale was told, Millie sat quiet for a moment, then shook her head. 'What are we going to do? I've signed everything, except this house and my Welsh cottage, over to Len. He has made me a generous allowance, but these things can be reversed at the say-so of the benefactor. I'm very afraid for the future.'

'Did he blackmail you, too?'

Millie nodded and went on to tell them about the

309

emotional manipulation Len had put her through. 'And I haven't a leg to stand on, as I would be judged to be of sound mind when I handed everything over. And I no longer have any control over it – unlike Len, who has full control over all the income that we have, and can do whatever he wants with it . . . Oh, how could I have been so taken in? I didn't even seek advice. When my new solicitor tried to caution me, Len shot him down. He even said he would be moving his business back to our old solicitor.'

'Anyone would have done the same as you did, Millie, in the same circumstances, even without the added pressure you were put under. I would have done anything for my Dot. That's what love does to you. But with someone as clever as Len, who I believe targeted you, then you don't stand a chance.'

'Targeted? I don't understand. Do you mean Len deliberately set out to woo me, just to get everything I own? My God, he could've done, couldn't he?'

Cess nodded. 'And I reckon he did the same to Jim too. To me, all of it was a part of Len's plan.'

Millie looked shocked. 'You're right! I feel in my bones that you are. It all fits . . . But how could Len have known that my father would die, and the circumstances I would find myself in?'

'Well, think about it, mate. He knew your father, and probably everything about him – including that he had a weak heart. He also knew that the jam factory was in a bit of a state financially – perfect pickings. As general manager of his father's bank, Len had access to everything. If I'm right, then he only had to await his opportunity, and it came the evening Elsie told me about, when them kids threw stones and made your horse rear up. Len knew that if he made you fall for him, he'd only have to bide his time. When that time came, he made sure he got his own man in – unsuspecting Jim – and the rest is history. I tell you, mate, you and Elsie were duped. I honestly believe that Len Lefton is the biggest conman I've ever come across, and I've met a few on the market stalls.'

A tear plopped onto Millie's cheek. 'I've been such a fool. Like I said, I did have suspicions – something Jim told me that Len had planned with him, when they went for a drink one evening. I had a gut feeling, but I ignored it.'

'Well, we can all do the right thing in hindsight. It's what we do now that matters.'

'But I don't know what to do, Cess.'

'Tell me, this solicitor you were talking about: is he any good?'

'He's excellent. I rang him first thing this morning and told him what had happened, and he went into business mode straight away, telling me that he would go to the factory and see what he could do. I told him the night-watchman would be there and would have let the women in, and how capable Peggy is. He proposed telling her there had been an accident, that you and I were all right, Elsie, and that is all he can say for now. Then he would make sure Peggy felt capable of keeping the production line going for today. He said he would take his office clerk over there with him, to answer the phone and take messages. But I'll have to go in tomorrow, even though I'm dreading it.'

'Well, I think we should take everything – and I mean everything – we know, and what we can surmise, to a good legal bloke. We can start with your solicitor and see what he thinks. He might put us onto to someone else or tackle it himself. There might be ways out of this. And we need a lawyer who'll take on Jim's case. He shouldn't be stuck in prison!'

'Oh, Elsie. In all of this I forgot Jim for a moment. Have you seen him? Can we go to see him now?'

'We're going after this. And yes, you can come. It might give us a bit of weight with our plea to see him, if you're with us.'

'Hmm, maybe we'd better go to my solicitor first and have a chat with him. These things are usually better handled by a lawyer, as Cess said. And yes, I think my solicitor will be able to recommend one to us. Though I might have the address in my bureau of the solicitor Mama contacted when you and Dot needed help, Elsie.'

Millie crossed the room to her bureau. Elsie was surprised to see it back where it used to be, but guessed that Len had probably ousted Millie from the office she'd made her own.

'Ah, here it is. Oh, he has his premises just over the river in Tower Bridge Road. Still, it can take a while to get there, so we'd better get a move on. I'm expecting my mama and Harold soon. They are on their way and will arrive around four-ish.'

'Do they know everything, Millie?'

'No. I didn't want to tell them on the phone, though it wasn't easy, as Harold was demanding to know what had happened to his son. But I said there was too much to explain and then made out that the phone line had gone dead. It's always doing that anyway. It kept ringing after that, but I ignored it, hoping they would think they couldn't get through. Now I'm dreading telling him. But let's concentrate on trying to see Jim, and sorting some of the mess out, first.'

Millie always surprised Elsie. She was what was termed a

tough nut, even though she hadn't been brought up that way – though she'd once said that she'd had a rough time in boarding school because she wasn't of the same class as the other girls, who were mainly from upper-class families. This had shocked Elsie at the time, as she'd imagined that anyone with a lot of money was upper-class. But Millie had explained that she was from what was called 'new money' – born to a man who was self-made, in the riches stakes. And this made her unacceptable to those of 'old money'. It was all a bit complicated for Elsie, but she could relate to those higher up the scale than you bullying you, as she'd experienced it many a time.

The lawyer's office was on the second floor of an imposing building of four storeys. When they got out of the car, Elsie looked along to Tower Bridge at the end of the road – to her, the tunnel going underneath it resembled a dark, gaping hole. She hadn't been this way often, but remembered herself and Dot, when they were about ten years old, going missing for the whole day, and it was here that they'd come to. They'd sat on the pavement not far from where she was now, and a gentleman had thrown them a penny. And then another had, until they had almost a shilling in pennies and ha'pennies. They'd gone home feeling like princesses – they were rich! Mum had bought pie and mash for them all, and Gran had played the piano. It'd been a wonderful evening, but although they'd prospered, she and Dot had been banned from doing such a thing again and had been told that the bogeyman would get them, if they strayed that far from home again. The memory made her see the pity of their lives, when something like being seen as beggars was a highlight in her memory.

'That was a big sigh, Elsie. Don't worry, dear. We're starting our fight back, and we'll win, you'll see. We'll soon have Jim out of that cell – after all, he didn't murder anyone, as the police thought he might have. And with the victim's own wife fighting on his side, then he'll stand every chance, as I will give a testimony at his trial, no matter what Len threatens me with.'

Millie had linked arms with Elsie. Elsie couldn't speak – that Millie should be on her side, after hearing everything that had happened with Len, was something she thanked God for. She thanked Him, too, for sending this wonderful sister to her side. Without her, she didn't think she would have got through all that she'd faced – and still had to face.

Chapter Twenty-Nine

Elsie

Elsie was shocked but pleased at how swiftly Mr Hepplethwaite, the lawyer, had been able to secure Jim's release. No sooner had they given him the facts than he'd made a telephone call, and he told them to go along to see Jim as they'd planned and leave everything with him.

He'd been surprised to see Elsie seeking his help again. A caring man, he told her he'd never got over all that had happened to her previously; and he had asked after Dot, showing great sadness at hearing of her passing. He'd shaken Cess by the hand and told him, 'I'm so sorry for your loss, but you should be proud of yourself for giving Dot some happiness towards the end of her life because, from what I saw of it, she hadn't had a lot before then.'

This had pleased Cess and helped Elsie cope with the memories that had been evoked of that awful time, when she and Dot had been imprisoned, suspected of causing the death of Ruth, their fellow jam factory worker.

By the time they'd arrived at the police station, they were told that Jim had been released on bail. Elsie wondered at how swiftly things could happen when you have enough money to pay for the best of everything, and she couldn't thank Millie enough as they stood waiting by the station front desk. When at last the door to the side opened and Jim walked through, his haggard appearance hurt Elsie.

'Oh, Jim, Jim. Thank God, luv.' Jim tried to smile but his lips quivered. Elsie ran to him. 'It's all right, now, Jim, luv.'

'There's still the trial, Elsie.'

'I know, luv, but Mr Hepplethwaite will see to everything.'

'He's a good man, but I'm not so sure.'

'He is, Jim. He told us that if you go to trial, he feels confident that he could secure you a probation order instead of a prison sentence. He thinks you'll have to work with a probation officer for a minimum of three months, to address the way you handled the situation with violence, instead of reporting it to the police and leaving it to the law to deal with.'

Jim didn't say anything to this, but Elsie thought he looked relieved as he went through the motions of collecting his belongings and signing for them.

Elsie clung to his hand as he sat between her and Millie in the back of the car, while Cess sat in the front seat next to Harry, Millie's driver.

When they reached Elsie's home, Rene was standing on the step of her shop. She greeted them all, before taking Elsie into her arms. 'Elsie, I'm so glad you got Jim out, girl. Are yer all right?'

'I am.'

'And you and Millie are together. I'm glad.'

'Yes, we're as if nothing has happened, but we've a lot

to sort out. I'll see you in a bit, Rene, unless you're able to come up?'

'I'll leave yer to it, darlin'. You can tell me all later on.'

Once in Elsie's flat, Cess, who'd skipped up the stairs first, had already put the kettle on, and Millie was helping him gather everything for making the tea. Elsie knew they were giving her and Jim a little time.

Jim stood looking out of the window.

'Jim? Jim, me darlin', everything's going to be all right, I promise.'

He turned. For a moment he just looked into her eyes, but then he opened his arms.

Elsie went into them. 'Oh, Jim, we'll get through this, we will.'

'That lawyer – when you said that he said "learn to deal with situations without using violence", it made me feel so ashamed, Elsie. It made me realize that I had done wrong. No matter what, you shouldn't hit out like that.'

'But it was my doing, Jim. Not yours. I was so wrong to try and keep everything from Millie. She is in a terrible predicament because I did that. Now the lawyer is saying that, although he will try, he doesn't think he can get her everything back. And she is stuck in a marriage that will give her God knows what pain – and she thinks she is pregnant, too . . . I've been such a fool, Jim.'

Jim, she could see, was helped by having to help her. He regained the strength that she was used to him having. 'Darling, you only did what you thought was right, and we all backed you. It was a situation that anyone would find difficult to handle.' He held her tighter. 'We all played a part and took wrong decisions. I was such a fool. Even though I thought I knew Len, and had told you lately what he was like where money and power were concerned, I didn't realize how ruthless he could be. To do that to you, and then to take everything from his own wife – why did she consent to it? Millie always seems so strong.'

'She is, but love can do funny things to you. And when you see another side to the one you love, and he is blackmailing you by saying he will stop loving you, then any one of us would give in.'

'You're not making sense, darling.'

She'd tried not to tell him all that Millie had gone through, but she could see that she would have to, for Jim to forgive Millie. 'He raped Millie too.'

'Oh God!'

'Well, it was a sort of rape. It broke her heart, and afterwards Len blamed her, saying he felt like a kept man.'

'That . . . I just don't have words to describe him.'

'There's more, darling. He's worse than all the names he can be called – and Rene's called him some choice ones.' Elsie told him Cess's theory.

'I think Cess is right: it all makes sense. And my part in it all, too! I hadn't heard from Len after I wrote to him, about a year previously, asking him if he knew of any positions in London that I might apply for. Then suddenly, out of the blue, he contacted me and told me he thought there might be something coming up very soon. Within a week he told me to pack a bag and get down to London and find myself a flat. I was a bit put out that he didn't ask me to stay with him at his father's house while I did so, but he said something about not getting on too well with his father at that time, and there being a bit of an atmosphere. But it's more likely that he didn't want his father to find out what he was planning! I gather his father can read him well.'

'All we can do now is try to put everything right – our part will be to support Millie during that. Are you up to going back to work tomorrow? I'm willing to.'

'Yes, we have to do that for Millie, and for the workers. But what shall we tell them?'

'Nothing for now, I shouldn't think. I wasn't due in till tomorrow anyway, so they won't surmise anything about me. But, well . . .' She told him the arrangements Millie's solicitor had put into place.

'Hmm, that makes it awkward. Something had to be done, of course, but the speculation will be rife.'

'Well, they're bound to find out one day. But until it's all sorted, it would be fatal to tell them now.'

'I'll think of something.'

Millie's voice called, 'All right if we come in?' This stopped any further speculation on how to handle the situation.

'Yes, mate, I've brought Jim up to date, and now we could do with your help. You see we've both decided to go back into work tomorrow. You've so much to sort out, Millie.'

'I have. And I can't stay here long. I have to get back to face Len's father with the truth about his son. As for my marriage, I just don't know. I can't face Len at the moment. Or make any decisions. I need the help of my mama.'

For the first time since they'd been in Millie's sitting room earlier, Elsie saw a crack in Millie's strength. She hurried over to her and took the tray of cups and saucers from her and put it on the table, then took Millie in her arms. 'We'll all be here for you, Millie. We'll help you all we can.'

Millie came out of her arms, 'I know you will. Thanks,

Elsie, but you and Jim have a lot to face. I'll be all right. Mama will help me – though she may advise staying in my marriage, and that isn't going to happen. I can't, Elsie. I never want Len back in my home. Oh, Elsie, that's all I have left: my house! How I am going to manage to pay for its upkeep, or for anything, until I sell it? Len won't give me an allowance if I kick him out.'

Jim stepped forward and put his arm round Millie. 'I'll help. I do have a little money, and I would advise taking whatever you have out of Len's bank now, before he can do anything to stop you and can transfer it to an individual bank. Then you can borrow money if you need it, putting your house up for collateral.'

Millie cheered up. She looked from one to the other. Elsie could see a little hope entering her and told her, 'I can help a little too, Millie. I've saved quite a bit out of me allowance.'

'And me,' Cess said. 'Though I have committed to a couple of things – a business interest with Dai. But looking for a house can go on hold, can't it, Else?'

'It can, Cess, there's plenty of room here.'

'I don't know what to say. You are all so kind. But don't forget there will be lawyer's fees, Jim. I can't take your money – you'll need some for that. But can I do all of that with the bank?'

'Yes. Of course. And I would suggest you do it now: get what money you have of your own out of Len's bank, as you'll never get a loan from him. Then, as you're right about my money being tied up, let Elsie and Cess loan you some in the interim while you put your house up for sale. Once it is, if you need more, then you will have a good case to put to your new bank, as they will see that they will get their investment back in the short term. They may charge a high interest, but you will come out in a very nice position if you buy – or rent something cheaper to live in. I know, because I have done it. Though most of what I made from my inheritance had to go towards the debts of my father's estate.'

'Oh, Jim, you've given me hope. Will you come with me to do this?'

'I will. We'll go this minute. Is that all right with you, Elsie darling?'

'It is. You get off. But will you come back here afterwards, Jim? I'll cook tea for you.'

Jim kissed her on the cheek. 'I will, my darling – we have a lot to talk about.'

When they had gone, Elsie sat down. She couldn't believe how everything could change in such a short time. Look at Millie – a rich young woman one minute, and looking at a very different life the next.

Guilt entered Elsie as she thought of how far Millie was going to tumble. In some way she felt it was her fault that Millie had suffered so much since the day they met Len by chance in St George's gardens.

'Sis, I can almost hear your thoughts, mate. None of this is your doing, and don't go taking it all on as if it is. You're the least deserving of all that happens to you. But there's hope for the future: for all of us. I haven't just been looking for a house to live in, I've been looking at stalls – the best market locations, visiting warehouses, looking at stock – and at buying a van. And I tell yer, mate, I'm excited about it all.'

'It sounds good, Cess. I always knew you'd make something of yourself. What about Dai? You mentioned him earlier – will he come down soon?'

'Yes, I've heard from him, and he thinks he's got a buyer for his guest house and will be ready to come down in about a month. He's been buying stock bit by bit, too. He's got an eye for a bargain, and wants to run the antiques side of the business on Petticoat Lane. I'm going into fabrics and household items. And I've taken a stall right outside here, where the other stalls are – Rene's going to be me first customer, as I've told her I've bought some batches of silk from an Indian wholesaler. You should see them, Else: the colours. Lovely, they are.'

'I hadn't dreamed you were up to all that, Cess. What me and Jim'll do, I don't know. We have to keep the jam factory going for now – not for Len's sake, but for the workers, and just in case there's a chance that Millie can get it back. After that, I don't know.'

'Who'll pay yer wages for doing that?'

'Well, I don't think anything has changed. Len didn't have time to change it – other than perhaps put the assets of the business into another account. He had expected Jim to carry on at that time, and me too, until me and Jim married, so he would have left the arrangements as they are, for paying our wages and the workers' wages.'

'So, what is that arrangement?'

'Every Monday, Jim submits to the accountant the hours put in by each worker the week before – ourselves included – and the accountant draws the money from the bank, then makes up the wages and brings them to us, to distribute on a Friday.'

'Well then, make sure Jim puts extra hours in for himself and gets plenty out of it, till the day Len is able to get back to running things. It strikes me that Jim'll have good grounds to stand on. If I was him – and I'll advise him of this – I'd use the fact that Len needs him. Len knows nothing about running a jam factory. And besides, he has a bank to run. What's he going to do without Jim? And where will he find another Jim? It might not suit Jim working for Len, but we've all got to work somewhere – so it's time to use a little blackmail on Len: he drops the charges or Jim walks out.'

Elsie felt a little hope come into her. She didn't want Jim to still have to be associated with Len, but what else was there for him? How would they survive?

'And another thing: if I were Jim, I'd be telling Len that if he goes to trial, Len's evil actions will all come out and the papers will love it, so his name will be mud – and that won't do his business any good.'

'Oh, Cess. There is hope, ain't there?'

'There is, mate. Come here, let's give you a hug.' Cecil sat down beside Elsie and hugged her to him. 'You'll marry Jim, mate. And you'll have a dozen kids and will be a smashing mum – you had plenty of practice. Where would our family have been without yer, eh? You were mum and dad to us. Mind, I'm not blaming our mum, but lovely as she was, the lifestyle she chose didn't do us any favours, did it?'

'No, it didn't. But no matter what I did, I didn't save little Jimmy, did I? I do miss him, Cess.'

'I know. He were a lovely kid. And it weren't anything you did or didn't do. Our Jimmy just weren't for this world, Else . . . Life's cruel at times.'

They were quiet. Elsie sat with Cess's arm around her, and her head on his shoulder. She knew that, like her, he was thinking of Jimmy, Dot and their mum and gran. All loved, and all missed so much.

A shout from Rene broke into their thoughts. 'Gertie's here with our lovely bundle of trouble . . . Oh, she's got two of them: double-trouble!'

Bert came up the stairs, laughing his head off, ahead of a smiling Gertie, who told them, 'I found this stray little boy, Duckie. He was trundling along – his socks at half-mast, as usual.'

Elsie and Cess rose off the sofa together, just as Bert threw himself at Elsie and knocked her back down again.

'You monkey, you don't know your own strength!'

'Well, I am six next week, Else. So I've got to get bigger.'

'Six! Where's the time going, eh? We better sort out a celebration for a very good and brave boy. How about I make some jellies, for you, buggerlugs?' Elsie suggested.

'And I could bake a cake – well, if I could come round here to do it, I could,' Gertie suggested. 'Oh, I'll be glad when you've found somewhere, Cess. I'm so stifled in that guest house.'

'Well, that may all change, Gertie . . .'

'Yes, we'd like to ask you to move in here, from tomorrow. We've not done up the bedroom at the top of the flat yet, but we soon can. In the meantime Cess can sleep on the sofa, I can move into his bed and you can have mine.'

Cess looked at Elsie in astonishment, then his face broke into a smile. 'Yes, and do you know, it's big enough up there to make it into a kind of nursery – well, we could get a cot up there, and a nice comfy chair for you, Gertie, and all that Kitty needs. Only we may not get a house just yet. I have to tie up me money in other things for a short while.'

'Oh? Well, whatever you have to do, me duck, you have to do, and it sounds wonderful to be with you all. But I won't put you all out like that. I'm all right at the guest house – well, at least until you can get my room ready. Ooh, it's going to be marvellous!' As she said this last, Gertie hugged Kitty to her and tickled her tummy with her head. Kitty giggled with delight, and Elsie felt the mood lift – whatever happened to them, they were a family, and that's all that counted in the end.

Chapter Thirty

Millie

Millie finished telling Harold and her mama the sordid tale of how Len ended up in hospital – well, the immediate cause at least; she'd yet to tell them about what she had gone through, or about being blackmailed into signing everything over to Len. She sat with her mama in her sitting room, although as soon as Mama entered it, it seemed to belong to her again. Harold paced up and down. For the first time since getting to know him, she saw a stern look on his face.

'And what does my son say about all of this?'

'I haven't asked him. He wasn't conscious for most of the time I was there, and not up to being questioned, but I have spoken to Elsie.'

'And no doubt taken her word against that which your own husband hasn't yet voiced?'

'I don't have to. I do believe her, as so much has happened that gives truth to Elsie's ordeal. In any case, why should she lie about such a dreadful thing? She knows now that if she had told me about Len's treatment of her in the very beginning, I wouldn't find myself in the plight I am today, as I wouldn't have married him.'

'Oh? And what plight is that? You make my son out to be a monster!'

'He is.' Losing control, Millie let everything come out: the rape of her, the blackmail. 'And now Len has everything . . . everything. I only have this house, of all that my father left me. I hate Len! He did all of this deliberately.'

'Hold on now. That's a massive accusation, and I want to hear his side of things, too. Is he well enough to come home?'

'I don't know, but if he is, he isn't coming to this home.'

'Millie, darling!'

'No, Mama, you cannot persuade me otherwise.'

'But maybe it can all be sorted. You're Len's wife now, for better or worse. I admit you are having the "worse" bit at the moment, but I'm sure we can sort it all out.'

'Yes. Well, I have to admit that my son has behaved abominably, but I can straighten him out. I can get Len to change his ownership of everything and give you equal shares. I have a very lucrative proposition for him, and that will change everything. Once Len feels that he truly is the man of this household, you will see a different husband. You loved him once, so surely you can find forgiveness for him and love him again?'

'But he raped my sister! What kind of a man does that? And all for greed. Elsie had a right to the shares that we agreed she should have, but Len didn't think so. He will never give Elsie her rightful place.'

'Millie, Millie, that's where your downfall lies: with that so-called-sister of yours – not with Len. You putting Elsie before Len has driven him to do all that he has done. It would drive any man to do what he has done.'

'Harold, what are you saying?' Mama rose. 'I am appalled

to hear that you hold such views. It's like listening to my late husband all over again. I – I can't take that. I can't go through what Richard put me through again, and now I know that, by agreeing with you, I am condemning my daughter to such a life. Please leave. Millicent and I will fight Len in the courts. He has extorted my daughter's fortune from her, and you are condoning his actions!'

'No, Abigail, please don't take that stance. I am nothing like Richard. You know I'm not. But faced with what we are, I am trying to help Millie see that she is looking at this all wrong.'

'All wrong? So it's not your son who has done wrong? No? You should be angry with Len. You should be taking Millicent's side, and changing your mind about gifting the bank Len runs to him, and giving him a chance to eventually buy out the partnership in Harlington & Lefton's Bank.'

'But he's my only son!'

'And Millicent is my only daughter. And you . . . you are not listening to her. You are treating her like any other man would – as if she had no rights – and I cannot believe that of you. I thought you were different.'

'Abigail. Wouldn't you do the same, if the boot was on the other foot?'

'No, not now I have thought about it. At first, I admit, I thought something could be salvaged from this, but I find myself appalled by it all. And if the boot was on the other foot, I'd be ashamed of my daughter. I wouldn't expect anyone she'd hurt, as your Len has hurt Millie, to toe the line and accept her behaviour – just the opposite. I would help them out of the crisis they are in, and let my daughter stew in the mess she had created.'

Harold sat down. He looked defeated. Millie had wanted

to stop their fight, but had chosen not to. Her mama was right, and Millie was glad to hear her standing up for her, and for herself. For a moment she hadn't thought she would.

Harold leaned forward and shook his head. 'I'm sorry. I didn't mean to come across like that. I do want to help you, Millie. Maybe I was misguided in the way I thought to sort all of this mess out.' He looked at Mama. 'Abigail, I *am* appalled by my son's behaviour. I have long worried about him . . . It's as if he isn't my son. As if he is a stranger to me, and always has been. I think he takes after his Italian family – they appear to be the most charming lot, but they are all gangsters. They make their money by extorting people, using any means possible to get their way. My dear Maria fled to Britain. Oh, it was with their blessing, as she convinced them that if she could study English, then they could start their racket here – not that she had any intention of that and, once she married me, they let her off the hook, happy that she had married well. But, you see, I have always known how much Len admires his Italian grandfather and uncles.'

Mama went to him. 'So you will now help Millie, and stop blaming her?'

'I will. Though I don't know what to do. At the end of the day, Len is my son. If I sell my business share to anyone else, it will break him. And then he could be pushed right off the edge and into a life of crime – and he has never, ever done anything underhand or dishonest at the bank. So my proposal may be the making of him. As I said, he will be what he wants to be then: a rich man in his own right.'

'Maybe if he is, he will give you back what is yours, darling?'

'Oh, Mama, Len is much more complex than that. I'm sorry, Harold, I know you are trying to salvage something, but what I have experienced tells me that Len won't reverse his decision to take everything that was mine. I will pursue my claim of being duped. My lawyer feels that I have a case, but he needs some concrete evidence. I am not holding out a lot of hope. Jim, Cess and Elsie have all offered me financial help, and I am going to put this house up for sale. I can do nothing else, as I know Len won't keep his promise of making me a generous allowance, once I tell him I want to divorce him.'

'Oh, my dear.' Mama came back to her and sat beside her, taking her hand. 'That this should happen to you – and so soon after your lovely wedding. I will help you all I can, but you know that your father didn't leave me much more than enough to run my household and maintain the house.'

'If you'll still have me, Abigail, I will take care of you. You will never want for anything. Have I gone too far down in your estimation?'

'No, Harold, dear. You were just being a misguided but protective father, and I understand what was motivating you. Of course I will still marry you.'

'Millie, I don't know how your father got away with anything – your mama can be a little tartar, if crossed.'

'That's because I intend to start as I mean to go on. I've "been through t'mill", as Ruby and her mother – well, most folk in the North – would say.'

Millie laughed at them, glad to see they weren't still at odds with each other. 'I miss Ruby so much. How is she?'

'Oh, Millie, with all this going on, my dear, I completely forgot. There's wonderful news. Ruby is having a baby!'

Millie gasped, and a painful reminder of what was adding to her troubles stabbed at her. She recovered quickly. 'But that's wonderful! I'll write a letter for you to take up to her.'

'Oh dear, my memory. Ruby has sent a letter to you. It's in my valise. I'll bring it down to dinner.'

'My dear, I would like to go to the hospital to see Len now. Will you come with me?'

'No, Harold. It would be like condoning his actions. I am very cross with him. And I hope and expect you to have a word with him, and to try and get Millie's heritage back for her. It's the least Len can do, to try and make amends.'

Harold didn't say anything to this. Millie knew that he didn't hold out a hope of doing so. He did turn to Elsie and ask, 'Can I give Len no hope of coming back here and making amends, my dear?'

'No. None at all. I never want to see him again, Harold.'

'He will have to go back to your Knightsbridge home, Harold. I don't want to see him, either.'

'Oh, Abigail, don't say that. He's my son.'

'I know. And I feel for you, but if I am even in his company, I will feel that I am saying it was all right for Len to do what he did to my daughter, and to dear Elsie.'

Harold left the room. Millie felt sorry for him. He looked as though the world weighed down upon him.

'How is Elsie, darling? And Jim? Poor man, facing a trial for doing something that a few years ago would have been considered the honourable thing to do. Will he still marry Elsie?'

'Yes. Jim's a tower of strength. If he suffers over what happened to Elsie, he keeps it hidden. Whether he does so from Elsie, when they are alone, I don't know. But, Mama, I have something else to tell you. I – I think I might be having a baby.'

'Oh, my dear. My poor darling.' A tear plopped on Mama's

cheek. 'I should be overjoyed, ready to welcome my first grandchild, but instead I feel so sad. I see history repeating itself, and I don't want you to go through what I went through.'

'I won't, Mama. I'll be fine. I have you and my sister, and Jim and Cess. I've never had so many friends in all my life, and they are good friends, Mama. They'll stick by me, no matter what.'

'But, darling, you'll have to go back to Len now. You cannot possibly manage with a child on your own.'

'I'm not on my own. I know the concept of friends isn't an easy one to grasp, but they are a wonderful asset in my life, Mama.'

'I know. I do have friends in Leeds, darling: proper friends and confidants. Life up there is not like down here in London. Everyone isn't just a social climber, clambering over others to get to the top of the pile. They are real people – caring people. Some I have known all my life, but your father wanted to leave them behind and never encouraged me to entertain them. We have a card school – it's such fun – and we do a lot of charity work together. I love that. Anyway, I wouldn't be without them now, so I understand how you feel. Only, for the child's sake, you have to take Len back. You can't let your child suffer because of its father's actions.'

Millie knew only too well how a child could suffer through its father's actions – hadn't she done exactly that? Wouldn't she have been happier with just her mama bringing her up? But for all that, she knew the stigma and shame of a broken marriage, and of a mother bringing up a child on her own because she'd left her husband. She didn't want that for her child, but what was the alternative?

'Don't cry, Mama. Something will sort itself out.'

'But where will you live? Would you consider coming home to Leeds? How can you support yourself and your child?'

'I – I don't know yet, Mama. I've had a good education, so maybe I could become a governess.'

'With a child in tow? That will be impossible.'

'I have Elsie, don't forget. She will help me.'

'You mean you expect Elsie to take your child in?'

'Only to look after it while I am at work.'

'Millicent, you're not thinking straight. How can Elsie do that? How will she and Jim live? Len isn't going to want them around him, is he? I mean, Len obviously won't run the factory in the sense that he'll be there physically, like your father was, but he will be in charge of all decisions and will have to work with whoever manages it. He won't want that to be Jim, and he won't want Elsie anywhere near him – let alone give Elsie the allowance that you did.'

Suddenly it all seemed so hopeless. By not having Len back, Millie was condemning her child to a life of poverty – and Elsie and Jim, too. Yes, she could save herself and her child by going back north with her mama, but that would still leave those dearest to her struggling to cope.

It was all too much. Leaning on her mama's shoulder, Millie sobbed her heart out.

When Harold came back from his visit, he was jubilant.

Millie had been for a lie-down and, although she hadn't slept, she had come to a conclusion about her future. She'd gained a kind of acceptance that, yes, she had married for better or for worse, so she must carry on. She'd tried hard to concentrate on Len's good points, and found that he had many. He could be very charming, he had a sense of humour, and he was a gentle lover, when he wasn't angry with her.

She hated herself for having given in to Len and for leaving so many people vulnerable. She felt pulled two ways, too. She knew that Elsie would beg her not to go back to Len, no matter what the consequences. And she knew, too, that her life with Len would never entwine with her life with Elsie, and she would have to keep the both separate forever. That would pose many difficulties. Somehow she'd have to overcome them.

'Millie, let us talk while your mama is resting, dear. I have had a good chat with Len. Everything wasn't how you believe. He cannot understand how you could think it was.'

Millie sighed. 'What part of it all does Len say isn't as I think?'

'Him extorting your estate from you – planning to do so – and, most of all, his supposed rape of Elsie.'

'So he hasn't behaved badly at all then? What about the way he treated me?'

Harold looked embarrassed. 'Len said . . . well, he explained that he felt dirty after what Elsie had done, and feeling that you were holding the purse strings made him act as he did. He wanted to be with you, and yet he wanted to punish himself and Elsie. He didn't tell me the details, but he wanted me to ask you to think about that afternoon – he said, do you think he could have done all that you did together if he'd already satisfied himself with another woman?'

Millie felt her colour rise. She looked away. Whether Len could perform the sexual act three times in such a short space of time or not, she didn't know. She had known him take her twice, straight after one another, and then again a couple or so hours later, so yes, maybe he could.

'Millie, try to give him the benefit of the doubt, dear. He's your husband. You're supposed to trust him. Anyway, I told Len my intentions and he was ecstatic. He actually hugged me – he's never done that before. I've felt nothing but resentment from him.'

Harold was smiling, but Millie felt sick. This was typical of what she'd learned of Len's nature. He could make you feel so rejected and then, once you gave him what he wanted, make you feel so good, so loved.

'I take it that you gifted him the bank that he now runs?'

'Yes, and I told him he would almost have enough capital in it to buy my shares. He just needs to either borrow funds or work towards getting them together and he could own a half-share in the biggest bank in England – a very lucrative business that will make him rich beyond his dreams. I also gave him my home in Knightsbridge: it's all a sort of legacy while I am alive and I can see him make good of it all. He will one day come into my estate in Kent, but for now I love it there and hope your mama and I can divide our time between there and her home in Leeds.'

'Will my mama's assets become yours when you marry, Harold?'

'Oh yes, without question. We're old-fashioned, and like the old-fashioned ways.'

This put a deep fear in Millie. The only inheritance that she had left in the world would eventually go to Len. 'And what about the assets that Len forced me into handing over to him – did he mention anything about giving them back to me?'

'No. Well, yes, he did. I wasn't going to discuss this with you, but Len says that if he does, then you won't have to stay with him and he couldn't bear that. He loves you with all his heart, Millie. Please reconsider your position, my dear. Len can be very ruthless and you will be left penniless.'

Millie felt so unsure on what to do. She felt her mind wavering yet again. But clarity came to her and with it a new strength as she answered Howard with a challenge. 'And you think that is right? You admire that in your son? You have deceived my mama and are just as bad as Len. Well, I won't let either of you win.' With this, Millie turned and ran up the stairs, and didn't stop running until she reached her mama's room. Knocking on the door, she opened it without waiting to be told to enter. 'Mama, you must listen to me.'

Her mama shot to a sitting position, removing her eye mask as she did so. 'Darling! What is it?'

'They'll take everything – all that you own, which should one day be mine, will end up being Len's, even if I am not married to him when you die.'

'Slow down, darling. For one thing, I have no intention of dying for at least twenty years; and for another, how on earth is that going to happen?'

Mama looked shocked as she told her what Harold had said. 'I can't believe Harold said that. We have never discussed our property or . . . well, yes, we have discussed money. I told him that I couldn't bring a lot to the table, and Harold said that didn't matter, as he would take care of me. I thought he meant that he would make me an allowance.'

'Well, he doesn't. Mama, don't make the same mistake that I did. Tell me, are you all right for money?'

'Yes, dear. Well, I'm not swimming in it, but your father left me well provided for – about the only good thing he ever did for me. However, it depends on how long I live. I do have returns on some good investments that Harold has made for me, though, and they keep my money-pot topped up.'

'But running the house in Leeds must cost a fortune?'

'It does, darling. But stop worrying – I'm all right.'

'Promise me that you won't sign everything over to Harold when you marry. Promise me.'

Throwing the covers back, Mama said, 'Let me get dressed for dinner, darling. We'll discuss all of this while we eat. Just make sure you dismiss your staff, once we have our main course.' Millie reluctantly went to leave, but her mama called after her, 'Don't worry, my darling, I will protect you. It's me and you against the world.'

Millie smiled. Her mama could be so funny. Not for the first time, she wished she'd spent the first nineteen years of her life enjoying the relationship they had now. But always she had taken her father's side and had blamed her mama for everything. How wrong she had been. But as she had learned, you cannot go back and undo what you have done – it was an all-too-painful lesson.

Chapter Thirty-One

Elsie and Millie

As she met Jim at the factory gates the next day, Elsie felt nervous, and knew that Jim did too. They didn't speak much, just greeted each other with a kiss, squeezed each other's arm and went inside.

'Elsie, girl, what the bleedin' hell's going on? We had a fright yesterday when neither of you turned up.'

'Morning, Ada. Where's Peggy?'

'She's nipped to the lav. She's got a funny feeling that everything ain't right and, when she gets that, she's on the loo till it's resolved.'

Elsie felt like laughing, but the concern on Ada's face and on all the faces turned in her direction changed her mind. 'I can't tell you anything at the moment, girls. You have to accept that we had a bit of a blip yesterday, but we're back to normal today. I hope you didn't slack, just because we weren't here?'

'As if I'd let 'em. Morning, Elsie, am I glad to see yer, mate. So it were a blip, was it?'

'Yes, you can stop your trips to the lav now, Peggy – besides, you'll smoke your ration of fags before break if you don't.'

338

'I had loose bowels, Elsie. All right, I had a fag or two while I relieved meself, but any girl's entitled to that.' She turned then. 'Not you lot, though, so don't come to me saying you've got the runs. Get your heads down and get back to work – I'm supposed to be hearing the clattering of jars, not silence and seeing a load of ugly mugs with their mouths gaping.'

The women resumed working without protest. Elsie did smile then, as she followed Jim up the stairs. 'I'll miss them all if we have to leave, Jim.'

'Well, it looks likely, from where I'm sitting.'

'I don't know – for me, yes, but you have a strong case for making Len keep you on.' She told him what Cess had suggested.

'Play him at his own game you mean?'

'Yes. Len's sort only understands that way of going on. He won't want to lose you and he won't want his name dragging through the mud – even if nothing can be proved about what Len did to me, folk of all classes will nod their heads and see that his wife must believe it because she's left him, and say that there's no smoke without fire.'

It was a saying that Elsie could apply to herself: her specu- lation about the possible outcome of Len's rape still filled her mind. She couldn't wait for the time of her monthly, and prayed for the umpteenth time, *Please, God, don't let me be having his baby*.

With this thought, and with Jim having nodded, saying he would think about it and then picking up the notebook left by the phone, Elsie realized that she must keep some of her money back, in case she needed to pay the woman that Rene knew.

Elsie's heart felt heavy. She didn't want to have her child

taken away, but she also didn't want to face having it. Her despair got her asking why men saw her in the animalistic way that both Chambers and Len did. But she knew she looked like her mum, and had that something that men craved – Mum had described it as voluptuousness. Well, whatever it was, she didn't want it. Whether it would be different with Jim, she didn't know. All she knew was that he loved her, and she couldn't imagine him treating her in the same way.

An hour later when Betty, the tea-lady, brought their tea, Jim sat sipping his, staring into space.

'Not going to read your paper, Jim?'

'No, I need to think. There's nothing but reports of trouble in Mexico and between the Austrians and the Serbs. Not to mention the Americans interfering in everything they can. It feels like all the world is stirred up. I'm expecting Russia to rear its head at any time, too, because already the Tsar is making noises about supporting the Serbs.'

'Oh, that's all a bit above me. I've enough to contend with in our own world, without worrying about the affairs of the whole world.'

'Exactly.'

This wasn't like Jim, and it made Elsie curious. She could see his newspaper sticking out of his attaché case. He'd rolled it up into a tight roll, which again she'd never known him to do – he usually folded it neatly next to him and often used it to swat flies.

When he excused himself and went to the bathroom, Elsie kept looking towards his bag. Was there something in the newspaper to worry her? Making her mind up to take a peep, she hurriedly pulled it out and unrolled it – then shot backwards as the words of the headline glared out at her: 'The Body in the Thames murderer to hang at noon on the eighteenth of October 1912.'

Dropping the paper, she felt a shiver go through her. She'd waited so long for this day to come, to see the rotten Chambers get his just deserts and now there was a date set and it was only three weeks away. Her throat dried and her eyes filled with tears. 'Justice at last, Mum.'

'Elsie!' Jim opened the door of the office, took in the sight of his newspaper on the floor and hurried over to her. 'I was going to tell you later, my darling.'

'I – I . . . Oh, Jim, I want this, I do, and yet I feel sick at the thought.'

'Don't, darling. I knew this would affect you, but don't let it. Oh, my Elsie, how will I ever help you to heal?'

'You are helping, Jim. You, more than anyone, are helping me. Just by loving me, you help me.'

But although she said this, the same thoughts she'd had earlier revisited Elsie: did she ever want to be properly loved by Jim, or any man? No, she didn't. Not in the way they wanted to show their love, because they used that in a lustful way, too, and it hurt. Not just physical pain, but pain in her heart and mind – more than anything, in her mind.

'Elsie? Let me hold you, darling. Don't reject me.'

'Not in the office, Jim. We have a few times, but we said we'd never show our affection in the office.'

'Is that all this is? You're not afraid of me, are you?'

'N – no . . . I, well, it's our rule.'

'Naughty me for wanting to offer comfort.'

'Don't . . . don't get upset, Jim. I – I couldn't cope if you did.'

Jim sighed. 'Sometimes I feel that I have to be all things

to all people, but I can't be, Elsie. I'm Jim. I'm an ordinary man, with ordinary feelings. And no matter what has happened to you before – and it is terrible, and rips my heart out to think of it – I'm not the same as those men. I love you, my darling. And if you never let me close to you, I will still love you.'

'Oh, Jim, forgive me.' Elsie stepped towards him, and he opened his arms. The hug he gave her was gentle and un-demanding. 'One day I'll be healed. One day we will give ourselves to each other. Be patient with me, my love.'

'I will be, darling, but it hurts so much when you reject me. It's like you're saying that I am no better than them.'

'I don't mean to. You're nothing like them. You're me mate – remember?'

They both giggled. Jim planted a kiss in her hair. Then he sighed deeply and let her go. She knew he was getting aroused and needed to distance himself from her. She loved him so much for that. But then the thought shuddered through Elsie that the next week, or just after, was weighted with anxiety. Her fear of not starting her monthly, and the agonizing truth that her mum had died in such a horrible way by the hand of Chambers, would be so vivid to her as he went to his eternal punishment.

Millie had been restless all night and had now been out of bed twice to be sick.

The scene at the dinner table played over and over in her head, and the sight of her mama crying had her feeling wretched. Harold had become very angry on her mama telling him that, before they married, she was signing her house and the estate in Leeds over to Millie.

This had shocked Millie as much as it had Harold. He'd

turned towards her. 'Well done, Millie. I'm beginning to see that you're more than a match for my son. So you have stopped your mama bringing her share to our marriage. What a good start for a couple about to venture on a life's journey together. You have virtually made it so that your mama will rely on being a kept woman!'

'This isn't my doing. I merely asked Mama not to sign everything over to you when you married. I made that huge mistake, and I didn't want her to. Besides, if she did, whether I am married to Len or not when my mama passes on, Len will get everything she owned, and me nothing – either through you, if you outlive Mama, because it would all pass to you, or if you die first she and I will be left destitute as Len will take the lot!'

'I would leave a provision in my will for your mama – what do you think I am? Did you think I hadn't thought of it? I had intended to leave you a legacy as well, but it seems I have no need to.'

'I still don't trust Len, whatever plans you put in place. I'm sorry, but despite all you said, I don't.'

'That's my son you're talking about.' Harold stood and threw his napkin down on the table. 'Abigail, I am going to my own home in Knightsbridge, and I will fetch my son out of that hospital and have him nursed at home. If either of you come to your senses, you know where we'll be. If you don't, then this is goodbye – you can both stew in the soup your daughter has cooked up!'

At the sound of her mama's sob, Millie jumped up and went to her. 'I'm so sorry, Mama. I didn't mean for this to happen. I knew Harold might be angry, but not that it would mean so much to him. He's a wealthy man – really wealthy, far more so than we are, or Father was. And he gave a large part of his estate to his son, so why should he think you shouldn't do the same for your daughter?'

'No Act of Parliament saying that women can own our own property, which we take into a marriage, will stop the Harolds of this world. They don't mean any harm; they just think it is right and proper that they should be the owners of everything within a marriage. There are a lot who think like them – a lot more than we know of. But I don't think Harold is the same as Len. You heard him say that he didn't understand the boy. He's always telling me that Len has some ways that he doesn't agree with. But you're right, darling. Whatever comes of this, we have escaped with my estate intact.'

'Are you sure you can afford the upkeep, Mama?'

'I am, darling.'

'These investments you told me about: does the dividend go into your own bank or Harold's?'

'My own bank, my dear. Harold set it up like that, and I get a really good return every month – surely he wouldn't have done that if he intended taking all that I own in his own name, would he?'

'I don't know. I only know what he said: that everything of yours would be in his name.'

'That isn't going to happen. I will go with you tomorrow to sign it all over to you.'

'Not yet, Mama. It's a wonderful gesture, but Len might take it from me.'

'He can't – not by law. The only way is if you sign it over to him, which I think is a lesson you have learned, my dear.'

'It is, well and truly. All right, we'll do it, providing your lawyer doesn't see a snag – if I am granted a divorce in the future, we have to make sure that Len cannot take it from me. But in the meantime, this is only to safeguard your assets, Mama. It isn't in any way giving me control over what you spend, or how you spend it. You must keep your own bank account, and your own money. But promise me faithfully that no matter how much Harold blackmails you, you won't give in.'

'I promise, darling. You know, with you using that word, it makes me think that father and son are cut from the same cloth – after all, when Harold left, his manner was threatening and his demand was a kind of blackmail.'

'I'm glad you see that, Mama, darling. I didn't with Len, or I would have handled things in a better way. I'd have stood up to him. Now I just don't know what is going to happen.'

When they'd gone to bed, after a couple of glasses of sherry to drown their sorrows, Millie cried herself to sleep.

Getting up the next morning, Millie felt very lethargic, but made it to the bathroom – only for the room to swim around her, and for her to be sick for a third time. As she sat on the stool next to the bath, tears streamed down her face. She missed Ruby so much. And Dot. If only she'd had more chance to get to know Dot. How sad that Dot suffered that breakdown. *Even when she lived here with Cess, I couldn't get to know her. The Dot that was here wasn't the real Dot.*

Wiping her eyes, Millie made up her mind that although she could no longer get to know Dot, she would get to know Kitty. She'd ask Cess if Kitty and Gertrude could come to stay for a weekend. Then she'd take Kitty out for a walk, using her own old pram.

Millie patted her tummy and told it, 'I'd better see about all the nursery equipment being ready for you, little one.'

But then it hit her that she couldn't possibly afford to stay in this house – she would have to sell it. *Where will I be living? Will I even have room for a nursery in my new home?*

Suddenly she knew where she wanted to be – anywhere that was close to Elsie.

Downstairs she found her mama in the breakfast room, and she looked bright and smiley. 'Feeling better, Mama?' As she asked this, Millie gently kissed her mother's cheek.

'Yes. Look!'

Millie looked towards where she pointed. 'Flowers! How nice.'

'They're for both of us from Harold. The note says: "Forgive me – Harold x" and on the envelope were both of our names. I think I have an old romantic on my hands.'

'I'm so pleased. Well, I suppose we'd better forgive him then.' But although she said this, Millie wondered if this was all part of Harold's scheme. Was he pretending, just ready to strike when Mama was least expecting it? To this end, she asked, 'Are we going to the lawyer's today, Mama?'

'Yes, we are – and before I go and see Harold. It will be a done deal then.'

'Thank you. Oh, Mama, I love you.'

'And I you, my darling daughter. I want to do this. I want to protect you. I know you won't interfere in any way with what I wish to do before I die.'

'That won't be for a long, long time, I hope, Mama. I would die myself, if I lost you. But you're right. Everything remains the same. You should forget that your house and land are in my name – it is, as you say, simply a protective measure. But I feel so relieved. I don't trust Len one bit, and I still think we have to be on our guard with Harold. As lovely as he is, it seems that his mindset is similar to his son's.'

'Don't you worry. Last night was an eye-opener and was very upsetting, but I'm glad it happened. I can have some fun – and enjoy life – but will always be aware of what was said. Now, have some breakfast and let's get ourselves organized. We are strong women, Millie, and together we can beat anybody.'

Millie laughed. She loved it when her mama dropped the formal way of addressing her. And she loved how she was now: so different from when she was suppressed by— Millie stopped that thought. She'd caught sight of the morning paper, sitting on the small stand next to the breakfast buffet. It was folded in its usual way, with the headlines facing upwards. 'Oh God!'

'What, dear?'

'Oh . . . nothing. I burned my finger on the hotplate. It made me jump, that's all. I . . . well, I'm not sure that I want to eat, Mama. Shall we order the car and get on our way?'

'But you haven't had a drink or anything to eat!'

'I have. That's why I'm a bit late down. I had tea brought up to my bed, and Cook had put a pastry on the tray – that often happens when they know I'm upset.' Millie didn't say that she hadn't been able to touch either.

'Ah well, that will be why you're not hungry. In that case . . .' Abigail rang the bell next to her. Barridge appeared, as always, as if he was one of those clockwork dolls and someone had wound his key and sent him gliding through the door.

When they reached the office of Mama's lawyer, Wilfred Hepplethwaite – given that he was already party to Millie's situation with Len, through the help he was giving them – Millie found that he totally agreed with them. He greeted them with surprised pleasure. 'So nice to see you, Abigail, darling. How are you? I thought you were lost to us.'

'Better than I've ever been, thank you, Wilfred. Well, I will be, when you sort out the problem we've come to you about.'

Wilfred was quiet for a moment and sat with his hands in prayer mode, with his pursed lips resting on them. When he spoke, it was Millie who was surprised. 'I can't say I'm pleased to hear that, as it means that my chances with you are still nil.' He gave a lovely smile at Mama, and she giggled like a young girl.

'Oh, you never know. If Harold doesn't toe the line, then I might come calling.'

Wilfred beamed. 'Well, he hasn't made a good start, has he, my dear? But at the risk of offending you, this is typical of him. And now, as you are aware of what his son has done, I can say that it appears Harold has taught Len to act in the same way.'

'Hmm, the problem is that I love Harold, so I will just have to be on my guard – as Millicent has already warned me.'

'Excuse me for saying this, but I do have to be frank with you: you were treated badly all your married life by Richard, so please consider very carefully. They say that a leopard doesn't change its spots, and I have known Harold for a very long time – he isn't a client, by the way, so I am not liable when I say that he has astounded me more than once with the shady deals he has gloated over, when I have been in his company. And to make my point, some of them were with – and others instigated by – Richard.'

Mama looked shocked. 'I – I didn't know. When I met Harold at social occasions I realized that he and Richard were on excellent terms, but . . .'

'Not always, and it didn't end that way, but Richard put a good face on things. He always knew how to do that, but he double-crossed Harold and was worried – he spoke to me about it. I could only advise him that he was better off not being involved with Harold and his wheeler-dealing. And now I'm going to say something that may mean you never speak to me again, but I care too much about you not to disclose what I know. Since I heard what his son has done, I have been worried that Harold is doing the same to you – and so far I haven't been proved wrong, have I?'

'But why should he? I am not a rich woman, and Harold is not trying to make his way in the world, as Len is . . . Besides, you are wrong. Harold told us that he has gifted Len the small bank he owns, and which Len is the manager of, and then will eventually sell him his share of the partnership in Harlington & Lefton's Bank. Harold would hardly go after more assets when he is doing that, would he?'

'My dear, please believe me, I feel terrible telling you this, but you are, well . . . What I mean to say is that I feel duty-bound, as one friend to another. Harold has a score to settle with your late husband. He told me how he cut him out of a deal.'

'Oh, that sounds typical of Richard. What happened about it?'

'Harold and Richard remained on speaking terms, Abigail, but only when necessary, and the atmosphere between them never improved. Richard was well and truly spooked and regretted his action, as Harold could have foreclosed on him a number of times – I think, from things Harold said, that he planned to get his revenge, but was waiting for the right moment. I warned Richard, but then Richard foiled Harold by dying. Now I ask myself: is what is happening simply Harold and his son completing the job?'

Millie had sat in complete awe through all of this – the revelation about the obvious feelings that Wilfred had for Mama had taken her aback, but to hear all that he'd said about her father and Harold left her speechless. Had she thought she was up to competing in the business world? Well, now she was doubting it. Hadn't she fallen at the first hurdle and lost the factory to her father's enemies? Whether of his own making or not, Millie felt she had betrayed her father. She looked at Mama and saw that her face was drained of colour.

Before she could react, Wilfred said, 'Abigail, my dear Abigail, I'm sorry. I shouldn't have—'

'Yes, you should. Thank you, Wilfred. I think I owe you a great debt.' Mama delved into her clutch bag and pulled out her pretty lace hanky. She dabbed her eyes.

'Mama. Oh, Mama.' Millie put her arm around her mother, at a loss as to what to say or do.

Wilfred stood. 'I – I'm sorry, please forgive me. Whether I should have spoken or not, I am mortified to have upset you so, Abigail.'

Mama nodded. 'Millie, will you leave us alone for a while, darling?'

As Millie got up and walked out of the room, she hoped with all her heart that her mama wasn't going to disassociate herself from Wilfred. And a huge part of her hoped that she'd do just the opposite, and take the love Wilfred was obviously offering her.

Chapter Thirty-Two

Elsie

The day seemed to be the longest Elsie had ever known. Now, as the factory came to a hush and Jim was doing his final rounds, making sure everything was safely switched off, Elsie stood and looked down on the women filing out – still gossiping as they clocked their cards, some with unlit fags hanging from their mouths, ready to light the minute they were outside, and others taking off their mob caps.

Watching them, the thought came to her of how devastated the women would be if the factory changed back to the way it used to be – or, worse, closed down, with the operations moved to a place they couldn't afford to travel to. Waving to one or two, who had looked up and caught sight of her, Elsie felt this even more keenly as they smiled and waved back.

As the building emptied, she could see the sinks where the washing of the jars used to be. She and Dot were once part of the team who did that job. Now most of it was done by a firm that collected the jars and returned them sterile – one of Jim's many brilliant introductions. It had left the jar-washers free to be able to help out wherever they were needed, and learn new skills: an altogether more efficient way of utilizing the staff. And it left the area free to put into operation Millie's plan to expand the stockroom space – if that ever happened now.

As she went to turn away, Elsie caught sight of the plaque commemorating Dot and the work she'd done. Her heart squeezed, so that she had to gasp for breath. *Oh, Dot. Dot, I miss you. And now I know first-hand how you feared who the father of your child was. But, if my monthly don't show, I'll be in no doubt.* Shaking herself, she thought, *I must stop calling it a child – it's a thing that I will rid meself of, and that's that!*

'Ready, darling?'

She jumped. 'You gave me a fright, Jim! I didn't see you coming up the stairs. How did I miss you?'

'Well, when I looked up, you seemed as though you were in another world. I followed your line of sight and knew what had taken you there. Come here, darling, and let me hug you. I've wanted to all day.'

She went willingly. When enclosed in Jim's arms, she felt safe and her world steadied a little.

'Darling. I – I want to talk to you. Shall we walk to your place through the park?' Jim's serious demeanour sparked fear in Elsie. Had he been thinking everything over and come to conclusions she didn't want to hear? Or maybe he wanted to tell her his fears. Her mind rested a little as he said, 'You had another shock today, darling. I want us to be together when the hanging takes place. But let's leave now, as the night-watchman has arrived.'

Once in the park, Elsie took a deep breath. She had no need to hurry home, as Cess would be there with Bert. He so wanted Gertie to move in that he'd said he would spend the day seeing what needed to be done to make it possible, and might even mix some whitewash and paint the walls.

It would be a relief to Elsie, too, as Gertie would take over some of the responsibility for Bert. Thinking of him, she told Jim, 'Bert has a birthday next week, Jim. I'd like to do something special for him.'

'Hmm. A piano concert maybe?'

Elsie hit him playfully. 'For goodness' sake, he's going to be six, not twenty-six.'

Jim laughed as he dodged her blow. 'I know, but Bert loves music. I'll come back with you and give him that lesson he missed.'

'Oh, would you? Ta, Jim. I can cook tea. Rene got me a nice piece of lamb, and said she would pop it in the oven at about four. It won't take me long to cook some veg, and I can put a rice pud in the oven to cook, too.'

'That would be lovely. I – I, well, I have to admit the lessons are a way of being with you in your home, darling.'

Elsie was quiet, afraid of where this was heading.

'Anyway, how about the zoo? I went there as a boy and loved it. I often go now to see the animals, and to check the same ones are there. Most of them are, but they've added to them. They have elephants and orang-utans, and gorillas – it's really fascinating. I love it.'

Elsie felt excited at the prospect, as she'd never been to a zoo. 'That's perfect! Bert seems to like anything that you like, so he'll be over the moon. When can we go?'

'This Saturday? We could take a chance on the weather being like it is now and take a picnic.'

Elsie felt cheered. This sounded like just the treat Bert needed – that she needed, even.

'Now, darling, I haven't asked you to walk with me to talk about zoos. Let's sit down on that bench.'

When they were sitting down, Elsie waited, but Jim didn't speak. 'I'm ready, mate, spit it out.'

'Well, I wondered – and hear me out, Elsie, as what I'm going to say I know you will be against, but I need to say it.'

Elsie looked ahead.

'Elsie?'

Sighing, she turned to him. 'I'll listen, Jim, but if you know I won't like it, why say it, as it seems to me you have yer answer?'

'No, I haven't. Elsie, I haven't cancelled the wedding arrangements for November. No, listen to me. The date is the first week in November – that's just five weeks away. If – if by any chance . . . Well, there's no easy way of saying this, but if you are pregnant . . . Elsie!'

She could sit there no longer. It was unbearable to talk to Jim about it.

'Elsie, wait, please.'

'Jim, don't make me face it – don't.'

'But it won't go away. We have to talk about it. Stop. Please stop walking.'

She couldn't, and marched on.

'Very well! Bury your head in the sand. But I can't, and if you don't let me help you, then there's no point to anything.'

Elsie stopped and looked round. Jim had turned and was walking away at pace, as if his life depended on getting away from her. She called his name. He stopped, but didn't turn round.

'I'll talk, Jim. I – I'm sorry. I do know that I have to.'

He came running back to her. 'We have to, darling. You're not on your own now. You have me. You have to share things with me. We're going to be man and wife.'

She nodded.

'Well, let's sit on this bench and see if another view of the park helps us.' Jim smiled as he said this. 'Elsie, my darling, I will do everything I can for you, I promise. Let me tell you my plan.'

Again she nodded. The tears were so close, but she didn't want them to overflow. She had to stay strong.

'Are you ready for me to carry on, darling?'

'Yes.'

'This is a terrible thing that you are having to go through. I want to be part of that. A supportive part. I can do that. We should be bringing our wedding forward so that you are protected – not putting it off. I don't see the point of that. And . . . well, I'm afraid that you're doing it because if you find you are pregnant, you won't want to marry me at all.'

'No! That's not the case. I – I have plans, that's all.'

'What plans? Weren't you even going to discuss them with me?'

'I can't, as you will persuade me otherwise.'

'Well, I'm determined to tell you my plan, and you can then compare it with yours. I want us to marry: at the earliest possible moment. I want to father the child – I mean, take your child on as mine, if there is one . . . No, don't inter-rupt me again, Elsie. I have to finish, then you can have your say. I don't know when you'll know, but if you don't by our wedding day, I promise that I won't consummate the marriage.'

'You won't what? I don't understand.'

'I mean that I won't make love to you . . . make you mine – though I want to, more than anything in the world. I will wait until you are ready. I want you to be sure of the parentage of your child. I don't want you forever wondering. I will wait until it is born before we begin to be a proper married couple, and still I will wait until you are ready. I just want to protect you and take care of you . . . Well, of course, I want more, but I am willing to wait. Then when your child is born, he or she will be presented to the world as ours. And I promise you that I will cherish it, and will always be a father to it.'

'No, Jim. I can't let you do that. I don't want to do it myself. I know what can happen. It will eat away at you over the years. And at Millie.'

'She won't know.'

'What if the child looks so like Len there's no mistaking it is his? He has such distinctive looks.'

Jim was quiet, then asked, 'So, what's your plan, Elsie?'

She couldn't tell him she planned to have the 'thing' – as she preferred to think of it – taken away from her, but she had an alternative now. She'd thought and thought over the last couple of days, and she'd remembered Dot's mum making arrangements for Dot to go into a convent and have her baby adopted. This had given Elsie the idea that she would go through with the operation, but then tell everyone who knew what Len had done that there had been no child. But to appease Jim she said, 'I will go away to a convent for wayward girls and have it adopted. Then we can start afresh from there.'

Still Jim didn't speak, and when he did he said, 'So this is why you want to cancel our wedding? You want to make sure, one way or another, before you decide what to do?'

'Yes. I do.'

'Well, so be it. But, Elsie, think about my plan, too. Please?'

'I don't have to, Jim. I won't do it. I cannot put you through that. None of this is your fault, and you're not going to pay for the rest of your life for something that beast did. A child is a lifetime commitment – that means that what happened will be in front of you, day in and day out, for years and years. No! You have to let me do this my way, mate. You have to.'

'When you call me "mate", I don't feel that I have any choice. It's as if you are asking me as your friend, as well as the man who loves you. Well, all right. But, Elsie, I will be by your side, no matter what.'

She took his hand. 'I know you will, Jim. That's the one sure thing that I have to hang on to, in all of this.'

His arm came round her and he pulled her to him. She looked around and then laughed. 'Come on, we'll be arrested for lewd behaviour in the park at this rate.'

Jim laughed with her, then stood and took her hands and pulled her to her feet. His voice lowered. 'I want so much to kiss you, Elsie.'

She looked away. The look in his eyes was all too familiar to her. The fear she tried to suppress overwhelmed her. Turning from him, she said, 'I can't wait to get home to tell Bert what his birthday treat is. Let's run.'

'Run? That's very unladylike!'

'Ha, I told you, I'm not a lady.'

Jim pulled her close, 'You're my lady, my darling, and I will always treat you like one. I promise.' His voice had deep, husky sound.

Elsie had to get away from the nearness of him. She pulled

357

away, and Jim's sigh was audible. To cover her action she said, 'Well, I'm going to run, I can't wait to see Bert to tell him!'

Not knowing what possessed her, she lifted her skirts and ran for all she was worth. When she reached home, she looked back. Jim was a long way behind her, but he was following her. Out of breath, she found her key and opened the door.

'What the blazes? Blimey, are the coppers after yer, Elsie?'

'No. I've some great news for Bert.'

Rene had stepped past her and looked down the street. Her knowing look as she raised her eyebrows made Elsie blush.

'Elsie, love, don't run away from them as love yer. I understand yer fear, mate, but look . . . Me and you need to have a talk, right? I'll come up later, when Jim's left.'

Jim came round the corner and Elsie made herself giggle. 'Slowcoach. I thought you would never catch up.'

He didn't smile. He greeted Rene, then followed Elsie up the stairs.

Elsie did her best to pass it all off. 'Let me tell Bert, please! I want him to see that good things, as well as tears, come from me.'

In a patient voice Jim answered, 'I wouldn't steal your glory, darling. You and Bert deserve that moment.'

She turned just before she opened the door to her flat. 'I do love you, Jim. I love you with all my heart. Give me time. Let me sort this all out in my own way, eh?'

He nodded. She bent from her higher step and kissed his nose. Jim wiped it away, but laughed as he did so. 'You wet my nose!'

'That means you're now my lapdog and must do everything I say.' This time she licked the end of his nose.

'Get off, Elsie . . . Oh, Elsie, I—'

She turned and opened the door. 'We're home! Where are you all?'

Bert came running and caught hold of her waist. Cess followed, carrying a screaming Kitty. 'Thank goodness you're here, Else. I can't do anything for her. I don't know what's wrong with her. I'm thinking of taking her to the doctor.'

'Ah, give her to me.'

Taking Kitty, Elsie could see that her cheeks were rosy-red and her little eyes were puffed up with crying. 'I think she's teething, Cess. I remember Bert being like this.'

'But she's got a temperature – she's all hot.'

'Yes, she may have. Let's try to cool her down. Get one of those nappies that are boiled, and rinse it in cold water. We'll give it her to bite on – it might soothe her gums.'

All problems were forgotten as everyone went into looking-after-Kitty mode.

'Mum used to rub a bit of her gin on Bert's gums. She did the same if any of us had toothache.'

'Did it help?'

'Well, it used to quieten Bert. And if he was really restless, she put a tiny drop in his milk.'

'She didn't!'

'She did, and probably did it to all of us, too. If the cold nappy doesn't work, we'll ask Rene if she's got a drop. She has a tipple now and then.'

A few minutes later, sitting holding the now-sleeping Kitty, Elsie looked down on her and felt the usual surge of love for her. The feeling made her gasp for a moment.

'Are yer all right, Else? Do you want me to take her?'

'No, I'm fine, Cess.' Although she said this, she was acutely aware of Jim's eyes on her.

'I made her sleep once, Elsie. I was playing the notes you showed me. I think she likes music, like us,' Bert said.

'More than likely, love. That's another thing Mum used to do: sing to you. You were always quiet when Mum sang, and even Jimmy used to curl up and have a nap on the sofa next to you and Mum.'

'Why can't I remember these things, Else?'

'Because you were always off somewhere, either playing football or wheeling and dealing.'

'They're nice memories to have, darling.'

She looked up at Jim and smiled. 'Yes. And we're about to give you something to remember, Bert. We've made our mind up on your birthday treat, mate.'

Bert jumped up and down when he heard what they had planned. 'I'm going to the zoo! I can't wait, Else. Can Kitty come too?'

'Yes.'

'And Cess and Millie, and Aunty Rene?'

Elsie laughed. 'Yes, we'll take a charabanc full. It's your birthday, and you can ask who you want to.'

'What, even George?'

'Who's George?'

'Me mate at school. His mum's poor, like we used to be. Sometimes I give him me sandwich, as he never has anything to eat and I can hear his tummy rumbling when we play marbles.'

'That's kind of you, Bert. Do you know where he lives, mate?'

'I do. He told me he lives on Salisbury Street.'

'That's where Aunty Rene used to live.' She turned to Jim. 'And Ada still does. And I still haven't found anywhere decent for her that she can afford.' Sighing, Elsie ruffled

Bert's hair. 'Poor George. Well, now that we know of him, we'll take care of him. We can visit him and take food and stuff for the family, eh?'

'He might be a bit grumpy about it. He is, when I try to give him me sandwich. He says, "I ain't no charity case."'

Elsie sighed. 'The old cockney pride. Well, I'll think of something. But now I know about him, I can't leave it at that.'

She caught Jim's eye. He was smiling at her and his eyes held such love for her. 'And no doubt you'll get Millie involved,' he said. 'This is just her barrow.'

'It is. Now, lessons for you, Bert. Go on. Take Jim up to the music room and show him what you can do. I think he'll be very surprised at your talent, mate.'

'I already know he's good, don't I, Bert? My aim is to make you better than good.'

When they disappeared, Cess asked, 'Is everything all right, Else?'

'It won't be if I don't get that lamb out of the oven and put the vegetables on to boil. I'm starving. Here, take Kitty, but be very gentle – try not to wake her. Lie her on the sofa, so we can keep an eye on her.'

Elsie hurried into the kitchen. Cess always had known when things weren't right with her, but the last thing she needed was having to tell him what had happened. She was in a turmoil over it all as it was, and she knew what he'd say. But marrying Jim before she'd sorted everything out wasn't an option for her. For now, she just wanted the next few days to sail by, so that she knew one way or another. She went to pray for the best outcome – no, beg for it, but she didn't. She was on the verge of stopping asking God for anything, as he never listened to her anyway.

Chapter Thirty-Three

Millie

Millie sat in her sitting room with the garden doors open. Every muscle in her body was tense, as fear of what might happen gripped her.

Mama had decided to drop all association with Harold. Both her own and Mama's nerves had been on edge for the past hour, as Mama had sent Harold a note asking him to visit. And now they were both in the living room just across the hall from Millie, and the moment Mama had dreaded was upon her.

Millie's fear stemmed from what Harold might do. He'd already shown that he had a quick temper. But she was ready: the moment she heard raised voices, she would run across the hall to her mother's aid.

Her thoughts went to yesterday: whatever her mama and Wilfred had been discussing after she'd been asked to leave them in private for a moment hadn't taken long, as she'd been called back into the office after about ten minutes – not to be told anything, other than Wilfred suggesting that she and Mama go and have a coffee while he prepared the paperwork, and then they were to go back to sign it.

Mama hadn't told her anything, either, as they'd sat sipping their coffee. The only clue she had was that when they returned to the office Wilfred looked a very happy man, and Mama had a glow about her. But then, Millie told herself, she was always trying to matchmake, so it might have been fanciful thinking. *Although I was right about Jim and Elsie!*

Sitting back in her chair, she played back in her mind the conversation she and her mother had when they were about to leave the cafe. Mama had shocked her by saying, 'I'm calling it off with Harold. I want to do that this afternoon. Will you be on hand, but leave it to me to deal with it, darling?'

This had worried Millie and she'd asked, 'Are you afraid, Mama?'

'Yes, I must admit I am, since Harold's outburst yesterday.'

'Well, I'm glad you're calling it off then. There can't be anything worse . . . Oh, but you know that.'

'I don't actually. I was never afraid of your father. I always stood up to him, but it never made any difference to his behaviour. He blamed me, of course.'

'I know. I used to hear him. He thought you should have been more tolerant of his behaviour with your maid, and should have forgiven him.'

'He did. But I couldn't, darling. I just couldn't forgive him. I felt betrayed and dirty.'

'That's exactly how I feel – though worse than that, as Len's betrayal was a filthy violation of my dear Elsie.' Millie stopped her thoughts for a moment as her heart leaked with pain once more.

Taking deep breaths, she relaxed a little. Clearing her mind of one pain didn't stop her speculating on what it all meant. Snippets from this morning kept coming back to her and she thought of how, as they'd walked back to Wilfred's office, she'd answered her mama's questions on how Elsie was, and what was happening between her and Jim, as quickly as she could. But she'd had a burning question of her own, about why Mama still felt the need to be so hasty in signing everything over to her, if she was going to break off her relationship with Harold. She'd argued that surely it wasn't necessary to, if the threat was removed. But her mama had said, 'It is important, darling. What Wilfred told us has frightened me. When someone holds a grudge as deeply and for as long as Harold has, that can be a dangerous thing.'

Suddenly Millie's fear became a reality, as the sound of Harold's raised voice came to her, cutting into her thoughts and catapulting her from her chair. Running across the hall, she opened the living-room door. 'What's going on? How dare you shout at my mama! Kindly leave at once, Harold.'

Harold turned towards her. 'You two owe me a debt, and I will collect it, don't you worry about that.'

'What debt? How can we possibly? I maybe did, when I owned the jam factory, but any debts attached to that are now your son's.'

'You think you've been so clever, don't you, Millie? Well, you're not as clever as me or Len. And don't you forget it.'

'Are you threatening me?'

'I have no need to. You may own this poxy house, and now your mother's estate, but I have tricks up my sleeve that you could never dream of.'

'Harold, please – just leave.'

At this plea from Mama, he turned on his heel and pushed past Millie, almost sending her flying and hurting her shoulder.

'What was all that about? I knew he'd be upset, but I never dreamed he'd react like that. Can he do anything to us, Mama?'

'Come and sit down, dear.'

Shaking and feeling lost – not knowing what was happening to their world, which just over a week ago had seemed safe and happy – Millie went to her mama and sat on the floor at her knee.

Mama stroked her hair, as she always did at times like this, when they needed to give and receive comfort from each other. They'd had many of those times in the last year or so.

'Darling, don't worry about what just happened. Wilfred told me there is nothing Harold can do to us. And whatever Harold threatens will be hot air: the kind that someone who is losing the battle will spout. But there was another reason for it – something I told Harold – and, darling, I don't know what you're going to think of me when I tell you.'

'Nothing but relief, I should think, after you saying there is nothing Harold can do to us. What is it, Mama?'

'Well, darling, you know that I have known Wilfred for many, many years? Yesterday was a revelation to me in many ways. But in one way in particular. I don't know what happened, but . . . I realized where my true feelings lay.'

'Wilfred! Oh, Mama, I'm so pleased.'

'You knew?'

Millie smiled – the news had so cheered her. She turned and looked up at her mother and tapped her nose. 'I have intuition, where who loves who is concerned.'

Mama laughed, but Millie thought how wrong she'd been in her own case.

'So you don't mind, Millie, darling? You don't think me fickle – flitting from one man to another when your father has only been dead just over a year?'

'Father was dead to you for a long time, Mama, and he didn't deserve the consideration of either of us. Our love was wasted on him. But I am curious as to why you still found it so urgent that you sign everything over to me?'

'Wilfred advised it. He said that none of us know what lies in the future, and it will safeguard you. You see, he not only declared his love for me, but he proposed, too!'

'What?'

'I know – I can't believe it. I feel so happy, and yet a bit silly, too. After all, I have not long announced my engagement to Harold. What will people think?'

'I should think they will be very happy for you. If Wilfred knew what Harold was really like, then so must all of his circle – I presume they are the people you are worrying about?'

'Yes. I don't know why, because they mean nothing to me . . . Except that, if I do become Wilfred's wife, I may have to mix with them again. Though not often, thank goodness. Wilfred said that now his dream had come true, he will retire as soon as he can – you know he is a widow with one son, of course? Well, his son is ready to take over his practice at a minute's notice, and apparently he is already the main lawyer within the firm.'

'That's wonderful. And I suppose Wilfred wanting you to give me everything now was him proving to you, after the experience you've been through, that you can trust him, and that he isn't after what he can get.'

'Yes, that and another reason. I know we weren't in there long without you, but we didn't need long – I have known for a long time that Wilfred was in love with me. And yet

366

me loving him only came to me in a flash yesterday, as I have held a torch for Harold for a good many years.'

All of this was such a revelation to Millie that she couldn't take it in, although she had realized yesterday Wilfred's feelings for Mama.

'I know that has shocked you, but stupid as it was of me, it's true. Anyway, all of that dissolved, and Harold's own behaviour contributed to that. I am so relieved now. I can see that he would have treated me worse than your father did. But I am supposed to be telling you why Wilfred wanted me to continue – and quickly – with my plan to pass everything to you. Well, once you left, I told him immediately that I had made a terrible mistake and had suddenly realized that it was Wilfred I loved; and that led him to propose and tell me that his ultimate dream was to travel around the world. And would I go with him?'

'Oh, Mama!' Millie jumped up as her mother did too, and they hugged. This turned into a little dance, prompted by her mama. They collapsed in laughter, ending up sitting on the sofa next to each other.

'You don't mind, darling?'

'No, I will miss you, but I am very happy for you. Only, you will be home when I have my baby, won't you?'

'Of course. And you, my brave darling, must go along to see the doctor soon, so we have it confirmed and the date.'

'I can't yet, can I?'

'Oh no, of course not. You've only missed one monthly. They can't tell until you are three months down the line. But we can work it out. You married on the third of August and you have signs now, so that points to it happening soon after you married.'

As Mama counted the months off, Millie felt sad. *How*

did I allow myself to be so taken in? I was so happy on my wedding day and during my honeymoon.

'That will mean we are looking at late April or early May. So Wilfred and I will have to do half of the world – if it can be done in that time. We'll do less of a trip, if it can't, and then do the other half once you are settled and can manage without me.'

'I will never manage without you, Mama dear. I will always miss you when you aren't here, but I am very happy for you to go off on your journey and hope it will be filled with love and happiness – no one deserves that more than you.'

They hugged again. When they came out of it, Mama said, 'Wilfred – well, to be truthful, he is usually known as Wilf in less-formal settings than his office – is coming to dinner tonight, darling. That is, he is awaiting a call from me to tell him everything is all right after the Harold episode, and with you, darling.'

'Well, you can make that call. But tell me one thing: will you still make Raven Hall your main residence?'

'I hope so. I don't know for sure, as there was no time to talk details – it was just a flurry of cuddles, a lovely kiss, a proposal, Wilf telling me his dreams and then you were back in with us.'

Mama giggled – a happy, relaxed giggle – and this gave Millie such joy that she forgot her own worries.

'Anyway, that place runs itself, and I have an account in place, as your father did, so that all bills are charged to it. I am also very lucky to have the loveliest housekeeper and really good staff, from Brigland, my butler, to my maid Rose. I know that everything I own – whoops, did own – is safe in their hands.'

'And all of that can, and will, continue, will it? As you know, I have hardly any funds and will struggle to keep this house going until I sell it, when I'll be in a much better position.'

'It can, don't worry. But you may consider selling that house too? I wouldn't mind in the least. It doesn't have happy memories for me, unless it does for you?'

'Not any more. They are all sour now.'

'Well then, darling, that would be the solution. Selling Raven Hall and this place would mean you will be very well off. You can either buy another house, or lease one. The choice will be yours. And that's just it: you will have choices, darling. You needn't ever consider going back to Len. You will be able to afford a lawyer to sort out your divorce – and you can be free to decide how to live your life.'

'Oh, Mama, I can feel a huge weight lifting off my shoulders. Thank you.'

'I'm so glad. All I ever wanted was for you to be happy, my darling Millie. I know I went about it the wrong way in the beginning. I was misguided in my thinking. But I hope now, with all my heart, that you will eventually meet someone you love, and who will love you and make you happy.'

Millie smiled. She didn't think she had a chance of that happening. Especially with a child in tow, but she made her mind up there and then that she wouldn't be unhappy. She would devote her time to her child, her lovely sister and her family, whom she now considered to be her own; and to the causes that were dear to her heart, but which she hadn't yet had time to get involved in.

At dinner Wilfred was so nice to Millie, and especially to her mama, but in an ordinary way. He'd always, since first meeting him when Mama engaged him to help Elsie and

Dot, shown that he was a caring man, not judgemental, but giving the impression that he thought everyone deserved justice, regardless of their standing. Thinking about this, Millie asked him about that time.

They were on their sweet course, and the conversation had turned to Wilfred's work. He'd related a few funny anecdotes to them when Millie said, 'Can I ask you something about when you helped my sisters?'

'Oh, you mean the death sentence that is about to be carried out?'

'No. I'm curious, as you were my father's lawyer at the time and their case was against him.'

'Ah, well, no, Richard wasn't a client of mine. Once someone dies, then my involvement ends, as it is their solicitor who sorts out probate. I would only have come in if there was a dispute that had to be taken to court. I was more of a friend – well, a useful acquaintance – and did help out on a few legal matters: Richard's run-ins with the employment rules, for instance, and the one deal I told you about, as there was a lot of legal entanglement that went with it, which might have ended up in the courts. So I was free to act for your sisters and was very glad to, especially as a favour for your mama.'

'Oh, I see.'

'May I ask something of you now, Millie?'

'Yes, of course.'

'Well, all of this must seem a bit rushed to you, because only a few nights ago you were having dinner with your mother and Harold. Are you happy about it all?'

She told Wilfred that she was very happy, and in return he offered a beaming smile. Millie thought him a handsome man, although his age, which she guessed was around fiftyish, was showing signs of encroaching on that. His hair was dark, but peppered with grey, and his bushy sideburns and moustache were grey, too. He had lovely twinkly eyes and his face, when he laughed – which he did readily – creased into many lines.

'Well, for my part, my dear, I am ecstatic. I never thought in a million years this would happen when you both came to see me yesterday – it was as if someone suddenly shone a bright light in my life.'

'I'm very happy for you both. And I can tell that Mama is so happy, and in a relaxed way, too. When I think about it, there was never this feeling that I get from you two, when Mama was with Harold. I couldn't have said so at the time, as all seemed well and I was glad for Mama – not to mention that initially I was swept off my feet by my own happiness, and then was plunged so deeply into trouble and unhappiness that I just accepted things.'

'I understand. I am so sorry for what you are going through. For someone you love to do such a thing, well . . .'

'I no longer love Len, and I realize, as Mama has done with Harold, that I never loved him. I was carried away by his attention – his looks, and even the love he gave me, which I now know was false. Len came into my life when I desperately needed someone and, as you know, we now believe that was orchestrated, which makes it all the more painful.'

'I'm truly sorry, my dear. And I, or rather my son, who is incensed by the case, will do all he can to prove a case against Len. I have to say that it's tricky, as there is no evidence to suggest you were duped. But if some is to be found, then either my son, or his wife Sally-Anne, will find it. She does all our research for us and is excellent. It is amazing what she finds out. She says it's all because she is nosy and loves to snoop into other people's business. Oh, I didn't mean that she will . . . I'm digging a hole for myself here, aren't I?'

Both Millie and her mama burst out laughing. Millie put him out of his misery by saying, 'Don't worry, I like that she will. I don't mind – I only hope she finds something. I'm only too pleased that you are forward enough to employ a woman in such a high-profile job, as she must have to delve into a lot of legal stuff.'

'She does. Sally-Anne is highly intelligent and knowledge-able – I found her, before my son did. She was working for a private detective agency and I saw her value. My son saw something more, and upped and married her.'

They all laughed at this, before retiring to the living room for after-dinner drinks. As they went, Millie realized that for well over an hour now she hadn't grieved about her own problems and the blow she'd been dealt. And that felt good – it made her realize that she could come out the other side of all this. And she told herself that she would. She would work towards carving a future for herself and her child.

Chapter Thirty-Four

Elsie

It was two days later that the letters arrived at the factory. Elsie and Jim were having their morning tea break when the messenger delivered them. They'd been talking about the following day's trip to the zoo, and Elsie continued to think about it as Jim went to receive the post.

Everyone was excited about the trip – especially Millie, who'd called round yesterday after they'd got home from work and had spent the whole evening holding Kitty till she had to go to bed, then telling them about the amazing change in her mama's life, and how Len's father had behaved and what he proposed to give to Len. It seemed that the Lens of this world would always fall on their feet, but they'd been so happy and relieved for Millie as they'd listened to her change of fortune that the family almost forgot to ask her to come to the zoo. When they did, her happiness was such that it almost made Elsie cry.

Jim's 'Uh-oh, these look like they are from the monster in our lives, Elsie' brought her back to the present, as she took the sealed envelope that he handed to her, keeping one for himself.

'Open yours first, Jim. I think we can guess what's in mine.'

Jim slit the envelope with a paper knife. The sound it made wasn't loud, but it grated on Elsie's fraught nerves. She waited, then listened anxiously as Jim read out what Len had to say:

'Dear Jim,
   I know what I am going to say will not be to your liking. We have been friends for a long time, and I want you to draw on that and try to see the truth in my words.
   Yes, I did have sex with Elsie, but it was at her instigation. And when it was over and I tried to apologize and ask her forgiveness . . .'

Jim lowered the letter. His anger made a small nerve twitch in his cheek as he gritted his teeth.

'Carry on, Jim. It's all right, I know you believe me. Nothing Len can say will alter that, will it?'

'No, it won't. How dare he? I wish that blow had killed him now – he doesn't deserve to live.'

Elsie didn't comment. Jim took a deep breath and continued:

'. . . she actually offered to forgive me if I carried on an affair with her behind Millie's back. This is the type of girl you are thinking of marrying, Jim. Please don't – she is a whore.'

At Elsie's gasp, Jim threw the paper on the floor. 'I can't bear to read it, Elsie. Oh, darling, how evil is this man?'

Elsie went to him. 'Jim, no matter what he says, you have to keep the upper hand. You have to. You may go to prison if he takes this all the way.'

'I know you're right, but, oh, Elsie, to read such filth about you.'

'Reading it don't matter. What matters is that you don't believe it.'

Jim picked the letter up and continued to read:

'I want to make you an offer, Jim. I can forgive you for what you did. Having been told lies, what else was there for you to do but what you thought honourable? I hope now that I have told you the truth, you can listen to my proposition and we can make a fresh start.

I am asking you to carry on running the factory for me, Jim. There will be a substantial increase in your salary, as well as other perks – a package that gives you access to private medical care and paid holidays. You will be known as the general manager, and I will employ office staff and a trainee supervisor for you. I want none of the workers having any greater responsibility than working on the factory floor.

In exchange for you taking on this position – which will really see me through the transition period of not being solely able to run the factory – I will not pursue your prosecution for the assault on me.'

Jim raised his eyebrows, but continued:

'I am going places, Jim. I will end up a very rich man, and if you do this for me, I will take you with me – shares in the business even. It's all up to you. Give it some deep thought, Jim. Choose to go as far as Elsie and her lot can drag you down, or come with me and help to build my empire and be a part of it – Swift's

will be no more. Instead, within two to three years there will be a modern factory, far from the slums where we are situated now. It will be called Lefton's. And it will be only the first of many.

Reply as soon as you can. I know you are holding the fort for me at the moment, and that gives me hope – carry on doing that and you will be laying the foundations for a life you never dreamed of.

Yours, Len'

Jim dropped his hands. 'I don't believe it, Elsie – the audacity of the man! Not one mention of poor Millie. And his only mention of you is not to apologize, but to rub your nose in the dirt. I can't do it, Elsie, I can't.'

'Yes, you can, Jim. You have to. At least until you are in the clear, and then you can have your revenge by walking out and leaving him in the lurch.'

'You're forgetting the workers in all this – our colleagues, because that's what they are, Elsie.'

'Of course they are, but I'm not forgetting them, Jim. I can't save them, and neither can you. If you refuse Len's offer, what will happen? The place will be shut, that's what. If you take up his offer, what will happen? The place will shut in a couple of years anyway. I think you should go along with it, get yourself in the clear and then leave. People leave all the time. The women do: some of them come and go, it's quite natural. They won't think you hold their destiny in your hands – and you don't, Jim. But you do hold your own destiny, mate. So please think about it.'

'You're right. I can see that. I hate what will happen here. But as you say, it will happen anyway.' Jim got up and walked to the window. 'It's such a great pity. Why did Millie sign everything over to him? Oh, I know the reasons, but if only she'd seen through Len.'

Elsie couldn't say anything, as she felt the guilt of that statement as she herself had been taken in by Len. She stood next to Jim and slipped her hand into his. At that moment Ada spotted them and waved. A tear plopped onto Elsie's cheek. But she knew there was nothing they could do to help the workers they relied upon. She had to hold on to that, as she did all she could to persuade Jim.

'Jim, luv, if Len can use blackmail to get what he wants, then so can you. Tell him you will take the job – even let him think that you'll drop me, if you have to. But say that none of it will happen until he has dropped the charges. In the meantime you will caretake for one week and, once you have confirmation there are no charges against you, you will sign on the dotted line.'

'Len will never believe that – though, wait a minute, I could make him believe it. I could tell him how much I believe in his plans, and in him, and how I didn't ever really believe you. And I could thank him for being honest with me. I won't write any of this down, but will ask him to meet me in the club. I will have to act all this out, when I will feel like stamping him into the ground, but I think I can do it. I told you, I am an artist really – a musician at heart, but I used to love to be in school plays. That's when I came into my own.'

There was a change in Jim as hope seeped into him, but then his face altered.

'But what will I do afterwards? What job, I mean? I could try the other jam factories, but I must admit I have looked for vacancies and there aren't any that I could take.'

'We'll worry about that afterwards. You said yourself

377

that you have a little money, and so do I. You won't need yours for legal fees, and Millie won't need mine. She even said that my allowance would carry on, once she'd sold everything – or she'd give me a lump sum. I can take the lump sum, and we could perhaps start something of our own.'

'You're right. Oh, Elsie, I love you.' Jim moved her away from the window and pulled her into his arms. 'I'm going to break our own rule, darling.' With this, his lips came down on hers, and to Elsie it was as if – but for one shadow – the light had come back on in her life.

When he released her, she picked up her own envelope and ripped it in two. 'I don't want to read it, Jim. It'll be full of threats and lies. I know the direction we are going in, my darling. And, come what may, I have decided to marry you on the date we have set.'

'Oh, Elsie, my love, my love. It will all come right, you'll see. I will care for you. It will be exactly as I said – if the worst happens, from the horrible experience you had.'

'I know, Jim. I know.'

None of their problems overshadowed their trip to the zoo – not even the fact that it drizzled with rain for a time. Bert was dizzy with excitement and could hardly stand at one enclosure before he got hold of George's hand and dragged him to the next, but then went back for more.

George was a lovely boy. And his mum, Jean, though looking weary, had a cheery disposition as she stood at her door with umpteen kids around her, saying, 'You mind your manners, George – oh, and your Sunday-best clothes,' then she laughed and added, 'But for all that, have a good time,

378

me lovely boy. And remember everything, so that you can tell us all about it, and we'll all feel as though we've been there, too.' She kissed him then and George glowed. Elsie wasn't sure if it was with embarrassment or pride in his mum, but his smile mirrored his mum's as he hugged her, before running to get into Cess's car.

Millie had already gone ahead with her driver, taking Rene. Elsie had wanted to stay with Bert all day, so she and Jim got into Cess's car. When they got there, they found that Millie had brought with her a stroller for Kitty. It was made of cane and had two large wheels. The body lifted off the wheels to transport it, and the whole thing fitted onto the back seat of the car. It amazed Elsie.

'It came from India. It was shipped over for me – but I bagsie that I push Kitty in it.'

This became a rivalry that made them all laugh throughout the afternoon, as they all vied to have a go, even Bert and George.

It was when they were waiting for Bert and George's turn to ride on the elephant that Elsie felt a sudden ache in her stomach. Her back had been painful all morning, but she'd carried on ignoring it while she packed the picnic – well, her half of it, which consisted of sandwiches only, as Millie was bringing a hamper, too.

The pain had eased as she'd lost herself in the wonderment of the animals, but now she didn't know whether to laugh or cry, because with the pain came a warm trickle into her knickers. She grabbed Millie's arm and whispered to her, 'I need a lav, quickly!'

Rene heard her and turned to look at Elsie. Her quizzical look turned to a smile and a wink. 'Come on, luv. I saw a block for the Ladies back there. I'll come with you.'

'Me, too.' Millie turned then and said to Cess, 'You can take the pram now, Cess. I need to visit the bathroom, but I want it back when I return, as it's still my turn.'

They all laughed at her.

Cess tutted as they left the group. 'You women. When one wants to go, you all do.' He nudged Jim. 'Giving us five minutes' peace, eh, mate?'

On the way Elsie told them what she thought was happening. Rene and Millie were so happy for her, though Rene sounded a bit put out as she said, 'I thought yer said yer monthlies were regular, Elsie, girl. By my reckoning, you've still got a few days to go.'

'I must have got mixed up, with all the stress of it. Anyway, I don't care. I feel as though someone has given me my life back. Only problem is that I'm not sure how I'm going to cope with it. I haven't got any rags with me.'

'I've got a couple of them of them big hankies on me. Yer know I don't like them little dainty ones that we're supposed to cope with. Blimey, you'd think we women had no need to blow our noses, with what they expect us to use.'

'That'll do, ta, Rene.'

When she'd fished them out of her pocket, Rene said, 'And I don't want them back.'

They all giggled.

'I've got a link of pins in my bag, Elsie, so you can secure the hankies in place. I always carry them, along with a few other items I never get to use.'

'I do that! I've a compact with a mirror, but I never look in it, mate – I'd rather not know what I look like.'

Elsie left them to it as they giggled and went on to compare other items they had with them. Once she'd shut the door she almost cried out with joy as it was confirmed that her monthly had arrived. Tears tumbled from her eyes – of relief, happiness and a little fear for the unknown. Though she'd consented to marry Jim on the date they'd already set, she wasn't sure she wanted to cope with all that entailed.

When she came out, it was to find that Millie had gone. Rene explained, 'I asked her to leave us alone, Elsie. I didn't get that chance to have a talk with you, did I? Well, I've made up me mind that I'm going to have it right now.'

'Oh, Rene, can you help me?'

'I'll try. Dry those tears away, luv. And listen to me. What a man who loves you will be like is nothing like what yer've experienced so far, I promise yer. Now would I lie to yer?'

'No, but I'm scared, Rene.'

'Not surprising, girl. And I know what yer've been through, believe me. There were men as didn't want to pay and so took what they wanted by force. And there were them as only enjoyed it if they knocked yer around a bit first, and got yer fighting them off. But I've known wonderful sex, too. There's a lot of gentlemen out there who think only of the woman. Apart from them, I've known love.'

Elsie listened as Rene told her about the love of her life, and how wonderful her time was with a man called Ian. They were to be married, but he was killed in an accident, leaving Rene pregnant. Her baby was adopted.

'Tore me heart out, it did, Elsie, girl. But I will never forget me little son, and I'll always remember Ian and the love we shared. You can have that love, Elsie. It's waiting for you over there by the elephants.'

Elsie looked over. Jim had Bert on his shoulders, and Cess had George.

'Jim's a good man, like my Ian was. You go to him and

take the love he's offering you, girl. And believe me, you will be happier than you could ever dream of.'

Elsie felt enlightenment dawn as she left Rene's side and walked towards Jim. The last piece of the broken jigsaw of her life slipped into place. Her walk turned into a run as she called his name.

Turning, he lowered Bert to the ground and ran towards her. His arms opened and he lifted Elsie in the air. Twirling her round, he laughed up at her.

When he lowered her, she smiled shyly at him. 'You know?'

'Yes, darling. Millie whispered it to me. Well, not in so many words, but she just said, "You and Elsie are going to be all right, Jim. She has news for you." Then she said, "We all are. We're all going to come out of this and make a new life. I'm convinced of that."'

'I have to go to her, Jim. But what she says is right. We are going to be all right. We're going to get married and be a proper couple . . . Oh, there's so much to do! But first I want to hug my sister. My Millie.'

The hug meant so much more than all the hugs they'd had in the past. During it they promised to support each other forever. And never to be at odds with each other ever again. When they came out of it, Millie said, 'And I will work towards getting the jam factory back. I have promised all our women, in my head, and I'll keep to it. If Len does move the factory, I'll buy our building back, or another close by, and we'll start again, Elsie. Jim and Peggy and Ada, and all of the women, will help us.'

'Millie, that's a wonderful idea. And it will work – I know it will. Oh, Millie, that factory has been the bane of me life and a place of happiness, but whichever it is at any given time, it is me life and I can't bear to lose that.'

'It can be again, but in the meantime we'll work at helping families like George's and will be ready when our lovely factory women are let down by Len. We'll support them with the charity that I'm going to set up – that is, until we go back through the doors of Swift's Jam Factory, Else. And we will. We will.'

Elsie hugged Millie to her again, but then she heard a cry of 'It's my turn, Else. Ooh, look at how big the elephant is!'

She turned and went to support Bert, whose voice held a mixture of fear and wonderment. 'Up you go, my lovely brovver. Enjoy it. Then we will have our picnic, eh?'

Bert's smile was all the reward Elsie needed. It had all been worth it, to see the love and trust he had for her. Life for Bert was going to be so different from her own.

When her wedding day dawned, Elsie looked lovely in her organza gown. Rene had sat up late into the night on several occasions to hand-stitch the rows of crosswise pleats into the bodice.

As the carriage carrying her and Cess to the church travelled along the Old Kent Road, Cess squeezed her hand. 'Life's changing for us all, Sis, with Dai arriving tomorrow and us taking over our first stall next week.'

'It'll be lovely to see him, Cess. I only wish we had room for him at the flat.'

'He'll be fine in the guest house. Besides, I haven't told you yet, but I think I've found us a place – it's a house near Millie's. I went to that estate agent she told you about.'

'That's good news. Gertie'll be in her element looking after both Kitty and you.'

'And that's not all. I may have some hope for Ada, and

for George's family. The estate agent thought I'd want a terraced house, and told me about a row that had been renovated, before he showed me the one I chose. He said they have three bedrooms in each, at three bob a week, in Grange Walk. Apparently there's three of them going for rent.'

'That's wonderful. Oh, Cess, will you get straight back to him and ask if he will consider housing Ada? I'll have to talk to George's family, as I'm not sure if they even want to move. But, oh, you've completed my happiness.'

'Well, don't get yer hopes too high, mate. But it's looking good, as I thought of Ada straight away and mentioned her. The agent sounded very interested, as the owner is looking to let the houses as soon as possible.'

Elsie smiled. It felt to her that everything was coming right – slowly, and they still had a long way to go – and from where she sat, the world had a rosy glow to it. And as they passed St George's gardens, she felt sure she saw Dot peeking out from behind a bush and waving to her. She lifted her hand.

'Blimey, I know yer look like a queen, Else – and probably feel like one, as you should – but waving to the crowd: that's going overboard, innit?' Cess laughed as he said this and squeezed her hand tighter.

Elsie laughed with him. The part of her that still held pain at missing Dot eased. Dot was happy now. Maybe Dot's mind would never have given her the peace that she had found at last.

Little Jimmy came to Elsie's mind then and, in her picture of him, she saw him holding Mum's hand. She smiled at them both. They too were at peace, and she had this feeling they were happy for her. To little Jimmy she said, *I'm marrying the loveliest man, and he's your namesake, little brother. He'll take care of me.* The voice of her mum came to her then: *He'd better, or he'll have Rene to contend with.* This was said in her mother's tongue-in-cheek way, and Elsie laughed out loud.

'I'm glad you're happy, Else. No one deserves to be more than you, girl.'

'I am, Cess. I am. This is a new beginning for us all.'

'I know. Me lovely Dot would have loved today. And she's here, Else. She wouldn't have missed it for the world.' Cess wiped away a tear. 'Be happy, Else. You've a good man in Jim.'

She kissed his cheek. 'I have two good men, as yer the best brother a girl could wish for, Cess.'

'Then why am I thinking that I can't wait to get to the church to get rid of yer?'

When they stopped laughing, Elsie sat back and let the last few yards to the church be peaceful ones. She felt bathed in happiness and so hopeful for the future. A future with Jim and surrounded by her lovely family, and one where all the promises they'd made to the women of the jam factory would one day come true.

Letter to Readers

Dear Readers,

Thank you for choosing my book. I hope you love Elsie, Dot and Millie as much as I do.

If you are new to the series, the book can be read as a stand-alone, but if you would like to follow Elsie, Dot and Millie's story, the first book in the series is *The Jam Factory Girls* and can be bought in Waterstones, WHSmith and on all online book stores. This is the story of the girls' younger years and how they met, the discoveries they made, their heartaches and their joys.

There will be further instalments in Winter 2021 and Spring 2022, so look out for these too.

Writing a book is like taking steps through the unknown for me, as my characters come to life, taking me on a voyage of discovery – an exciting, but sometimes tense, experience through many emotions. This is what I want for my readers too.

I love the research process, and have often combined my love of travel with visiting the area I am writing about. However, the circumstances that prevailed when creating this trilogy meant having to rely on the internet. I became engrossed in learning about the lives of the girls who worked in our factories in the late nineteenth and early twentieth centuries – their fight for better conditions and their down-trodden lives, which the cockney girls tackled with the true grit and humour they are known for. If you would like to know more, I have listed the resources overleaf.

If this book is your first introduction to my work and you would like to read more, you can find a list of my titles in the front of this book, and you can order online and from all good bookshops or find them in your local library.

To find out more about me, my work, my talks and my book-signing events – or to book one of these with me – I can be found here:

Website: **www.authormarywood.com**
Email: **marywood@authormarywood.com**
Twitter: **@Authormary**
Facebook: **facebook.com/MaryWoodAuthor**

I look forward to hearing from you.

Much love to all,

Mary x

Research

My thanks to the following sources:

www.exploringsouthwark.co.uk – a wonderful source of information on Hartley's and Pink's jam factories and the practices of the time – Hartley's came out with flying colours, not so Pink's on whom I based my Swift's Jam Factory.

Amanda Wilkinson's 'J is for Jam Maker' – www.victorian occupations.co.uk

The strong and caring Mary Macarthur and the National Federation of Women Workers – spartacus-educational.com/ TUmacarthur.htm

Ada Salter, a woman of strength, courage and conviction. Millie is set to be in the same mould as this remarkable woman – menwhosaidno.org/context/women/salter_ada.html

Acknowledgements

Many people have a hand in bringing a book to publication and I want to express my heartfelt thanks to them all. My agent, Judith Murdoch, who stands firmly in my corner, whilst propping me up when I need it and encouraging me forward. My editor, Wayne Brookes, who is always there for me, whose care means the world and who makes me laugh. I love him to bits. Victoria Hughes-Williams, who does a wonderful, sensitive structural edit of my books, keeping my voice and tightening my work. Editor Alex Saunders and his team, Samantha Fletcher and Mandy Greenfield, who all do an amazing job of editing and checking my research, till my words sing off the page – I always say, an author is nothing without her editors and I am so lucky in mine. Thank you.

Thanks, too, to the publicists, who work towards getting exposure for my books and me, and meticulously organize events to ensure I am taken care of on my travels. The sales team, for their efforts to get my books onto the shelves. The cover designer for my beautiful covers. And last but by no means least, a special thanks to my son, James Wood, who reads so many versions of each book, advising me on what is working and what isn't as I write my draft manuscript, and then helps with the read-through of the final proofs when last-minute mistakes need to be spotted. All of you are much appreciated, and do an amazing job for me.

My thanks, too, to my special family – my husband, Roy, who looks after me so well as I lose myself in writing my books, and is the love of my life. By my side for almost sixty years, I couldn't do what I do without him or the love and generous support that he gives me. My children, Christine, Julie, Rachel and James, for your love, encouragement and just for having pride in me. My grandchildren and great-grandchildren, too numerous to name, but all loved so very dearly and who are all in my corner cheering me on. My Olley and Wood families, for all the love and encouragement. You all help me to climb my mountain.

And I want to thank my readers, especially those on my Facebook page – 'Mary Wood Author'. The love and encouragement you give me, the laughs we have and all the support you show makes my day. You are second to none. Love you all, thank you.

If you enjoyed

Secrets of the Jam Factory Girls

then you'll love

The Jam Factory Girls

by Mary Wood

Book one in
The Jam Factory series

Life for Elsie is difficult as she struggles to cope with her alcoholic mother. Caring for her siblings and working long hours at Swift's Jam Factory in London's Bermondsey is exhausting. Thankfully her lifelong friendship with Dot helps to smooth over life's rough edges.

When Elsie and Dot meet Millie Hawkesfield, the boss's daughter, they are nervous to be in her presence. Over time, they are surprised to feel so drawn to her, but should two cockney girls be socializing in such circles?

When disaster strikes, it binds the women in ways they could never have imagined. And long-held secrets are revealed that will change all their lives . . .

Available now

The Forgotten Daughter

by Mary Wood

Book one in
The Girls Who Went to War series

From a tender age, Flora felt unloved and unwanted by her parents, but she finds safety in the arms of caring Nanny Pru. But when Pru is cast out of the family home, under a shadow of secrets and with a baby boy of her own on the way, it shatters little Flora.

Over the years, however, Flora and Pru meet in secret – unbeknown to Flora's parents. Pru becomes the mother she never had, and Flora grows into a fine young woman. When she signs up as a volunteer with St John Ambulance, she begins to shape her life. But the drum of war beats loudly and her world is turned upside down when she receives a letter asking her to join the Red Cross in Belgium.

With the fate of the country in the balance, it is a time for bravery. Flora's determined to be the strong woman she was destined to be. But with horror, loss and heartache on her horizon, there's a lot for young Flora to learn . . .

Available now

The Abandoned Daughter

by Mary Wood

Book two in
The Girls Who Went to War series

Voluntary nurse Ella is haunted by the soldiers' cries she hears on the battlefields of Dieppe. But that's not the only thing that haunts her. When her dear friend Jim breaks her trust, Ella is left bruised and heartbroken. Over the years, her friendships have been pulled apart at the seams by the effects of war. Now, more than ever, she feels so alone.

At a military hospital in Belgium, Ella befriends Connie and Paddy. Slowly she begins to heal, and finds comfort in the arms of a French officer called Paulo – could he be her salvation?

With the end of the war on the horizon, surely things have to get better? Ella grew up not knowing her real family but a clue leads her in their direction. What did happen to Ella's parents, and why is she so desperate to find out?

Available now

The Wronged Daughter

by Mary Wood

Book three in
The Girls Who Went to War series

Can she heal the wounds of her past?

Mags has never forgotten the friendship she forged with Flora and Ella, two fellow nurses she served with at the beginning of World War One. Haunted by what she experienced during that time, she fears a reunion with her friends would bring back the horror she's tried so desperately to suppress.

Now, with her wedding on the horizon, this should be a joyful time for Mags. But the sudden loss of her mother and the constant doubt she harbours surrounding her fiancé, Harold, are marring her happiness.

Mags throws herself into running the family mill, but she's dealt another aching blow by a betrayal that leaves her reeling. Finding the strength the war had taken from her, she fights back, not realizing the consequences and devastating outcome awaiting her.

Can she pick up the pieces of her life and begin anew?

Available now

The Brave Daughters

by Mary Wood

Book four in
The Girls Who Went to War series

When Sibbie and Marjie arrive at RAF Digby, they are about to take on roles of national importance. It's a cause of great excitement for everyone around them. Perhaps they will become code-breakers, spies even? Soon the pair embark on a rigorous training regime, but nothing can prepare them for what they're about to face . . .

Amid the vineyards of rural France, Flors and Ella can't bear the thought of another war. But as the thunderclouds hanging over Europe grow darker, a sense of deep foreboding sets in, not just for their safety but for the fate of their families . . . With danger looming, as the threat of war becomes real, Flors and Ella are forced to leave their idyllic home and flee. Can they make it to safety, or will the war have further horrors in store for them?

'Wood is a born storyteller'
Lancashire Evening Post

Available now